W9-BKA-039

MARGARET WEIS was born and reared in Independence, Missouri. She received a BA in creative writing in 1970 from the University of Missouri, Columbia. Weis worked at Herald Publishing House in Independence, going from proof-reader to editorial director of the trade press division in almost thirteen years. Her first book, a biography of Frank and Jesse James, was published in 1981. In 1983, she moved to Lake Geneva, Wisconsin, to become a book editor at TSR, Inc., where she met Tracy Hickman. The rest, as they say, is history. Weis is currently a free-lance writer living in a converted barn in Wisconsin with daughter Elizabeth, two collies, Laddie and Robbie, and a cat, Nickolai Mouse-slayer.

TRACY HICKMAN was born in 1955, in Salt Lake City, Utah. His parents encouraged him to try everything good in life. He became a sailplane pilot at seventeen, sang and played guitar in a local folk group and, at nineteen, became a missionary for his church. His two-year mission was served in Hawaii and Java, Indonesia. Upon returning home, he married his childhood sweetheart, Laura Curtis, and began a whole new adventure in raising his family. Tracy has worked as a stockboy, assistant TV director, glass shop worker, movie projectionist, theater manager, drill press operator, dark room technician and, for five years, as a game designer for TSR. He and his wife coauthored the original RAVENLOFT® adventure while he spearheaded the DRAGONLANCE® game design team. With Margaret Weis he is the coauthor of over twenty novels. He now lives amid the tall Ponderosa pine trees of northern Arizona with his wife and four children.

NANCY VARIAN BERBERICK is the author of *Stormblade*, *The Jewels of Elvish*, and *Shadow of the Seventh Moon*. Her fourth novel, *A Child of Elvish*, is due out in April 1992. When she is not writing, she is gardening—a hobby that has become a year-round pleasure now that she and her husband have moved to the cordial climates of North Carolina.

RICHARD A. KNAAK is a longtime contributor to the DRAGONLANCE® novel series, including several short stories in the first Tales Trilogy and the novels *The Legend of Huma* and *Kaz, the Minotaur*. He also is the author of a popular fantasy series for Warner Books.

ROGER E. MOORE joined TSR, Inc. in 1983 and has been the editor of DRAGON® Magazine since 1986. In his free time, he runs amok with his six-year-old son, John, writes articles, practices aikido, and bakes bread in the shape of trilobites.

DOUGLAS NILES is the kind of writer who likes extra cheese on his pizza. He is a free-lance author and game designer who has written numerous FORGOTTEN REALMS® novels, as well as *The Kinslayer Wars* and *Flint, the King* (with Mary Kirchoff) for the DRAGONLANCE novel line.

NICK O'DONOHOE is the author of several DRAGONLANCE stories, the Nathan Phillips detective series, and a science-fiction novel, *Too, Too Solid Flesh*, published by TSR, Inc. He has published several other short stories and novellas, the most recent being in *Alfred Hitchcock's Mystery Magazine*. He taught for several years but has not, to his knowledge, ever taught a kender—though one student was awfully close.

DAN PARKINSON has had twenty-four novels published during the past eight years and has had bestsellers in several genres, including western, high seas adventure, science fiction, and, recently, fantasy, with his DRAGONLANCE novel *The Gates of Thorbardin*. He also is the author of the TSR® Book *Starsong*. "Off Day" is his second published short story and his first visit to the "surprising realm of Krynn's least acclaimed citizens," the gully dwarves. A native Kansan and longtime Texan, he was author guest of honor at the 1991 GEN CON® Game Fair.

MICHAEL WILLIAMS was a member of the original DRAGONLANCE game design team, and has written four fantasy novels, of which *Weasel's Luck* and *Galen Beknighted* continue the saga of Krynn. His early adventures of Sturm Brightblade, *The Oath and the Measure*, is forthcoming as part of the Meetings Sextet. He recently returned from a tour of pre-Norman ruins in the British Isles and Ireland, gathering images for a future work.

DragonLance Saga

THE REIGN OF ISTAR

Tales II Trilogy
♦
Volume One

With an introduction by
Margaret Weis and Tracy Hickman

Cover art by Larry Elmore
Interior art by Stephen Fabian

DRAGONLANCE® TALES II

Volume One

THE REIGN
OF ISTAR

©1992 TSR, Inc.
All Rights Reserved.

First Printing: April 1992
Printed in the United States of America
Library of Congress Catalog Card Number: 91-66508

9 8 7 6 5 4

ISBN: 1-56076-326-4

TSR, Inc.
201 Sheridan Springs Rd.
Lake Geneva, WI 53147
U.S.A.

TSR Ltd.
120 Church End, Cherry Hinton
Cambridge CB1 3LB
United Kingdom

TABLE OF CONTENTS

INTRODUCTION

Paladine, you see the evil that surrounds me!
You have been witness to the calamities that have been
the scourge of Krynn. . . . You must see now that this
doctrine of balance will not work!

" . . . I can sweep evil from this world! Destroy the
ogre races! Bring the wayward humans into line! Find
new homelands far away for the dwarves and the kender
and the gnomes, those races not of your creation. . . .

" . . . I demand that you give me, too, the power to
drive away the shadows of evil that darken the land!"

So the Kingpriest prayed on the day of the Cataclysm.

He was a good man, but intolerant, proud. He believed his way to be the right way, the only way, and
insisted that everyone else—including the gods—follow
his thinking. Those who disagreed with him were, by
definition, evil and, according to the law, must be "converted" or destroyed. The stories in this volume deal
with the effects of such edicts and beliefs on the people of
Ansalon at the time prior to the Cataclysm.

Michael Williams begins this series, appropriately,
with a prophecy for the last days in "Six Songs for the
Temple of Istar."

"Colors of Belief," by Richard A. Knaak, tells the story of a young knight who travels to Istar in search of the
truth. He finds it, though not quite in the way he expected.

A crusty old trainer of young knights must cope with
a most unorthodox recruit in "Kender Stew," by Nick
O'Donohoe.

"The Goblin's Wish," by Roger E. Moore, is a tale of a
disparate band of refugees, driven together by need,
who almost find the power to overcome evil. Almost.

"The Three Lives of Horgan Oxthrall," by Douglas
Niles, continues the theme of unlikely allies, forced to
band together in the face of a common enemy, as told by
a clerk to Astinus.

Nancy Varian Berberick writes about alliances of a
more intriguing nature in "Filling the Empty Places."

Dan Parkinson tells how the small and seemingly insignificant can end up playing an important role in history in "Off Day."

Our novella, "The Silken Threads," reveals the fate of the true clerics and tells how Nuitari, the guardian of evil magic, attempts to thwart the ambitions of the black-robed wizard known as Fistandantilus.

We are delighted to be visiting Krynn once again, along with many of the original members of the DRAGONLANCE® game design team and some new friends we met along the way. We hope you enjoy *The Reign of Istar* and that you will join us for further journeys through Krynn in subsequent volumes in this series.

Margaret Weis and Tracy Hickman

Six Songs for the Temple of Istar

Michael Williams

According to legend, the author of these songs is the obscure Silvanesti bard Astralas, born about the time of the Proclamation of Manifest Virtue. Well over a century old when his voyage commenced, the elven prophet supposedly set sail for Istar shortly before the Edict of Thought Control, returning with a series of confused and confusing visions of an impending disaster. He vanished under mysterious circumstances around the time of the Cataclysm; some say that he was destroyed by the elven priestesses of Istar, acting in accordance with the edict. Some also say that in the nightmare days of chaos that followed the Cataclysm, Astralas traveled the forests of Ansalon, forever reciting these songs. The fifth of the songs—the account of the visions themselves—occurs in more than a hundred oral versions throughout the continent. This, however, is the only known manuscript version.

Quivalen Sath
Archivist of The Qualinesti
Poetic Records

I

Astralas, called into song
by the fluted god
Branchala of the leaves,
called when I haunted
the woods of Silvanost,
two thousand and sixty years
since the signing of scrolls,
since the sheathing of armies.

O when the god called me,
the twin moons crossed
on the prow of my ship,
and the ocean was red on silver,
encircling light
upon inarticulate light
from the settled darkness
rushing, awaiting my song.

And O when the god called me,
this was my singing,
my prophecy compelled
in a visitation of wind.

II

The language of wind
is one tongue only,
pronounced in the movement
of cloud and water,
voiced in the rattle of leaves
in the breath between waiting
and memory, it stalks
elusive as light and promise.

The language of wind
is the vanishing year
preserved in recollection,
and always it yearns
for a season the heart
might have been in its wild anointing.
And the wind is always your heartbeat,
is breathing remote
as the impassive stars,
and it moves from arrival to leaving,
leaving you one song only:
Oh, that was the language of wind,
you say, and *what does it mean*
to the leaves and the water,
always, *what does it mean?*

So it found me the first time
at the banks of Thon-Thalas,
at the last edge of river,
after the ministries
of inkwell and tutor,
after the damaged heirloom of days,
when the long thoughts burrow
and the childhood dances
on dark effacements of memory,
losing the self in the dance.
I remembered too much, unabled
for the sword and buckler,
for spellbook and moon,
for altar and incense,
for the birds' veiled grammar
and the seasons' alembic,
and always the river
was telling me telling me
Come, Astralas, come to the waters:
I am the last home, it was saying,
the refuge of dreams
and the sleep of reason.

Come to midcurrent, Astralas.
I shall carry you past your failures.
Come to midcurrent and open your arms
as you fall into spindrift,
to movement, to light on the water,
to water itself, enraptured and lost
as the whole world vanishes.

And always the river
spoke like this, always the dark current
lulling the heart and the mind
into that undertow
where the homelands shift
behind you and fade,
and you think they have vanished
in the necessity of rivers,
in the battlements of forest,
so that if you return
to recover your path
you are lost in the maze
of leaf and inevitable current,
of fore and aft,
of the homelands always receding.

So spoke the river,
and darkly I hearkened,
suspended in darkness,
in the heart's surrender.

A boat for the passage
I began to fashion,
hides stripped in the lime pits
sealed with tallow
and stitched by the tendon of flax
as the awl and the needle
passed through and over
the supple and skeletal wood:

The sails bellied forth
in carnivorous winds,
and in dark, in surrender,
the ship moved rudderless,
launched on insensible currents,
borne to the South
where the Courrain covers
the edge of the world.
And borne to the South
I lay on the deck,
and the boat was a cradle, a bride's bed,
a gray catafalque carried into the night,
it was strong wine and medicine,
sleep past remembrance
and past restoration,
and as I lay down
in the veinwork of halyards
I decided to rise up no longer.

And the date of my death
was my embarkation.

III

Something there is
in the rudderless sailing,
abandoning hope
as the husk of desire,
architectures of boat and body
coalesce with the water
and the disburdening wind.
In the south, the sails filled with words
and the boat took wing
above the denial of waters.
Softly the wind spoke
under the pulse of the sails:

Come, Astralas, ride into prophecy:
I am the breath of a god,
the wind was saying,
the source of dreams
and the webwork of reason.
Astralas, open your arms:
I shall pass through your fingers
as brindled light,
as a vision from the brows of a weary king.
Hasten to Istar, domed and templed,
where sunlight refracts
on bronze and silver,
on crystal and burnished iron.
Ten visions there
you shall read and interpret,
in that comfortable city
where truth without pain
governs the span of the hand,
glitters like moonlight
over immovable waters.

But you, Astralas,
impressed for your terrible voyage,
cannot make truce with the wind and the water
in the breath of your veins,
because they are with you forever.

The trees wept blood
at my departure,
staining the whiteness
of birches and butternut,
glittering dark on the maple and oak,
blood that was falling
like leaves in a thousand countries,
greater than augury,
sprung from prophetic wounds,

as I sailed through the mouth
of ancient Thon-Thalas
like a prayer into endless ocean.

In the mazed and elaborate swirl
of omens, of long prophecies,
comes a time when you stand
in the presence of oracles,
but what they foretell
is mirrors and smoke.

When I reached the Courrain
I was standing on deck,
despair having moved
to the country of faith,
and slowly the coast took a shape
and a name, as the forest
dwindled to Silvanost,
green on water on green.

At long last, to portside
lay the watch fires of Balifor,
the manhandling country of kender,
of hoopak and flute
and rifled treasuries.
The smoke from the coastline
mingled with clouds from the mountains
in the high air resolving
to nebulous hammer and harp,
to veiled constellations,
as the shores of Balifor
sighed with departures of gods.

North and west along the coast,
cradled by pine-scented wind,
by infusion of hemlock,
the long plains climbed
into mountainous green,

and everywhere forest and ocean,
ocean and forest twined
with the westernmost haze
of the damaged horizons,
until the traveler's fancy
supposes Silvanost rising again
in dreams of retrieval,
but instead it is priest-ridden Istar,
sacrifice-haunted, where freedom is incense,
the long smoke rising
destroyed in its own celebrations.
There in the branching seas,
in warm waters harmful and northern,
the wind took me westward
skirting a desolate land.

IV

Now the sea is a level
and heartless country,
boiling with unsteady fires:
The salt air smothers
the coastal lights,
but the mast, the shipped oars,
ignite with the corposant,
and all through the water
a green incandescence,
and often at night
the coastline is dark, obscured
by the luminous reef
by the Phoenix of Habbakuk,
low in the canceling west,
and the wind and the water
are borrowed and inward as light.

And on those same nights,
on the face of the waters,

unexplainable darkness
embarks from the starboard to port
like a dream beneath memory
as though from the ocean
a new land is rising, proclaimed
by the distant and alien
calls of the whales.
The compass needle
flutters and falls
into vertiginous waters,
and waking to sunlight
fractured on spindrift,
the impervious jade
of the ocean below you,
you dismiss the night, you turn it away,
which is why this song
returns to you quietly
at full noon, when the assembled sea
is changing past thought and remembrance
above the eternal currents.

And now the northerlies
rising fierce, equatorial,
the madman's wind,
the mistrals of prophecy,
guiding me into the bay.
Karthay tumbled by to the portside,
the city of harbors
where the sorcerer's tower
waits out the erosion of mountains,
as the northerlies lifted
my boat from the waters' embrace.
Into the Bay of Istar we rushed
like an unforeseen comet,
like a dire thing approaching
the webbed and festering streets,
the harbor's edge
where the wind sailed over me,

calming the vessel
at the feet of the mountainous piers:
where the wind sailed over me,
catching the web of the kingdom
as it blew where it wished,
and none could tell
where it came or went,
and it dove through the alleys,
vaulted the towers,
and lay waste the house
of the last Kingpriest.

The augurers took it
as one immutable sign,
to add to the bloodtears
of alder and vallenwood,
to the pillared eruptions
of campfire and forge,
to the flight of the gods
and the gods returning.

And the sound of my coming
was a warning sign.

Ten visions, O Istar, lie sleeping
in the great crystal dome
of your Kingpriest's Temple,
where the walls recede from the plumb line,
where foundations devolve
through corundum through quartz,
through limestone through clay,
to the half-fallen dreams of foundation.

Ten visions lie sleeping
and my song has awakened them all.
For my words are the leveling wind,
are the blood of the trees
and the fire on the shores,

the gods walk in my song,
where ten visions waken
in the hands of my singing:
I offer them, glittering, shattered,
and the gods break in my hands.

V

Istar, your army in Balifor
is a gauntlet, clenched
on a quicksilver heirloom.

Your priests in Qualinost
are dazzlements of glass
fractured on red velvet.

Your light hand in Hylo
steals breath from the cradle:
Ice on the glove.

In Silvanost, the white thighs of the women
wade through the muddied waters
of Thon-Thalas.

Your sword arm in Solamnia
entangles in filaments,
in the spider's alley.

Your children in Thoradin
dream away ancestries
of green earth and sun.

The shards of remembered Ergoth
collect to a broken vessel
from dispersion they call the planet's twelve corners.

One name on the lips of Thorbardin
the rows of teeth
unmarked gravestones.

Your fingers in Sancrist
fumble the intricate hilt
of a borrowed sword.

But, Istar, the last song
is yours, the song at the center of songs:
A bleached bone on the altar.

VI

And last generation of Istar,
pure generation,
born of bright stones
drawn from the crown
of a mountebank's hat,
whose goodness is ordinance,
precise, mathematical,
stripped of the elements
in the heart's fire
and the earth of the body,
in the water of blood
and the air's circumference:
You have passed through your temple
unharmed until now,
but now all of Istar
is strung on our words
on your own conceiving
as you pass from night
to awareness of night
to know that hatred is the calm of philosophers
that its price is forever
that it draws you through meteors
through winter's transfixion

through the blasted rose
through the shark's water
through the black compression of oceans
through rock
through magma
to yourself to an abscess of nothing
that you will recognize as nothing
that you will know is coming again and again
under the same rules.

So says the wind
in one tongue only,
pronounced in the movement
of cloud and water,
given voice by the rattle of leaves.
In the breath between waiting
and memory it stalks
elusive as light and promise.
So says the wind
in the long year preserved
in the heart's recollection,
and always it yearns
for another and blessed year
that the heart might have been
in its wild anointing.
And the wind is always your heartbeat,
is breathing remote
as the impassive stars,
and it moves from arrival to leaving,
leaving you one song only.
Oh, that was the language of wind,
you say, *and what does it mean*
to the leaves and the water,
and *always* is what it means.

Colors of Belief

Richard A. Knaak

ARRYL **T**REMAINE **STEPPED INTO THE COMMON** room of Timon's Folly, the inn where he was staying, and immediately noted the eyes that fixed on him. He was clad in simple traveling clothes. Those in the inn could not know for certain that he was a Knight of Solamnia, but they *could* mark him as a foreigner. That in itself brought attention enough. Had he not prudently decided to leave his armor back in his room, the rest of the patrons would not have pretended that they were looking anywhere but at him.

Ignoring the others, he marched toward the innkeeper, a heavy, bustling man named Brek. The innkeeper was the only one to give him any sort of greeting, likely because he felt a kinship with the young knight. Brek's grandfather had been the Timon whose folly had earned the inn its name—and likewise drove the family to leave Solamnia. Timon had been a Knight of the Sword, like Tremaine.

Tremaine was of the opinion that Timon's line had grown much too soft in only two generations.

"Good evening, Sir Tremaine," the man said in a voice that carried well. Now all the patrons looked up.

"Master Brek." Arryl Tremaine's own voice was low and just a hint sharp at the moment. "I have asked you

---

to not use my title."

Solamnic Knights were a rare sight in the land of Istar, much less the holy city of the same name. Arryl, coming from the more secluded southwest of his own country, had never truly understood why. Both the knighthood and the Kingpriest—he who was ruler of Istar—served the same lord, the god of light and goodness, Paladine. Once compatible, the two servants no longer seemed to be able to work side by side. There were rumors that the church had grown jealous of the knights' power, and the knights jealous of the church's wealth. A Tremaine never bent low enough to believe such rabble-rousing. The House of Tremaine might have seen better days, but the pride of the family was still very much in flower. The young knight had come to Istar three days earlier to learn the truth.

"My apologies, Master Tremaine. Have you decided to take your meal here? We've not seen you since you arrived. My wife and daughters fear you find something amiss with their cooking."

Arryl had no desire to talk about either food or the innkeeper's family, especially where Master Brek's daughters were concerned. Like many a woman, they were taken with the young knight's handsome, albeit cool, visage and his tall, well-honed form. Arryl in no way encouraged them and, in point of fact, found the thought of mixing base desires with his holy trek to Istar sacrilegious.

"I have come merely to ask some information of you before I retire for the day."

"So early? It is barely dark, Master." Brek thought the knight a little odd. It was clear that the innkeeper either had forgotten or had never been told by his grandfather about the daily rituals of a Solamnic Knight.

Arryl frowned. He wanted answers, not more questions about his personal habits. "I saw a man arrested by the city guard, a man who had simply been standing by his cart and selling fruit. I have made purchases myself from him in the past day. The soldiers gave no reason for his arrest, something unheard of in my country. He was chained and dragged—"

"I'm certain there was a *proper* reason for it, Master Tremaine," Brek interrupted quickly. His smile suddenly seemed strained. "Will you be staying for the Games, Master? Rumor has it that there will be something special going on this time. Some say the Kingpriest himself will attend!"

"I do not believe in these so-called Games. And I've seen enough of the Kingpriest, thank you." Everywhere Tremaine wandered through the vast city, with its tall white towers and extravagantly gilded temples, he saw the benevolent image of the holy monarch smiling down at him. The many majestic banners, which had initially reminded Tremaine of his training days at Vingaard Keep, all bore a stylized profile of the Kingpriest. Sculpted faces, like the one that hung high on the wall behind Master Brek, invoked a frozen blessing on the knight.

Worse yet were the statues, especially the one portraying the Kingpriest holding a smiling baby in one hand and a writhing, many-headed snake in the other. The snake was some artist's interpretation of the dark goddess Takhisis, Paladine's eternal nemesis. Arryl was outraged. All knew that Huma, a Knight of Solamnia, had defeated the Dragonqueen! Huma had invoked the aid of the gods—Paladine—not the Kingpriest!

As for Paladine, the god for whom Istar had originally been erected, he was represented, but not nearly as often as the master cleric. In fact, many of Paladine's tributes had him standing shoulder to shoulder with the Kingpriest, as though they were equals!

"Holy Istar seems more concerned with the greater glory of the servant than it does of the one who is his master," said Arryl sternly.

Brek paled, cast a darting glance sideways at three men seated in a booth. "If you'll be excusing me, Sir . . . Master Tremaine, I—I must be about helping my wife."

Master Brek was gone before the knight drew another breath. Apparently speed was not one of the traits diluted by two generations of sloth.

Shrugging, Arryl turned and headed for the stairs leading to his room. He had much to think about. The pilgrimage to holy Istar had been a great disappointment. Tremaine hoped that his evening prayers would give him the answers he needed.

The knight had taken no more than a dozen steps when a voice from a corner table asked dryly, "Could you spare us a moment, Sir Knight?"

Arryl would have declined, then he noted the silver-and-white robes worn by the three men.

They were clerics of the Order of Paladine. Arryl acknowledged their presence with a polite nod. "Good evening to you, brothers."

"May the blessings of the Kingpriest be upon you, brother," responded the smallest of the trio. His companions said nothing, merely nodded. It was clear that the one in the middle was the senior. "Am I correct? Do we have the honor of addressing one of our Solamnic brethren?"

The two acolytes, for that was what they must be, looked more like soldiers than priests. Of course, the Order of Paladine contained capable fighters, even if they were forbidden to use blades. They fought with blunt weapons, such as maces, like the ones these two had resting on the table. Arryl suspected that these two acted as bodyguards for the third, which said something for his authority and power.

Not that he looked all that powerful. The priest was thin, with slightly hunched shoulders. His face was long and narrow and reminded Arryl of a rat. Nevertheless, the man *was* a holy brother.

"I am Arryl Tremaine, Knight of the Sword," he answered politely.

"As I thought. A Solamnic warrior." The cleric clasped both hands together. Arryl noted that the priest wore thin leather gloves that matched the cleric's robes. The index fingers pressed tight, forming a steeple. The knight wondered if there was something wrong with the man's hands, that he should hide them under gloves. The weather was certainly not cold enough to make protection desirable. "Forgive me for not introducing myself," said the cleric. "I am Brother Gurim."

Although it might be a sin in the eyes of Paladine, Tremaine could not help feeling repulsed by the man's countenance. Brother Gurim had eyes like a rat that watched everything. His nose was long and crooked. It looked as if it had been broken and had not healed properly, which made little sense, considering that Gurim should have been able to heal himself. The priest was nearly bald, his sparse hair combed into a poor semblance of a monk's crown.

A twisted smile stretched Brother Gurim's thin lips, which only made the resemblance to a rodent even stronger.

The knight realized he'd been staring impolitely. He finally remembered to acknowledge the cleric's introduction. "I am honored by your acquaintance. If you will forgive me, I must retire to my quarters to prepare for evening prayer."

Gurim nodded in understanding, but did not bid the knight farewell. "How pleasing it is to meet one of our brothers engaged in the struggle against the Dark Mistress. How pleasing to know that not all of you knights have lapsed in your faith."

Arryl was angered, but careful to maintain his poise. "We knights are faithful to the tenets set down by Paladine. Our faith lapses in man, not the god."

Gurim nodded and smiled unpleasantly. "Is that so?" The gloved hands separated. Brother Gurim placed them on the table, palms down. "I shall not detain you from your vigil, then, Sir Knight. I merely wished to state that I am pleased you are visiting Istar. I pray for the day when the knighthood once more takes its rightful place as His Holiness's tool against the minions of evil. Your presence has encouraged me in that respect."

"I am glad I have pleased you, Brother." Tremaine bowed low so that the look of disdain was not visible. The knighthood a *tool* of the Kingpriest? The Knights of Solamnia were as strong in their beliefs as any in holy Istar. Strong and *independent* . . . as Paladine ordained when he and the gods Habbakuk and Kiri-Jolith appeared before Vinas Solamnus, the knighthood's founder, and instructed him to break from his evil master, the emperor of Ergoth.

There had been a knighthood long before there had ever been a Kingpriest.

Tremaine started toward the stairs. Brother Gurim drew a symbol in the air. "Go in peace, Sir Knight. May the blessings of the Kingpriest be upon you."

Arryl glanced back. "And may Paladine watch over *you*, Brother."

Brother Gurim's rat smile remained in Arryl's mind all the way up the stairway and down to where his quarters were located. Only when he began his evening prayers did the sight at last fade, and only when he was deep within his own mind did Brother Gurim's distasteful countenance disappear.

The memory of the man, unfortunately, did not.

* * * * *

By the end of his fifth day in the holy city, Arryl Tremaine had seen enough. He doubted the sanctity of Istar and its leaders. Istar was not the bastion of good that he had imagined during his childhood. It was not the city of miracles. Parts of the city were beautiful, certainly, but parts of it were ugly, filled with unfortunates living in poverty and squalor. The bad parts were ignored, however, by most of Istar's citizens, who seemed to think they might pray them away.

That day, Arryl told Brek he would be leaving Istar on

the morrow.

That night, Arryl was within sight of the inn when he heard a stifled cry and a grunt. A warrior experienced in combat, Arryl recognized the sound of someone being beaten or stabbed. It came from an alley to his right.

This being holy Istar, the law forbade men to carry weapons, unless they were part of the priesthood or the city guard. Daggers were allowed, since no one liked to go about the city completely unarmed, but they were to be bonded, strapped securely in their sheaths.

Arryl struggled with the bond that held his dagger in place as he hurried to the alley. Whoever had bound the dagger had done a good job, however, and he finally gave up, deciding to rely upon his other skills instead.

Solinari shone brightly. By the moon's light Arryl could see three men fighting among themselves. Or rather, two of them were beating a third. The two attackers wore swords at their sides.

When he was almost within arm's reach of them, the knight shouted, "Stand away and surrender!"

The two men released the third, who lay unmoving. One attacker already had a knife out. The second assailant drew a broadsword. In the shadows, Arryl could not make out the features of either man, but he guessed their type: bullies, who relied on brute strength and quick results. Skill was unimportant.

The first slashed with his blade, then tried to follow through with a meaty fist. Tremaine let the dagger pass him by, fended off the oncoming hand with a sharp blow of his own, and kicked out with his foot.

The hard toe of his boot caught the man just below the kneecap. Yelping, the attacker fell to the street, his empty hand clutching his leg.

The tip of a sword grazed Arryl's forearm. Tremaine, rather than stepping back as most people would have done, dove forward while the second assailant was still completing his swing. His adversary realized what was happening, but by the time he began to pull his sword back, Arryl had him by the waist.

The two men crashed against the alley wall. The swordsman, caught between the wall and the Solamnian, grunted, dropped his blade, and tried to regain some of the air that had been shoved out of his body by the crushing blow.

Tremaine gave him no quarter. With his left hand balled into a fist, he struck his hapless opponent hard in the stomach.

Folding over, the second man fell.

Arryl heard movement near him, and he kicked out to the side with his foot. The first attacker, just about to leap, went flying against the opposite wall.

There was no resistance after that.

Barely breathing hard, Arryl looked for the victim. It did not surprise him when he found no one. The unfortunate had likely crawled off as soon as he had been able to do so. Arryl could not blame the man. There were few whose courage and abilities matched those of a Solamnic Knight.

Arryl was just debating what to do with his two charges when a group of armed soldiers, obviously the city guard, appeared at the end of the alley.

"What goes on here?" asked another man, stepping forward. Unlike the others, he wore the robes of the priesthood.

"These men were beating another. I ordered them to surrender, but they chose to attack *me* instead."

The soldiers began to filter into the alley. Several men reached the two dazed assailants and half-dragged the limp forms away. The cleric, meanwhile, ordered a torch brought so that he might better survey the scene. After observing the alley and the weapons dropped by Tremaine's adversaries, the cleric turned his attention to the waiting knight. Seen by the flickering light of the torch, the priest's pale face and emaciated countenance made him look like a week-dead corpse.

"Why did you not call the guardsmen?"

"They wouldn't have arrived in time. A man's life was in danger."

"So you say." The cleric sounded skeptical.

Arryl's temper rose a bit at the thought that someone would dare question his word, but he reminded himself that the priest did not know he was a Knight of Solamnia.

"Is the sword your weapon?" The cleric pointed at the blade lying on the street.

"I had no weapon. These belonged to them."

The cleric was genuinely impressed. "You took on two men without a weapon?"

Tremaine shrugged. "I am a Knight of Solamnia, a Knight of the Sword. I have been trained to fight with or without weapons. The two who attacked were hardly a threat." Arryl shrugged. "Swords and knives in the hands of novices are generally more dangerous to themselves than to anyone else."

The city guardsmen glanced at each other and muttered among themselves. The cleric demanded quiet. Arryl noted the silver stripe running across the man's chest, the same stripe he had seen on Brother Gurim and several other clerics since his arrival. He wondered briefly about its meaning, but the priest demanded his attention again.

"Your name, Solamnian?"

"I am Arryl Tremaine."

"Arryl Tremaine, I want you to come with us."

"Excuse me, Brother, but I would like to return to my quarters. I have been negligent in the performance of my evening prayers."

The cleric smiled. "I commend your dedication, but this is a matter of justice. The laws of His Holiness and the great Paladine have been broken. Surely you see that this is of much greater import than missing one day of prayer?"

Arryl hesitated, then nodded. The cleric had a point. The law had been broken and Tremaine was a witness.

Likely they wanted him to testify against the two.

"Come, then, Sir Knight," said the cleric pleasantly. "Walk beside me. It is not often that we have one of our Solamnic brothers among us."

Very understandable, Tremaine thought. When he left Istar tomorrow, he certainly would never be back.

The city guardsmen suddenly closed in around him and jostled him roughly. Angered at their effrontery, Arryl started to reach for his sword, then reminded himself that not only was he not the prisoner, but that his sword was back in his quarters.

*   *   *   *   *

To his astonishment, the guardsmen took him to the Temple of Paladine.

"Why are we here?" Tremaine asked. "I would have thought felons would be taken to the headquarters of the city guard."

The emaciated priest, who still had not introduced himself, gave Arryl a look that said that only a foreigner would ask such a question. "The city guard is the physical arm of justice. Defining and overseeing the law is a matter for the Order of Paladine."

Despite the merit of the statement, the Solamnian had his doubts. "You have not yet explained my purpose here. Am I to act as witness?"

"That is up to the inquisitors to decide."

Inquisitors? Arryl disliked the sound of that.

The temple itself was as splendid as anything in Istar. Immense marble columns rose high in the air. Intricate friezes representing both the history of Istar and Paladine's glory decorated the walls. Sculptures and other valuable artifacts lined the halls. The temple had been built long before the present Kingpriest. The additions made since his rise to power were gaudy and seemed out of place. His banners and masks were everywhere, but here the true wonder of Paladine overwhelmed that of his servant, as was only proper.

A pair of tall silver—*true* silver—doors led to the chamber where the inquisitors meted out justice. Tremaine and the others waited for several minutes, the knight trying not to grow impatient.

The doors suddenly swung open. Two large acolytes, armed with very solid-looking maces, pushed the doors aside and stood guard. One of them nodded to Arryl's guide.

"Enter."

The guards shoved Arryl forward, as if *he* were the prisoner! He glared at them angrily.

The room was lit by only a handful of torches, but it was still enough light to allow Arryl Tremaine to study his surroundings. The contrast between this chamber and the rest of the temple was astonishing. It seemed that the original builders had forgotten to finish this room once the walls were up. To be sure, the familiar banners and masks commemorating the Kingpriest were present, but little else. The only furniture consisted of a table and three chairs atop a dais.

The doors behind them closed.

Three hooded and robed figures entered from a side door that the knight had not noticed in the dim light. They all wore the same robes that Brother Gurim and the cleric beside him wore, white with a silver stripe running across the chest. Tremaine guessed now what that symbol meant. These specific clerics served as the keepers of justice in the Kingpriest's city.

Their hoods masking their features, the three newcomers sat down in the chairs and faced the group. The one in the center clasped his hands together and asked, "Is this the one involved in the struggle, Brother Efram?"

Arryl's companion stepped through the line of guards and took a position two or three feet in front. The knight tried to follow him, but the soldiers formed a tight ring around him. Arryl frowned, but did nothing more, assuming that this was merely a matter of protocol.

Brother Efram bowed respectfully and answered, "This is the one."

The spokesman for the triumvirate signaled someone beyond the side doorway. Arryl was shocked to see the two men he had beaten enter on their own. The knight was the one being guarded!

"This is the man?" the center figure asked them.

They nodded.

"You are dismissed."

The two departed. The hooded clerics focused their attention on Arryl, who was growing extremely angry. He was forced to remind himself he was in a temple of Paladine.

"You are Arryl Tremaine, Knight of Solamnia?" the cleric demanded.

"I am!" he answered proudly.

The center cleric folded his hands together again. "You appreciate the letter of the law, do you not, Sir Knight?"

"I do. What—"

"Then you realize that you have transgressed."

"I—" Arryl stiffened. He could hardly believe what he was hearing. "I am *innocent* of wrongdoing! What do you mean by saying that I have transgressed?"

A second inquisitor spoke. "Arryl Tremaine, you are charged with preventing two members of the city guard from performing their duties. Further, you assaulted and injured both soldiers."

"This is preposterous!" Tremaine retorted. "They were beating an unarmed man senseless! When I called to them to stop, they did not identify themselves. They attacked me! I defended myself!"

"Where is this third man?" asked the same cleric.

"I . . ." Tremaine had no answer. His only witness had vanished during the struggle. "How could I know these men were guardsmen? I am innocent! This is madness!"

"None of us are truly without sin," the center cleric intoned. The third inquisitor, who had not spoken yet, nodded agreement. The spokesman added, "And you of all people, Knight of Solamnia, should know that ignorance of the law is no excuse. Think of the chaos if we allowed that."

For Arryl Tremaine, the world ceased to be. All that existed for him were the three men and their incredible accusations. What was *happening* here?

They took him then, realizing he was weakest at this moment. Two guards caught hold of his arms and pinned them, while two more clamped manacles around his wrists, ankles, and throat. Arryl was too proud to resist; against so many, his struggles would have been useless. In less than a minute, the knight was shackled.

"Arryl Tremaine," said the inquisitor, "you have been found guilty of crimes against the laws set down by the Kingpriest of Istar and Paladine himself. To argue against those laws is to argue against your very faith."

Arryl said nothing, his mind dazed as he tried to understand what was happening.

"You are hereby sentenced to the Games, there to train and fight for your eventual freedom . . . if Paladine deems you worthy of salvation."

The Games? As with everything else, even Arryl's sentence bordered on the absurd, the unbelievable. The Games were death itself, senseless, bloody conflicts that were *against* the laws of Paladine, as set forth in the Oath and the Measure.

"Place him in a cell for the night and see to it that he is sent to the arena first thing in the morning," the inquisitor ordered. Brother Efram bowed. To Arryl, the inquisitor said, "May the Kingpriest watch over your soul, Sir Knight."

The three hooded clerics rose. Arryl shook free his guards' hands and marched out, glaring balefully at the inquisitors. His mind noted and locked on one feature concerning the third inquisitor, the silent one. Arryl tried to hold back to get a better look, but the guards shoved him toward the doors.

Nonetheless, Tremaine was certain that the third

inquisitor—and *only* the third inquisitor—had worn a thin, elegant pair of gloves.

*   *   *   *   *

Arryl Tremaine stood outside the tall walls of the arena, staring at it with disgust and loathing. Until his misguided pilgrimage to Istar, he had considered the Games the one aberration, the one pit of darkness he had been willing to admit existed in the holy center.

Certainly he had not thought to ever find himself inside, sentenced to fight for a crime he had not committed. Now he was just one among a group of dour men, standing in a wagon that had drawn up just outside of the stonework leviathan. The arena looked massive enough to seat every citizen of Istar. From where he stood, he could see a portion of the field where men killed one another for the amusement of the masses.

In Istar, holiest of holy places.

"Step down, step down!" ordered an ugly, scarred dwarf, who apparently was in charge of the arena. "My name is Arack. This here is Raag." Raag was an ogre. Yellowish of skin, he was taller than even the tall Tremaine and had a warty face that Arryl doubted even the proverbial mother could love. The ogre was the most monstrous thing the Solamnic warrior had ever come across.

The knight, with his proud air and stiff, upright stature, stood out in comparison to the slouchy, slovenly half-dozen others. Most had the hang-dog expression of long-time felons. Arryl took an interest in only two—a boy dressed in motley, who obviously had no idea what was going to happen to him, and a half-elf, whose face was that of a man who knows he is doomed. Having studied the rest during the short, bleak trip from his cell to this place, Arryl guessed that most would not survive long enough to win their freedom.

Arryl Tremaine glanced about and grimaced at the exterior of the arena, adorned with the benevolent visage of the Kingpriest. Brother Gurim came immediately to mind.

Brother Gurim. The rat-faced cleric was responsible for his being sentenced to this place, of that Arryl was certain. A night in a dank prison cell had been long enough for the Solamnic warrior to question the law and authority by which he had been judged. Something was amiss. It was too coincidental that the same man who had spoken to the young knight only a day prior, and who had overheard what Arryl was forced to admit may have been injudicious remarks about Istar, should be one of the inquisitors at his sudden, mad trial.

Marble masks lined the arena walls, each visage gazing down in sculpted tenderness upon the monarch's spiritual children when they entered on the days of the Games. Through the open gateway Arryl could see the faces that adorned the inside of the arena. Probably the countenance of each succeeding monarch replaced that of his predecessor. Not at all to Arryl's surprise, he saw very little tribute to Paladine.

Once again, Tremaine wondered whether Istar, stronghold of Paladine, had forgotten exactly who it was its citizens were supposed to worship.

"You there!" The dwarf walked up to him. For one of the hill folk, Arack was surprisingly lean, like a small cat. Knowing the strength of Arack's kind, Arryl wondered if he could take the dwarf in combat. One did not gain authority in an arena without some prowess. "Which are you?"

"I am Arryl Tremaine."

"The knight." The dwarf looked him over, pausing at one point to eye Tremaine's flowing, well-groomed Solamnic moustache. "Yer in good shape. Last o' yer kind I saw looked more like a merchant man than a fighter. Round as a tub."

Raag laughed. Arryl kept silent, figuring the dwarf was only trying to provoke him into a fight.

"I understand you took on two of the city guard," Arack pursued.

"I did what I thought was right. I did not know they were guardsmen," Arryl replied sternly.

The dwarf snorted. "Yeah, that's what they all say!" Arack pointed the knight out to the other prisoners. "Ya see this man? Fought the city guard. Beat 'em both . . . and bare-handed, yet!"

There was a subtle movement away from the Solamnian, as if anyone who had crossed the guard was unclean.

"What's yer best weapon?" the dwarf asked, all business again. His eyes sparkled with some scheme.

Arryl had the uncomfortable feeling the scheme involved him. "Sword."

"Just that? 'Sword,' he says. Any particular *type* of sword?"

"Broadsword. Short sword." Tremaine decided not to tell him more.

Scratching his chin, Arack considered. "You'll be going to Nelk's bunch, then."

"I will not fight. I will not become a part of this barbaric ritual! This place, these Games, are an affr—"

"You'll go to Nelk's group, whatever you end up doin'!" That was the end of the discussion, as far as Arack was concerned. He stepped away from the knight and moved on to the half-elf, who was surreptitiously observing the Solamnian.

Arryl Tremaine knew that arguing would be a waste for now. He kept quiet, turned his mind to other matters. He wondered what Master Brek would think when he did not return. It occurred to him that maybe the innkeeper knew exactly what had happened to the knight, perhaps had had a hand in it.

The fight . . . outside the inn . . . No, Arryl couldn't believe something so monstrous, not even of Brother Gurim. The knight wondered about his belongings. . . .

My armor! Arryl was horrified that he could have

gone so long without thinking of the armor passed down from his grandfather. "Master Arack!" he called.

The dwarf glanced over his shoulder. "What do you want, Sir Knight?" he asked with a sneer.

"My armor! What has become of it?"

"The guard'll return it to ya, if it's decided ya should wear it in the arena! Now keep yer place!"

The city guard *did* have his belongings, then. Arryl was most concerned with the armor. Those who had seen him ride into Istar in full armor might have thought him an elegant, rich knight, but the truth was that, while the House of Tremaine was not poor, like so many of its cousins, it had learned to be frugal. He had been fortunate in that his grandfather's suit had fit him with very little alteration and had also borne the symbol of the order to which the young Tremaine had always aspired to join. Among many Houses of Solamnia, armor, when still serviceable, was a treasure to be handed down until the day when someone else might be able to don it.

Of course, if such a suit did not fit, then a new one had to be put together. Some knights preferred new armor. Arryl considered it an honor to wear the armor of a noble ancestor.

There was nothing he could do about his armor, save hope that someone in the city guard did not take a fancy to it.

Raag's leering visage loomed before him. The ogre's rancid breath struck Arryl like one slap after another. "Knight!" Raag grinned, revealing sharp, yellowed teeth. "You come."

"Take these two as well," Arack called, jabbing a thumb at the half-elf and the confused-looking boy, dressed in the sort of loose, colorful clothing worn by peasants in the villages far to the southwest of Istar. Arryl recalled hearing that those places were very relaxed in their worship of the gods. They were even said to worship the gods of neutrality, despite the Kingpriest's efforts to alter their thinking. Arryl wondered what sort of crime brought a mere boy, who couldn't be more than fourteen, to the arena and how the gawking boy was expected to take part in the Games.

The Games at this time consisted of both live combat and tournament battle, with more of the former than the latter. The difference between the two was that "live" combat usually meant "live" death as well. Tournament battles were fought between gladiators of exceptional skill, who were too valuable to let themselves get killed, and generally ended when one of the men was disarmed. None of the prisoners were to be a part of those tournaments. The Games Arryl and his fellows had been chosen to play would be very, very real.

Raag led them into the arena and out onto the field. The sound of two weapons ringing against one another was almost deafening. A group of fighters—obviously veteran gladiators—stood in a circle, cheering on two combatants. The battle sounds stirred something inside Arryl. He craned his head to see. It was evident from the frequency of the strikes that here were two opponents who not only fought with speed, but with skill.

Despite the noise, someone noticed Raag's approach. It paid to notice the ogre before one became a temporary obstacle in his path. The gladiators gave way for the oncoming ogre. Arryl made a quick study of the men. Hardened fighters all, but lacking in the grace and elegance of a knight. If not for the arena, many of them would have ended up mercenaries or highwaymen. More than a few had probably worked as one or both during the course of their lives.

Raag, gruff as ever, turned to Arryl and pointed at the duelist to the left.

"Nelk. Arack say, you fight with Nelk."

Arryl stared, amazed.

Nelk was an elf.

A maimed elf. Arryl wondered about the sort of elf who would deal in death, decided he must be a dark elf, one of the outcasts of elven society.

Tremaine studied Nelk. He seemed no different from the few elves the knight had met, except that the arrogant, delicate features were marred by a sardonic twist of the mouth, as if Nelk—that could not be his true name—had seen too much of the world and not found it to his liking. But he handled a mace with a skill becoming that of a Solamnic master, a necessary skill, since the elf lacked the lower half of his right arm and could not, therefore, have used a shield to any real purpose. His natural grace and agility also served to compensate for his physical handicap.

Nelk's opponent was a human, a thin, brown-haired man who both looked and moved like a snake. He fought with a sword and Arryl, who took an instant dislike to the serpentine man, grudgingly had to admit he was skilled.

It was a strange duel, mace against sword. Both men were caught up in their practice and it was evident that here were two masters. Arryl forgot his troubles, watching the two skilled fighters at work. Although Nelk had only one arm, his mace was nearly three feet long. He moved with a speed that few humans could match. His heavier adversary compensated for a lack of elven speed by utilizing both sword and shield as few men in the knighthood could have managed.

The weapons clanged together again and again, never remaining motionless. Each time one duelist seemed about to break through the defenses of the other, a counterassault brought them back to their standoff.

Then, Arryl saw the human make a blunder. An overextension of his arm left his side vulnerable. It was a very slight mistake, but a master such as Nelk should have been able to capitalize on it easily.

Nelk ignored it. The gap in the human's defenses vanished instantly. Once again the two were on even footing.

"Hold, Sylverlin!" The elf stepped back, still guarding himself. His serpentine counterpart did the same. Both men saluted each other, then smiled grimly. Nelk was not breathing hard at all; his human adversary seemed only slightly put out by the strenuous activity. Arryl silently applauded their abilities.

Turning, the elf eyed the newcomers. The rest of the gladiators melted away as he walked over to inspect the small group Raag had brought him. "What is this?"

"Arack said," was all the ogre commented.

"Mine, then." The elf surveyed the trio of prisoners. He seemed amused by the boy, and sneered at the half-elf. Most elves—even dark ones—looked down upon half-breeds as being less than either of the two races from which they had sprung.

Nelk paused when he came to Arryl. "You are a fighter, I see."

"Solamnian," Raag offered.

"Ah. The knight," said Sylverlin, coming up behind. Both instructors studied Tremaine with interest.

Tremaine straightened. "I will not fight in your Games."

"Won't you?" Nelk shrugged. "We'll see. Arack gave you to me and that is all that matters."

"Too good for us?" Sylverlin hissed. He even sounded like a serpent.

"Arack waits," Raag grunted.

Satisfied that Nelk was now in charge of the three, the ogre turned and departed without another word. Nelk watched him go, seeming to appraise the ogre's every movement.

"He'd still beat you, my good friend," the reptilian man commented offhandedly. "Raag's quick in the head when he needs to be, not to mention having a skin as tough as a breastplate."

"I am well aware of both my limitations and his, Sylverlin. Best to worry about your own. If we had been dueling to the death, I would have crushed your rib cage after that last ploy of yours."

"You mean the opening I left? Wasn't a mistake, my

good friend." Sylverlin bowed in mockery to Arryl, then slid off in the opposite direction Raag had gone.

"I knew it was not," the elf commented with a wry smile, his voice loud enough for the knight to hear. "Why else would I have avoided it?" The elf's slanted eyes returned to Arryl. "As for you, you will fight, human. You will fight for the simple reason that you will die if you do not. You . . . and others because of you." His glance went, as if by accident to the half-elf and the boy. "For now, you should get something to eat, I think. You will need your strength today. That is a promise. Go with them."

He pointed to several gladiators who leered at the newcomers and made crude comments about "last meals." Arryl stiffened and reached for a sword that wasn't at his side. Nelk laughed and sauntered away.

The half-elf leaned toward Arryl and whispered, "They will kill us on the spot if you choose to give them trouble now! Best to live and find a better moment, human!"

Tremaine reluctantly gave in and started walking. The half-elf's words made sense to him, but he wondered exactly when that better moment might come. Escape seemed impossible. The arena was well protected; archers and sentries were everywhere.

An indrawn breath from the half-elf made Tremaine shift his gaze. "What is it?"

"The senior inquisitor is up in the stands with the arena masters!" his companion muttered. "Pray he is not here concerning us! If so, we go from having little chance to *none!*"

Following the direction of the other prisoner's eyes, the knight focused on a man who had been watching the duel between Nelk and Sylverlin from the stands.

Brother Gurim!

Arryl Tremaine tripped and nearly fell. He stared and stared at the rat-eyed priest. Arryl was certain now. He had stepped into a nightmare whose master was the gloved cleric.

Was this *truly* what Istar had become?

* * * * *

Sylverlin marched Arryl out into the arena after the meal and handed the knight a sword. Arryl dropped it at the man's feet. Sylverlin told him to pick it up. Arryl told him the same thing he had told the elf earlier: "I will not fight." The knight fully expected to be beaten or tortured. Sylverlin clenched his fist, seeming to enjoy the idea.

"Leave him be," ordered Nelk. He made Tremaine stand aside while the elf took the half-elf and the boy and added them to another group of mixed unfortunates. Sylverlin glowered, obviously disappointed. He obeyed Nelk, however, though he flashed the elf a vicious glance that Nelk saw but ignored. The abandoned sword remained at the knight's feet, as if a challenge of some sort. Arryl folded his arms and stood unmoving the rest of the afternoon.

At the end of the day, he again expected to be punished. Nelk ordered Arryl into the line with the others. That was all. No mention of punishment. Sylverlin joined Nelk; the two seemed as attached as two branches of the same tree. They walked off together, now apparently the best of friends.

During the evening meal, the half-elf chose to join Arryl. No one else sat near them. The other men, both veteran gladiators and newcomers, were unwilling to sit next to either a Solamnic warrior who had fought the city guard or a half-elf whose crime was the fact that he existed. The only one who seemed to want to join them was the peasant boy, who also sat alone. He gave the two of them a shy, nervous smile, obviously hoping to be invited. Tremaine started to signal him over, but his companion shook his head.

"I would like to talk to you alone. My name is Fen

Sunbrother," the half-elf said in a low voice. He had a swarthy complexion and his mixed background gave him exotic features. A thin beard attested to the fact that his human half had at least some dominance. "What are you called?"

Tremaine hesitated. While Solamnia had been built on the principles of justice and fairness, mixed breeds like Fen Sunbrother were not accepted members of society. It may have been that his own desperate situation made the knight more tolerant, for he found himself replying, "I am Arryl Tremaine."

"We are both outcasts, it appears." Fen indicated the empty benches around them. "You hardly seem the type who should be here. Knight of Solamnia, yes?"

"I am a Knight of the Order of the Sword."

"Thought that." Fen glanced warily around, as if he expected someone to be spying on their conversation. "You need not tell me, but I would be interested to know for what reason you are here."

"I am innocent of wrongdoing. I came to the aid of a man being beaten. I did not know the bullies beating him were city guardsmen."

The half-elf gave him a sour smile. "Crime enough here, depending on the situation. Tell me about it." —

Arryl did, leaving nothing out. After a day of having no one willing to hear his side, he was gratified to find a sympathetic ear. Fen Sunbrother listened, and as he listened, his expression turned dark and bitter.

"I have all the luck. I am constantly allying myself with those who draw the ire of the mighty." The half-elf took a bite of his food, grimaced, but swallowed it nonetheless. The food at the arena was designed to keep the men fit enough to fight; taste was not a priority. "You have brought the attention of the inquisitors down upon you. Worse, you have attracted the personal wrath of Brother Gurim."

"What have *I* done to the man?"

"What have you done? It could be any number of

things." Fen poked the gruel with his finger. The hole formed did not fill in when he pulled the finger out. "The worst part of being in the arena is not the possibility of death—it's the food."

Arryl did not smile.

The half-elf shrugged. "There is something that you must understand, Tremaine. In Istar, the clerics are the law. Among the clerics, the inquisitors are justice. It is they who define the words of the Kingpriest and how those words affect the citizens."

"Would that they were as concerned with the word of Paladine as much as that of the Kingpriest," said Arryl sternly.

Fen's eyes widened, then he nodded in understanding. "You knights are very strong in your faith, not to mention vocal about it. You've been talking like that for the past few days, haven't you?"

"What of it? I am within my rights—"

"In *Solamnia*, you would be within your rights, but not here. . . ." Fen shook his head. "Istar is another matter. A Solamnic Knight, one of the legendary warriors of justice and good, rides into the holy city and finds it not so holy. Small wonder that you incurred the wrath of Brother Gurim. To him, you are a threat to the order."

"For speaking out?" Arryl realized his voice had risen. He glanced around, but everyone else was working hard to pretend they had not heard him. "I am only one man! What sort of threat could I be?"

The half-elf grunted, began eating his gruel again. Between bites, he muttered, "You come to a place few of your kind ever visit and you immediately question the ways of the priesthood. Those who rule Istar have long seen the Solamnic Orders as rivals, jealous of the priests' wealth and power."

Tremaine recalled Brother Gurim's words at the inn. *I pray for the day when the knighthood once more takes its rightful place as His Holiness's tool. . . .*

"Brother Gurim may even think this a plot by your

kind to undermine the authority of the Holy One. That alone would be enough to have you executed," added the half-elf.

It was such a preposterous thought that Arryl could not take it seriously. He decided it was time to turn the conversation. "And you, Fen Sunbrother? What harm have you done that sentences you to the arena?"

He had expected something on the order of thievery, but the half-elf shrugged and said, "I'm a 'breed.' A mongrel."

"That is hardly a crime."

The half-elf turned his attention to the unappetizing gruel. "Welcome to Istar, Sir Knight."

* * * * *

Another day dawned. Arryl refused to take the sword Sylverlin handed to him. Sylverlin taunted, jeered, insulted him. The knight ignored him.

Nelk watched in silence.

Sylverlin shoved the knight a couple of times, but did him no harm. Tremaine wondered at Nelk's ploy. It would have been simple enough to execute the knight, but someone appeared to want more. Someone wanted Arryl to fight in the arena. He thought he understood. If he gave in, it would be as great a victory for his captor as if he *had* died in battle. It would mean that Gurim had broken the knight, could claim he was weak.

Arryl had no intention of bowing to the will of the senior inquisitor.

Eventually Nelk sent Sylverlin off to instruct some of the gladiators in the finer points of swordplay. The snakelike man was showing them how to *pretend* to strike an opponent. None of the veteran gladiators wanted to accidentally die or kill one of their comrades during tournament combat. The prisoners, of course, had no choice. They could only hope to survive long enough to either win their freedom or be offered a place in the tournament combats.

"This will avail you naught, Solamnian," said Nelk, glancing at the sword.

"I will not fight. Execute me if you will, but I will not go against the Oath and the Measure by fighting for the pleasure of others."

Nelk laughed. "Do they teach such arrogance in the knighthood or is it something you were born with?" Arryl refused to respond. The elf stepped closer, his voice lowered. "You *will* fight in the Games, Knight! Listen to me! I had hoped you would not force me to this, but I want you to know that—"

"Nelk!" Sylverlin shouted. "Spectators!" With his blade, he pointed to their right.

Brother Gurim was once again in the stands. The hood covered his unsightly features, but Arryl had now learned to look for the gloves. Brother Gurim gestured to Nelk.

The maimed elf gave Arryl a long, intense look and whispered, "You may have lost your last chance, human fool!"

Nelk and Sylverlin went over to talk with Brother Gurim. The two had barely departed when Fen Sunbrother and the boy, struggling beneath weaponry enough to arm a legion, joined the knight. Arms full, the boy smiled cautiously at Tremaine, who nodded in return.

"What did the Cursed One want of you?" Fen asked.

Arryl's brow knitted. "Cursed One?"

"You don't know what 'Nelk' means in Elvish, do you? Never mind. Did he threaten to have you beaten?"

"He said nothing of that, but I think something is going to happen soon."

The half-elf shook his head. "And you'll just let it happen to you! You'll take their punishment . . . or the axe if they decide you're not worth the time. Mark me, Tremaine. Brother Gurim has let you live this long for a reason. He has a reputation for playing games with his victims."

"Is he really that bad?" the boy asked shyly. It was the first time Arryl had heard him talk. "But he's a cleric!"

"Yes, he is," Sunbrother snarled. "So?"

"Do not frighten him unnecessarily," the knight warned.

"You there, *breed*!" One of Sylverlin's trusted gladiators struck Fen on the side of the head. "The guards don't like quiet talk! Get movin'. Arack'll count all those swords before he lets you back out of the storeroom!"

Fen Sunbrother staggered beneath the blow, grimaced, and moved on, his younger companion struggling to keep up. Tremaine thought over the half-elf's warning, but remained unmoved. He could and would continue to resist, despite whatever punishment Nelk or—more likely—Sylverlin decided to mete out.

Arryl stared at the cleric, trying to will the man to meet his gaze. Not once, however, did Gurim glance at him. The inquisitor knew the knight was watching him, was deliberately ignoring him. Arryl felt his temper rise. The cleric was baiting him, and it was working.

The conversation between the gladiators and the cleric was short, which might have been good or might have been bad. Nelk and Sylverlin returned to the field. Brother Gurim, accompanied by his two large shadows, departed the arena. Nelk's countenance was carefully indifferent. Sylverlin gave Arryl a serpentine grin.

Nelk did not talk to the knight again that day. No one spoke to Tremaine or asked him to pick up the sword. A decision had been made, obviously, and the instructors were only waiting for the proper moment to carry it out.

That night, Arryl Tremaine made his peace with Paladine. He did not expect to live out the morrow.

* * * * *

Arryl was certain of his fate when the groups were rearranged. The half-elf, the boy, and most of the veteran gladiators were sent to the opposite end of the arena in order to commence with a series of practice duels. Nelk, Arryl, and a much smaller but distinct group remained in the area where the knight had stood the day before. Nelk was instructing the group in the uses of a mace against a sword. He seemed preoccupied. Tremaine guessed something of far greater import had possession of the elf's thoughts.

Nelk ignored Arryl, save to tell him where to stand. From his vantage point, the knight could see clearly the elaborate box set aside for the Kingpriest. Fen had informed him that the Kingpriest seldom appeared at the Games, but that other high-ranking clerics often sat in the box.

He was not very surprised, then, when Brother Gurim and his two acolytes entered the box only a couple of hours into the day's training.

The senior inquisitor seated himself in the very center of the box and, looking rather bored, settled himself to observe the practice. His hood had been pulled back. As with the day before, he seemed to pay no attention to Arryl. The cleric was intent on watching Sylverlin's group.

Nelk ordered one of his subordinates to take over. His eyes flashed to Brother Gurim, then to Arryl. The maimed elf, mace still in hand, walked slowly over to the knight, who regarded the elf with cool disdain.

"I tried to warn you," Nelk said in a low voice. "He knew all along that it would be useless to threaten *your* life, but he enjoys his own games almost as much as he does those in the arena."

"What do you mean?" Tremaine frowned, convinced it was a trick.

"One way or another, he will make you do what he wishes, no matter how many lives it costs." He glanced in Sylverlin's direction.

Arryl understood. Fear gripped him. He stared at the large group on the opposite end of the field. The gladiators clustered about, staring at a body lying on the ground.

"Sometimes," Nelk was saying, "there are those who do not make it to the Games."

The boy! was Arryl's first thought.

"Blessed Paladine!" He started to run, but the elf's foot tripped him up.

Arryl tried to regain his feet, but found the hooked and jagged head of the elf's mace against his throat.

"It's already too late, Sir Knight. It was too late before I even started to speak." Nelk stepped back and allowed Arryl to rise. Several gladiators from Sylverlin's group were heading toward them, carrying a limp form.

"It seems there's been another training accident," Sylverlin shouted jovially.

The victim was not, as Arryl had feared, the boy.

"Fen Sunbrother," he murmured. Part of the half-elf's body had been covered by an old, stained cowhide, but blood had already seeped through it. Arryl guessed he had died instantly.

Nelk called out, "What happened?"

"What always 'appens?" retorted the lead gladiator, a grizzled bear of a man with scars all over his arms and face. " 'e fairly threw 'imself on the blade! 'e was warned about movin' like that, but 'e wouldn't listen!" As an afterthought, the bulking figure added, "Master Sylverlin couldn't 'elp but run 'im clean through."

Sylverlin!

The head of Nelk's mace rested, as if by accident, on Arryl's shoulder. The knight took the hint and watched in impotent rage as the gladiators carried the body from the field. Tremaine's gaze shifted to where the senior inquisitor sat. For the first time, Brother Gurim stared back.

"Accidents could happen at any time," Nelk was saying casually, "especially to those who are not familiar with weapons. Take the boy, for instance. . . ."

The knight turned sharply. "You wouldn't!"

"*He* would," the elf replied, indicating Brother Gurim. "Can you stand by and let others die because of your stubbornness?"

The Oath and Measure of the knighthood said otherwise. To allow others to die in his place would be tantamount to cowardice.

"The boy can be saved," Nelk said softly. "Brother Gurim wants you, not him."

To prove that a cleric could make a Solamnic Knight yield his principles. To make a knight bow to the cleric's will. Brother Gurim's countenance might be expressionless, but his eyes were not. The senior inquisitor would order the boy's death if Arryl rejected his demands.

Arryl turned away, faced Nelk. "What will happen to the boy?" the knight asked.

"A mix-up. He should have been sent to work cleaning the temple floors for a month in order to make his penance. These things happen." Nelk shrugged. "Sometimes the mistakes are rectified, sometimes not."

Holy Istar! Arryl thought bitterly. There was no choice. The Oath and Measure demanded he protect the innocent from harm. "I agree, providing you personally guarantee the boy's life."

"It will be guaranteed. I swear to that. You have not dealt with the eccentricities of the inquisitor as I have. He will be happy to give the boy back his life, if only to prove how benevolent he can be."

There was relief in Nelk's eyes, a strange thing, the knight noted. The elf removed the mace from its resting place and, turning it upside down, sank the head into the dirt.

It was a signal, a signal of Arryl's defeat. The moment the mace touched the ground, the inquisitor rose and departed the arena. No backward glance, no lingering. Brother Gurim had seen his adversary bend knee to him and that was all the cleric wanted. For now.

The maimed elf smiled. "Pick up your sword and join us. I want to see what you can do."

Tremaine knelt and picked up the sword that had been handed him each day. They will see what I can do, he vowed. He had been forced to this decision, but now that the barrier had been breached, he had no intention of holding back. The gladiators would see what it was like to face a true knight.

Brother Gurim would see what being a Knight of Solamnia truly meant.

*　*　*　*　*

Nelk made certain Arryl was present when the city guard marched the boy away. It took some time for the guard to explain to an annoyed Arack that there had been a mistake. The dwarf evidently did not like mistakes. He lit into the hapless guard commander with a tongue that lashed out as hard as his fists. Tremaine could see that Arack's anger was genuine. This helped convince the knight that the boy would indeed receive lighter punishment.

"I gave you my word," said Nelk.

It was on that same day, shortly after the boy's removal, that the swordmaster issued his challenge to the knight.

Sylverlin watched the two duel with avid, jealous attention. He did not interrupt, but stood patiently by. Nelk finally called a halt. "What is it you want, Sylverlin?"

The tip of the snaky human's sword pointed at the knight. "I've come for him. I need to see if he'll be ready for the Games."

Arryl, still burning over the half-elf's murder, started forward. Nelk darted between the two.

"He'll be ready. I will see to him."

"You?" Sylverlin scowled. "You're mistaken, friend Nelk. This one is definitely mine."

"It is you who are mistaken, friend Sylverlin."

Sylverlin glanced at the wary knight. "A pity," he said,

shrugging. "I'd hoped that our blades might cross. Now, no such luck. You'll be dead before I get the chance."

Arryl would have replied, but Nelk was quicker. He brought the mace around and pushed the swordmaster's blade away. "Never wish ill, Sylverlin. The gods have a habit of returning such wishes to their makers."

The serpentine fighter laughed, bowed mockingly to the knight, and left without another word. Arryl was barely able to restrain himself from charging after.

"He has marked you for his own sport. This changes everything," Nelk muttered.

Tremaine studied the elf's features. A sense of foreboding washed over him as he noted his companion's dark expression. "What do you mean?"

"Sylverlin has never really cared about those I choose to fight. But you, Knight, are something special to him. He hates your kind and always has. He murdered the last knight quickly enough. Some say he is one of your cast-offs. Who knows? The only man he wants to fight more than you is me and that is forbidden to him. Sylverlin never argues with Brother Gurim."

Arryl stared. "I am to fight you in the arena?"

"You *must* fight me, human!" Nelk paused, then quickly whispered, "I could not save the half-elf, but I might be able to save *you*, Knight of Solamnia!"

At first, Arryl thought his ears had betrayed him.

Nelk gave him a barely perceptible nod. "I can save you from the arena, Arryl Tremaine, just as I have saved others. You won't be the first."

Tremaine had already had enough treachery. He pulled away from the elf. "I will not fall prey to any more traps set by Brother Gurim! Give me to Sylverlin, who does not pretend to be other than he is! He still owes for Fen Sunbrother's life!"

"This is not a trap! I have saved others and, if it had been in my power, I would have saved even the half-breed! Listen, for I doubt we will have long to talk! There is a way for you to escape the arena and Istar, but to succeed you must put total faith in me!"

"Why should I?" Arryl scoffed.

Nelk dropped his mace, reached out, and grabbed the knight's sword by the blade's sharp edge.

"Are you mad?" Arryl snatched the weapon back, but blood was already streaming from the wound in the elf's palm.

"Watch," Nelk commanded. His eyes closed and he whispered something. Arryl felt a tingle in the air.

The elf's wound began to *heal*! First slowly, then with ever-increasing speed, the deep cut closed and sealed itself. A scab formed along the wound, but it only remained a moment. In the matter of a breath, a thin scar was all that was visible of the cut, yet Nelk was not finished. Even the scar dwindled away, ever shrinking until the only evidence of the self-inflicted injury was the blood that had stained the elf's hand.

Nelk wiped his palm on the sleeve of his shirt. "You're a cleric of Mishakal!" Arryl gasped.

"I serve the goddess."

"But . . . your maimed arm . . ."

"I chose not to heal myself in order to hide the fact that the goddess still favors those who keep the true faith. Have Brother Gurim perform the same miracle and see if he can heal himself. You will find that the inquisitor seems to be lacking somewhat in his faith, or perhaps his god lacks faith in him." The elf eyed his companion. "Will you listen to me now? Will you believe in me?"

Tremaine lowered his sword blade. "If I thought my sentence just, I would still ignore you, but there is no justice in Istar." He shook his head. "And little faith, other than yours. What must I do?"

Nelk nodded his approval. "Sylverlin is eager to match blades with you, but I have been granted the right to face you in the arena. When open combat begins, we must be certain that Sylverlin does not come between us. The battle must be my mace against your blade." Nelk shook his head. "Always before I have trusted my skill, never mentioned my plans to those I rescued for fear they would weaken and betray us both! This situation with Sylverlin, though, and your own worthy abilities, have made this change necessary. I find I must trust *you*, Knight!"

"What about Sylverlin? He cannot be allowed to go unpunished for what he has done!"

"Leave the swordmaster to me. The time is fast approaching when he and I will clash. He might call me friend, but there is no love between us. We are marking the day. You might wish his death now, Knight, but rest assured I have prior and greater reasons than you. What concerns us now is making certain that it is we two alone who face each other during the Games. No one else must be allowed to come between us."

Arryl was still not pleased about leaving Sylverlin to the elf, but Nelk *was* a cleric—a true cleric. "I will abide by your decision, but tell me, why do you risk yourself here? Why do you do it?"

The elf considered his answer well before giving it to the knight. "Because there is a balance to maintain . . . and Istar threatens to tip it too far the wrong way."

"Very well, then. Tell me now your plan. What happens when we come to blows?"

Nelk tapped Arryl's chest with the tip of his mace. "Then, while the crowd and Brother Gurim watch, I will kill you, Sir Knight."

* * * * *

So eager for blood!

The day of the Games came too soon, yet not soon enough. Arryl stood in the line of anxious gladiators, his eyes scanning the packed stadium. Istar seemed especially eager to watch the blood flow this day. Tremaine had heard rumors that *he* was the attraction. It had been rumored that a Knight of Solamnia was among the fighters. Despite the fact that his armor was still a prize of the city guard, he had no doubt that most of the crowd had picked him out already.

Across from him stood Nelk . . . and Sylverlin.

The Kingpriest's box was filled, but the holy monarch himself was absent as usual. Today the box played host to a group of men garbed in identical silver-and-white robes. In the center sat the only one wearing gloves, Brother Gurim. Arryl could not clearly make out his features, but he guessed the senior inquisitor had a smile on his face. For Gurim, all was right in the world. This day was to mark yet another triumph.

Arryl wished he could drag the false cleric down to the field and tell him the truth.

The tournament had been played, the exhibitions had finished. All that remained was the final mass combat. A free fight, in which a man could only hope that he survived the time limit. Arryl heard some of the prisoners plotting desperately to keep in the back, away from the rest of the combatants. Their plans collapsed when Arack informed them that hesitation would not save any man here. The archers on the walks had orders to shoot any gladiator who shied from battle. The prisoners had to fight. As long as they did, they had a chance. Arack emphasized the last, and the prisoners looked more hopeful.

Arryl could have told them the truth. They were doomed. Most were unskilled fighters, even barring the days of training. They had learned enough to hack and slash, but the skilled fighters were few and far between. The masters of the Games did not want their hand-picked gladiators killed.

Arryl knew the outcome, having been forewarned by Nelk. The skilled fighters had already been picked out by the veteran gladiators. Two, even three, would converge on the newcomers while the rest took on the other prisoners. It might look as if the sides were even, but the experience and brutal skill of the gladiators would almost immediately turn the tide in their favor. The crowds would cheer because most of their favorites would win and no one would pay any mind to the dead, who were convicted criminals, anyway.

Sylverlin was grinning with anticipation. Nelk was eyeing Tremaine with an almost indifferent expression. He had armed himself with a sinister-looking ball-and-chain mace that gave him almost half again the reach of his other weapon. Tremaine was somewhat startled by the change, and tried not to think of what an accidental blow might do to him. His only protection lay in a rusting shield, his sword, and his skill.

The horns sounded their death knell. The gladiators charged their chosen opponents. They all avoided the knight, knowing he was reserved for Nelk.

All except Sylverlin. He ran up behind Nelk. Tremaine shouted a warning.

The elf turned. Sylverlin shot past him, sword ready. "You are mine, Knight!" Sylverlin hissed.

Tremaine moved to meet him.

Nelk ran up alongside his friend as if he now planned to join Sylverlin in the duel against Arryl. The spiked ball of the elf's mace swung back and forth, a wicked-looking pendulum. It grazed Sylverlin's leg.

The swordmaster howled in pain and collapsed into a writhing heap on the now-bloody surface of the field.

"The goddess has blessed it," said Nelk, smiling at Arryl. Nelk was on him, mace cutting a deadly arc. The one-armed elf moved with far more speed than the Solamnian was expecting, struck at him with lethal skill. Had he not trusted Nelk, Arryl would have suspected that the elf was indeed trying to kill him!

Arryl brought up his sword and jabbed, keeping the other at bay, as they had planned. Nelk nodded and, his back to the crowd, he winked at Arryl. The two circled one another, feinting strikes, but, as far as onlookers were concerned, they were too expert to fall prey to such tricks. The crowd cheered.

Suddenly, out of nowhere, Sylverlin appeared. Sword raised, he headed for Nelk, prepared to stab the elf in the back.

Arryl had no time to shout a warning. Nelk could not have heard him if he had. The knight thrust forward. Nelk reacted to the attack by stepping aside, still unaware of the true danger. Sylverlin's blow caught the elf's shoulder, but Nelk's movement left the human gladiator open to Tremaine.

The knight's blade sank to the hilt in Sylverlin's stomach. Arryl jerked his sword free. Sylverlin slid off the blade to the ground.

Arryl heard a rattling sound behind him. Instinctively, he started to turn, and forced himself to stand still. This was Nelk's plan.

A thick chain wrapped around his throat. Arryl pretended to struggle to free himself, then suddenly realized Nelk wasn't pretending to kill him!

The crowd had hushed, breathless with excitement.

"Sylverlin was mine!" Nelk shouted loudly, and wrenched the choking chain tighter.

Once more, Arryl thought, my beliefs have been betrayed . . . and this time it will be fatal.

He tried to lift his sword to strike the elf, but he lacked the strength. The blade slipped from his nerveless fingers. He tried to speak, to curse Nelk, to plead. All that escaped his lips was a pathetic gasp.

The dying knight saw the silver-and-white figure of the senior inquisitor rise to his feet in anticipation.

The chain crushed Arryl's windpipe. Bone crunched; the pain was horrifying. He fought to breathe, but he was choking on his own blood. He staggered and would have fallen, but the cruel chain held him upright. He saw the stands and then the sky, and then he was falling. Fire burst in his eyes, his head, his lungs. When the flames died, darkness.

"Trust in me," a voice whispered . . . and laughed.

* * * * *

When Arryl woke, he realized two things.

The first thing was that, despite the knowledge that he had died, he was not dead.

The second was that he was lying on his back in a field that must be far from the arena, for he could neither hear the crowds nor see the high walls.

Dazed and confused, his hand instinctively reaching for his throat, Arryl sat up. He was well, whole, no trace of injury. Just like the cut on the elf's hand . . .

Arryl looked around, saw Nelk seated astride a tall black horse. In his hands, he held the reins of Arryl's own horse. Armor—his grandfather's suit of armor, packed neatly and strapped to a packhorse—glinted in the sunlight.

"The terror of death must have been worse for you than for most of the others I've brought back. I wondered if you were ever going to wake up."

Brought back! The knight stood. He glowered at the amused elf. "What do you mean, brought back? You killed me!"

"Yes. Then I brought you back to life. That is within my powers as a true cleric."

"You are *not* a cleric of Mishakal!" The knight recalled his last thoughts. "You told me you were a cleric of the goddess!"

"Ah," said Nelk cunningly. "You never asked *which* goddess!"

Arryl reached for his sword and immediately discovered that it was not at his side.

Nelk held up the scabbard and weapon. "*You* chose to make me a follower of the gods of good, not me. I am not a cleric of Mishakal, true. I am a servant of Kinthalas, whom you term Sargonnas."

Sargonnas, consort to the Dark Lady, Takhisis, Queen of Darkness.

"Why did you bring me back?" Tremaine demanded

suspiciously. "Why? For what purpose?"

Nelk considered the matter. "What I said to you in the arena holds true, Knight. There *is* a balance to maintain, though I must admit the Dark Lady would like to see it shift in her favor. I do what I can to help those I think will aid the cause. Those I rescue are beholden, however little they may realize, to my own patron."

"You expect such thanks from me?" Arryl asked harshly.

"I expect nothing. I find it amusing to think that a Knight of Solamnia, imprisoned by the Order of Paladine, owes his life to a servant of his god's eternal foe."

Tremaine could not deny what the elf said, but he was determined that neither Sargonnas nor Takhisis would ever own the knight's soul. He would die first . . . again. "I am not your slave, dark elf! Give me my sword and we will fight. Fairly, this time."

"I will return your sword, Sir Knight, and the rest of your belongings, which took some doing to procure. As for a battle, that may yet be what the future holds for us, but not now. I will not fight you. And I do not think you will strike me." Nelk tossed the sword to the knight.

Tremaine caught the sheathed blade, but did not draw his sword.

"If it will ease your conscience, I have no hold over you. You may continue your way, free once more, but with perhaps a little more understanding of the world." Nelk smiled. "You have my word."

"What happens now? Where am I?" Arryl asked gruffly. His greatest desire at the moment was to return to the master keep of the knighthood and reorient his own beliefs. The world that once had been black and white had become too complex, too gray.

"We are a half-day's ride northwest of Istar, a safe place, though we should not stay too long. You need to be on your way, and I have to return—"

"You are *returning* to Istar? To the Games?"

"Of course. I was on leave of absence to take

Sylverlin's body to his kin," Nelk said grimly. "His kin were jackals. They enjoyed what was left. You did me that favor, Knight. Sylverlin had discovered my secret and threatened to reveal me. Sylverlin is dead and my secret is safe . . . for a time. Only you know that I am a cleric, and I doubt you would be willing to inform Brother Gurim, would you?"

Tremaine did not reply.

Nelk nodded. "I thought not. It may be that Brother Gurim or Arack or some other will discover that I have been saving lives, but, until then, I will continue to serve the goddess. There will be more like you. The inquisitors are very busy men." The elf smiled, looking much like Sylverlin at that moment. "If you are strong enough to ride, I recommend you do. Best not to take chances." He tossed the reins of both Arryl's steed and the pack animal to the confused and bewildered knight.

"I refuse to thank you."

"I do what I must." Nelk waited until Tremaine had mounted before adding, "If you could forego wearing your armor until you are farther from Istar, I would recommend it."

"I . . . understand."

Nelk took a tighter hold of the reins in his hand. "May the blessings of Kinthalas and Chislev be upon you, Arryl Tremaine."

The Solamnian glanced up at the mention of the latter name. Chislev was a neutral goddess who had a fondness for the elven race. She was the goddess of nature, of life in the forest.

Nelk met his gaze. "Yes, I will not deny that my own blood, however darkened, might also be responsible for my desire to maintain the balance of life."

Turning his horse, the cleric started to depart. Arryl, though, felt he needed something solid to cling to, something to explain the inexplicable.

"Nelk, wait. I need to know . . . Fen told me . . . Nelk is not your true name, is it?"

"No, Sir Knight." Bitterness crept into the elf's voice. He halted his steed. "It was given to me when I was cast out. There is no direct translation from my tongue, but it essentially means 'of no faith, lacking in belief.' To my people, that name was the greatest punishment they could lay upon me."

"How could they—"

"By their beliefs, I was ever a betrayer of the way. Even though I still followed the gods, I did not follow them in the manner elves deemed proper. In that, my people are more like Istar's clerics than they want to admit." The elf raised his good hand in farewell . . . and blessing. "May your own beliefs stay strong, Knight of the Sword. But may they not blind you to truth."

Arryl Tremaine remained where he was until the elf had vanished over a nearby hill. The knight was still at a loss concerning the elf, who was and was not everything Arryl would have expected of a worshiper of the Queen of Darkness.

To Tremaine's surprise, he found that despite the corruption and insanity that he had seen in the holy city, his faith *was* still strong . . . and it was the dark elf's doing. Arryl didn't understand exactly how, yet. Perhaps he never would. But Nelk had been right. From now on, Arryl would champion his faith and help fight injustice—wherever he found it.

"May Paladine watch over *you* as well, Nelk," he called as he mounted his own steed. "You are right. Someday, we *will* meet again."

For he intended, someday, to return to Istar, holy Istar.

Kender Stew

Nick O'Donohoe

MORAN MOVED A SWORDSMAN FORWARD, FEINT-ing the game piece sideways to prevent ambush. "Your mercenary is endangered."

Rakiel's mouth quirked. "For the first time in our lives." He stretched a slender, thinly muscled arm out and withdrew the mercenary down an alley.

They were playing Draconniel, said to have been invented by Huma himself to keep knights ready for war. The game grid was laid over a map of Xak Tsaroth, and the dragon side was moving small raiding parties through the back streets, down the storm drains, and inside market carts. Moran, accustomed to the open play favored by Solamnic Knights, was intrigued by Rakiel's underhanded style—and a little appalled.

He brought a second swordsman forward. "I'm preparing a sortie down Grimm Street."

"Your frankness does you credit." Rakiel withdrew a previously concealed bowman from Grimm Street. "Perhaps it's just as well that you honor-bound knights no longer fight wars."

Once the cleric's caustic remark would have cut through Moran. A long, thin man, Moran awakened morning after morning in a lonely, wide bed, knowing that he had spent his life training for a war he would never fight: a grand and glorious war on dragonback, a war such as the great Huma had fought. No more. The dragons were driven away. Istar was bringing "peace" to the world. He had thrown himself into drilling squire novices with a ferocity that had earned him the name "Mad Moran."

Now in his fifties, "Mad Moran" was a legend, parodied for his sternness, revered for his teaching. He seldom smiled. He never laughed.

A door, opening far below, distracted Rakiel from the game. He peered out the tower window. "Someone's coming in. More novices?" He said the word with distaste. Istar was beginning to resent the Solamnic Knights' claims to piety, as well as, perhaps, their wealth.

Moran fingered his moustache thoughtfully. "The boys are not due till tomorrow, and I've interviewed them all and read their references." He considered who the late caller might be. "The meat and fruit and other supplies were delivered yesterday, and the cook quit this morning." All sensible cooks quit before drill season. "Probably someone volunteering for knighthood," he decided.

Rakiel snorted. "You're dreaming. These days the volunteers go to the clerics. The knights only get disinherited second sons and," he added with a hint of a sneer, "the needy poor, the people who think that the knights' treasury will open up to them when they sign on."

Moran winced. Rakiel was a "guest," here in the Manor of the Measure in Xak Tsaroth to prepare a report for the clerics on knighthood and training methods—or so he claimed. Actually, he never missed an opportunity to discredit the knights, and he seemed to take an uncommon interest in the treasury.

"These novices aren't like that," Moran said stiffly.

"Not after gold, I grant you, but what about that first one, Saliak? Power hungry, if anyone ever was."

"His father's a knight," Moran said. "His son will learn

to lead." In fact, the father was impoverished and bitter, and that had affected Saliak, the son. Moran had found Saliak arrogant, self-centered, and—Moran suspected—a trace cruel. Without the discipline of the knights, the boy's obvious talent and courage would never come to anything.

"So Saliak will learn to lead," Rakiel said dubiously. "Well, 'lead us not into evil,' as has been said. And what about Steyan? A tall and clumsy oaf of a boy."

Moran waved that aside. "I'm tall. I was clumsy. He's quiet and a little sensitive. He'll do just fine."

Steyan had won Moran's heart when, instead of asking first at the interview about swords or armor, the boy had blurted out, "Is it hard seeing friends die? I'd want to save them."

Moran had said simply, "Sometimes you can't."

The tall boy had scratched his head and muttered, "That's hard." And he'd still agreed to learn to be a knight, as his father and mother wanted. He was the fourth son and, obviously, would inherit nothing. He would have to make his own way in the world.

Moran shook himself back to the present. "What do you think about Janeel and Dein? Their parents are fairly well off. Their pedigrees are fairly established."

Rakiel mimicked, "Their minds are fairly easily led. See if they amount to anything." He folded his arms. "At least they stand a better chance than the fat one. He won't last a day."

"The fat one," Moran said, annoyed, "has a name, too." But he couldn't remember it. The fat one, at the interview, had the habit of ducking his head and letting his older brother do all the talking—and the brother had never mentioned the other boy by name. "He'll find self-respect here."

"Only if the others let him look through the blubber." Rakiel laughed at his little joke. "And these are the 'flowers of youth' that come to the knights. Once it was probably different, I'm sure, but how can you care about these . . . these . . . dregs? They're hardly worth the money spent on them. Do you really think you can make knights of them?"

Before Moran could answer, he cocked an ear to the sound of footsteps far below. "I was right. A volunteer."

Rakiel said acidly, "Aren't you going to rush down to meet him?"

"If he really wants to be a knight," Moran said, "he'll climb all the way. You don't think my rooms are in the tower just to keep me above the heat and the dust, do you?" Mad Moran was dropping into character. "Training begins on the walk up and never stops." He added with satisfaction, "Put that in your report."

The footsteps stopped outside the door and loud knocking began immediately. No hesitation, Moran noted to himself. Good. He waited at the door, putting on the Mask, the fierce, moustache-bristling, confidence-draining facial expression that the novices came to know and dread. Moran always thought of the Mask as hanging over the door, where he could grab it and "put it on" over his real face before striding down to the lower hall for lecture and drill.

The knocking stopped. There was an odd scraping sound, then nothing. Moran, sword in hand, threw open the door, swung the blade across at chest height on a young man.

The sword arced at eye level past the boy in the doorway, who didn't even blink.

A child, Moran thought disappointedly. Then he saw the eyes: clear and innocent, but thoughtful, set in a face that had its first (premature?) wrinkles. The boy's hair fell over his forehead in a tangle, all but blocking his vision.

Moran studied him as a warrior studies a new opponent. The boy wore a baggy jerkin and faded breeches. He held a battered duffel in one hand and a stray piece of brass that Moran thought he recognized in the other.

The boy stared interestedly at the knight. Moran had

a hawk nose and bristling white moustache; he looked fierce and remote except on the rare occasions when he smiled.

"You could have killed me," the boy said.

No fear, Moran thought. None at all. "I may yet. What have you come for?"

Rakiel half-rose at the daunting boom of the Voice, companion to the Mask.

The boy said simply, "I want to become a Knight of Solamnia."

Rakiel chuckled aloud. The cleric's laugh ended abruptly when Moran, with a single wrist flick, sent the sword flying backward to *thunk*, quivering, in the wall opposite him.

Moran resisted the temptation to see where the sword had landed. Always assume, Moran's own mentor, Talisin, had said, that it landed well if you still have work in front of you. Part of Moran was pleased that his skill had impressed Rakiel as much as it had the boy.

"Name?"

"Tarli. Son of"—he hesitated and said finally—"of Loraine of Gravesend Street. She sewed funeral clothes."

The Mask nearly cracked for the first time in Moran's career. "Loraine of Gravesend. A dark-skinned woman, one-half my height, slender, red hair?"

Tarli shook his head. "Gray and red when they buried her. It's been a year."

Moran felt as if the Mask were looking at him; Moran's own sternness was piercing him. "We met. She did work for . . . a . . . friend of mine." He added gruffly, "You're holding my door knocker."

"So I am." Tarli turned it over in his hand, as if startled to see it. He passed it to the knight. "It came off."

The boy peered beneath Moran's arm and stared at the bound books that stood on the simple shelf above the bed.

"*The Brightblade Tactics*? Bedal Brightblade?" Tarli ducked around the knight, entered without being invited. He reached past the startled cleric, pulled the book out. "Handwritten." He turned to a careful drawing of an intricate parry-and-thrust pattern, trying to follow it through with his left hand. "Did you write this?"

"I did." Moran tried not to sound proud. It had taken years of reading, and more years of testing technique, until he was sure of how the legendary Bedal Brightblade had fought. "There are twelve copies of that book, one for each trainer of squires plus the original."

He had unintentionally dropped the Voice and Mask, and immediately brought them back. "Swordplay is nothing. If you want to be a knight, there is the Oath and there is the Measure, and they are all. The Oath is four words, the Measure thirty-seven three-hundred-page volumes. Which is more important?"

"The Measure," Tarli said firmly, then added, just as firmly, "unless it's the Oath."

Moran pointed a single finger at the boy. "*Est Sularus oth Mithas.* My honor is my life."

Tarli looked at him blankly. "Isn't everybody's?"

Moran stared at him a long time to be sure he wasn't joking. Rakiel regarded them both with amusement, which he didn't bother to hide.

"Put your gear in the barracks downstairs, Tarli," Moran said. "Classes begin tomorrow."

"Yes." Tarli added quickly, "Sire." He bowed, bumping the writing desk and bouncing the Draconniel pieces. As he headed toward the door, he gave Rakiel a nasty whack with the duffel.

"Tarli," Moran began.

The boy whirled, knocking over a candlestick. In picking up the candlestick, he shattered the water jug on the dresser.

Moran regarded him gravely. "The book."

"Oh. Right." Tarli handed it over. "I'd like to read it."

They could hear his dragged duffel bump behind him all the way down the stairs.

Rakiel stared at Moran in amazement and disgust. "Surely you're not admitting him?"

"He admitted himself."

Rakiel laughed, a nasty noise. "Are the knights as desperate as all that?"

Moran was looking down the stairs. "The knights choose first for honor, and second for noble family." It hadn't always been true.

"But you don't even know his father." The cleric's lip curled. "*He* may not even know his father."

"Then I'll judge the boy and not his family."

Rakiel sniffed. "It's insupportable. He's not only common, he's probably a bastard."

"Not nearly as much as a cleric I could name," Moran muttered, well beneath his breath.

Rakiel was ranting on. "And so short. He hardly looks human. Do you suppose he's . . ."

Moran, staring out the window, said absently, "Loraine was very short."

*　*　*　*　*

It was the hottest summer anyone could remember. All the travelers who had tarps put them up and were lying under them. The others trudged as far as the city walls and lay in the narrow midday shadows.

Only Moran rode on, a thin, tired knight pulling a cart that held a sword, a shield, and a corpse. The body had been reverently wrapped in a blanket. Moran had kept it cool with water from his precious travel ration. He passed the obelisk at the edge of town, glanced at the final line on it:

the gods reward us in the grace of our home

He turned away.

Moran rode past the nearly completed Temple of Mishakal. Several wanderers gawked at it, all of them more impressed with the stonework than a single dusty Knight of Solamnia.

He knocked at a shabby wooden building. Its stone rear wall was a side wall of the entrance gate for the staircase called "The Paths of the Dead." A young girl answered.

"I'm looking for Alwyn the Graver," said Moran.

"He's bought into his own wares," the girl said simply. "The business is mine now. I'm Loraine."

Moran looked at her and thought at first, "Nothing but a child." He looked at her eyes and quickly realized that she was a woman—just grown shorter than most.

Loraine couldn't see over the cart sides. She climbed one of the wheels, stared in, then gasped at the sight of the sword and shield. "Who is it?" She was like a child at a puppet show, waiting for the next surprise.

Her shining red hair spilled over her shoulders as she leaned in, watching Moran unwrap the body: Talisin, his black moustache even blacker against his ice-white skin. The back of his helm was split in half.

Moran said dully, "The greatest swordsman since Brightblade, killed by a thrown axe."

He turned on her, shamed by the sting of tears in his eyes. "Mend the robe, patch the cape, give him new leggings—everything. He'll be entombed with his family; he's noble, and a hero, and the best—" Moran couldn't talk anymore.

Loraine, surprisingly strong, rolled the cart inside by herself. She quickly measured the body and figured cloth and labor costs while Moran stood by, empty with grief.

"Come back in two days," she said.

As he turned to go, she laid her hand on his arm. "And come back often after that." He noticed how clear her eyes were, how soft her voice could be. "You'll need to talk, and I—" She looked suddenly embarrassed and straightened her gown, patted her hair over her ears. "You're like no one I've met. I love strange places and *strange men."*

As he left, he heard her singing, in a clear, young voice, " 'Return his soul to Huma's breast . . .' " Moran had sung the song himself, in a voice cracked with grief, two days ago.

To his surprise, he came back to see her within a week after the funeral.

*   *   *   *   *

On the front wall of the classroom hung a tapestry (on loan from the permanent gallery of the city fathers) picturing knights riding silver and gold dragons, aiming lances at red dragons and riders. The dragons, woven in metal thread, glittered disturbingly in the grim gray hall.

The novices were excited. Two of them were leaping benches in mock swordplay, and almost all of the rest were ringed around the term's first fight: two boys, rolling on the floor.

Moran strode into the room, carrying two breastplates. The boys froze in place, then drifted to seats. Tarli's lower lip was bleeding. Another novice—Saliak, Moran noted—had bloody knuckles.

Oh-ho, Moran thought. It's starting already. He walked in silence to the flat table below the tapestry and turned to face the novices, who were now sitting quietly on the low wooden benches. Only Tarli, sitting apart from the others, was too short for his feet to touch the floor.

Two other novices sat apart: the ungainly tall boy, and the fat one. Moran, from long experience, knew that the three would be targets in the barracks.

He slammed one of the breastplates on the table. It clanged loudly. All the boys jumped.

"This," he said coldly, "is the armor of a Knight of the Sword. The hole you see was made in combat, by a lance."

"This," he said, slamming the second breastplate on

the table, "was worn in the last week of drill by a novice, training to become a squire. The hole was made in practice, by a lance.

"The holes are exactly alike. So were the wounds—both fatal."

In the silence that followed, a number of boys glanced at each other nervously.

"Can a lance really go through armor like that?" Tarli asked with interest.

Silently, Moran turned the breastplates around, showing the small exit holes the lance points had made. One of the novices gagged.

Moran looked and found him. "Janeel. You have something to say?"

The boy coughed, cleared his throat. "Sir, if it would help the training, my father knows a true healer."

Moran said flatly, "While you are training there will be no plate armor and no healers."

He let that sink in. "The greatest favor that I can do the Knights of Solamnia is to kill any of you who can't defend yourselves, before you fail in the field, where other knights are depending on you. When a novice dies, I offer thanks to Paladine that it happened here and not later. That is why"—he lowered his voice slightly—"I give you every chance to die that I can manufacture, before you are even squires."

Moran moved to the door at the back of the room. "I'll be back. If any of you want to leave, do it now." He eyed Saliak, who already had the look of a leader. "Don't shame anyone into staying. That's a little like murder."

He walked out and went to reinspect the drill equipment.

A short time later he walked back in and went straight to the front. When he turned around, he saw a group of frightened but determined novices, who had just learned that honor could be fatal but were willing to be honorable.

Where Tarli had been, he saw an empty space.

He was relieved, both for the boy and for himself, but he also felt a sudden, sharp disappointment that only the Mask kept him from showing.

"Those of you who remain," he said, "may die for it. Some in training, some in service, and some in combat—yes, even in these times." The pain of this next story was duller after all these years. "The knight I first squired for was killed in combat. I have vowed, since then, to prepare each novice well for an honorable life and a fitting death."

They stared at him, and he let it sink in. For the first time, these boys were getting some sense of what their deaths might look like. They were also feeling, for the first time in their lives, grown-up courage.

He looked at the faces in front of him and felt relieved that Tarli had left; the boy had an innocence that would be destroyed by training—

A terrible growl came from directly underneath Saliak, who let out a startled, high-pitched shriek, leapt straight up, and scrambled over the second and third row of benches to find the door. Most of the others jumped, but settled back embarrassedly.

Saliak made it almost to the door before he turned to see. Smiling innocently, Tarli crawled out from under the front bench. He took a seat in Saliak's place.

Saliak slunk back and sat next to Tarli.

Tarli, bright eyed and grinning, said to Moran, "Excuse me, Sire."

The Mask stayed in place, not acknowledging what had happened, but Moran didn't miss the stony glares of the embarrassed novices, or the utter hatred on the face of the humiliated Saliak.

Tarli, Tarli, Moran thought with a surprising rush of exasperated fondness, I couldn't have charted a rougher path for you than you just mapped out for yourself.

When class was over, Rakiel stepped out from behind the dragon-covered tapestry. He'd been observing. "What do you think of them?" he asked.

"The usual," Moran answered shortly. "Too much ambition, too much energy, not enough thought."

Rakiel chuckled. "And can you make them think?"

"Fear can." Moran looked out the window, saw Saliak take an ill-advised swipe at the back of Tarli's head. Tarli heard it coming—how, Moran couldn't imagine—and ducked the blow. Saliak stumbled. Tarli, stepping aside, let him fall. Saliak, without getting up, threw a well-aimed stone, which struck Tarli in the shoulder.

Moran turned from the window. "This afternoon we start with the first lance drill. That would scare anyone. They'll think about what they're doing, from then on."

"Even that Tarli?" Rakiel shook his head. "Face it, he's not fit to be here. He's a head shorter than any of them, and he's making enemies already." He grimaced with distaste. "Moreover, he plays jokes like a kender. Frankly, I don't think some paltry lance drill will make him think."

" 'Some paltry drill'? Perhaps you should try it, then."

Rakiel glanced at the tapestry; his eyes lingered on the lance points. "Some other time. Draconniel tonight?"

Moran glanced pointedly at the niche behind the tapestry. "I'll be observing the boys tonight. Over dinner? It would be my pleasure." And, oddly, it was a pleasure. At least Rakiel was someone to talk to.

The oddity didn't escape Rakiel. " 'Your pleasure'? Really, Moran, you must be starved for company."

* * * * *

He was lonely for the first time in his life. He spent most of the summer with her.

First he told her about places he'd visited, then he talked about Talisin and how it had hurt to see him die in some minor skirmish with a bunch of goblins.

Finally he told her his deepest secret: that he was no longer sure what being a knight meant, and that he wondered whether or not, by doubting the Measure, he had violated the Oath.

Loraine laughed, as she often did, and told him he was too serious. He tried to ruffle her hair, as he often did, and as always she ducked away under his hand.

Every morning that summer, Moran woke up angry. At night, anger turned to passion, as it sometimes does to make aging men feel young. He lay awake for hours the night Loraine, leaping up, kissed his nose (he caught her, as he always did) and said, "I hope your honor is never as soft as your touch."

Is it, he wondered? Do I want to stay a knight and live for a war that will never come, or would I rather give my whole life to Loraine?

That was eighteen summers ago, shortly before Tarli was born.

*   *   *   *   *

In the afternoon breeze, the wooden saddle-mounts creaked on the ropes and pulleys. The squires looked from the mounts to the rack of shields and metal-tipped lances, and stared uneasily at the suspicious-looking rust-brown stains on the courtyard stones. The stones had been scrubbed well, but the stains were too deep to come out.

Moran was proud of those stains; he'd spent much of last week painting them on and aging them. "Right."

All heads turned. He stood in the archway, a twelve-foot lance tucked under his arm as easily as if it were a riding whip.

He saluted with the lance, missing the arch top by inches. He flipped the lance over his right shoulder, then his left, then spun it around twice and tucked it under his arm, all without scraping the arch.

Tarli applauded. His clapping slowed, then stopped, under his classmates' cold stares.

"The lance," Moran said loudly, "is the knights' weapon of tradition. Huma consecrated one, called Huma's Grace, to Paladine. A single knight, with a single lance,

69

defeated forty-two mounted enemies during the Siege of Tarsis."

He looked over the group with disdain. "Let me also mention that your lance may—just may—keep you alive while you are squires. Later you'll train with footmen's lances. For now—" He pointed the lance suddenly under Saliak's nose, then transferred the lance to his left hand and all but stabbed Tarli. "You and you, choose lances and mount up."

Saliak flinched. Tarli, to Moran's pleasure, did not even blink.

"On the barrels?" Tarli cried in excitement. He stared at the wooden mounts, whose reins ran through eyelets to join the pulley ropes.

"They're not barrels, runtlet," Saliak hissed.

Tarli shrugged. "They're not horses, either. What are they supposed to be?"

Saliak said, "Who cares," and pulled the first lance from the rack. He snapped it up, then down, in a clumsy salute. He was long-limbed and strong. Despite his inexperience, he could control the lance well.

Tarli lifted his own lance upright and staggered as the weight toppled him backward.

"It's too long," he complained. His classmates snickered.

Moran regarded him solemnly. "Grow into it."

Saliak laughed loudly.

Carrying his lance clumsily by the middle, Tarli walked over to his mount, which was scored with lance hits. A stubby board projected from under each side of the saddle. He studied them. "If these were bigger, I'd say they were wings."

He turned to face Moran, his face alight. "It's supposed to be a dragon, isn't it? You're training us to fight dragons, like in the classroom tapestry."

Good guess, Moran thought. Once that was probably true; now the drill was kept to honor Huma and to make beginning squires feel clumsy and humble.

Aloud he said only, "Spotters," and passed the ropes to the boys. "When I give the signal, raise the mounts into the air. Riders, mount up, take reins and shields, and fasten your lances."

The two combatants straddled their mounts. Saliak sat easily and comfortably with bent knees, the unmistakable pose of someone who had owned and ridden horses. Tarli could only reach the stirrups by half-standing.

They set the lances in the saddle-mounted swivels. The greater weight of the lance was in front. Tarli kept his weapon upright by putting nearly his full weight on the butt end. He swung the point up clumsily.

Saliak swung his sideways, up, down, and circled it. He smiled at Tarli. "Say good-bye."

Moran paused before signaling the start. "Yes?" he said to Steyan. "Did you want to say something?"

Steyan, who looked as if he hadn't slept in nights, glanced back at Saliak speculatively.

"Nothing," he mumbled finally. Several of the other novices looked relieved.

Moran turned to the riders, dropped his raised hand. "Now." The spotters tugged on the ropes. The mounts swung into the air.

Tarli nearly dropped his lance when his mount jerked upward; his spotters had pulled too hard, possibly intentionally. He recovered, but his lance popped out of the swivel, and he was forced to bear its full weight. The tip dropped to where it couldn't threaten anyone except Tarli's own spotters.

Early days, thought Moran. Let him make his mistakes here, where he might survive.

On the riders' first pass, Saliak speared Tarli's shield, knocked it to the ground. His classmates cheered.

Tarli stared down at the shield, then, brushing his hair out of his eyes, he looked up at the exultant Saliak. Tarli's expression was excited and confused, but unafraid.

At a tug on the reins, Saliak's spotters dragged him backward, then launched him straight at Tarli.

Saliak swung his lance sideways. Tarli crouched against the saddle, avoided being slashed.

By intention or by accident, Saliak sliced through Tarli's reins. Tarli's spotters, given no signals, tugged wildly.

Tarli lurched from side to side, trying to avoid being smashed against the courtyard walls. He glanced at Moran, the boy's eyes asking for help or advice.

Moran watched silently.

Saliak pulled back on his reins and hung motionless, watching Tarli's flight. Drying his palms on his legs, Saliak grasped the lance firmly. His spotters slowly pulled him backward, preparing for his forward arc.

Tarli glared in frustration at the lance he could barely hold. Suddenly, he took the reins in his mouth. Holding the lance crosswise, like a balance pole, he smashed it against the saddle pommel. The lance broke in two.

The watchers gasped. Tarli threw down the lance point, tied the broken reins hastily around the butt, and whirled the stick over his head by the leather thong. The stick whirred like a living thing. Tarli's mount swung crazily. Saliak dove toward him.

Saliak aimed the lance straight for Tarli's unguarded chest.

Tarli leaned away, brought the whirling lance end down on Saliak's lance, breaking it. The pieces bounced over Saliak's shield, struck him in the forehead.

Stunned, Saliak dropped his reins. Tarli shifted his small body to the center of the saddle, whirled the lance butt faster.

The mounts, both out of control, swung past each other. Tarli got in four more good hits before Saliak fell off into the arms of his spotters.

Tarli slid off his mount easily, catching the footrest and lowering himself to the ground to shorten his fall. He ran to where Saliak sat, dazedly rubbing his eyes.

Tarli bent down and patted the bigger boy. "Don't cry."

Moran had seen one man look at another as Saliak did at Tarli. It was in a seaside tavern in Tarsis. The ensuing fight involved marlinespikes, and the memory made Moran queasy still.

Saliak staggered to his feet, turned away. Tarli shrugged and went to join the others, but they edged over to Saliak. Even the tall, thin one and the fat one, possibly fearing their classmates, shunned Tarli.

Moran looked impassively at them all. "Drill is over until we can repair the mounts." The other boys looked more relieved than disappointed. "Go to your barracks."

Tarli stayed behind to pick up the thonged stick he had made. He looked up and noticed the knight standing over him.

"I've made an enemy," the boy said.

Moran nodded. "Only one?"

A grin flickered across Tarli's tired face. "Saliak is the best-liked boy in Xak Tsaroth. Maybe in the world. His father hosts his own festival in autumn. His father and grandfather were both knights."

For just a moment, Tarli sagged. "I wonder what that feels like, to have a father so important that everyone respects you before you even do anything."

He left the courtyard, swinging the stick on the thong. Moran stared after him, aching inside.

*　*　*　*　*

They walked through the market by evening, Loraine tugging on his hand. They looked more like father and daughter than lovers. From time to time, a breeze would sweep the marketplace, and she would carefully, almost primly, pat her beautiful hair in place over her ears. Moran loved watching her.

He enjoyed telling her about the market's various wares. "That gadget, that's gnomeware from Mount

Nevermind . . . It's probably illegal to sell it, and it's certainly dangerous. That axe, the dwarves use those up north to cut firewood. The blades'll last a dwarf's lifetime, let alone ours. That hammock, that's made by net weavers from Tarsis. Talisin and I went there once, when I was young. . . ." He stopped.

Loraine reached up and touched his arm. *"You miss him all the time."*

"When I was young, he was everything to me. He took me everywhere, and people were good to me just because I was with him. I learned all I know of the world from him."

"He was like a father to you. Everyone needs someone like that." She regarded him critically. *"You'd make a wonderful father."*

He looked down at her nervously. *"What makes you say that?"*

She laughed and swung on his arm like a small girl. *"Because it worries you. You don't like jokes, do you? Someday, 'Sire,' I'll make you laugh again."*

*   *   *   *   *

Late that night, Moran stood brooding in the courtyard. He had dined with Rakiel, then watched the novices from one of the Manor of the Measure's observation niches.

Moran expected hazing and abuse, but the novices seemed crueler than those in past years. To some extent, Tarli was to blame. Tarli's presence, Moran corrected himself. Novices always attacked those different from themselves, and Tarli was so different. . . .

As if Moran had conjured him, Tarli appeared in the barracks window. "Good evening, Sire. By the way, I did you a favor."

"Favor?" Moran was learning, already, to be leery of Tarli's initiative.

The boy nodded. He must have been standing on tiptoe to be seen from below. "I made you more of those short lances like I used today."

"Did you, now? Wait. Made them how?"

"From the other lances. I told you they were too long. I broke them into thirds, mostly . . . some halves for the larger boys."

"You broke the lances?" Moran gasped. Huma, pray for us all! "All of them?"

Tarli shifted uncomfortably. "I did my best. Besides those on the rack, I found just the one storeroom full— the one with the lances in colors. Was that all?"

Sweet Paladine! "The ones in colors . . . You mean red, silver, and gold? For parade dress, for the full knights?" Moran shook his head, not wanting to believe. "Those were locked up."

Tarli waved a hand. "Don't thank me. They weren't locked up that well. It was easy." He dropped from the window; he must have been standing on a stool. "Good night, Sire."

Moran dashed, panic-stricken, to the weapons store. He spent the evening going through the lances and confirming that they could not be reassembled.

The treasury would cover replacing the lot, but the paperwork would be a quest in itself.

In the end, Moran gratefully accepted Rakiel's offer to write the requests to release funds. Rakiel's help almost, but not quite, made up for the cleric's sour I-told-you-so smile.

"Breaking and entering should be a handy skill for the boy's future. Tell me, can the treasury really afford to train a bastard *and* a vandal?"

"The treasury," Moran snapped, "could afford to replace the entire manor."

"Really. Just with the funds available to you?" Rakiel raised an eyebrow, not believing. "Well, let's hope Tarli isn't that ambitious."

* * * * *

Rakiel moved a spy across the grid. "So what are they calling him?"

Moran munched a breakfast roll. " 'Kender Stew.' They claim he's not human." He moved a footman, casually speared the spy. "They've hung his pack above his reach, and they call him an animal and chain him up. I'm not supposed to know."

Rakiel stared at him, shocked.

Moran buttered another roll. "Oh, and the tall one, Steyan, is 'Mount Nevermind.' Night before last, they sawed partway through his bed legs and, when his bed broke, made him stay up fixing it. Maglion, the fat one, is 'Gully Gut.' They make him eat table scraps and pretend that he's part gully dwarf and that they're doing him a favor."

"Aren't you going to stop them?"

Moran looked surprised. "Why would I? I spend all day drilling them to death, then chew them up and spit them out. They're frustrated all the time. They take it out on each other at night."

He pointed the butter knife at Rakiel. "Then, one night, one of them will start to think about the Measure. Really think about it. He'll be afraid, but he'll stand up to the others and say, 'This is wrong. We shouldn't do this.' The next day they'll all be living the Oath."

Rakiel's expression was dubious.

"It happens every year," Moran assured him.

"And in the meantime," Rakiel retorted, "you let them torment each other, even when they pick on your own—"

"My own what?" The butter knife was still a butter knife, but suddenly the blade glittered in the light from the window.

"Nothing," Rakiel said with a nervous smile. "I can't imagine what I was thinking."

* * * * *

the fat boy's nostrils. He choked and sputtered.

"And now"—Janeel waved a cake in front of Maglion like a conjurer—"a nut cake! Made with real honey. Don't you want it? Or should I feed it to Kender Stew?" He held it to Tarli's nose. "Poor Kender Stew. Has to beg for treats." He spun, and mashed it into Maglion's face. "Gully Gut gets them for nothing."

He pulled the fat boy's hair, forced open his mouth, and shoved the entire cake in. Then he mashed Maglion's jaw up and down on the cake. A single angry tear leaked from the fat boy's eyes.

"Wait." The voice sounded weary, embarrassed, and ashamed. To Moran's surprise, it was Saliak who spoke. "This is wrong. I've been wrong."

He wiped Maglion's face clean, using one of his shirts as a towel, then untied his arms. The fat boy took the shirt from him without a word and finished cleaning himself.

"I thought it was fun." Saliak bent down and undid the strap buckles on Steyan's knees and elbows. "I thought, they're strange, and we're not, and it's only . . . fun."

Steyan, free of the trunk, stumbled and fell. Saliak massaged Steyan's arms and legs to bring the feeling back.

"We all thought that." Saliak looked around anxiously. "Didn't we? We all laughed." He looked as far as Tarli and looked away, flushing. When Steyan groaned and rolled over, Saliak stepped to Tarli.

"I never thought about the Oath." Saliak unlatched the chain. "And the Measure was just, well, classroom stuff." He unbuckled the muzzle and said, as he untied the gag, "I wouldn't blame you if you wanted to hit me."

"Fair enough," Tarli said, and kicked Saliak in the groin.

The others gasped, in surprise and in sympathetic pain. Maglion and Steyan looked as though, after a rainy spring, the sun had broken through.

Saliak, when he could rise to his knees, gasped, "Is

that any way for a knight to fight?"

Tarli shrugged. "You'd rather fight face-to-face?"

Saliak looked green. "I'd rather not fight just now."

"But you insulted my honor. Repeatedly. And now you know it."

Saliak blinked several times; he was having trouble focusing. "The Measure says that if I choose not to fight, and have apologized, then you must accept my apology."

Tarli nodded. "So it does." He added, so casually that Moran's heart froze within him, "But my own code is more important than the Measure. Face-to-face?"

Saliak nodded, grunting with the effort.

"Good." Tarli tilted Saliak's head up. With the taller boy on his knees, the two boys were on eye level. Tarli clenched his hands together and swung them both into Saliak's face, knocking him backward.

"This may hurt a little—"

After a few more punches, Tarli propped Saliak upright with the thonged stick and began a systematic top-to-bottom dismantling of Saliak, punches only. Moran, watching in dismay, had to admit that what Tarli did not know about mercy or the Measure, he clearly made up for with his knowledge of anatomy.

At length, Tarli, staggering under the weight, carried the beaten Saliak to bed. Steyan and Maglion shook Tarli's hand several times. Then, to Moran's immense relief, the two larger boys dressed and bandaged Saliak. Everyone but Tarli seemed at last to understand what the Measure was, to a knight.

* * * * *

Moran hated doing it.

He could see Loraine's laughing face, quizzical and completely trusting. All that summer, she had never looked as though she thought anyone would hurt her, and he had tried very hard never to be the one who did.

After breakfast, Rakiel, with every show of sympathy

and every indication of smugness, went down the stairs and sent Tarli up.

Moran argued with himself a final time. The best I could hope for, he said to himself, is that it would be many years before he failed. And then it would be trial, and conviction, and the black roses of guilt on the table.

He sat quietly, rehearsing what he would say. As many years as he had sent squires from the manor, Moran always hated good-byes—unexpected good-byes the most.

* * * * *

At the end of the summer, Loraine came to him. "I'm going away. Don't ask, and don't follow."

He argued, but she stood firm. "You have your duty. Your honor is your life, remember? Keep your honor for my sake. Remember your promise to me."

She kissed him. He tried to catch her, but she twisted out of his hold and was gone—both from his arms and from Xak Tsaroth. She was carrying a duffel that he hadn't even noticed she'd brought. Hurt, he watched her walk away. As the winds from the side streets blew across her, she carefully patted her hair in place over her ears. She did not look back.

Moran returned to his studies. Years later, when he heard that Loraine had returned, he didn't go to visit her.

* * * * *

Tarli knocked. For once, Moran didn't put on the Mask, but left his face as gentle and weary as he'd seen it in the mirror. "Come in."

Tarli had his duffel and thonged stick with him. He looked at Moran quizzically. "I've never seen you at your desk. Is that where you wrote *The Brightblade Tactics*?"

"Yes." Moran gestured at the other chair. "Sit down."

Without further delays, he began: "Tarli, I've watched your progress these past few weeks. You've done wonders, in spite of your size."

Tarli nodded proudly.

"And in every situation—and I know that in some training sessions you've faced real danger—you haven't shown the slightest fear."

Tarli looked puzzled. "Of course not."

"Most of your classmates found it harder. In three decades of novices, you're probably the most courageous boy I've ever taught."

Tarli beamed.

Moran did not smile back. "However, your courage showed itself in—well, in strange ways. Instead of using weapons, you broke or . . . took them. Instead of accepting training as offered, you took it and reshaped it. It would not be too much to say that you changed everyone else's training, too."

Tarli sat rigidly. "I did my best for them." He seemed not to understand what was happening to him.

"There has also been a problem of property"—Moran tried to dance around it—"private property. You don't seem to acknowledge others' property as off-limits, unavailable."

Tarli frowned, irked. "If people would just label things—"

"We can't label everything, and what with one thing and another—" Moran waved his arm. "Lances, daggers, miscellaneous books, and foodstuffs—this has been the costliest term I can remember."

Tarli scratched his head. "I've heard people saying that costs are going up all over the city."

Moran said more diffidently, "Finally, in private, you've faced a certain amount of . . . of hardship from the other boys. For the most part, you endured it patiently."

Tarli's eyes widened. "You knew, then."

Moran nodded. "I needed to know how each of you

would respond. Being a knight is learning to act like a knight." He finished, watching Tarli's face, "Not just in training or in combat, but at all times."

He waited.

Finally Tarli said, unembarrassed, "Then you know about last night, too."

"I do." Moran cleared his throat. "You fought in direct defiance of the Measure. What you said, even more than what you did, shows that you don't believe in the Measure."

Moran sighed. "Believe me, Tarli, I'm sorrier than you can imagine. But you just weren't meant to be a knight. You have your own way of doing things, your own view of others' rights, and your own code of honor, and they'll never square with becoming a knight." Righteous but unhappy, he faced Tarli.

"You're absolutely right, Sire. The knights are all wrong for me." Tarli made it sound as though it were the knights' fault.

Moran stared at him. "You don't mind?"

"Not anymore." Tarli frowned. "I would have minded when I started. Did you know, I promised my mother that I'd try to become a knight?"

Moran shook his head, partly to clear it.

"She said it would be good for me and for the knighthood." He sighed loudly. "Sometimes, these past few weeks, I've wondered if she meant it as some kind of joke."

Possible, Moran thought, smiling sadly. Very possible.

"Ah, well. Time to go." Tarli stood up, but he didn't leave. "By the way, I do have another name, Sire."

Moran stiffened. "So I assumed."

"I just don't use it, since my father and mother weren't married." He looked, clear-eyed and innocently, at Moran.

"Your mother's name was good enough," Moran said gruffly. Since that summer, Loraine had become elevated in Moran's mind into a sort of spirit-woman, someone whose love was too wild and pure for Moran.

"By rights I can use the other name." Tarli didn't sound bitter or ironic, merely stating a fact. "Did you know that?"

Moran nodded. "I assumed you didn't know the name." He added quickly, "Which is not an insult to your mother. She was a wonderful woman. I knew her well, you know."

"I knew that."

Moran licked his lips, which were suddenly dry. "Of course you have the right to use your father's name. I think"—he paused and braced himself—"I think he'd be proud."

"Are you?" Tarli asked quietly.

Moran was stunned by the simple directness of the question. Tarli had to repeat it.

Finally Moran stammered, "I . . . uh . . . She never told me . . ."

"Well, my mother told me. And she always told the truth." Tarli looked tolerant of someone else's failing. "She said you probably wouldn't like it if I took your name. She said you might feel awkward about it, training boys like you do. It didn't make sense to her, but she thought you'd want it that way."

Moran nodded. "She was good to me when I needed her most. Except for leaving, she was always good to me." He asked a question he'd wondered about for eighteen years. "Did she know that I would have married her?"

Now Tarli looked startled. "She never told you? She knew, but she didn't think it would work. You're very different from her." He added calmly, "But I think she loved you."

"I think so, too." Moran thought, briefly and with regret, of the demands of knighthood, of bastardly scandals in the knighthood, and of the fact that conflicts of duty can be every bit as painful as conflicts of honor.

"You have my permission. Use my name if you wish."

Tarli smiled. "Thank you, but I think I'll keep using my own name, plus my formal name, now that I'm an adult."

Moran, amused by this sudden eighteen-year-old adult, said, "And what name is that?"

Tarli answered easily and calmly, "Tarli Half-Kender."

Moran's jaw sagged slowly, like something settling into a swamp. "Half . . . kender?" he repeated faintly.

"That's right." Tarli flipped the broken lance end-for-end.

Moran remembered Loraine's words. *No matter who the child is, or what it's like?* And her laughter. *I love strange places and strange men.* Even her constant patting of her hair, over her ears. "Half-Kender?"

"I suppose I could use 'Flamehair.' It's a respected name among her people, you know. I didn't want to use it at first, since it would look like social climbing."

Moran's room reeled around him. "Half-Kender?" How could he have been so stupid? Or was it that he just wouldn't admit it to himself?

"That's right." Tarli stared off into space and said reflectively, "But my mother left her people and came here. Kender all love wandering. That's why she left here, too, partly."

Tarli walked around the room with his duffel, looking absently at things. The shaken Moran would later discover that a bottle of wine, a table knife, and a copy of *The Brightblade Tactics* had disappeared. "I'd better get going."

But Tarli stopped and rummaged in the duffel, which seemed disturbingly full. "Could you give these back to your cleric friend?"

Moran took the offered scrolls. "He gave these to you?"

"Not exactly." Tarli grinned. "I just needed something to read one night, and his room was unlocked—or almost." He trailed off, then brightened. "The parts about the knights' treasury are pretty good."

Moran unrolled the top scroll (the seal was already broken) and read:

> *Most revered Cleric Ansilus, in Istar. Greetings, and the blessings of the Only True Gods, from their servant and your brother Rakiel; may you and they speak well of him.*
>
> *Written when the moon Solinari is on the wane in the month of the moon Lunitari ascendant in the Queen of Darkness.*
>
> *So far, things go well. I have learned the extent of the knights' wealth here in Xak Tsaroth and believe that it is more than is needed for a defensive training force in peace time. I will recommend that the church could make better use of it.*
>
> *I have gained access once to the treasury, and have enclosed an itemized list of its contents. I am unsure how the money and precious metals are transported from the treasury and where the knights' main store is, but I hope to find out soon. The old man who trains these peasants is a fool . . .*

Moran closed his eyes, remembering Rakiel asking questions, Rakiel filling out forms, Rakiel offering to handle requisitions for the lances.

"Plus this. I kept it because of the map—I love maps—but I don't suppose I'll be back here ever."

The "map" was a floor plan of the Manor of the Measure, with the storeroom marked in red. On the bottom of the scroll was a careful tracing, from the top, bottom, and end, of the treasure room key.

"I'll kill him," Moran muttered, but even as he said it he recoiled. There was no honor in Solamnia's best-trained weapons master killing a cleric who trembled when the knight brandished a butter knife.

Moran turned the paper over thoughtfully. If he could soothe his honor somehow and refrain from slaying Rakiel, this page alone, sent to the Order of the Rose, would humiliate the clerics and probably keep the knights in Xak Tsaroth free of their influence for years to come.

"Thank you for showing me this," Moran said.

Tarli smiled, looked at the knight affectionately. "Uncle Moran, you've been good to me."

"Uncle Moran? You may call me 'Father.'"

Tarli nodded, almost shyly. "I'd like that. You know, you've been almost a spiritual guide to me—"

Moran, holding Rakiel's tracing of the knights' treasury, had a wild idea.

"I may still be your guide," he said slowly. "Tell me, Tarli, where will you go from here?"

Tarli frowned, considering. "No idea," he said finally. "Maybe to meet my mother's people again. I've been with them, and they're nice." He frowned still more, and Moran was reminded forcibly of himself. "But sometimes I think I ought to make something of myself."

Moran took a deep breath and said carefully, "Have you considered the clergy?"

From his blank expression, clearly Tarli never had.

The blankness turned to wonder. "You know, you're right," Tarli said excitedly. "They're perfect. I'd have a wonderful time. The more I know of clerics, the more their code seems more like mine than the knights' does." He looked up suddenly at Moran. "No offense."

"Oh, none." Moran hid a smile.

"Tell me, do the clerics accept common—accept people like me?"

Ah, Tarli, Moran thought fondly, there *are* no other people like you. His hand closed in a fist around Rakiel's letters. It was hard, not killing a man for a debt of honor, but this way might be better.

"I'll write your recommendation myself. The clerics owe me a large favor. You'll get in, sight unseen." He pictured, briefly, Tarli in a classroom of fledgling clerics. This was better than murdering Rakiel in uneven combat.

"Thank you." Tarli was genuinely surprised and pleased. "Mother always said you would be good to me."

"Ah. And what will you do as a cleric?"

Tarli's eyes looked far away and dreamy. "I'll go to my mother's people. Something tells me they'll need clerics in the future."

He swung the stick at his side. "And I'll take them this weapon I've designed. It's a great thing for short people in a fight. I need a name for it." He spun the stick over his head. "Isn't that a wonderful sound? Hoop," he said happily. "Hoop."

Moran scribbled a quick note. "Take this to the clerics and wait. I'll be sending . . . some other items . . . on to the Knights of the Rose." After a brief moral struggle, he added, "I hope the church will open many doors for you."

"If it doesn't, I'll open them myself." Tarli stuffed the note in his duffel, which by now was bulging ominously.

He said quickly, "Good-bye, Father."

Moran's arms remembered what eighteen years could not erase. He caught Tarli and held him. Tarli kissed his cheek. Not even the Mask could have kept a few tears from Moran's eyes.

Tarli dropped back to the ground and, in a gesture surprisingly like Loraine's, patted his hair back over his ears. It didn't matter, since his ears—however well they heard—looked exactly like his father's. He walked to the door, turned back suddenly.

"Maybe I'll be able to teach the clerics as much as I've taught the knights."

And he was gone.

Moran, watching from the window as Tarli rode off on Rakiel's horse, laughed out loud for the first time in many years. "Maybe you will, Tarli. I know you will!"

The Goblin's Wish

Roger E. Moore

The human carried a broad-headed spear with a crosspiece mounted behind the spearhead. The crosspiece would keep a speared boar from running up the shaft and mauling the hunter, but the human didn't think the crosspiece would be necessary when the spear ran the kender through. If the spear went in right, it shouldn't make any difference what the kender did.

The little guy was only a hundred paces ahead now, and the chase was obviously getting to him. The man, on the other hand, had run after prey all his life. He knew if he could just get on a good, firm, downhill slope, he was sure to put the little unbeliever on a spit and collect on his hair. There was a five-gold bounty paid on kender scalps in Aldhaven. That was ale for a month. Good-bye, kender.

The kender was fast, though, the man had to give him that. The little guy's filthy brown hair whipped back and forth as he ran through briars, splashed through creeks, and vaulted over rocks in his panicked flight, and his bare feet were quick and sure, even up dirt slopes. But the kender didn't have the long legs the human had. The hunter knew that was how the gods of evil marked their lost children, with misshapen limbs that mirrored their souls. Some people killed kender and their wicked kind out of righteousness, but righteous causes did not impress the hunter much. Bounty money was reason enough.

The kender disappeared around a ridge, nearly falling over an exposed tree root. The man put on some speed, sensing his time was near. He'd never killed a kender before, though he'd once stabbed an old drunken goblin behind a barn and had gone for a lost elven boy two summers ago with a club, battering the lad until not even his own mother would have recognized him. The hunter had gotten only two gold for that scalp, which infuriated him to this day. He wouldn't be cheated this time, or the fat priest in Aldhaven who paid out the bounties would get a little lesson in the consequences of not keeping his word to honest men.

The hunter rounded the ridge, arms tensing for the throw or the thrust, and there was the kender—down. The unlucky little guy had fallen over a log in an old creek bed covered with dead leaves, and he was trying to get up but was crying out because he'd hurt his leg. It wouldn't hurt much longer, the man thought, and he lifted his spear to run it through the willowy kender's rib cage. The human was so close he could see the kender's wide brown eyes. The kender put up his hands to ward off the blow, but thin palms had never stopped a spear.

A thing like a red-and-black spider leaped out of the bushes on the low creek bank to the hunter's right. In a red fist it held a steel machete that swung down too fast to see or block. Pain jolted the hunter's body from his right thigh where the blade hacked its way through trousers and skin and muscles, biting into the hard bone. Blind with agony, the hunter went down. The spear jammed into the dirt and fell from his grasp, landing behind him. Then all he could do was scream.

The scalp hunter was able to think a little bit as he screamed, because he didn't want to die here. He tried to get up to run but had lost all feeling in his leg below the wound. He looked down in terror and saw his thigh cut open right down to the broken white bone. He gripped the flesh to pull it shut and stop the bleeding, but his hands and arms were slippery with blood. The air was full of the sharp tang of gore. There was movement down the trail behind him. The hunter looked through pain-dimmed eyes and saw the goblin there, walking casually, its red-splattered machete dangling in one hand.

It was a goblin, the hunter knew, because it looked a lot like the old drunken one he had killed, but this goblin was big and young and did not look drunk at all. It wore a ragged black tunic with a thin rope belt. Wiry muscles flowed under its dirty red skin. Its black eyes were relaxed and seemed to smile, though its round face was as cold as stone. The goblin eyed the now-silent kender, then bent down and picked up the boar spear with its free hand to examine the tip. The goblin tossed its machete aside.

"Don't kill me!" the man screamed in the trade tongue. "In the gods' names, don't kill me! I was after the kender! Please, get a me a healer! I'll give you anything, anything at all, but please don't kill me!"

The goblin snorted gently and looked down at the hunter. "Get priest? What you think maybe priest do for me when I knock door, eh? Think maybe priest say, 'Hey, goblin, here silver for you. Be good, you go home?' "

"Don't kill me!" The man sobbed, tears running down his face. The pain in his leg was unearthly, and the blood just kept coming out. "Please don't kill me. Please."

The goblin hefted the spear, feeling its balance, then gripped it hard in both hands and upended it, ramming it into the hunter's abdomen, pushing it through and twisting it until the man's last screams and spasms had passed and his head fell back on the leaves, his mouth and eyes open forever.

The goblin jerked out the spear and stuck it in the ground. He recovered his machete and wiped it off on the hunter's stained trousers, then stood up and looked at the kender again. The kender was on his feet down in the gully, staring at the dead human.

"Rats," said the kender. "You got him too quickly."

The goblin lifted his chin, judging the distance to the kender. The spear could reach him with a good toss, and the machete with the right spin. But the kender was doing nothing to require immediate action, and he had no obvious weapons. "Too fast, say?" the goblin asked, mildly curious.

"Yeah," said the kender. "He would have run right into my pit in another three steps." The kender stuck out his bare left foot and nudged at the thick patch of leaves before him. A stick shifted, revealing a long, dark split in the ground. The goblin carefully took a step closer and saw that, indeed, there was a pit in the center of the dry gully. It was an expertly done pit, at that.

The goblin stepped back, eyeing the kender with a faint amount of respect. He hadn't seen a kender in years and had thought they were all dead in these parts. Pointing down with his machete at the dead human, the goblin asked, "He want hair bounty on you?"

"I guess so," said the kender, still looking at the man. "I was about to skin a deer when he saw me. He just started running after me, and I ran away." The kender sighed and looked up at the goblin, the hunter forgotten. "Say, are you hungry?"

The goblin's empty stomach lurched when the deer was mentioned. He could go for several days with no solid food, but it had already been two days and the taste of grass and leaves did not appeal to him. He had been an informer and extra muscle for a human moneylender in East Dravinar when the Kingpriest's men had broken into the warehouse, with magical lights and swords in their hands. The goblin was the only one to get out through the skylight before the vigilantes seized the rope. The screams of the thieves and other thugs had grown faint behind him as he fled across the rooftops to escape into the countryside. Stolen food from farmhouses had helped for a while, but the farmers, after the first half-dozen break-ins, had been prepared for raiders.

"Are you hungry?" the kender repeated, still waiting for a reply. "I mean, I've got a whole deer, and the meat won't go to waste with two to eat it. Do you want some?"

The goblin thought about it some more, fearing a trick, but his stomach won. "Yes," he said simply, marveling at the novelty of it all. No one had ever asked him if he was hungry before. No one had particularly cared.

He'd just make sure the kender didn't try anything without catching the wrong end of the machete first. Just to be safe, he picked up the spear, too.

"Well, let's be off, then," the kender said, waving the goblin on to join him as he set off into the woods. "Mind the pit. It took me a week to make all the stakes."

*   *   *   *   *

"We really should go back and bury the human at some point," the kender said, kicking through a big pile of brown leaves. "I mean because of the wild dogs and wolves and things. And the smell, too. I don't live here, so it wouldn't bother me much, but I have some pits here, after all, and there are always humans about, you know. I wonder if anyone will miss him—the man, I mean. No one ever seems to miss us, people like you and me. The humans have each other to look after. We have no one. We just have to stay alive when the humans come. That's the way it's always been, hasn't it? My parents told me it wasn't, but I learned different. They said some humans were nice. I never saw the nice ones. Maybe my parents were telling me a story, right? They always used to tell me stories about heroes and dragons and ghosts and elves. They told some good ones. Do you know some stories to tell? I bet you do, the way you handled your sword. I was sure glad to see you, even if I had the pit ready. You never know what might happen. I found a wolf in one of my pits once and I nearly fell in looking at him. The wolf was almost dead, and I felt sorry for him, so I had to kill him. I forgot that other things besides humans might fall into the pits. It would have been . . . um . . . i-ron-ic if I had fallen in. My father taught me that word. He was good with words. What's your name?"

The goblin hesitated. The kender's chatter was more than a little annoying and was bound to grow worse, but playing along with the charade of friendship would keep the kender off guard for now. Kender were supposed to be trusting, if unbearably nosy. "Do not have one," he said stiffly.

"No kidding? No name at all? I've never heard of that before. Didn't your parents call you anything?"

The goblin had never known his parents, having been sold into slavery as an infant and having escaped in his teens. He had been called many things by the human thugs who had also worked for the moneylender, but none of the names were worth remembering.

"Eh," the goblin said at last. "Do not know why."

"How strange," the kender said. "I thought everyone had a name. Mine is . . ." The kender stopped, then looked down in sudden embarrassment as he walked. "Well," he finished quickly, "what's important is that we're alive, and that's what counts. My father always said that. He was smart."

The deer carcass lay on a hillside among a pile of leaves. A broken arrow shaft protruded from the space behind the deer's front left shoulder; a bow leaned against a nearby tree. The deer had been cut half open, and flies swarmed about the entrails. The kender searched in the leaves for a moment, bent down to pick up a long-bladed knife with a bone handle. The goblin tensed, but the kender merely sat down by the deer to finish dressing it.

The kender continued talking throughout the whole

process. His easy patter about the forest and its secrets were of more than passing interest to the goblin, who suspected that he might have to live in the wilderness for some time to come. The kender had obviously lived here long and had learned much.

In the back of his mind, the goblin knew that one of these days it might be necessary to kill the kender, particularly if food became too scarce to be shared. Until then, he would listen and learn, and would watch his back just in case the kender's syrupy friendship turned out to be as false as a human's.

The goblin watched his back, and the kender talked and talked. The kender borrowed the goblin's things, and the goblin took them away again. Three weeks flew by. The winter rains were now six weeks away.

*　*　*　*　*

The minotaur had fallen into a stagnant pool of cold water and red leaves, where it lay unconscious. Its breath rasped slowly and heavily as the leaves endlessly rustled around it and flies feasted on the open, filthy wounds across its back and shoulders. The twenty-foot length of mud-choked iron chain, linked to the manacles on its wrists, had gotten snagged on a log, which the weakened minotaur had been unable to pull loose before collapsing.

The goblin caught the kender by the arm as the latter approached the huge brown figure. "Damn, you crazy!" he growled. "What you do, eh? One bite, we all bones." He hefted the boar spear in a muscular red fist. "I finish it and sleep good."

"No!" The kender grabbed the goblin's arm and pulled it down. For a second the goblin started to resist, almost turning the spear to run it into the kender's chest, but holding off. Instead, he simply shoved at the kender with his free hand and sent him sprawling.

The kender immediately got to his feet, face filled with

rage. "No!" he shouted. "I want to help him! If it was you, I'd help you! Look at his chains! He was a human's slave! I want to save him!"

"We have no food to feed him in winter!" the goblin retorted. "We live good, bellies full now, but food gone when rain come. You say you hungry in cold rain, hunting bad. He hungry, too. What you feed him, eh? You like him chew off leg?"

The heated argument continued unabated for several minutes. Finally, the goblin cursed and turned his back on the kender, walking the two miles back to the cave where they lived. Damn the little bastard! Did he want to start a city out here in the forest? The fool was not thinking with his head. The minotaur was more dangerous than a company of city guardsmen. The goblin once saw a chained minotaur bite off the arm of its slave overseer, though it knew it would be killed for its crime. The minotaur had roared with laughter until the massed humans had beaten it unconscious with clubs before dragging it away to its fate.

The goblin fumed and stamped around the cave, finally realizing it was cold. The kender had always gathered wood in the evening while the goblin sharpened their weapons and relaxed. Everything had been just fine until now. The goblin knew how to use the fire-starter bow, but he didn't know where the kender found all the wood for the fire pit. When he went outside, all he could see were sticks and leaves, no burning wood.

And the kender did most of the hunting and cooking, too.

The goblin stamped around some more.

Maybe the minotaur could be bargained with. The goblin had no illusions about whether or not the minotaur would be a grateful and friendly ally, but even a brute like that would see the value in having two lesser beings tend to its wounds and hunt for it. And having a monster like that around might not be a bad idea, if it could be managed. Minotaurs were as savage and brutal as could be imagined. They were damn strong, mightier than humans. They hated humans more than they hated any other being, and they hated the slave-taking, holier-than-all Istarians most.

The goblin cursed himself for believing this would work. The kender was infecting his brain. He should just kill both the kender and the minotaur and let them rot.

But the kender did almost all the hunting and cooking.

The goblin sullenly picked up his weapons again and left the cave. Life wasn't fair. He hated that.

The tired kender looked up, knee deep in the water alongside the minotaur, and a grin broke out on his face. "I knew you'd help," he said with relief.

They made a crude sledge before nightfall, roping two long rough poles together with a ragged length of hemp that the kender recovered from disassembling an animal snare. It was past midnight when they got back to the cave with the minotaur and set him down inside. The huge brown beast had never once stirred. The goblin staggered off to collapse in a corner and fall asleep.

When he awakened, it was long past sunrise. Cold, cooked venison was spitted over the fire pit; the fire itself had long gone out. The minotaur's festering wounds had been carefully cleaned and dressed with old rags from the cave's rag pile, donated by many farmhouse clotheslines. The kender apparently had found nothing to cut the huge chain the minotaur was dragging around. The chain was carefully wound into a loose pile by the minotaur's side.

The goblin rubbed his face and got up. He noticed the kender had succumbed to exhaustion and was asleep, sitting upright against a cave wall, some rags in his lap, a bone needle and sinewy thread in his hand. He'd been stitching together a crude blanket.

Then the goblin saw that the minotaur, still lying flat on its stomach, was watching him. The beast's dull eyes were as large as a cow's, with the same deep brown color. Long scars crisscrossed the monster's muzzle and low forehead. One broad nostril was split open from an old wound. Long yellow teeth gleamed dully against its thick lips.

Trying to pretend he hadn't been caught off guard, the goblin nodded at the beast. Suddenly the idea of having a live minotaur in the cave did not look as good as it had earlier. The goblin could almost feel the monster's enormous teeth tear into his flesh. The minotaur made no move to get up, and the goblin took care of a few minor chores with an air of forced casualness. The minotaur must be very weak to skip a live meal. The goblin made his decision.

Chores finished, the goblin walked over to the fire pit and carefully sawed off a piece of venison with his machete. Very slowly, he moved over to the minotaur and knelt down near its scarred, long-horned head. He could see no readable expression on the creature's bestial face.

If this worked, they would have a new ally. The goblin was sure that the minotaur would eventually kill both the kender and himself if they weren't careful or if it went hungry. But the goblin had worked with the strong and brutal all his life, and he knew the value of strength in numbers. He hoped the minotaur knew this lesson, too. At least the minotaur wasn't a human. It was poor consolation, but in these days, it helped.

The goblin held out the piece of venison near the minotaur's muzzle, letting it smell the food. Then he moved the venison closer to the monster's mouth.

The huge nostrils flared and snorted. The minotaur stirred slightly, then grimaced with pain. Its teeth were bared as its lips drew back and it closed its eyes, but it quickly forced itself to relax and open its eyes again.

With a carefully measured move, its gaze fixed on the machete that the goblin gripped in his other hand, the minotaur opened its mouth, revealing a set of teeth that rivaled those of the largest bear. Its breath was unspeakably foul. Very gently, it took the venison and began to chew.

* * * * *

Four weeks passed. The minotaur recovered. The kender was overjoyed and talked until the goblin dreamed of killing him just to shut him up. Both goblin and kender hunted now; the minotaur sat silently in the cave. Though the minotaur never spoke, the goblin feared that the beast would react violently the moment the two smaller beings asked anything of it, so he worked more than he had ever worked when it was just him and the kender, and he grumbled about it under his breath. But deep inside he was satisfied. He began to think that bringing the minotaur to the cave had been his own idea. He had a boss again, a strong boss who could eat humans for breakfast if it chose. It was worth the trouble for the added power and safety—just as long as the minotaur didn't go hungry.

The wind grew colder. The kender raided some of his old caches, laid more traps, and brought more food and supplies to the cave. The goblin was able to build a windbreak of huge branches and rocks at the cave's entrance, and this doubled as camouflage for the cave in case humans were about. The minotaur ate a whole deer now every three or four days, and its muscles bulged until they were like huge knots of steel under its ugly brown hide. It still never spoke, though the kender talked incessantly now, a beatific look on his face as he gladly tended his new friends.

The kender still borrowed the goblin's things, but the goblin no longer cared. He had too much else to worry about. The winter rains were almost upon them.

* * * * *

The goblin watched his quarry—a large buck worth half a week of food for them all—leap out of bow range and bound away. The cry had startled it. Cursing softly to himself, the goblin leaned forward in the bushes and strained to hear against the stirring leaves.

He heard nothing now. A bird? His grip on the bow and arrow relaxed.

No. Not a bird. He could hear it again. It was a human, maybe, crying out. He'd probably fallen in one of the kender's pits. Perhaps the kender heard it, too, but the kender was nowhere to be seen. Figured. He was probably distracted by something again when he should be hunting. It was amazing that the kender had lived this long.

If the human was alone, it wouldn't take much to finish him off and pick through his belongings. He might even have some money. The goblin didn't plan to live in the forest forever. It wouldn't hurt to save a little change for a future day.

Crouching low, the goblin moved through the crackling brown undergrowth, sliding from tree to tree. Cool wind blew over his face and through his black rags. He kept an arrow nocked. He had only three more arrows if the first one missed, which it often did. He wasn't the experienced hunter the kender was.

Laughter reached his ears, human laughter. The goblin stayed down, listening, then moved forward more slowly. Hidden among rock outcroppings and thick briars, he climbed up a low hill. Someone was saying something in a nonhuman language. It sounded like an elven tongue, Silvanesti. The speaker mumbled; his words were unclear.

"I can't understand you," said a human voice in a language the goblin remembered well from his days in East Dravinar. "Talk Istarian, boy."

Someone mumbled again. The goblin was almost at the top of the hill. No guards were visible. He carefully checked his bow, arrows, and machete, then began to crawl toward a fallen tree trunk overgrown with briars and thick vines, slightly downslope on the hill's far side. The wind covered the sounds of his movements.

"Talk to me, gods damn you!" Beefy smacks sounded

from the hill's other side.

A few seconds later, the goblin reached the fallen log and looked down the slope.

There were three humans, two men and a woman. All wore the brown and gray leather of Istarian free rangers. Once the defenders of Istar's forested west, the free rangers were now no better than mercenaries and bounty hunters. A thin, blond-haired man was leaning into the face of a male elf, whose arms were wrapped back around a tree trunk and presumably tied there. The elf's head sagged; cuts and bruises were visible through his long, sun-bleached hair. Both his eyes were blackened and swollen. The elf's fine clothing, too light for the weather, had been deliberately cut and ripped to shreds.

"You listening to me?" the blond man demanded. His right hand gripped the elf's hair and pulled the prisoner's head up and back. "Anything getting through your pointy ears? Why were you trailing us, elf? What were you after?"

The elf started to mumble through thick, puffy lips. His knees had given out, and he hung upright only because he was tied in place.

The goblin chewed his lower lip. An elf and some rangers. Great. Two of a goblin's worst possible enemies. Maybe there should be a dwarf here, too, to round things out. But it looked like there soon would be one less elf, and that was fine with the goblin. Damn shame the rangers had probably robbed their victim first. This day was nothing but bad pickings all around.

"The elf said something about a sword," said the massively built, dark-haired man standing nearby. He sounded uncertain. "Didn't the captain find a long sword, a ceremonial thing of some kind, in a box with that elf the boys caught yesterday?"

"I thought he said sword, too," said the woman with them. She had the plainest face the goblin had ever seen on a human, but she was heavily muscled, too, with short, stringy hair the color of old hay.

"Hey, elf!" yelled the thin, blond man, his mouth against the elf's left ear. The elf winced and tried to turn his head away. "Hey, can you hear me? Did you want that pretty sword with the gems on it? Was that what you wanted?"

When no response came, the blond man slammed his fist into the elf's abdomen. The three humans waited as the elf vomited and choked and gasped for air.

"This is taking all day," said the woman. "We gotta get back to the troops. We should just take this sword and sell it to the clerics in Istar, make our fortune! Either gut him here or take him with us."

"Shhh!" said the blond man. He leaned close to the elf, listening as the elf's lips moved. The goblin heard no sound.

"So it was the sword, right?" the blond man said. Without waiting for a response, he added, "Is that sword magic, boy? Does it got magic powers?"

The other two humans stood a little straighter, startled by the question. They watched the elf intently.

After a pause, the elf nodded, his face slack. He was nearly unconscious.

"Damn," said the blond man. He looked up at the other two humans, a smile crossing his face.

There was a whisper in the wind, followed almost immediately by a thump. At the same moment, the huge man with the dark hair bent back, his hands clawing behind him at the dull-colored arrow that had struck him directly between his shoulder blades. The arrow was sunk in almost to the feathers. The man made a strange wheezing sound, then pitched forward on his face.

"Oh, great Istar!" the woman said, wide-eyed. Her hands pulled her sword free, and she and the thin, blond man ran for cover behind separate trees. They crouched down, both clearly visible to the goblin. The man on the ground did not move. The elf hung limp from the tree, his chin against his chest. The wind started to blow harder.

The goblin slowly reached down to his side. His fingers touched the curved wood of his bow.

The blond-haired man, his nerve gone, made a break for it. He took off from his tree, running in a straight line for a clump of bushes about a hundred feet away. The woman started after him, but she must have heard the arrow as it went past her, for she dropped to the ground, rolling until she was behind a pair of close tree trunks. From there, she could hear the blond man scream as he writhed in the leaves and dead ferns.

"I surrender!" the plain-faced woman cried in the trade tongue. "Don't shoot! I've got kin who'll pay my ransom!"

"Then come out!" the kender's voice called. (It figured, thought the goblin.) "Leave your sword!"

"I've got a big ransom!" the woman yelled again. The goblin could see the white in her face, as pale as a drowned man's skin. She looked as if she would be blubbering any time now. The blond man was not so much screaming now as making short, gasping cries, trying to pull out the arrow buried deep in his lower back.

"Just come out slowly," said the kender. "Very, very slowly."

The woman tossed out her useless sword, then got to her feet. Her legs shook as she placed her hands on her head. "Don't shoot me!" she yelled again, looking around with huge eyes and a trembling lower lip.

"I'm over here," said the kender. He stood up, his bow lowered but his arrow nocked.

The woman saw him and stared, surprised at his size and obviously reconsidering her chances of survival. The goblin could see it on her face. If I can get close enough to that little bastard, he knew she was thinking, I can make hash of him. It's my only chance.

"My kin can pay a big ransom for me," she said, her voice gaining strength. "Lots of gold, I swear it. Just don't hurt me. Promise me that you won't hurt me."

"I promise," said the kender.

The long arrow that thumped into the woman's chest took her by surprise. She staggered back, her hands still on her head. Her eyes grew terribly big and round before she fell over backward. She never made a sound.

The goblin lowered his bow. It was the first time in four days that he'd hit anything on the first try. He waved at the kender, then started down the slope toward the gasping blond man.

* * * * *

The goblin found the minotaur sitting in front of the cave, gnawing on a deer's thigh bone. The overwhelming odor of dried blood and ripe manure carried on the air. The goblin was actually getting used to it.

"Eh," said the goblin, almost apologetically.

The minotaur, ears up and alert, glanced in the goblin's direction. Yellow teeth tore away a scrap of deer meat. The thick chain links hanging from the beast's wrist manacles swung and clinked.

The goblin swallowed the bile churning in his stomach, but he went on, even daring to smile. "Kender and me hunt deer, but kill humans. Shoot three. We find damn elf, much bad hurt, bring him back. Elf no good, eh? I know, but maybe elf know woods, good ways to hunt. Maybe we make him teach us. Want maybe keep elf alive for now. OK?"

The goblin hesitated, wondering if any of this was sinking into the minotaur's brain. It hadn't spoken a word since they'd found it. Humans said minotaurs weren't very bright, but this one had to be dumber than dirt.

The minotaur continued chewing on the bone, watching the goblin with its dull brown eyes. The goblin felt he had done all he could to safeguard the elf's survival, at least until the issue of the magical sword was cleared up. After that, the minotaur could dine on Silvanesti meat when the kender's back was turned, for all the goblin cared. The goblin nodded to the minotaur, then went back to help the kender carry the elf up to the cave. There they laid the elf out on the kender's bed—a pile of rags on the packed-earth floor.

The kender was frantic to do things for the elf. Before long, the elf was undressed, wrapped cozily in the kender's own blankets. The goblin busied himself by going through all the loot that he had taken off the bodies of the rangers and the elf as well. The kender gently washed the elf's face. The goblin carefully counted thirty-six Istarian gold pieces, ten Istarian silver coins, and two rings. It was more money than he'd ever had, even in East Dravinar in the good old days. He couldn't spend it, but it felt awfully good. He wrapped the money in cloth to muffle it, placed it in a pouch, then tied it inside his clothing behind his belt, where not even the kender's light fingers would find it.

He lifted the elf's backpack and looked it over. Its quaint, elaborate tooling and stitching occupied his curiosity briefly, then he undid the straps and looked inside.

He snorted. Books and papers . . . and a small bag of gold coins, twelve of them, each with an elven king on one side and a swan on the other. Silvanesti for certain. The rangers must not have gotten around to searching the elf's gear if they had missed this. The goblin palmed the gold and was about to empty the rest of the backpack's contents into the fire pit when he noticed the biggest book.

Except that the book in the elf's backpack was white, it was just like the red spellbook the goblin had seen a Red Robe reading one day, three years ago, on the banks of a mountain stream. Of course, the goblin had given that wizard a wide berth. It wasn't smart to mess with wizards.

The goblin eyed the book before gazing at the battered elf. If the rangers had found the book, the elf would have been dead long ago. The goblin wondered if that wouldn't have been best. A minotaur knew but one way to kill you and would at least be quick about it; a wizard knew a thousand, and he often took his time. The Istarians burned wizards at the stake, but it was not uncommon for whole Istarian villages and towns to go up in flames themselves shortly after such events. Better to turn away from a wizard than to raise your hand against him.

The goblin chewed his lower lip.

Better to turn away, but maybe better still to make a wizard your ally—even an elf—if you could do it.

The kender, muttering to himself all the while, finished cleaning and dressing the elf's wounds. The goblin, coming out of his reverie with a start, made a production of relighting the fire until the kender went outside to wash off in a stream. Once he was alone, the goblin carefully replaced all of the Silvanesti coins and made sure the elf's things were in order inside the pack before strapping it shut. He then took both the backpack and the elf's pouch-laden belt and stored them in the back of the cave where the minotaur and kender weren't likely to find them. (The kender had already fully explored the shallow cave and was unlikely to search it again.) Then there was nothing to do but wait—and think.

The elf regained consciousness later that afternoon. The kender was beside himself with joy and talked without stop for two hours afterward, pestering the elf with questions that he lacked the strength to answer. This gave the elf a chance to eye his surroundings and take in the goblin and minotaur; upon seeing the latter, the elf's eyes widened and he seemed too afraid to move. The goblin kept to the background and took care of minor chores that the kender usually handled, saying nothing. The minotaur merely grunted when it saw the elf, then went outside and sat down to dine on a freshly killed boar taken from a pit trap, noisily tearing into its dinner with its bare teeth.

When the kender ran off to fetch some water from the nearby stream, the goblin ambled over and sat down on the ground next to the elf, who tried to edge away. The goblin pretended not to notice.

"You feel good?" asked the goblin in the trade tongue. He knew only a few Silvanesti words, and he had never had the chance to learn the goblin tongue—not that an elf would have appreciated it. "No human beat face for fun now, eh?"

The elf looked as though he couldn't think of anything to say. His eyes were blood-red spheres nestled in great black bruises that covered nearly his entire face.

"No need worry, eh," said the goblin with a squint-eyed grin. "The humans you meet, they get sick. Bad sick. We can do nothing. Maybe bury them later. More humans maybe out in woods, looking around, but you safe here." The goblin reached over and gently poked at the elf with a stiff finger. "Eh, you Silvanesti?"

The elf stared in tight-lipped silence at the goblin.

"Yes? No? Not matter," said the goblin, looking down to check his fingernails for dirt. "You think, eh, goblin not like elves. Maybe he do for me hard." The goblin looked into the elf's eyes with a knowing smile. "Maybe goblin want you to live. Maybe we all help each other. You wear robes, eh?"

The elf licked his lips, seeming to overcome some obstacle inside him. "Yes," he whispered. He was obviously afraid, but the goblin could tell the elf wanted to come out with it. Pride, no doubt. And perhaps an arrogant honesty. "I wear the wh—" The elf coughed painfully and swallowed, then continued in a weaker voice. "I am of the White Robes."

"Hmmm." The goblin made a face, looked down at his fingernails. It figured. "Good magic not help much, eh? You maybe looking for something when humans catch you?"

The elf started to reply, then stopped. His wide-eyed gaze locked onto the goblin.

Gotcha, thought the goblin. "Humans that beat you say they take magic sword from elf, maybe not long ago.

Maybe humans go to Istar with sword, give Kingpriest. What you think Kingpriest do with sword? Maybe cut off little elf, goblin heads?"

The elf's face twisted. He made an effort to get up, without success. "No," whispered the elf, rolling back in despair. "Did they take it? Are you sure they have it?"

"Eh," said the goblin, feigning indifference. "They say they have sword with gems. Pretty sword. Humans gone now."

The elf's eyes closed. "My cousin," he whispered. He took several deep breaths, then continued. "They must have caught my cousin. I was looking for his trail when my horse broke a leg. Then the humans found me. They asked why I was following them, but I wasn't. I just wanted my cousin and the sword." He roused himself again, looking at the goblin. "Did they say anything about my cousin?"

The goblin shrugged and shook his head. He knew what must have happened. He knew the elf knew, too.

The elf groaned and again tried to get up, but he was very weak and fell back limply. Sweat beaded up on his forehead. His breathing became labored, but soon evened out as he fell unconscious and slept.

For several minutes, the goblin sat by the elf in silence. Instinct confirmed that the sword had to be magical. An elf, especially one who was a wizard, would not waste time worrying about a simple weapon. What could the sword do, though? Magical weapons were capable of doing anything, the goblin had heard. Some were said to hurl lightning, others to burn like torches, still others to cut through stone. The goblin had never before dreamed he would have the chance to get a magical sword of his own. He was certainly thinking about it now.

"How is he?" asked the kender as he came in with the full water bucket. "Is he still alive? Did he say anything?"

The goblin snorted and got up, dusting off his hands. "Still alive. Not say much, need sleep. Maybe all right soon." He looked down at the sleeping figure. "Not bad elf. Maybe we get along, eh? First time for everything."

* * * * *

"Running no good," the goblin observed the following morning. Leaving the cave, he found the elf standing upright by the entrance. A cold wind moaned through the branches. The sky was overcast, as usual.

The elf turned and almost fell over, but he grabbed for support from the rock face behind him. The elf wore stolen clothing that the kender had provided. The outfit was old, mismatched, and ill fitting, but better than nothing.

"I wasn't going to run," said the elf softly. He looked with a trace of anxiety in the direction of the minotaur, who was slowly wandering among the bare tree trunks some distance away. The beast had wrapped its chain around its waist and tied it there, like a belt, allowing its hands and arms some range of movement. The chain links clinked together lightly as it walked.

The goblin nodded in approval. "Good you stay. No horse, no luck." He waved a hand at the forest. "Nice new home, eh? You like? Stay long time with us, maybe?"

The elf looked away, his hands clenching and unclenching. His breathing was short and shallow.

You're exhausted and in pain, but you want to escape, thought the goblin. You want to escape and get that sword back. It's so obvious, it's laughable.

"I—" began the elf. He wrung his hands, seemingly unaware of what he was doing. He was watching the minotaur, who was casually breaking off tree limbs as thick as a grown man's arm, then dropping them or hurling them away. The kender would use them for firewood later.

"Tell me story, why you here now," said the goblin, sitting down on a rock. He was relaxed even though he didn't have his machete or spear. He knew he wouldn't need them.

The elf was silent. He looked down at his clenched hands.

"No story, eh?" said the goblin in mock disappointment. "Maybe tell good story about magic sword. Make no matter now. Sword gone. Humans got it. Tell about sword. Good to hear story, start day."

The elf unclenched his hands. "It was just a sword," he said without looking up.

The goblin grinned mirthlessly. "Just sword, eh?" he said. "Dirty sword, no good? You sure you wear white robes?"

Stung, the elf flushed, but still did not look up. "It was a gift for a friend," he said. "It . . . had a lot of personal value for me, too."

"Hmmm," said the goblin, after a minute had passed in silence. "Not much story, eh. We find you, shoot humans, save life, fix you up, and you have no story. Eh! Wizards all alike." He made a gesture with his hands, resigned to the ingratitude of the universe. "We save white book, even. You throw many spells all you want. Play good wizard all day. Still sword gone. Still no story. Eh!"

The elf blinked and looked directly at the goblin. "My spellbook?" he asked in astonishment. "You have my spellbook? Where is it?"

"In cave," said the goblin easily. "All safe for you. Eh, some goblins not stupid. Work together, maybe live. Fight each other, all die. Winter coming, you know. Rains start soon. Maybe you use spells, we live to spring. You stay, grow strong. We safe from humans here. You leave, eh, we not care. But humans, maybe they not so nice next time."

It would be tricky, the goblin knew. If the elf had the magic to obtain the sword, he would certainly have done so by now. But he didn't have the sword, he hadn't stopped the rangers from beating him up, and he hadn't managed to escape even now. He might not have the magic to do much of anything. But maybe he did and just needed time to prepare. It would be tricky, baiting him like this, easing him into the circle, making him give up his secrets.

"You not trust me," the goblin said at last. "Maybe good thing. Elves, goblins like water and fire. Humans, they kill us both, but we not care. That fine with you, maybe?" The goblin gave a short laugh. "Look! You see me, you see kender, you see minotaur. We work together. You alive also. Think! Wizards good at thinking. Real enemy is who, eh? Think!"

The elf did not answer for a minute. He looked embarrassed as the goblin spoke. "I apologize," he finally said. "I'd just never imagined that . . . well, that—"

"That goblin get smart, eh? Or kender? Or—" The goblin jerked a thumb in the direction of the minotaur. "Istar make us smart. No time for stupid things. We stick together or Istar collect our hair. You, wizard, maybe worth more gold than me, minotaur, kender." The goblin grinned, rubbing his own short, wiry hair. "My head, I like much, eh?"

The elf actually smiled. Then he looked around, and the smile faded as he saw the bare trees and low clouds and seemed to look beyond them.

"Cousin gone," said the goblin softly. "Why you risk life for sword?"

It was the moment of truth. The goblin's eyes narrowed as he leaned forward on the rock.

The elf looked down at his hands and wrung them together for several long minutes.

"It was a gift for my cousin," he said at last, looking at something only he could see. "I made it with the help of my brethren in the Orders of High Sorcery. Over the years, my cousin had shielded many in the orders from Istar, defying his own family to do it, and we wished to reward him. I asked that we make him a sword, one that he could use as his wisdom saw fit."

The elf took a deep breath and let it out, never looking

up. His eyes seemed to glisten. "I rode out to meet him at a prearranged place south of here, but an Istarian patrol chased us. He got the sword, but didn't have time to undo its case before we split up. I tried to find him. Then my horse . . . You know the rest."

The goblin nodded solemnly. The sword, he shouted inside. Tell me about the sword, you maggot elf.

The elf licked his lips and went on. "The sword was named the Sword of Change. We wanted to fulfill my cousin's dearest dream, whatever the gods would grant, so we gave the sword the power to do just that. It will grant its user one wish. It is not all-powerful, but the gods of magic will grant the user what he asks for if it is within reason." He grimaced at a thought. "I've been guilty of worrying more about the sword than my cousin's life, but the sword could do much harm in the wrong hands. The Kingpriest no doubt could find a use for it to build his power. He could root out traitors, gain victory in battle, grant himself many more years of life. Now it's . . ." He lifted his hands, then let them fall, his shoulders sagging.

The goblin quietly digested this. The idea that a sword was capable of so much power was almost too ridiculous to believe, but the practical aspects of having a sword like that were not lost on him at all. A parade of wishes flowed through his head. Food, riches, women, physical might, rulership, immortality—he would ask for any of these if the sword were his—or if it became his, one day. It began to seep into his mind that perhaps the sword wasn't totally out of his grasp. It certainly couldn't hurt to find out if the elf knew anything more that would be useful in obtaining the sword. The goblin would have to prepare himself for the journey, though it meant abandoning the elf, the minotaur, and—

"Wow," said the kender.

The elf spun around and nearly fell again. The goblin jumped in surprise. Eyes full of wonder, the kender was sitting on the hillside over the cave mouth, beside a few small saplings only thirty feet away. The goblin had never seen him.

"A sword that can do all that," said the kender in awe. "And you cast magic, too? I can't believe it. That's incredible. Are you going to capture the sword? Can we see it if you do? What's it look like? My mother and father told me all about magic, and they said it was the best thing. I'd love to see a magic sword. Where is it? Can you find it?"

The elf slowly swallowed, appearing confused and unsure. He glanced from the goblin to the kender. "If I knew where the men who took it were, I might have a chance to get it back," the elf said. "If my cousin is . . . if he is dead, then I should see that the sword stays out of Istarian hands. I could not sleep, knowing they had it and could use it."

"Great!" shouted the kender, leaping to his feet. "Can we go with you? He and I are great hunters"—he pointed to the goblin—"and we can track and set traps and do all kinds of stuff. And the minotaur can carry things. He's strong! We won't get in the way, I promise. We'll be good! Are you going to cast spells to get the sword back? I can't wait!"

Both the elf and the goblin stared at the kender in astonishment. The goblin looked at the elf. The elf looked back at the minotaur, who was now sitting under a tree, taking a nap.

"Well . . ." said the elf.

"Then let's get going!" shouted the kender. "I'll grab my stuff!" He scooted down the slope and ran into the cave, past the camouflage branches.

The elf and goblin stared at each other. Each seemed to be about to ask a question. Neither did.

The elf cleared his throat. "I really should recover that sword. The Istarians will use it against us and against everyone not of their faith, and we will suffer for it. Making that sword was foolishness. Letting it go to the likes of them is worse."

The goblin shrugged and glanced at the minotaur. "You know, that fine by me, you get sword. Fine that we go for walk. But maybe big one not like to take walk with us," he said in a very low voice, nodding in the minotaur's direction. "Hard to tell with big one."

The elf thought. "Maybe I can do something about that," he said. "I don't like doing this, but . . . could you find that white book you said you found? I think I have a spell there that might . . ." He let his voice trail off.

The goblin made a show of looking up into the trees, then motioned for the elf to follow him into the cave.

Everything was working out so perfectly that the goblin had trouble believing it. The possibility that he would soon have the sword in his hands made it hard to think. He'd have to calm down and use his head. There was too much at stake to blow this. And he'd have to start thinking about the wish he would make the moment his hand closed on the sword's hilt. There were so many things he had always wanted, and now . . .

There was no sound in the forest but the rustling of dry leaves and the cold wind in the bare branches. Beneath the tree where it rested, the minotaur leaned back, eyes almost closed, perfectly still except for the gentle rise and fall of its barrel-sized chest. One of its broad, cupped ears flicked away a horsefly, then curled back like the other toward the cave mouth.

* * * * *

They traveled east under a dark sky for the rest of the day. Behind them were the woods that the kender had known all his life. The kender was quite excited about the trip and talked incessantly, though he looked back now and then, too, and was sometimes silent. Nervously eyeing the placid minotaur, the goblin marched along quickly to keep up with everyone else. The elf's spell of charming did indeed seem to have tamed the huge beast, though the goblin was careful never to annoy it. There was no sense in pressing one's luck. Once the elf felt certain of the minotaur's obedience and that it understood the widely used trade tongue, the elf paid little attention to the beast and merely had it carry their heavier supplies. These included a few bags the elf had dropped when the humans had captured him. The elf fussed over these for several minutes before assuring himself that they were safe and unharmed.

The Istarian free rangers had left a remarkably clear trail behind them. The goblin spat on the ground as the kender traced it back with ease. In the old days, the goblin had heard, no living thing could find the path a ranger took. Obviously, that had been a *very* long time ago.

They bedded down that night, too exhausted to talk. The kender took first watch in the evening, unable to sleep from excitement. He talked to himself a lot, however, which kept the elf and goblin awake until the elf relieved the kender and forced him to get some sleep himself.

On the afternoon of the second day, the foot trail of the rangers merged with that of a larger party of humans with horses and wagons. The signs of a camp on the edge of the forest were fairly fresh, abandoned not more than a day ago. A bonfire had been built in a broad clearing; the large ash pile was still smoking slightly.

There was a grave, too, with an elf's battered helmet pounded into the soil above it. The elf rested his hand on the soil for a few moments, then stood, said nothing. The goblin noticed, though, that the elf's eyes seemed unusually red thereafter. The goblin shrugged; vengeance would make the wizard fight all the harder. And it meant one less elf in the world.

"We've got to move more carefully," said the kender, scuffing his bare feet through some flattened tall grass. "If they rest in the evenings, we could catch them as early as tomorrow morning. But they could catch us, too. We killed three of their scouts, but they might not miss them right away. It looks like they have about twenty men, probably in armor. They might have slaves, too. Those footprints right there are barefoot. The slaves probably stay in the wagons when the Istarians are traveling. Looks like children, maybe a woman, too."

"Where are they heading?" the elf asked, shading his eyes to look into the distance. The sky was overcast, but the cold sun managed to peek through irregular breaks in the clouds.

"East, probably back to Istar. It looks like a regular patrol, border checkers. They must all want to get back home. They used to come into the woods when I was small, but not so much lately. We should stay low and near trees whenever possible." The kender turned to look up at the elf. "Say, what spells are you going to use when we find the humans, anyway?"

The elf looked down with a faint smile. "This was all your idea. I thought you knew."

"No, really," said the kender. "You're a wizard. You should know about stuff like this. Are you planning to throw a blast of fire at them? Are you going to blow them up just like that? Can I watch if I'm quiet?"

The goblin, who had turned to continue the trek, stopped to hear the elf's response. The same thought about their tactics had been going through his mind, too, but he had planned to ask about it this evening when they made camp. Would the elf do all the work for them?

The elf's lips pressed tightly together. His face was now less puffy, but it was an off-green color, the bruises and cuts fading away slowly. "We'll see," he said. "I have a few things with me that might help. I'll need to think it out, but we should be able to put on quite a show. I doubt that the patrol will ever forget it."

The kender nodded with excitement, the goblin with satisfaction. The minotaur wandered on ahead to kick at some rocks.

The kender's guesswork on the location of the Istarians proved to be reasonably accurate. By late evening, even the goblin could tell that they were not far behind the humans. The oddly assorted companions elected to camp for the night, forgoing a fire to prevent their being spotted. They planned to catch the humans on the following night. The elf guessed it would be their last chance to do so before the humans entered territory that was more heavily defended.

That evening, before the light in the sky was gone, the elf carefully outlined the plan he had developed for assaulting the Istarian camp. He brought out the things that the order had gifted him with before he had left with the Sword of Change, and he went over their uses, point by point. It would be difficult to take on the Istarian force, especially since the four of them were far outnumbered. But the elf pointed out that they had the weight of magic and surprise. If a kender and a goblin could kill three rangers, they certainly had a chance against the rest.

The kender was beside himself with excitement at the plans; the minotaur seemed indifferent and uninterested. The goblin listened carefully to the explanation and fought to control his mounting tension. He mentally thanked himself for not having burned the wizard's books and for the silver tongue it had taken to open up the elf's foolish trust. This elf was truly dangerous. It seemed he could do everything.

And it was that very thought that brought back a tale the goblin had heard, and his blood ran cold with fear. Nonetheless, he asked the question with earnest innocence.

He cleared his throat to get everyone's attention. "Hear talk from men of Istar, back when, that priests of Istar hear you think when you not talk." The goblin tapped the side of his head with a red finger. "Maybe they do this to you or us, find us out?"

"I doubt that they have a priest with them, but it's possible," the elf replied, unhappy with the thought. "I've heard about the priests' mind-reading, too. Only the more important priests can do that, but . . . let's hope for the best."

The goblin grinned. "Eh, hope for best, yes. Maybe you can do this listen-to-thoughts trick also, eh? You hear their thoughts so we know what they think?"

"No, I'm afraid not. There were a few spells I was never able to learn, and the mind-reading spell was one of them. I couldn't learn to cast a fireball spell, either, but I think I've taken care of that. I've always wanted to throw a fireball, but what I've got is better."

The goblin laughed and nodded. His mind was safe. His plans were secure. The relief he felt almost left him light-headed. He knew a White Robes wizard would not lie, and he was grateful for that flaw as much as he despised the elf for it.

The goblin busied himself, setting up camp without even being asked, which was unusual for him, but welcome by the elf and kender. The goblin had already come to terms with what he needed to do to get the sword at the least amount of risk to himself. All he needed was to lay his hands on the sword for a few seconds, long enough to make his wish, which he now knew by heart. After that, he'd have no worries at all.

The elf took first watch that evening. The others bedded down in the darkness of a thicket at the foot of a hill. The minotaur simply stretched out on the ground, chains rattling, and was asleep almost at once. The goblin and kender bedded down as well. After long minutes of forcing his tension-tight stomach to settle down, the goblin closed his eyes and prepared to take a much-needed rest.

"Are you still awake?" came the kender's voice. The goblin jerked, and his eyes opened instantly. Then he realized the kender wasn't talking to him. The soft voice came from where the elf had gone on guard duty.

"Of course I'm awake," the elf said.

The goblin sighed and lifted his head slightly. With his night vision, he could see the elf settle down on the ground next to a log, about fifty feet away. The kender wandered out of the dark undergrowth and sat down by the elf. The little nuisance was wrapped in a blanket he had brought from the cave. The goblin tried to close his eyes to sleep, but found rest impossible now. He resigned himself to staying awake a while longer, watching the elf and kender and listening to them talk.

"I can't sleep," the kender said, scooting closer to the elf. "I'm a little excited about tomorrow night. I've been in fights before, but never one like this. Is it bad to be excited like this?"

"No," said the elf. "I'm feeling a little . . . er . . . excited myself, but it will pass. Just remember your part, and when the time comes, you'll be ready for it."

The kender sighed. "I hope so. I keep thinking about what it will be like, and I can't seem to make my mind slow down enough to drop off. My head's all full of things."

Your head is full, yes, thought the goblin. It is full of briars.

The elf grunted. "You know," he said, "I never did ask you what your name was. We've been so preoccupied that I never got around to it."

There was a little silence. "Well, I wasn't really going to tell you, because I was talking with the goblin a few weeks ago when we first met, and he said he didn't have a name. I figured it would be im-po-lite to tell him my name when he didn't have one to tell me. My father taught me that word."

"Hmmm," said the elf. "Well, so you're worried about offending what's-his-name, the goblin?"

"Yeah," said the kender, scooting a little closer to the elf. "So you can't tell me your name, either. We have to be fair."

The goblin gently shook his head in disgust. He had long ago given up trying to plumb the depths of the kender's bizarre mind. It simply made no sense. Still, he felt odd hearing the kender's reason for never telling his name. It made the goblin vaguely uncomfortable, and he couldn't say why.

The little guy was now practically stuck to the elf's side. The elf raised his arm and hung it back over the fallen log to keep from poking the kender in the head with his elbow.

"Magic is great," said the kender. "I never knew you had so much magic. I've wanted to see magic all my life because my parents always told stories about it. They said it was the most marvelous thing, but it wasn't fair because kender couldn't cast magic, no matter how hard they studied. But elves and humans knew how. Is that true?"

"I'm afraid there's some truth to that," the elf said. "Kender can cast spells if they serve the gods, but the Orders of High Sorcery are closed to them." He shrugged his shoulders, but his voice betrayed a certain relief at his words.

The goblin was appalled. A kender casting spells? The very idea was chilling. Gods above, there was enough trouble in the world already. Istar would be less of a threat than a kender wizard.

"By the way," said the elf. "That's mine."

"What? Oh! I'm sorry." The kender handed something back to the elf. "It fell out of your pocket."

The elf put the item on the ground far away from the kender. "If I lose anything else, I won't be able to cast any spells tomorrow," he warned.

"Oh," said the kender. There was a pause. "Here. I found these, too."

The elf took the offered items with a deep sigh. "Thanks," he said, and all was quiet for a while.

"I used to ask my parents if I could learn to cast magic when I got older," the kender said. "My mother said maybe it was a good thing I couldn't, since if you want to become a magic-user, you have to pass a test, and they make you do terrible things in the test. Is that true?"

The elf was silent for perhaps a minute. It was a different kind of silence than merely thinking. The goblin found himself turning his head to hear better, straining to hear more.

The kender poked the elf gently in the side with an elbow.

"What?" asked the elf blankly. "Oh, the test. Yes, we do have to take the Test of High Sorcery. The test doesn't really make you do terrible things, but you . . . you have to . . . um . . . go through some terrible things. The bad things just . . . happen to you. I don't think I want to talk about my test right now. I want to keep my mind clear and ready for tomorrow."

"Oh." There was a brief silence. "Would I have made a good magic-user? I'm thirteen now. Is that old enough to be a wizard?"

The news surprised the goblin. He had seen very few kender in his life, but because they had all looked to be the size of human children, he never thought twice about this kender's age, assuming it was about thirty or so. Thirteen was far younger than he had expected of someone, especially a kender, with so much ability at wilderness survival and lore.

"Thirteen is a little young," the elf finally commented. "But a few wizards start not long after that age. Some slightly younger."

The kender seemed to be thinking hard about something after that. Finally, he blurted out, "Could you cast a spell for me?"

The goblin blinked in shock. What?

"Well, I could," said the elf slowly, "but most of the spells I have right now should be saved for tomorrow night." He paused for a moment, then said, "I suppose I could try one small thing. I can relearn a new spell in its place in the morning."

The kender leaned forward in excitement. "Really? A real spell?"

He dropped his voice, glancing back at the goblin and minotaur. The goblin closed his eyes, though he figured they'd never know if he was awake or not unless he moved around.

"All right, I'm ready!" the kender whispered. "You won't set anything on fire, will you? It's awfully dry out here and it hasn't rained in the last five days. Anything but that is fine."

"Don't worry," the elf said softly, and he raised his hands. "*Impilteh peh.*"

A faint blue light—a tiny ball the size of a fingernail—began to glow in the darkness between the elf's fingers. The goblin caught his breath, not daring to make a sound and reveal himself. He had never seen magic before, either, and the sight of it frightened him as much as it excited and fascinated him.

The elf's fingers began a slow, waving dance around the ball, and the ball responded by moving from one hand to the other, swaying back and forth. In a moment, the ball divided into two balls of equal size, then each ball divided again and there were four, then eight, each rolling to the rhythm of the elf's hands. By the faint, mobile light, the goblin could see the kender's eyes shining.

The elf's hands moved, altering the pattern. The eight blue balls began to chase each other in a small circle, changing colors from blue to violet, then to red, orange, yellow, green, and blue again. The balls began to change colors out of sequence with each other, whirling around between the elf's outspread fingers as he manipulated their magical essence. They formed an oval pattern in the air, chasing each other faster and faster, until they were a single, unbroken cord of golden light that gyrated like a coin rolling on its edge in a tight circle, just before falling flat.

The elf's lips pursed, concentrating on the pattern. The circle began changing shape as it revolved in the air, taking the form of a square, then a triangle, then a five-pointed star. Then its shape altered even more: a flying bird, a leaping rabbit, a swimming fish, all whirling around without sound.

The elf's fingers changed the pattern again. Now it was deep glowing green, a narrowing column that revolved more slowly until it stopped over one outstretched palm and began to grow leaves like a live plant. Each leaf appeared in outline, then filled in with soft color; thorns formed on the main stem. The top of the plant bloomed into a bright red bud, which slowly grew until a rose of crimson light reached up toward the sky.

The elf uttered a soft word, and the plant collapsed into a small ball of pale white light. In moments, it formed a mouselike shape that scampered around on the mage's palm with lifelike curiosity. When it had finished exploring the hand, the mouse stood up on its back legs, did a short dance, took a deep bow to the kender and wizard, and vanished into a dot of light that slowly faded from sight.

It was completely dark now. The goblin had forgotten how to breathe. He slowly shut his mouth, unable to believe it was over. He blinked and resisted the urge to rub his eyes. It was magic. Real magic.

Then he heard the kender sniffle.

He looked at the little figure by the elf's side. Both of the kender's hands were pressed to his face, covering his eyes. The kender suddenly drew in a ragged breath and began to cry.

The elf's arm dropped over the kender's shoulders. "What's wrong?" he asked in confusion.

The kender leaned into the elf's chest as he wept, his thin body shaking. Long minutes passed in the night as the goblin watched.

"My mamma and daddy told me magic was beautiful," the kender sobbed. "They said they had never seen it before, but they knew it was good. They wanted to see it so badly but no one would show them. They told me that humans weren't all bad, and maybe someday a human or an elf would show us some magic if we were patient with them. They didn't think humans would hurt them, but the humans did. The humans hurt them, they hurt my mamma and daddy a lot and I couldn't help them because I was too scared and I hid, and when the humans were gone, I had to bury them and say the good-bye prayers like they taught me. I was too scared to help them, even when they were really hurt bad. I wish I had magic then so I could have helped them. They wanted to see magic so bad." He shook as he wept, his face hidden in the elf's clothes.

The goblin realized that his hands were clenched into cold, trembling fists. Something burned in his eyes; it was hard to see. Slowly, the goblin unclenched his hands and covered his hot face with them. He hated weakness, he had hated it all his life, and now he was filled with it. He hated himself for it, and it was all the kender's fault— the damned, weak, stupid, wretched kender. Wet streams flowed down the goblin's cheeks, and he bit his lower lip until he tasted blood.

Tomorrow, he thought. Let tomorrow come fast.

*　*　*　*　*

No stars were out. A tall fire burned just up the slope of the hill, visible through the thick trees and under-brush. The crickets called from all around.

"So you think you know how to handle that elf girl?" the grinning guard said. "You think she's not too much of a match for you?"

The smiling guard had turned to face his companion, who was bending over to pick up firewood. The goblin drove his knife into the grinning man's lower back, straight through his leather armor. The guard knew in-stinctively he was going to die, the pain was so great. He was terrified and tried to scream, but the scream wouldn't come out through the goblin's calloused hand that was clamped over his mouth and face, twisting his head back with incredible force. The man reached back to grab his attacker, but agony filled his head and made him forget everything. The goblin let the body sag to the ground.

"You bet I can handle her," said the guard picking up the firewood. He crouched down to adjust the load in his arms, reaching for a few more pieces. "Good redeems its own, they say, and I'm gonna redeem that elf girl before she gets to Istar. She's gonna know the ways of man, and I'm gonna be the head priest. They can have the other slaves. I've waited too long to pass this one up."

He picked up the last piece of wood, and the goblin slapped his hand tightly over the man's mouth and pulled him into his hard chest. The razor-sharp blade sliced swiftly through his throat. The man knew what was happening, but could do nothing to stop it, and trying to scream did nothing useful at all.

Then it was quiet again in the night woods, and soon the crickets began to chirp. Everything smelled of blood.

The goblin grinned, wiped off his blade, and moved on through the wood. He felt no weakness at all now, not with the spell of magical strength the elf had cast upon him. He thought he could lift a horse now if he wanted to, maybe ten horses. And he wore a ring that altered the sounds around him, so a man would think he had heard an owl hoot if the goblin spoke, or heard the wind blow if he walked up. It was too good to be true. In his excitement, he barely noticed the cold.

The main encampment of Istarians was on the hilltop, packed tightly around the bonfire in the chill air. Down the slope, in a clearing, half hidden from the hilltop by trees, was a cluster of several wagons and all the Istarians' horses. The elf had scouted ahead with his spells and reported finding slaves in one wagon: an elven woman, an old dwarf, and three children—human or elven, he couldn't tell. The other three wagons were empty. The kender's estimate of twenty men was close; the goblin guessed twenty-four—twenty-one now that he had killed three men in the last few minutes of circling the camp.

The elf and minotaur were down by the wagons, attacking the guards there. The elf cast a spell that silenced the minotaur's rattling chains. The goblin crouched down, pulled a thin, ceramic flask from a leather pouch on his rope belt. It was time. Uncorking the lid, he drank the contents, screwing up his face at the bitter taste. Wiping his mouth, he stood up, tossed the flask aside, and moved toward the firelight in a crouch. He had to reach the top of the hill before the kender arrived with the fireball.

Every step of the way, the goblin pictured the sword. He saw himself holding it instead of his machete, and saw himself after he made his wish, the one wish, the only wish. The thought almost made him hurry too fast and give himself away to the humans, who were directly ahead of him. He dropped down behind a tree and faded into the darkness. He was only two hundred feet from the fire on top of the hill.

"It's not like we're killing real people, you know." The human who spoke kept his voice low, but his tone was sure and knowing. He shifted his stance, and his armor clinked. Chain mail, maybe with plate. "You and I, we're real people. We know the difference between right and wrong. The great gods blessed us with vision that no other race has. That's the vision to see our destiny. We're not like the mongrel races who see only to the next day's meal. They don't deserve to breathe our air. By the blessed gods, do you want to live in a city with goblins?"

There were two men ahead of the goblin, thirty feet away, near a pile of brush and branches from a fallen tree. He could see them well in the firelight. One wore metal mail, the other riveted leather. The goblin guessed that the one in mail was a leader, maybe a knight. The man would be hard to kill if this wasn't done right. The goblin wondered if he should just go around them, but he hated leaving anyone alive behind him, especially people who didn't want to live with goblins or breathe their air.

The man in the riveted leather looked away from his companion, his grip loosening on his spear. "No, Your Reverence," he mumbled.

The goblin froze. Gods of Istar, he thought, a priest. Perhaps a priest that could tell what you were thinking!

"Well, neither do I," said the mail-armored man, looking at the other with a half-grin. "No one does. You know what kinds of evil things goblins do, don't you? Well, certainly. We have to destroy them, and you know that's right. And kender. Forgive my asking, but would one of the gods of good ever have created a kender?"

"They—" The other man stopped, obviously trying to think this out carefully. "They aren't . . . I mean . . . kender, they cause trouble, I know, but—"

The mail-armored man snorted good-naturedly. He looked away at the distant bonfire in the center of the camp, surrounded by the secure clutter of bedrolls. The dim firelight was reflected in his polished steel breastplate. "You're trying to tell me that kender aren't as bad as goblins, right?"

The leather-armored man took a breath, thought better of his answer, and said nothing.

"So you *do* think kender aren't as bad as goblins." The mail-armored man sighed. "You think we're doing wrong, is that it? We're doing the will of the gods of good and the Kingpriest of Istar, and it's wrong?"

"No." The man seemed badly frightened. The goblin could barely hear the answer. "No, that's not it, Your Reverence."

"Ah," the cleric said, the misunderstanding apparently cleared up. "The captain said this was your first campaign. I know it's hard, and everything seems confusing at times. Maybe all the time, right?"

The other man looked at the ground and seemed to nod in the affirmative, unwilling to speak.

The goblin's worst fear was eased. If the priest could read minds, he wasn't doing it now. The goblin studied the ground ahead of him, then reached into a side pocket and pulled something out. He couldn't count on a clean kill through mail armor, so he'd have to use the potion's powers and work around it. He slowly crept out from the tree's shadow.

"It was confusing for me, too, when I started." The cleric suddenly sounded strangely vulnerable. "It was terrible for me at first. I wasn't worried about fighting goblins, but other things threw me. We had to fight dwarves once. They put the fear of evil into me, with their shifty little eyes and ratty beards and stumpy bodies. They fought like"—the cleric dropped his voice and turned his dark eyes on the recruit—"like the Seven Evil Ones were in them."

There was only silence after his words, except for the distant crackling of the fire. The wind seemed to be picking up around them.

"It was a terrible war in the mountains," said the cleric in a low voice. "I saw my friends crushed by avalanches, shot by bolts and arrows. They lay in my arms with their limbs hacked away, begging me to heal them. The dwarves did this to us in the mountains. They didn't fight like humans. They weren't human. They were evil reborn. I saw it all then, and I came to believe at last in their evil. I wish to the gods even now that there had been a better way for me to learn than to have gone through that. I'll not see my friends die in my arms for that again, bleeding away and me not able to stop it because all my spells were gone to others wounded earlier." The cleric's eyes were like dancing black flames.

The cleric reached up, patted the other man on the back. "I like you, boy. You remind me of the way I was, before the war in the mountains. I wish you could always be like that. I really do. You're a lot happier for it."

The leather-armored man coughed and dared a weak smile. The cleric smiled back at him. The leather-armored man reached up to wipe the sweat from his forehead.

Something moved across his feet and crawled up his

legs.

The man jumped when he felt it. Something had him by the feet, and he lost his balance and fell over, dropping his spear. The cleric began struggling and slapping madly at his thighs. He was seeing tall grass and vines and roots and briars and saplings knot themselves around his calves like iron chains. The two men opened their mouths to shout or scream. No cries sounded. Instead, the crickets chirped more loudly, the wind blew harder, night birds called. The men on the hill by the fire went on about their business.

The goblin came swiftly out of the darkness. He whipped a flexible wire over the cleric's head, twisted the wire around his neck, and pulled it tight in less than a second, snapping the cleric's head back with great force. The cleric's eyes bugged out; he fought to get his fingers under the wire but found no space. His tongue came out between his teeth, and his eyes stared, white, at the stars. The man on the ground struggled to get free of the vines and grass that tightened over his legs and chest and arms and reached up for his face, and he screamed and screamed and heard only the crickets and the night birds and the wind in the trees above.

Then the cleric collapsed, falling backward into the grasping grasses and vines, and the dark shape released the garrote and looked at the fallen man with cold eyes. The leather-armored man saw it and believed the cleric about the evil then, he believed it all, and he screamed like a madman right up to the end. And no one heard him.

It's all too good to be true, thought the goblin.

* * * * *

"Where in the Abyss are they?" muttered the captain, heedless of the sleeping men around him. He had to be the captain, the goblin decided, though the man wore no armor. His bearing and movements marked him at once as a man who was in charge. "Hey, you!" he shouted to the sentry standing across the camp. "Get out there and tell those two dung-eaters that the fire's dying, and they're to get their fat asses back up here with the wood right now. And tell them I want to see them afterward, too. If they've got time to hunt squirrels, they've got time for a few other things I've got in mind for them. Go!"

The sleeping men slept on. The chosen soldier saluted with a grin and took off into the woods, passing the unseen goblin and leaving the bearded captain to slap at mosquitoes and gnats. "I hate being out here," the captain muttered. "I hate all of the camping out crap, with little things that bite and sting. The wilderness doesn't give a damn about me or my rank or anything. I can't fight back."

The goblin looked at the soldier heading into the woods. The man wasn't likely to find the last two bodies, covered up as they were, but if he kept going he'd soon find the first three. Time was running out. Hidden behind a cluster of saplings, the goblin rubbed his arm muscles and looked back at the camp. He counted twelve sleeping rolls around the clearing; the captain was standing guard now by himself. The other men must be down the slope with the horses and wagons, if they were still alive—which the goblin doubted very much.

The kender was due. The goblin had to get there first, to look for the sword. He took the time to squint against the firelight and search the clearing for any sign of a box or crate that might contain a sword. There was only one pile of belongings and supplies, and that was on the edge of the clearing, about two-thirds of the way around to the left. He couldn't make out what was in the pile very well; the fire interfered with his night vision. His only hope was that the captain had thought the sword valuable enough to bring it into the camp to prevent its being stolen.

The goblin carefully moved back from the light and

began making his way around the camp's edge toward the left side. He tried not to think of the possibility that the elf, the minotaur, or even the kender would find the Sword of Change first. He had dreamed about the sword so much in the last two days that he couldn't imagine not having it. There was so much to gain, and he deserved it so badly. The wish would pay for a lifetime of loneliness, deprivation, and brutality. It would set him above all worries ever again.

He still felt as if the strength spell was working. He didn't know if the plant-control potion was active or not, but he didn't care. If he could get close enough to the supplies and find that sword, he wouldn't need to entangle the soldiers with plants again; he could just take off and run with his prize. No. He changed his mind. He would use the potion's effects if it still worked. Better to snag everyone with weeds until he had time for his wish. Then it wouldn't matter anymore.

The slope in the woods behind the supplies fell off steeply, dropping at least twenty feet straight down through the tree limbs. The goblin kept as low to the ground as he could while he moved, taking his time. Any minute now, the guard in the woods would find someone's body and set up an alarm. But the goblin couldn't afford haste. He reached the edge of the grassy cliff. It was bathed in shadows cast by the supply crates and chests, blocking the fire's light. The goblin decided to risk standing up in a crouch, and he took a much better look around the camp.

Right then, the kender flew down out of the sky and landed in the middle of the camp, not a pike's length away from both the captain and the goblin himself.

It happened so fast that the goblin froze in the act of taking a step, and the captain didn't even shout to wake everyone up. The kender merely landed and looked around, then waved a hand at the captain and gave him a devilish grin. The kender, his dark hair full of tangles and his scarred face smudged with dirt, came up to the captain's breastbone. The kender wore his usual filthy mix of torn clothes and animal hides, and he held a huge bag cradled in his arms: the fireball.

"What in the Abyss!" whispered the captain. His right hand slowly edged up his back toward a dagger sheath. Keeping his face blank, he waved at the kender.

The kender hopped into the air, did a smooth back flip, and landed on his feet again, his face alive with excitement. He nodded at the captain and made a motion of looking briefly toward the sky, as if urging the captain to try it, too.

The captain licked his lips. His fingers were working on untying the dagger straps. "I'm . . . I'm afraid I can't fly like that," he said, forcing a smile. "But that was real good."

Out of the corner of his eye, the goblin noticed an arm snake quietly out of a bedroll about ten feet behind the kender, reaching for a sword on the ground. The captain seemed to see it, too, but he kept from looking in that direction after the first glance.

"Do you know any other tricks?" the captain asked, almost conversationally.

"Sure!" said the kender, then looked instantly contrite. "Not supposed to talk," he mumbled apologetically. "My mistake. But here's my last trick anyway."

The soldier in the bedroll behind the kender lifted the sword, then slowly rolled forward to get within striking distance. The goblin tensed. He hadn't the faintest idea what to do next.

The kender crouched and leaped into the air. Still carrying the bag, he flew straight up into the darkness. The soldier in the bedroll flung himself forward. His sword whipped down, missing the kender completely.

"Camp awake!" roared the captain, forgetting the dagger and pulling his long sword free instead. "To arms! Get the rocks out of your asses and get up! To arms, the gods damn you!"

The kender was gone now, lost against the starless

black of the night sky. The goblin backed farther into the undergrowth until he was on the edge of the cliff. There was nowhere to go. He kept the bulk of a tree between him and the awakening camp, and silently cursed the kender for nearly getting himself killed.

Sleepy, frightened men tore at their bedrolls, flailed about for weapons and armor and helmets and shields. The captain, swearing at all the gods, stared up into the sky for the flying kender.

"Sorry I missed 'im, Cap'n," said the warrior. "I had 'im right there before he took off. Was he a wizard?"

"Had to be," said the captain tightly, still looking upward. "He flew."

"What's going on, Captain?" one of the men shouted, his armor half-on, an axe in his hand.

The bearded captain looked down. All his men were up now, crowding around. "You," said the captain, pointing to a red-haired man. "Get down the hill and get the priest up here; we could be having some trouble. Tell him there's a wizard loose. Take three men with you. Don't—ow, damn it!" The captain clapped his hand over his eyes, rubbed them vigorously with his fingers, and other men around the camp nearest the fire did the same. Sparks flew up from the bonfire's flames as a black, powdery rain began.

It was the start of the fireball.

The goblin realized his danger when the black dust came down and the men in the camp swore. He knew he should get away, but he hesitated just a moment before escaping, because he couldn't figure out where to go without being seen. That was all the time he had and it was gone.

The fireball was an explosion of white and yellow light half as big as a city block. It billowed out over the bonfire, filled the entire clearing, framed the flying bodies of men at its base for an instant before it swallowed them whole.

A solid blinding wall of superheated flame and air

reached for the goblin through the black branches and leaves, incinerating the trees as it came. The flames found him and burned the hair from his arms and face, set his rags on fire, and roasted every scrap of skin that faced the inferno. In agony, the goblin instinctively flung up his hands to ward it off. There was no time to be truly afraid. He had no time to react, except to move.

He turned and threw himself off the cliff. He fell through space, bathed in firelight, the wind roaring for a moment in his ears, the distant sloping ground rushing up to meet him.

The ground slammed all of the air from his lungs when he hit. He rolled in a crazy tangle of arms and legs down the slope until he struck a tree with his back. He couldn't breathe. A million thorns and sticks had torn his burned skin. A flaming mass of leaves landed around him. He forced himself to his knees without thinking at all. He fought for air and felt a dozen sharp knives stab him through the lungs. It was the worst pain he had ever known, worse than the burns and cuts. He got numbly to his feet, not daring to breathe again, and staggered forward, heedless of everything, until he fell over a log. Something struck his forehead like a hammer, and the world went out.

* * * * *

For a minute, the goblin could not remember what was going on or why he was even here. All he knew was a peculiar numbness. Strange images began to filter back to him, part of some awful dream that ran around and around in a storm inside his head. He remembered who he was, but nothing about where he was or what he was doing here. He lay back, feeling some of the numbness slip away into a slowly building pain that covered his whole body. He dreamed that he had bathed in lava and been beaten with clubs.

I am out in the night in a forest, he thought. There's a

big fire on a hill above me. I should get away from here, but I don't know where this is or why I'm here.

He started to roll over but didn't, wincing from the awful pain that started deep in his chest. He slowly began to remember the kender, then the minotaur and elf. He even remembered the sword, but he had no idea why he should care about it.

After a while, he remembered that, too.

He finally got to his knees, but stayed there, his bruised chest aching with every wheezing breath he drew. The blast had been the elf's coal-dust fireball, the one he said he'd worked on with the help of gnomes, who had provided the coal for the enchantment. The goblin wondered if the kender could have survived the blast, being so far up in the sky. The elf had warned the kender about staying aloft too long. The spell would fade and drop the little guy from the clouds to his death. Maybe the kender wouldn't have to worry about that possibility, if his curiosity had gotten the best of him and he'd tried to watch the blast close up. The goblin found himself hoping the kender was still around somewhere. After all, he told himself, the kender did all the work.

Then the goblin remembered the elf and the minotaur. The elf would be looking for the sword right now, and he had the minotaur's help as well as his spells.

That's all right, the goblin thought suddenly. I'm going to kill that elf. I'm going to kill that elf and the minotaur, too. I can do it; I've killed lots of men tonight. I'll just kill everyone. I'm so strong, nothing can get me. I just need to get that sword, and that's all I'll ever need. I have to do it now.

Carefully, using a tree trunk for support, the goblin got to his feet and began to stagger back up the hill.

* * * * *

Smoke drifted across the countryside in the night as flames leaped through the dry trees, sending yellow sparks skyward by the thousands. The bottoms of the clouds glowed orange.

The goblin began climbing the hill, pulling himself up foot by agonizing foot. His burned, aching hands clung to branches, bunched weeds, and stones. He climbed until he knew he had been climbing for years without end. Somewhere along the way, he lost his magical ring. Several times he felt delirious and babbled about things that seemed to make lots of sense but never stayed long in his mind. He yelled and sang and grasped a last handful of grass, pulled himself up on his stomach, and saw that he had made it. He was still singing something, a tune he'd heard the thugs sing in East Dravinar, but the song faded away as he coughed on the smoke and the stench of burned flesh. He rested for a moment, then pulled himself up to look around.

It took a while, but eventually he realized that the fires on the hilltop were going out. It took a few moments longer to realize that it was probably the doing of the elf wizard. The goblin watched dumbly as a small fire in front of him died away into a blackened smear of ash and smoke. Only the much-weakened bonfire still burned with any heat and light.

The goblin shivered as a violent chill passed through him. He knew it was from both fear and the beating he'd taken, especially from the burns. He had to find the sword. He couldn't go on much longer. He moved forward on his hands and knees, his body alive with pain, looking for the supply pile.

As he did, he heard someone stumbling toward him through the scorched remains of the camp. The goblin coughed and looked around.

A blackened apparition in guardsman armor held out its arms to the goblin as it approached. Its face was burned beyond recognition, and its fingers were gone, leaving only the black stumps of its hands. The figure walked stiffly toward the goblin. The man was blind and unaware, trailing smoke from the remnants of his smoldering clothes.

The goblin shrieked in terror. He couldn't even think of fleeing or fighting. All he knew was that it was a dead man, a dead man he had helped kill, and it wanted him. He knew all the stories about dead men. He didn't want to know any more.

The burned apparition stumbled over a body on the ground before it collapsed with a muffled cry. For a moment it tried to rise, then it fell flat and was still at last.

The smell hit him then, and the goblin retched, but he forced himself to look away from the dead man and began crawling again. He knew he'd find worse as he got closer to the blast, but it didn't matter. He had to find the sword.

A jumble of blackened wood appeared in the dying firelight, only thirty feet away. With a burst of energy he didn't think he could find, the goblin gave out a gasping cry, then hurried forward on hands and knees, heedless of what he had to crawl over or through to get there.

Restless fingers reached for the smoldering boxes. He saw that they really had been camp supplies, but it was still possible that the sword was among them. He was so close now, so close to the only power he would ever know, that he couldn't stop looking. He got to his knees and tried to examine the boxes in the dimming firelight.

And, almost at once, he saw one that stood out from the rest. It was a weapons case, once covered with fine elven carvings in the wood but now half-charred. It was just a little bigger than a sword would be. He snatched at it with an agonized, inarticulate cry, dragging the case to him as he fumbled for latches or locks. His fingers found one, snapped it open, and emptied it out.

But it was already empty.

He blinked.

It was already empty.

He checked the inside of the box again.

It was still empty.

Empty.

Empty.

Someone moved through the camp behind him. The goblin turned around, shivering but feeling no pain at all from his wounds.

"Oh, gods!" cried the elf's muffled voice. His face was white with shock, and he held a cloth to his nose and mouth with his left hand to ward against the awful stench in the air. "You're hurt! Don't move!"

The goblin dully dropped his gaze to the elf's right hand, which held a gleaming, jewel-encrusted long sword, point down, at his side.

The elf sheathed his sword in a scabbard that the goblin did not recognize.

"I found the Sword of Change with one of the guards by the horses," the elf said hastily, coming up to kneel and check the goblin's injuries. "The man must have won it in a dice game or something. The minotaur's just down the slope. The slaves ran off into the hills. Let's get you to a creek and get you washed off. If that kender's around anywhere, we'll get him to bandage you up. Damn, you're really hurt. How close were you to the fireball? Couldn't you get away from it?"

The goblin's shoulders slumped, and he seemed to melt into himself. The elf reached out and gently took the goblin by one arm, trying to help him up. The goblin flinched at the painful touch, but didn't get up. He sat on the ground and stared at the elf's feet without a trace of expression.

"Come on," said the elf. "We have what we came for, and now we must look after your wounds." He reached down again with both hands. The goblin looked up stupidly at the elf's face. Then he looked down and saw the sword.

"Come on," the elf urged.

The goblin stirred, reaching up to the elf with both hands as he sat back on the balls of his feet. He took a sudden deep breath and lunged forward through the elf's arms. As he hurtled past the elf's side, he snatched at the sword hilt with both hands. The sword snagged, then pulled free of its sheath.

He had the sword. *He had the sword!*

"Gods, no!" shouted the elf, starting for him.

The goblin stumbled backward, nearly falling before he caught himself. The elf almost grabbed him, but the blade came up. The elf dodged and jumped back, almost a moment too late.

"Please!" pleaded the elf. "You're crazy! You don't have any idea of what you're holding!"

The goblin stared for a moment, then laughed—a wild, mad, painful laugh that rang in the night across the hilltop. His eyes were glistening balls of blackness in his burned, filthy face, his mouth open to the black sky. His chest shook as if each breath was killing him.

"Give me the sword!" the elf shouted. "Give it to me!"

The goblin still laughed and shook his head. He felt giddy, as if his soul were leaving his body. He seemed to hurt all over. "It my sword," he managed to say, though the pain in his lungs stabbed him with every word. "It my sword! My sword!"

"You'll ruin everything, you fool!" the elf yelled. "It's a wish sword! We can fight Istar with it! We can save ourselves and our people from Istar if we use it right! We have the chance now! Give me the sword!"

The goblin shook his head slowly. He kept the sword point facing the elf, ready to thrust in case the elf did something stupid like charge. But the goblin was feeling very tired now. It seemed like a year since he'd slept last. The sword was very heavy, and his chest was starting to hurt more than usual. He tried to swallow, but it hurt too much.

The elf held his pose, his arms reaching out to the goblin from a crouched stance. Then he slowly let his arms drop, and he stood up. "Fine," said the elf in a different, flat voice. "I should have known better. I should have known. This is the way you want it, so"—the elf raised his hands into the air—"I have no choice."

The elf's hands began to glow.

The goblin's mouth fell open. He raised his sword—and he couldn't remember his wish.

"*Aliakiadam vithofo milgreya!*" shouted the elf. "*Somalitarak ciondiamal freetra—*"

A huge, dark shape arose from the brush behind the elf, its massive brown bulk and long horns silhouetted against the light of the dying fire. The goblin saw the minotaur and fell back with a wild cry. He landed on his backside and knocked the wind out of his lungs. He didn't release the sword, simply held it before him.

The minotaur swung its arms in a huge, rapid arc. The black iron chain whipped around, struck the elf in the back, smacking him like a giant's hammer. The elf was thrown forward into the air, crashing in a heap on the ground. The magic on his hands flared up—and died out.

The elf writhed on the ground, gasping for air. He managed to roll onto his chest and pushed himself up to face the minotaur. The elf's chest heaved, and his face twisted in grotesque pain. The goblin could see in the firelight that the back of the elf's shirt was stained dark and wet where the thick chain had struck him. Not daring to move or think, the goblin stared at the minotaur, which was standing upright now, facing the elf. From the minotaur's large hands dangled the long black chain, readied for another strike.

The goblin tried to remember his wish, but it wouldn't come to him. He couldn't think of it at all.

"Well," said the minotaur in the trade tongue, as it looked at the elf, "aren't you going to throw a spell at me?"

The elf wheezed, seeming to find it hard to breathe. The goblin stared at the huge brown monster and forgot about breathing entirely.

"You . . . can talk," the elf gasped at last.

"Very good," the minotaur said. It spoke lazily, but with a perfectly precise grasp of the trade tongue. "You have learned something about your world that you did not know before. I've heard that elves value knowledge, so this information will serve you well in the afterlife."

"Wait," said the elf, trying to catch his breath. "Just wait. We set out . . . to get the sword . . . so that we could . . . use it against . . . our common foe . . . Istar. We have to—"

"No," said the minotaur. "We each set out to gain the sword for our own purposes." The minotaur flicked a glance in the goblin's direction. "I would guess that our friend the goblin merely wants power. Maybe he wants to be a god. But my need of the sword is far simpler."

The goblin wondered if he was dreaming. The elf pulled himself up a bit, but couldn't seem to sit upright now; he grimaced as he settled down, chest against the earth again, his breath coming shallow and quickly.

"You don't appear to have heard me," said the minotaur. The chain in its fists swung slightly.

"No! I heard!" said the elf quickly. "Why? Why?"

"Because this is the way of the world: Only the strong deserve to rule, and the strong should use any means at their disposal to accomplish this. Because true strength is revealed in chaos, in the destruction of all borders and laws and boundaries, so that each being may challenge every other for the right to rule. Once I take that sword, I will ensure my chance to rule the world, from sea to sea and beyond, for all time, by wishing for the doom of the civilized world. My brethren and I will have our freedom at last, and we will command what's left of this sad, tortured land."

The elf stared at the minotaur. "Madness," he whispered.

"No more mad than your hope to destroy a part of Istar's power with this sword. You'd open the gates to chaos in your own way, but you'd leave justice and order in the world intact. Those who make the laws and govern the armies would probably find minotaurs to be as inconvenient as do the Istarians—and they might not be as willing to save our race for enslavement."

The goblin figured that the elf's back was broken, and indeed it might be, but the elf seemed to gather some strength as he spoke next. "If we use . . . the sword together, we . . . can break the hold . . . Istar has on us!" he pleaded softly. "We can start to . . . throw down slavery . . . and killing and prejudice everywhere, and be free! We can . . . have a new world!"

"Did you not attempt to enslave me with one of your spells before we left on this quest?" asked the minotaur, raising a thick eyebrow. "If that's a sample of how your new world is going to be, I confess I find it lacking. I threw off that spell, thanks only to my willpower—the same willpower that allowed me to survive long enough in this mad wilderness to be found by that pathetic kender. Besides, I really have no quarrel with slavery or killing—as long as it is the minotaurs who are doing the enslaving and murdering. It is the way of the world. You elves should really come out of your forests once in a while and see what the world's all about."

Sweat dripped from the minotaur's broad snout. "This has gone on long enough. You have had your fun tonight. And now I'd like some fun myself." It stepped forward, arms and chain swinging back and around.

The elf raised a hand. "*Elekonia xanes*," he said, pointing his index finger in the minotaur's direction.

A pulsing stream of white light burst from the elf's finger, flashed into the minotaur's chest. The beast flinched and threw back its head, roaring in agony. Then it came on, maddened, the long chain lashing down to strike at the elf's head. The goblin came to his senses and rolled to get out of the way.

The elf gave a strangled cry when the chain struck him. The goblin heard the chain lash down again, and again, and he kept rolling to get away.

Then he remembered his wish.

He remembered it perfectly.

He stopped rolling and held onto the sword's hilt as he

lay on his chest, facing away from the smashing and rattling sounds as the minotaur flailed at the fallen elf.

"I wish," began the goblin in a choking voice, his chest burning and his hands shaking, "that I would be—"

He heard the minotaur's earth-shattering roar directly behind him. Panicked, he brought the sword up as the minotaur leaped at him.

* * * * *

It was cold, but the goblin didn't feel the cold very much. The chill from the ground seeped into his body and through his bones, but it seemed very distant and not very real. It was odd that he felt no pain. For some reason, he thought that he should.

Someone was calling, someone close by. The goblin opened his eyes and saw dark gray clouds rolling overhead, heard the wind tossing the tree branches. Something cold and wet struck him on the forehead. Rain, maybe.

A new sound began. It was the stupid kender. He was crying. The goblin stirred, trying to look in the kender's direction, but he couldn't move very well. He found it hard to breathe.

Footsteps thumped over to his side. Small, cold hands touched his cheeks, wiping away dirt and blood. Turning his head, he saw a thin face with tangled brown hair and brown eyes.

"Are you alive?" the kender asked, his voice almost breaking. "I saw you move. Please say you're alive."

The goblin licked his lips. His mouth felt very dry, and it tasted awful. "Yes," he said. It hurt to speak; the wind almost carried his voice away.

"I'm sorry I wasn't here," the kender said, choking back his sobs. His hands continued to clean the goblin's face. "I got lost last night because of the explosion and the wind, and I crashed in some bushes. I came down far away and kept falling over things and getting stuck in briars and almost twisted my ankle. What happened?"

"Fight," the goblin managed to say. Was the kender going to talk him to death? He suspected that he was dying anyway. Then he remembered. "Minotaur," he whispered fearfully, trying to look around.

"The minotaur's over there." The kender waved an arm blindly to his right. "I'm sorry. He . . . he's dead." The kender started to cry again but fought it down. "The humans killed him with the gem sword. The elf's dead, too. The humans beat him up. I don't want you to die, too."

With a sudden effort, the goblin forced himself to sit up a few inches and looked in the direction the kender had indicated. The minotaur lay collapsed in a dirty brown heap, the sword's silver blade protruding from its back. The goblin remembered now the minotaur's roar as it had leapt upon the blade, its full weight smashing into the goblin's face and chest. Then the awful gurgling howl as it arose and tried to breathe with a shaft of steel through its lung and heart.

The goblin eased himself back down, fighting the dull pain that came from his chest. I should be happy, he thought. I killed a minotaur. But I feel so tired. It isn't worth it to move. I just want to . . . Oh. The—

"Sword," whispered the goblin. He tried to reach toward the dead minotaur. "Sword."

The kender wiped his eyes and leaned closer. "What?"

"Sword," said the goblin. He tried to reach for it. Things seemed to get dark and that frightened him, but his hand caught the kender's hand, and he felt less afraid. Stupid kender, he thought, and the world slowly drifted away.

*　*　*　*　*

One of the wagons carried shovels. It took the rest of the day, with intermittent droplets of rain falling all around, for the kender to dig a pit large enough to bury his three friends. The goblin had asked for the sword, so the kender carefully cleaned it after removing it from the minotaur's chest, never touching the blade. He held it by its hilt as he prepared to lay it at the dead goblin's side.

"I wish . . ." the kender whispered, then closed his eyes to better remember the words that his parents had taught him. He could remember only the end of the good-bye prayers, so he said that. "I wish you peace on your journey, and hope you will be waiting for me at the end of your travels."

Because his eyes were closed, he did not see the sword glow briefly as he spoke. The light faded away when he set the sword into the goblin's hand.

The kender filled the pit halfway with dirt, then covered it with rocks to keep out wolves and other creatures. It was dawn the next day before he was finished.

He left the Istarian soldiers where they lay. Then he went home.

Raindrops began falling all across the hilltop. Within minutes, the land was awash in a cold, blinding torrent.

The Three Lives
of Horgan Oxthrall

Douglas Niles

Research of Foryth Teel, scribe serving Astinus Lorekeeper

My Most Honored Master:

Regretfully, information detailing the history of the Khalkist dwarves during the century preceding the Cataclysm is sparse and, for the most part, of questionable veracity. Nevertheless, I shall endeavor to collect the scraps that yield themselves to me and present them to you in as sensible a manner as possible.

The tale begins with the Istarian invasion of the Khalkist Mountains in 117 PC, following the dwarven reaction to the Proclamation of Manifest Virtue (118 PC). The Khalkist dwarves' refusal to renounce Reorx and swear obeisance to only the gods of good was viewed as a direct challenge to the authority of the Kingpriest. The resulting disastrous campaign is, naturally enough, given scant treatment in the surviving human histories.

The few traversable routes through the crest of the high Khalkists—most notably, Stone Pillar and White Bear passes—were the only overland roads connecting the eastern and western portions of the empire of Istar.

Angered by the effrontery of the human proclamation, the dwarves turned their backs on a lucrative income (from tolls on the passes) and closed their realm to Istar.

The emperor invaded late the following summer (117 PC), delaying the assault until then in order to minimize the difficulties presented by the deep snow in the heights. He sent two of his legions against each of the two major passes—a total army of some forty thousand men. The rugged terrain confined each force to a single deep valley, and though each marched but a score of leagues from the other, neither was in a position to support its counterpart in the event of difficulty.

The dwarves capitalized on this disadvantage quickly, meeting the two southern legions with some eight thousand doughty warriors. Meanwhile, the northern wing of the Istarian army advanced over rougher ground, pushing toward the lofty divide at a snail's pace.

Making his attack in the south from ambush, at the fording of a rapid stream, the dwarven commander timed the onslaught perfectly. (Incidentally, reports indicate, but do not confirm, that the dwarven field army was led by High Thane Rankil himself.) Waiting until half of the Istarians had crossed, the Khalkist army annihilated an entire legion and harried the second all the way back to the lowlands. There the remnant of the human legion remained, its fighting spirit shattered on the granite foothills. The heights loomed like jagged daggers to the west, casting shadows of an early sunset over Istar. (I beg Your Excellency's forgiveness of my metaphorical excess!)

By this time, the northern legions had penetrated to Stone Pillar Pass, without seeing a single dwarf. Then, abruptly, the attacks began—sudden strikes from concealment. There seems to have been a simple sameness to the tactic:

A wedge of stocky, bearded dwarves bearing keen battle-axes or steel-headed hammers charged from a ridge line or ravine, slashing into the human column, then disappearing before the Istarian army could concentrate its forces. The attacks were repeated; the position of the legions became untenable. The human troops endured short rations, harsh weather, and constant harassing combat, but their generals ordered them to stand firm.

After several weeks of this treatment, during which every grown, able-bodied male dwarf was drawn into the Khalkist army, the centurions commanding the two trapped legions gradually came to grips with the precariousness of their situation. Food had begun to run low, and the icy menace of winter was a constant reminder behind the harsh autumn winds. Desperate, the commanders ordered a march back to Istar.

The humans surrounded their heavy, ox-drawn supply wagons with many ranks of guards and rumbled down the high valleys. The oxen led the charge against the dense dwarven formations when the Khalkist forces strategically chose to block the Istarian army's retreat.

Reports from Istarian sources, Excellency, confirm the truth of this last tactic, claiming that the oxen presence was often effective against dwarves. It seems that the wagon handlers fed the beasts a gruel laced with rum before the battle—a goodly dose reputed to have made the normally equable oxen most disagreeable. They are great creatures, of course, and must have loomed over the dwarves in elephantine proportion!

Nevertheless, the stocky mountain dwellers tried to stop the Istarian army, even as roadblock after roadblock crumbled before the lumbering beasts of burden as the oxen scattered the dwarves. Still, High Thane Rankil remained stubbornly determined to obliterate the two legions.

The humans finally were cornered before the last river crossing—a historical site called Thoradin Bridge, which I have located on a pre-Cataclysm map—leading to the safety of the Istarian Plains. Here a company of young dwarves stood, and once again the oxen were drawn to the fore.

At this point, Excellency, it becomes difficult to sort the legend from fact. We know that the human force was lost in total—the greatest military defeat suffered by Istar to that date. As for the course of the battle, little is known.

However, I have uncovered a somewhat implausible tale. Dwarven legend has it that a young dwarf, one Horgan of Squire, employed some great magic—often referred to as the power of Reorx—to lure the oxen away from the bridge, diverting the fateful charge that would have ensured the human escape. It is said that this Horgan wore a tunic embroidered with silver thread, portraying as its symbol the Great Forge of Reorx. It seems, indeed, Excellency, that the youth was host to a miracle! Many accounts have been cited—dwarves who saw the blessing of Reorx ignite in young Horgan, leading the enemy army to disaster!

Reports of specifics vary here, Your Grace, but I am assured that witnesses attested to beams of silvery light emanating, sometimes from the ground, at other times from the clouds. Others heard choruses of heavenly voices—songs that tore the hearts of even stalwart dwarves with their pure beauty! O Exalted One, it makes me tremble to think of it!

But, excuse my rambling. In any event, with the failure of the oxen's charge, the defense of the bridge held and the human army met its grim fate. Legend has it that the river was tainted blood red all the way to Istar itself. (A precursor, if you will, of the great bloodletting that the gods would send against that unholy city! Indeed, Excellency—a sign of the coming, the making of the very Bloodsea itself! How splendid is the will of the gods—shown to us through the window of history!)

The tale concludes with the young hero dubbed, by the high thane himself, as Horgan Oxthrall.

It seems that, technically, Horgan Squire was too young to serve in the army. But, as the war gradually had developed into an epic victory, every young dwarf who could break free from his hearth and home hastened to bear arms. Apparently, Horgan wove a beard of goat hair over his own sparse whiskers to give the appearance of maturity. The ruse worked—he was accepted into one of the last companies mustered for the war.

It was this company of young dwarves, formed with virtually no training, that was sent to the valley of Stone Pillar. This untried, inexperienced unit found itself standing astride the final link in the human escape route. Then, the miracle occurred—the oxen followed the youth into the ditch, and the human charge was stopped.

At the ceremony, Horgan seems to have been given some official post, perhaps honorary. I'm not certain. Nothing further of him appears in the histories.

I have enclosed this legendary note, Your Grace, for your enjoyment as much as anything else; I cannot swear to its veracity. Yet I *feel*—and I hope you do as well—that there is a least of hint of real destiny in the tale.

As to the rest of my assignment, I can report little progress. Many have heard tales of a brave courier of the Khalkists—one who carried historical texts of the dwarves into the mountains on the eve of the Cataclysm, there to conceal them for some future age. But no one can give me even a hint of the whereabouts of such a cache.

As always, I shall continue my labors to bring to light more of this obscure phase in the history of our world!

Your Most Humble Servant,
Foryth Teel, Scribe of Astinus

*   *   *   *   *

O Exalted Historian!

Please forgive my inexcusable delay in the filing of this report. I beg your indulgence, only to hear the tale of my recent discovery—and of the light it sheds upon our earlier image of history! I write to you by faint candlelight, from a windswept vale in the high Khalkists. My reasons for coming here, and my news, I shall endeavor to communicate while blood still flows through my cold-numbed fingers.

I have not sent word, Excellency, for I have been on the pathways of history for many months. I journeyed into the mountains to investigate a report that had filtered down to me from the most convoluted of sources—a young stable hand, who has a cousin who visits the high country, and there hears tales of the shepherds, and so forth.

The gist of the tale that reached my ears was the story of a cheesemaker who kept a herd of milk cows in the highest valleys of the Khalkists. In search of shelter one day, this humble dairyman stumbled upon a cave that had lain hidden since the time of the Cataclysm and had been only recently revealed by avalanche.

Within the cave he found a skeleton and a bundle of tightly wrapped scrolls. A shred of the wrapping was brought to me. Your Grace can no doubt imagine my excitement when the pattern of dye marked the scrap as dwarven—*pre-Cataclysmic* dwarven!

Could this be the lost messenger? The one who carried the records of the dwarves into safety, even as the Cataclysm showered death across the lands of Istar? I hoped, but could not believe for certain. Yet the piece of evidence could not have come at a better time. Due to my ceaseless and uncomplaining diligence, I had exhausted every other bit of documentation in my local sources. It had begun to seem that the tale of the Khalkist dwarves would vanish into legend a full century before the Cataclysm, but now—now I had *hope*! Indeed, the proof was profound enough to draw me from the comfort of my study, uncomplainingly, to make the strenuous pursuit of knowledge for the library.

My journey into the heights has been arduous in the extreme. I wish you could see, Excellency, the slopes that yawned below me, the dizzying spires of rock poised above, as if waiting for the moment to cast a crushing javelin of stone onto my poor and unprotected head! Always I kept in mind my duty, to be borne without complaint, as you command.

But I digress. I finally reached the small, remote village of Saas Grund, still some miles below the cheesemaker's farm. Here, however, that worthy dairyman met me and provided me with one of the scrolls he discovered. That volume piqued my hunger for more, and so it is with resolute and uncomplaining vigor that tomorrow I accompany the man even higher into the mountains, to his lofty abode. No matter the precipitous slopes before me, nor how deep the depths of snow! Not even the icy bite of the killing wind shall deter me, nor make me long for this comfortable fire . . . the fire that even now sends its warmth to my bones and soothes my weary muscles and promises to restore life to my poor, benumbed fingers. The fire, and a little spiced wine . . .

Forgive me—once again I lose my path.

In short, I pen this note to you tonight, Most Esteemed Historian, in the hopes that you soon shall receive the remainder of my tale. But even in the one scroll I have perused I have discovered a story of relevance to my earlier work. I admit, however, that I present it to you with some embarrassment, since it seems to contradict an incident I had earlier reported.

The scroll I read is the family journal of Horgan Oxthrall—-the young warrior I told you about who miraculously drew away the oxen at the Battle of Thoradin Bridge. It was written later in his life, in 92 PC, to be precise, as he worked in the service of his thane.

Horgan recalls, in this journal, the story of that day of

battle, when the human invasion had been broken. He described that sturdy wooden river-crossing that he had only later learned was called Thoradin Bridge. The battle of twenty-five years ago was a memory that had been etched, vividly, against the canvas of his brain. In his mind he could still hear the white water frothing below him. He saw, as if it had been this morning, the snorting oxen lumbering toward him, steaming breath bursting from the monstrous creatures' black nostrils.

And, as always with the memories, came the guilt, the lingering sense of shame that would never quite give him the room to breathe.

He knew the tale that legend had created, of course: the power of Reorx had blessed him at the moment of battle-truth, and he had cast a thrall over the massive oxen leading the human train, luring them away from the charge that certainly would have opened the escape route across the bridge. Horgan even remembered the looks of awe upon the faces of his comrades as they witnessed the "miracle."

Yet, in his own mind, he recalled the stark terror that had seized him like the coils of a constricting serpent, threatening to crush his chest and squeeze his bowels into water. All he could think of was escape, but shock prevented his legs from responding even to this, the most basic of emotions. Even as his comrades streamed away from him, panicked by the oncoming beasts, Horgan stumbled numbly until he stood, alone, before the lumbering charge.

We see proof of one thing in his words, Excellency: oxen did indeed inspire a panicked terror in the dwarven troops—a terror that seems peculiar to their race. Of course, most of the Istar War had been fought in terrain too rough for the beasts to play any major role, but on flat ground the huge, buffalolike creatures loomed over the dwarves and were truly intimidating.

Horgan's mind reeled, and here—in his own words—we learn of another source of his shame. It seems that the young hero was stinking drunk! Before the battle—quite against orders—he and several in his platoon had snitched a bottle of potent rum. Horgan claims to have guzzled far more than his share. Indeed, he states that his hands shook so much that he spilled the stuff all over himself.

Now he stood there, dumb with shock, gesticulating wildly—to some mysteriously. Finally, his brain's frantic messages to flee reached his legs, and Horgan turned toward the ditch. The bridge stood open to the human wagons.

But the oxen ignored their drivers' commands and veered sharply from the road. Bellowing loudly, pawing the earth with their great hooves, and snorting in agitation, the beasts lumbered after Horgan, following the dwarf determinedly into the ditch. To the other dwarves, it had seemed a miracle. The wagons were immediately mired, blocking the road and the bridge, and the entire human army was crushed. Only Horgan Oxthrall knew the real explanation.

The oxen stared at him stonily, their eyes glazed, their breath putrid . . . and rank with rum. You will remember that the poor creatures had been fed a goodly dose of spirits themselves. Now, in the midst of battle (probably starting to sober up), they sniffed out this equally intoxicated dwarf and followed him in eager anticipation of more rum!

Of course, none of the other dwarves figured out what was going on. Horgan was a hero. After the battle—when presumably, *every* dwarf stunk of rum—the thane appointed Horgan to the elite order of Thane's Scouts.

As one of the scouts sworn to High Thane Rankil, Horgan's job was to routinely patrol the rugged Khalkist heights, which formed the border of a dwarven nation surrounded by enemies. The scouts were drawn from the finest, proven veterans of the Istar War. It is in the service of his thane that Horgan Oxthrall labored for twenty-five years, a full quarter century after the victorious war. Lonely patrols through the heights, battles with groups of human brigands and trespassers—it was a solitary and adventurous life that seemed to suit Horgan well.

Incidentally, My Lord Historian, it appears that Horgan performed well among the scouts. He mentions that he held the rank of captain and was assigned to patrol the most remote areas of the realm. He was one of the few dwarves who worked alone.

His words tell us of the way his service changed in the years preceding 92 PC. He patrolled the mountains as always, alert for human incursion. But lately there had come another foe, one that presented a grave threat to the lonely scouts, isolated in their posts on the frontier.

Ogres. For long years the dull humanoids had avoided the mountains, since the inherent hatred between ogre and dwarf ran deep and universal among both races. The dwarves, with greater organization and led by heroic fighters, had banished the ogres in earlier centuries, but now they came again, fleeing from the even greater menace of the Kingpriest's bounty hunters. Those ruthless killers sought them out, together with hobgoblins, minotaurs, and other creatures that had been branded as "evil" by the ruler of Istar. The scalps and skulls of these unfortunate beings—including females and young— were taken to Istar, where a handsome bounty would be paid in the name of the gods.

Horgan Oxthrall began his journal while he was on the trail of one of these ogres. Apparently many thoughts had been churning in his mind for some time, no doubt agitated by his long periods of solitary marching. His writing shows a need to communicate, for he shares the tale of these days in some considerable detail.

He first spotted the ogre from a distance of many miles, across the expanse of a high basin. To the best of Horgan's knowledge, the ogre had not seen the dwarf. Only through the most diligent efforts did Horgan locate the creature's trail.

For three days, Horgan tracked his quarry along the valleys and slopes of the Khalkists. The ogre worked his way through a series of low, brushy vales, moving slowly and cautiously. The dwarven scout gradually shortened the gap between them, though during the pursuit he did not spot the ogre again. Horgan wondered if the creature knew he was being followed. If so, he might be leading the dwarf into a trap. But then the dwarf shrugged, accepting the threat implicit in that possibility but undeterred from his single-minded pursuit.

In any event, Horgan *always* eyed his surroundings as if he expected an ambush at any moment. The dwarf's keen eyes examined each patch of rough ground, each shallow stream bank or nearby ridge, considering them for lines of fire, potential cover, and routes of retreat— all the while steadily pumping his stocky legs.

The trail wound downward from the lofty crests. The ogre and, some miles behind, the dwarf, skirted the foothills of the Khalkist Mountains near the borderlands, where the outposts of Istar asserted the Kingpriest's arrogance at the very feet of the dwarven realms. Alert for humans, Horgan nevertheless maintained his pursuit, steadily closing the gap.

On the fourth morning, Horgan reached the ogre's most recent campfire to find the ashes still warm. His quarry, he deduced, was less than four hours ahead of him. The monster's trail led along a crude pathway that followed the floor of a narrow, winding valley. A deep stream alternately meandered and thundered beside Horgan, in the same direction as the ogre's trail.

The mountainsides to the right and left loomed so close, at times, that the place became more like a gorge than a valley. The view before Horgan was often restricted, though sometimes the dwarf would come around a bend to see several hundred yards of the path before him. Every once in a while the route crossed the stream on a crude but sturdy log bridge.

It was as he approached another of these bridges,

where the stream had dropped through a deep chute some fifty feet below, that his long pursuit reached its climax. A trio of tall, straight pine logs had been lashed together to form a crossing. Horgan's instincts tingled, his senses heightened.

The dwarf saw footsteps leading to one side of the path, before the bridge. Turning to investigate, he peered between a pair of sharp boulders. The trail of the ogre led to the mouth of a narrow cave, less than a hundred feet away, and disappeared within.

Shrewd, thought Horgan Oxthrall, studying the shadowed niche. The vertical slash in the rock stood perhaps nine or ten feet high, but only half that in width. The ogre might lurk anywhere inside, perhaps armed with a crossbow or spear. Either weapon, hurled at the dwarf, could end the fight before it began.

Then, to his surprise, Horgan saw movement within the cave. A dark form loomed in the entrance. Tension surged through Horgan's body. His right hand clenched the smooth shaft of his axe, while his left reached behind to pull his shield from his back.

The hulking shape moved forward, abandoning its sheltering darkness. Horgan saw it, felt the ancient racial hatred that lay so deeply within the dwarven character. An urge to attack the ogre swept through the dwarf with frightening intensity. The monster's great mouth dropped open; the thick gray lips moved grotesquely. Horgan noticed that the creature had three great teeth jutting from its lower jaw—an extra tusk near the center of its lower lip.

"Gobasch fight."

The words—crude Common spoken in a deep, guttural voice—shocked Horgan. He had pictured his opponent as a dull beast, incapable of communication or articulation. The dwarf stared at the ogre, too surprised to reply.

The creature loomed over Horgan. The ogre's barrel torso rested upon legs as thick as gnarled oak roots. The face, despite its trio of sharp tusks, did not look bestial. Arms, bulging with straps of sinew, rippled downward to hamlike fists that swung nearly to the ogre's knees. He wore a jerkin of stiff, dirty leather and, in his right hand, held a battered long sword. The ogre's eyes were small but surprisingly bright, and they glittered at the dwarf with frank appraisal.

Horgan claims that he felt no fear of his opponent's size. (Indeed, Excellency, nimble dwarves with their diminutive stature had historically outmatched much larger ogres in hand-to-hand combat. Too, there is no reason to suspect that he would be less than candid in his private journal.)

Then the dwarf astonished himself by feeling a grudging awareness of respect. The ogre had emerged from concealment—where he could have lurked in ambush—to confront his enemy in a fair fight.

"Unless you want to surrender to the rightful authority of Rankil, High Thane of the Khalkists," the dwarf told the ogre, after a few moments of mutual assessment, "you don't have any choice except fight me."

The ogre snorted scornfully. "Gobasch not quit—Gobasch *kill!*"

Despite his bluster, the ogre did not advance. Gobasch raised his sword and Horgan saw that the weapon was longer by several feet than the dwarf's entire body. The blade was mere bronze, marked with many nicks and grooves. The ogre held the weapon across his body, ready to parry but not to attack.

Horgan hesitated. He recalled feeling pity for the homeless creature before him, driven here by the same humans who had harassed the dwarves. At the time, Horgan felt ashamed of the impulse.

For several seconds the two creatures, mortal adversaries by race and heritage, remained frozen. Horgan sensed that the ogre desired escape more than battle. Horgan himself was oddly reluctant to fight. He couldn't understand why.

Then, in a flash, he recalled the bitter memory of his cowardice at Thoradin Bridge. His face flushed with shame and anger. Clenching his axe, he raised it and took a step forward, his shield couched carefully at his chest.

Gobasch raised his great sword.

Suddenly, by mutual consent, both combatants halted. Another sound intruded into their tightly focused concentration.

"Horses!" grunted Horgan, as he heard the unmistakable clattering of hooves upon rock.

"Men!" Gobasch snarled, his voice louder than Horgan's but still hushed.

With a flash of irritation, Horgan realized that the ogre's observation was more acute—it was the humans, not their poor, dumb mounts, who mattered.

Carefully the dwarf backed away from the ogre, determined to investigate the new intrusion without giving this monster a fatal opening. But Gobasch sought the shelter of his dark cave again, vanishing into the shadowy entrance. Horgan imagined that he could see those two tiny, bright eyes glittering outward at him and the valley.

Instantly the dwarf whirled, crouched low, and scanned the trail below him. In another moment he saw them: three humans on horses, moving up the valley at a walk. They wore silver helmets and breastplates, and the one in the lead wore a bright red cloak. A matching plume trailed from his helm. The pair who rode behind were clad in billowing capes of green and bore no badge of rank upon their heads.

Horgan cast another glance at the cave. All was still within. Boldly, he raised his axe and shield and stepped onto the pathway. He had advanced to the beginning of the crude log bridge before the riders, on the other side of the stream, saw him.

"Hold," cried the human in the crimson cloak, raising his hand. His two comrades reined in and regarded

Horgan suspiciously. His tunic, emblazoned with the hammer sign of the high thane, clearly marked him as an official, and this apparently did not please the humans.

But it was the tall man, the one who had commanded the halt, who spoke first. Horgan identified him by the gold-hilted short sword resting, for now, in the man's scabbard, as a centurion of Istar.

"Greetings, dwarf," the centurion said, making the word sound like an insult—to Horgan's ears, at least. The man shouted to be heard over the sound of the stream surging through the gorge fifty feet below and between them.

Horgan studied the human silently. He rode a huge horse, a bay that pranced and pawed the earth in apparent agitation at the delay.

"You have crossed the borders of our realm," Horgan Oxthrall shouted back, curtly. "This is the land of High Thane Rankil of Khalkist, and you are trespassers. In his name, I bid you depart!" He fingered the axe easily, just to show them that he was not afraid to back up his words with action.

"We cannot depart," replied the human loudly, his tone still firm. Horgan figured the fellow was having a hard time trying to sound persuasive when he had to shout in order to be heard. "Our mission is a holy one!" the centurion concluded.

Horgan blinked, momentarily nonplussed by the reply. Then his anger took over. "Nothing of Istar can be holy!" He sneered.

"It's worth gold!" added the officer, though his face flushed angrily. The two other riders dismounted casually, stood next to their horses, and talked quietly to each other. Horgan concentrated on the centurion.

"Istarian arrogance!" Horgan snapped bitterly, his voice ripe with scorn.

"Watch your tone, dwarf!" ordered the officer in warning. "The power of Ultimate Goodness shall not be mocked!"

"Get yourself back down the valley, and you'll hear no words to offend your ears—or the ears of your precious priestking!"

"The *Kingpriest* has offered a bounty for the slaying of the evil races. Earlier today, we spotted an ogre moving along this trail. We are god-bound to kill him and carry his skull to the high throne of Istar!"

Horgan's mind churned. Istar! How well he remembered the legions marching into the heart of the Khalkists a quarter century earlier—and on just such a spurious quest! Then it had been the dwarven insistence on the worship of Reorx, their traditional god all across the face of Ansalon, that had pitted Istar against their race.

In the arrogant eyes of the Kingpriest, Reorx, as a neutral god, was no better than a deity of evil. How many humans had perished as a result of that arrogance? Horgan didn't know. (We do, however, Your Grace; the figure was somewhere around thirty-two to thirty-four thousand men.)

Horgan's dwarven blood rose to his face as he considered the scope of the Kingpriest's newest arrogance. The would-be emperor of all the world dared to send bands of his agents into dwarven lands to pursue his edicts!

"Any enemy found here is the rightful prey of High Thane Rankil—be it human, ogre, or any other trespassers!" Horgan shouted.

"Your impudence will cost you, runt!" growled the human officer. His hand flexed and, in a fluid motion, he drew a long sword of gleaming steel from beneath his crimson cloak. The great bay reared eagerly.

Horgan immediately looked for the other two humans, who had been chatting idly beside their horses. This instinctive alertness saved his life for, with astonishing quickness, one of the standing humans twisted free from his green cloak and raised a weapon—a crossbow!

The scout stepped backward, setting his cleated boot

firmly against the slippery surface of the log bridge. Horgan ducked, raising his shield to cover his face. The bolt from the small crossbow punched into the circle of protective metal with such force that it knocked the dwarf onto his back. He struck the logs of the bridge heavily, barely retaining his balance on the edge of the span.

Horgan's heart leaped into his throat as he teetered over the brink of a fall. Below him he saw icy water through a barricade of sharp-edged granite boulders. In another instant, he recovered to crouch low on the bridge.

Feverishly, the crossbowman placed another bolt in the groove of his weapon and began to crank back the heavy spring. The centurion, still mounted, stared at Horgan with eyes that bulged white, over lips twisted by fanaticism. Yet he had enough discipline to hold his horse in check.

For a dizzying second, Horgan writes, he was frozen with fear. He recalled another bridge, a quarter century earlier. There, too, he had looked into the snorting nostrils of a great beast that had been lashed into the service of humans. The beast was different now, as was the bridge, but the humans, he saw with sudden and crystalline clarity, were the same. (This point, Excellency, seems to have dawned on Horgan with the brightness of a clear sunrise. Indeed, he goes on and on about it. I have summarized pages in the above paragraph.)

Perhaps it was this new recognition, or perhaps simply the additional experience of his years in the thane's service, that imbued him with the will to act.

"For Reorx and Thoradin!" he bellowed, his legs pumping as he rushed across the bridge—straight at the humans! The steel cleats of his boots chipped into the logs, propelling him with a quickness that obviously stunned the trio of Istarians.

"Stop him!" cried the centurion, his voice a mixture of alarm and surprise. "Shoot him!"

The crossbowman lowered his weapon, sighting with difficulty on Horgan's chest. Fortunately for him, the target grew larger with each passing second. Unfortunately—again, from the bowman's perspective—the target did not behave predictably.

At the end of the bridge Horgan dove forward, tucked his body into a ball, and executed a forward roll. He heard the *clunk* of the crossbow and the curse of the shooter as his missile sped over the compact bundle of the dwarf's body.

Completing one somersault, the dwarf bounced to his feet, shield and axe poised and ready for battle. "Hah!" he shouted, looking up at the snorting bay. The quivering horse reared away from the strange figure.

"Heathen! Paladine will curse your impudence!" bellowed the centurion, struggling to control his horse as the steed danced in agitation.

"Flee! Run back to Istar!" bellowed Horgan. He darted past the centurion and lunged at the two horses held by the second footman. The poor beasts stared in terror at the bounding, sputtering dwarf. In another instant, they broke and turned to gallop down the trail. The two footmen hesitated, then ran after them, not wanting to be left to walk through hostile territory.

"The fires that are evil's reward will be your just end!" The officer shrieked his curse as he tried to whip his horse through a tight turn. But Horgan circled faster, until he once again stood before the narrow bridge.

Furious, the centurion urged his steed to the very brink of the gorge, took a vicious cut at Horgan with his sword. The dwarf dodged underneath the singing steel. Chopping savagely, Horgan hacked his axe into the rider's leg.

The man screamed in pain and terror as he struggled to keep his balance. The horse skipped away from the cliff's edge. The wounded man toppled to the ground, landing heavily at the brink of the precipitous drop.

"You're no better than that ogre!" hissed the centurion.

His fingers grasped and tore at the grass as he slipped toward oblivion. "The gods curse all of you who would thwart the Kingpriest's justice!"

Horgan watched the human slide over the lip of the cliff, uprooted grass tufted in his clenched fingers as his feet kicked empty air. The centurion twisted into space, his face a mask of stark terror. Then, his red cloak billowing around him, the man smashed onto the boulders of the stream bed. The dye of the robe blended with his blood, flowing downward through the rapid stream.

(Note, Excellency, if you will forgive my aside, that once again we have this image of blood flowing downhill to Istar. A foretaste of the Bloodsea, rendered in the hand of an adventuring dwarf, nine centuries before the Cataclysm! Oh, poetry and prescience!)

Wearily, Horgan clumped back across the bridge. He remembered with a sense of vague detachment the ogre who had started this fracas.

Here, in his journal, Horgan Oxthrall records that he reached a point of decision in his life. He was filled with disgust and loathing for the humans and their arrogant lord. Considering the ogre, the dwarf found it hard to muster the same kind of antipathy—despite the racial hatred that was so much a part of his being. He wondered if the human had spoken an inadvertent truth in his dying breath. Were dwarves any better, truly, than ogres? Did they not have more in common with ogres, in some ways, than they did with their so-called civilized neighbors in Istar?

He came back to the clearing and found Gobasch standing before the cave mouth and looking at Horgan with an expression of bewilderment on his great, three-tusked face.

"Why you fight for me?" asked the ogre.

Horgan scowled. Why, indeed? So that he would have the honor, the pleasure, of slaying the ogre for himself? There had to be a better reason than that, he told himself.

"No human has been allowed in these mountains for twenty-five years!" he huffed, angrily.

The ogre stood before him, his huge sword held defensively across his chest. Chin jutting in determination, Gobasch regarded the dwarf, the ogre's three tusks bristling in Horgan's eyes.

"And ogres? How long for them?" grunted Gobasch.

Even as his mind grappled with the question, Horgan knew the answer. If he carried out his duty now, he would be no better—in his own mind—than the human bounty hunters he had just confronted.

"Go on," Horgan said to Gobasch. "Get out of here!" He indicated the valley, the ogre's route before Horgan had caught up with him. There, through the foothills, lay wild country—and beyond, the plains of Istar.

The ogre blinked, suspicious.

"Move, by Reorx! Before I change my mind!" shouted Horgan Oxthrall.

Still blinking, Gobasch looked cautiously over his shoulder. He kept looking, all the way down the trail, until he disappeared from sight.

At this point, Horgan sets his journal aside. It is not for another year that he again takes pen to paper, and then it is to record, briefly, the events of the intervening annum.

Horgan Oxthrall, being a dwarf of true honor, reported the incident to his thane. The closing words of his journal are difficult to read, but indicate that his gesture toward the ogre cost him his post in the scouts, and he was banished from the high thane's court.

Nevertheless, as I read his words, penned in the year following his banishment, I see no sign of regret, no desire to change the decision he had made with regard to Gobasch, the ogre. If anything, the words of Horgan Oxthrall fairly swell with pride.

This is the first scroll of the cheesemaker's find. It leads me to believe, Excellency, that the tales of the Last Messenger are true! Somewhere in the heights above me lies the tomb of this hero who preserved the history of the Khalkist dwarves. I go to seek this trove, an opportunity that any historian would seize—though not all, I dare to venture, with as much stoicism as I!

With the coming dawn, Master, I set out for the icy ramparts that have framed my view for these past months. I will send further word with all the haste I can muster, though I doubt that ready accommodation will present itself for the passage of messages.

Until my next word, I remain,

Your Devoted Servant,
Foryth Teel, Scribe of Astinus

*   *   *   *   *

My Most Honored Master:

I can only beg the gods of good and neutrality to see that this missive retraces the path I have recently traveled. My own survival I take as proof of divine providence—and should this brief note reach your hands, I shall claim no less than the benevolent intervention of Gilean himself!

Of course, Your Grace, as always I press forward without complaint, but—by the *gods*, Excellency!—the summits that have loomed above and below me! The thundering avalanches spewing their deadly weight across my path a dozen times a day! And this, along a route imperiled by monstrous bears—beasts that could tear the limbs from a man without apparent effort, jaws that could snap off a head. . . .

Forgive me, Lord. My nerves are not at their best. Truth to tell, we saw no bears. Still, the knowledge of their presence, you may be sure, robbed me of even a single decent hour of sleep.

Now I have reached this cheesemaker's place, and before me are spread the scrolls of the Khalkist dwarves.

As soon as my hands thaw out enough to unroll the parchment, I shall continue my perusal. (In the morning, hopefully, the sun will come out and, by its pale heat, I may manage to save a few of my fingers.)

In the meantime, I await this humble dairyman, for he has ventured out into the night. He promises to bring me something of interest. But until his return, the scrolls around me shall keep my attention. I turn to them now.

* * * * *

Excellency, hours of reading allow me to present a summary of the additional scrolls. Further efforts yield a wealth of material, all relevant to the history of the Khalkist dwarves—-but alas, little of it relating to the decade immediately preceding the Cataclysm. The mystery left by their disappearance remains.

I have unearthed a few items of note, mostly gleaned from the tales of dwarven lore. I have endeavored, as always, to cull these legends into the most conclusively indicated facts:

Extensive financial records were saved by the bold messenger, who gave his life to carry these scrolls to safety. It is clear that the dwarves were taxed by their thane at an extreme rate during the years 60 PC through 10 PC. Then the tax records end. Was this massive treasure expended? For what? Is it hidden somewhere? Destroyed in the Cataclysm? Or taken by the Khalkist dwarves when they left . . . wherever they have gone?

One dwarven record postdates 10 PC, and this is unusual for not only the date, but that once again we encounter our friend, Horgan Oxthrall—though only in a peripheral sense. The record itself is the history of a battle that was fought at Stone Pillar Pass, around 7 PC. It is the last known contact, in human records, with the Khalkist dwarves.

It seems clear, as claimed by Istar, that the Kingpriest's invasion of the mountains in 7 PC was considerably more successful than had been the attempt of a century and a decade before. However, the Istarian tales of great victories and righteous massacre of the "dwarven heathens" are, at best, grotesque exaggerations.

For one thing, evidence indicates that this was a war with few battles. Indeed, I can find evidence of only one major skirmish. It occurred on the Stone Pillar Pass road and is hailed by the Istarian histories as the Kingpriest's greatest victory—a "rout" of the defenders.

There is a note in one of the scrolls about this battle, however, and it is interesting to contrast the dwarven point of view with that of the humans. From the dwarven perspective, the engagement is regarded as a moderately successful holding action. A gorge in the road was held for one day, and then abandoned—as so many dwarven positions were abandoned in this war.

Indeed, it seems as though the dwarves fought merely to gain time for a withdrawal into a more remote, unassailable position. Finally, they were able to fall back so far that the humans could no longer find them.

In his arrogance, the Kingpriest declared the war "won," his enemies "destroyed." The truth seems to be that the dwarves simply yielded the mountains to the humans and disappeared. Their escape route and destination remain one of the great mysteries of the world.

Forgive me, Your Grace, I wander. There are two unique points associated with the Stone Pillar Battle. I feel confident enough of their veracity to report them.

First, the curious reference to Horgan Oxthrall, who once again plays a role on the stage of history. He was the commanding general of the dwarven army standing against Istar. (I get ahead of myself, Your Grace. A new thane, Rankilsen, had taken the throne. Oxthrall's banishment ended in 12 PC. The venerable warrior had been readmitted into society. He took command of the field army shortly thereafter.)

Second is a tale that defies ready explanation, yet is referenced enough to compel its inclusion here. As the battle waned, the human forces—with rare initiative—attempted to encircle the dwarven army. Reports indicate that this tactic almost succeeded, save for the intervention of a sudden reinforcement. An unexpected brigade marched out of the mountains in support of the dwarves, breaking the human flanking action and allowing the dwarven army to escape.

The curious thing is the identity of this rescuing brigade: you see, all of my sources are adamant in their insistence that the army of Khalkist was saved by a brigade of *ogres!* Where they came from, where they went—these are questions that will entice future historians. What I know is this: The ogres fought as allies with the dwarves against Istar and then, like the dwarves themselves, disappeared.

Implausible? Certainly. But it seems to be a fact.

I have to wonder, as I know you, Excellency, yourself, must be wondering: Could this have been a return of the boon, a life for a life?

Gobasch and Horgan meet again on the field, the bodies of the shattered human army scattered like trampled weeds around them.

"I come onto your lands again, dwarf," says the three-tusked ogre, his jowled face wrinkling into a wry grin.

Horgan looks up at the beast as his army escapes, filtering into their caves and tunnels, turning their backs on a sun that most of them, during their lifetime, will never again behold.

"I thank you for coming," Horgan says, quietly.

The two clasp hands awkwardly. The sun sinks, casting mountain shadows across the human camp in the valley. Multitudes of fires blink in the darkness, and drunken revelry begins. To the humans, it was a "victory."

"They are your mountains now," adds the dwarf, turning to join his people. "Care for them well."

"We shall do our best," Gobasch replies.

* * * * *

I hear a noise at the door, Your Grace. It is my host, returning with his mysterious burden. I see—he brings me the skull of the messenger, this lone courier who brought the secrets of the dwarves into this remote range before the Cataclysm! My historian's heart thrills for their brave hero, perishing so that his words could be read in a future age.

Who is this brave soul? Why did he strike out, alone, to carry the tale of history?

Imagine my shock, Excellency, when the cheesemaker holds out the whitewashed skull, the remains of this courageous figure. For the skull belongs to an ogre! From the jaws jut three yellowed, but clearly recognizable, tusks.

As always, Excellency, I seek the truth in your name;

Your Humble and Devoted Servant,
Foryth Teel, Scribe of Astinus

Filling The Empty Places

Nancy Varian Berberick

The minotaur fell to his knees on the cracked, filthy cobbles of Beggar's Alley. Covered with rough red fur, the man-beast had the head of a bull, horns as long as my forearm, hair like a mane growing down between his shoulder blades. He foamed from the corners of his mouth like an animal.

I'd taken the minotaur two days before in an unexpected end to a fruitless search for heretics. He'd come at me like a storm, rising up out of the tall savannah grass, a knife in each fist; charged me roaring, dark eyes afire with battle-joy. Minotaurs don't much like humans or anyone else, and they do love to fight. But this one, it seemed, hadn't reckoned on my horse. The gray reared high, hooves flailing, and the minotaur went down before he knew what had hit him. He stayed senseless long enough for me to get the manacles, hobbles, and chains on. They have a strength beyond believing, those horned man-beasts. Bound and hobbled is the only way you can take 'em prisoner.

I never liked bringing live heretics to Istar, but sometimes—like in the heat of summer, when you don't really want to be traveling with the dead—you have to. That's the way of things and seasons, and that's the way I was working in that long, hot summer of my thirty-fifth year. By then I'd been fifteen years in the bounty trade. I'd had good times and bad, pockets filled with gold and just as often empty. In Istar they called me "Hunter-Doune," and I was good at my work.

Fair quiet it was in Beggar's Alley that evening, but for the minotaur cursing and panting on the cobbles. Rats ran in the filthy gutters. Tumbledown shacks and unpainted, drab houses huddled together, empty and looking lonely. At sunset the panderers and pickpockets did a better trade over by the great temple. From a distance— beyond the alley, beyond the market and the slave auction—rose a hymn, a gathering of elven voices, as soft and sweet as any dream of what song should be. The holy choir was beginning evening devotions. Elven women, famous throughout the world for their piety, lifted eerily pure voices in praise to the gods of good. Tonight they celebrated wise Paladine and his gentle, compassionate Mishakal.

The minotaur, struggling to his feet again, lifted his dark, horned head. He spat in the direction of the temple. I should have kicked him for it, but because no one was near to see what could be considered my own heretical omission, I let the minotaur have his way. I wasn't one for tormenting prisoners. It's bad business.

I had a partner once—a mountain dwarf. That was all right, no chargeable heresy in those days to be seen with a dwarf. Toukere Hammerfell, his name was. He'd been in the bounty trade longer than I had, and I remember all the advice he gave me.

"One thing you need to know in the trade, Doune, my friend," he once said. "Don't let feelings become part of the hunt. Now, some people think this means don't let softer feelings get in the way. No pity, none of that sweet nonsense. But the harder feelings are just as much a trap. If you want to do well in this business, you'll empty out all those places where your feelings are, the soft and the hard. Mercy costs you money, Doune. So does taking time to plague a man with kicking and beating when he's going to be dead soon anyway."

Toukere would pause to take a long drink of ale and wipe the thick foam from his black beard. We were taking our meal in the Hart's Leap that day, a tavern known for the goodness of its ale. He always liked his ale, Toukere did, and he held that no one could talk well or wisely unless he had some in his belly.

"A heretic's a heretic, Hunter-Doune, whether it's some woman weeping over her babe or some ugly minotaur all chained up and looking like an easy thing to kick. The only thing you want to worry about is how much you're getting paid for 'em. Worrying about feelings—theirs or yours—is a waste of time."

A heretic's a heretic.

As it happened, Toukere had found out that this simple definition worked to the Kingpriest's advantage, too. Not long after that night the Kingpriest spun a new twist in his religious logic. He decided that since most dwarves worshiped the gods of neutrality—the crafter-god, Reorx of the Forge the most honored among them—then the whole race must be evil because they would not worship the gods of good. Notice went up in the paymaster's den that a bounty hunter could make sixty gold on a dwarf. Now, I never knew how Touk worshiped—or even whether he did—but the night the notice went up, he parted with more gold than I'd ever known him to, got me and everyone in the Hart's Leap drunk enough to forget where we were—or who we were—and sneaked out the back door.

He left Istar without me, and with no word of farewell.

Ah, yes. He robbed a minor shrine to Mishakal on the way out of Istar, getting himself some traveling money, and likely needing it after his trick at the Hart. The cleric at the shrine resisted, was dead of his wounds before morning. And so the bounty on Toukere Hammerfell was larger than that on the average dwarf—one hundred gold, a sixty-forty split between heresy and murder.

That was years before. Since then, I'd heard a few rumors that someone over Xak Tsaroth way had finally claimed the gold on Touk. For the most part, I got over missing my partner, but I lost my taste for ale, learned to like wine. Ale didn't taste like ale after Touk left.

So at the end of that long, hot summer day, with sunset's gold shining on the broken cobbles of Beggar's Alley and the air filling with hymns, I didn't kick the minotaur. I took care of business as Toukere and I used to: jerked the chain and got my prisoner moving again.

I hustled him down the alley, out into the wide avenues where the wealthy and the pious live. The tall, beautiful towers of Istar rose gleaming and shining around us. I herded the minotaur along the broad, tree-lined street where flower beds made lush and fragrant medians, and hummingbirds danced in the air like living jewels. The street led to the great temple, and beyond that holy place was the jail.

People on their way to prayer stopped to cheer as we passed, and in an excess of zeal, a young man, dressed in brocades fashionably cut to imitate hunting gear, scooped up what my horse left on the cobbles and hurled it at the heretic. But the fancy bravo didn't know what to do about the mess on his hands after that. I laughed about it all the way to the jail, was still laughing when I turned the minotaur over to the guards and went to the paymaster's den to collect my gold. A small place, the den; a little wooden shack crouched behind the jail where the Kingpriest wouldn't see it. He didn't mind that his clerics and clerks paid bounty on heretics. He just didn't like to see it done.

The walls of the den were filled with the usual notices that reward would be paid for those who served the gods of neutrality or the gods of evil; for kender and elves and humans, dwarves and ogres and goblins, minotaurs, and any cleric who declined to worship the gods of good.

The bounty had been doubled again on Kell, the infamous outlaw-heretic who professed to revere the gods of good, but who scorned the Kingpriest's practice of using torture and execution to convince people that they must worship those wise and gentle gods.

(Some holy defender of good that Kell was. Ask anyone about Kell and you heard the tale of how he robbed and murdered a whole family of pilgrims on their way to Istar to worship at the great temple. Or the one about him looting wayside shrines and slaughtering the clerics. A real favorite was that he liked to sneak into wakes and steal the silver pennies off dead men's eyes. All in all, Kell didn't sound like he was much better than the Kingpriest.)

Every bounty hunter knew that he could retire richer than an elf lord if he managed to capture Kell, but, though everyone knew what his crimes were, no one knew where in all of Ansalon this fellow, Kell, was hiding. No one even knew what he looked like. Was he a dwarf or human or elf? It depended on which rumor you liked best.

I didn't do more than glance at Kell's bounty sheet that day. There was a time when I'd been eager to hunt for Kell, but that was a while ago, and now I remembered what Toukere used to say about him:

"When you think on it, Doune, my friend, no one really knows whether this terrible heretic, Kell, is much more than a bad dream the Kingpriest has from time to time when his food is too rich. I like the gold as much as the next one—maybe more, eh?—but I stick to the easy prey. No sense wasting time chasing savannah-wind that's all the time changing direction."

Then he'd called for another tankard of ale.

*   *   *   *   *

There was a kender at the Hart's Leap. The race's heretical status didn't bother kender enough to keep them out of Istar, though no few of that free-worshiping kindred had met the heretic's fate there. Ah, but you know kender: those light-fingered thieves don't worry about much. This one was young, a likable-looking fellow, the way kender can be when they're not torturing you with their eternal chatter and endless nonsense. Red-haired and slim, with a thief's long, nimble fingers, he wore kender motley—yellow leggings, blue shirt, green cloak and purple-dyed buckskin boots. He had six or seven pouches and wallets about him, all stuffed full with pack-rat junk.

Except for me and the kender and the barman, the tavern was empty. Careful people were still at devotions or keeping discreetly out of sight. There were plenty of tables to choose from, but the kender was sitting at the table by the Hart's only window, the one with the knife-scarred top, where Toukere and I used to sit reckoning a bounty's split and drinking ale. Chance, the barman, always kept that table clear for me, no matter how crowded or empty the place was. Now he only shrugged when I scowled to see the table occupied.

"He's here lookin' for you, Doune."

That was thirty gold in kender topknot sitting at the table. Ah, life is mighty sweet, I thought, when the bounty comes looking for the hunter. I fingered the hilt of my sword, told Chance to get me some food, and said that I'd like to have it by the time I got back from hauling the kender's butt to the jail.

But Chance closed his hand round my wrist, gripping hard. "Maybe you should eat first, eh, Doune?"

The kender cocked his head, eyes alight and grinning as if he was expecting to have some fun.

Then someone told me—a woman's voice, as soft and deadly as a steel blade cutting cold air—that no one would be hauling kender anywhere tonight.

I turned fast on my heel, sword half drawn, and nearly spitted myself on her blade. The tall swordswoman set the point of her steel gently against the base of my throat. Chance never lifted voice or hand in my defense.

"How much did they pay you, Chance?" I asked bitterly.

"Just exactly enough," he said, not even bothering to try for shame. He said no more, and I heard him leave for the kitchen.

"Gently," the swordswoman said, smiling and flattening out her words so that they were a taunt. "Gently, Doune, if you like living."

I like living well enough. I dropped my sword point, but not the sword.

She was human, like me, but dressed and geared like an elf whose family had some means. Silk and buckskin and low-heeled riding boots of the finest cut. I'll tell you now, she was well made, long-legged and slender of waist. She was round in all the best places, and there wasn't much need to guess about that. The cut of her blouse showed more than the silver-and-sapphire necklace she wore.

I tried a question. "How do you know my name?"

"Who hasn't heard of Hunter-Doune?" She grinned, as cocky as a scamp bent on mischief. "You're a legend where I come from."

Light from an oil lamp gleamed on the steel between us, hers high, mine low and useless. She gestured to the kender.

"Peverell," she said, "relieve him of his weapons."

The kender did what kender love to do. He got my dagger, found the small knife I always kept sheathed in my boot, lifted the sword from my hand before I knew he'd reached for it. He also took the bounty notices I'd gotten at the den and the fee I'd collected not an hour ago. He would have taken the teeth from my head if his companion hadn't called him off.

"Now, Hunter-Doune," the swordswoman said, "come join Peverell and me for a drink and a bite, eh?" She sheathed her weapon. "It could be to your profit."

I eyed Peverell, back at the table and happily sorting through his take. "Hasn't been so far," I said.

"I suppose you're right. Pev! Give Doune his purse."

The kender screwed up his face in protest, but he emptied the gold coins onto the table, then tossed the purse to me.

"*And* the gold," the woman said firmly.

Long eyes bright, the kender cocked his head. Something needing no words passed between the two and—for a wonder—Peverell scooped up the coins, came and gave them all to me. I took the gold, pursed it, and stashed it in my deepest pocket, watching him trot back to the table. He was uncannily quiet for one of his kind. I smiled sourly.

"Someone cut out his tongue?"

"No," she said, "someone slit it. Works out the same. A bounty hunter who took him and couldn't stand the chatter. Didn't keep him, though. Kender are hard to hold. But I expect you know that. Now," she said, cold and no longer pretending courtesy. "Do you want to know where the heretic Kell is hiding, or is that little bit of gold enough to keep you happy?"

* * * * *

Chance brought us platters piled high with mutton and cabbage and potatoes, a jug of wine for me, and a great pitcher of ale for the others. Fair pleased with himself, old Chance was, and acting like I should thank him.

Outside the window, high up in the sky, I saw the two moons—the red and the silver—shining brightly. Chance had barred the door, lighted only the few lamps we needed to see what we were eating. The swordswoman told me that her name was Alyce. She said she was a mercenary's daughter, that since her father's death she'd taken up the family trade, hired her sword to merchant caravans needing to make their way through the goblin-haunted passes of the mountains ringing the Plains of Istar.

Now some might think that mercenary work is a

strange way for a woman to keep herself in sapphire necklaces, but I had no reason to doubt that Alyce was capable of the work she claimed to do. She'd gotten up behind me quickly enough, and that fine jeweled sword was no stranger to her hand, but, for all that, I'd heard no reason to believe that she knew more about Kell's whereabouts than anyone else.

"Well," she said, tucking into a second helping of mutton with a wharfman's appetite. "There's not much I can do to convince you that I know where Kell's hiding— except to say that a friend of mine tracked him to his lair not longer that two weeks ago."

"But this friend didn't kill or capture him?"

She laughed, and the kender clapped his hands in delight, his brown eyes kindling with merriment.

"My friend's not foolish enough to go out alone after a man who's supposed to have done all Kell is accused of." She smiled slyly. "If Kell were an easy take, surely some bounty hunter would have snatched him by now, eh? Pev and I were supposed to meet our friend here, go after him together, but our friend is . . . not available."

I snorted. "Not available to make himself rich?"

"He's been jailed." Alyce downed her ale, all business now. She nodded to Chance, who quickly refilled the pitcher. "The barman says you know the jail well— having helped fill it up often enough over the years. Help me break out my friend and you can come along."

"You want me to arrange a jailbreak? Sorry. I put 'em *in* jail—I don't break 'em out."

"Exactly," she said, "that's why you're the perfect choice. You'd have it done before anyone even suspected what was going on."

I thought about that for a while, and she— impatient—leaned across the table, her blue eyes alight.

"A quarter share, Doune! Help me get my friend out of jail and we'll be on our way to claiming a bounty so great that no place you could stash the treasure will be empty."

Well, she wasn't much exaggerating about the bounty, and I was always tracking the gold. But I was also careful.

"Supposing I do this jailbreak? What's to keep you and your friend from getting rid of me and going after the bounty yourselves?"

Alyce's eyes grew sharp and cold. She drew her sword and I reached for where mine should have been. She made no threat, only laid the jeweled weapon flat on the table between us.

"This is my father's sword," she said, ignoring my own gesture. "I have never sworn an oath on this steel that I didn't mean to keep."

I believed her. Maybe it was the way her voice sounded, low and freighted with fierce pride. Or maybe it was the look in her eyes, straight on and unflinching, like the light gleaming along the blade's keen edge. Out of the corner of my eye I saw Peverell idly tracing some old calculation Toukere or I had carved in the oaken table-top.

I'm honest when I want to be, Doune, my friend. And when a man reckons the split with his partner, he'd best want to be honest or he'll deserve to be dead.

Toukere had had the same straight-on look in his eyes as Alyce did now when he'd said that. By that look—its absence or its presence—I'd always judged a man's nature. Or a woman's. I guess I reckoned on it this time, too.

"Who's this partner of yours?" I asked. "A lover?"

She tossed her head, and her short, dark hair swung and bounced. "Dinn's a friend. Sometimes he acts like a hotheaded fool, but I love him dearly. He comes from people who have only one word for both loyalty and honor. Hard enemies, these people, and good friends. My father earned his friendship, and Dinn says that I inherited it." Her voice dropped low. "On his soul and my father's sword I swear that I'll deal honestly with you, Doune."

It was a powerful oath. I knew none like it to offer her.

She asked if I had a father; I told her I must have at one time. A mother? Dead, I said. No sister or wife, she supposed. I told her she supposed right, and none of the women I knew had the kind of soul I'd care to swear an oath on. She looked at me with a mocking, exaggerated expression of pity.

"Well," I growled, "I don't expect they're swearing any oaths on my soul either."

The kender whistled a rising note, like a question, to catch Alyce's attention. When he had it, he hit his two fists against each other, then clasped both hands together. Alyce shrugged with the air of someone who has come to the bottom of the coffer and expects to find nothing but dust. To me she said: "I don't suppose people in your line of work have many friends."

"Not many," I said flatly, "and the one who was closest to me is a long time dead."

"Was he a good friend?"

A good companion, an honest partner, and one who made his escape from Istar in such a way as to leave plenty of witnesses to the fact that I'd had nothing to do with it.

"Yes," I said quietly. "He was a good friend."

She thought about that for a long moment, her blue eyes no longer bright and jeering, but soft and very serious.

"Swear by your friend's memory, Hunter-Doune. Swear that you'll deal honestly with me." Then I couldn't see her eyes at all for the veil of her dark lashes. Only her lips moving in a secret little smile. "It'll be well worth your while."

That's all I needed to hear. I placed my hand over hers and took an oath on a friend's memory.

Good thing she waited until I'd sworn before she told me that her partner was the minotaur I'd brought to Istar's jail only hours ago. Good thing for her, but not so good for Peverell. The mute little kender laughed so hard that he fell out of his chair. And not so good for me. I'd been two days in the minotaur's company and I suspected he'd not readily agree to become my partner in the hunt for Kell. But I was sworn now, and by Touk's memory.

Too, there was all that gold to consider.

*   *   *   *   *

Peverell was hot to pick every lock on every door in the jail. When I told him that we wouldn't get in that way, he showed me how deeply he resented this slight to his thievish abilities. Mute he might be, but he'd raised the skills of obscene and insulting gesture to high art. Alyce calmed him, and from there the night's work was no more than the usual game: Get some weapons for the minotaur, some mounts for Alyce and me—no sense getting horses for Peverell or Dinn; Alice said that neither would ride if you paid 'em—then bribe the right guard and pay off the right cleric. The bribe and the payoff were huge, took all the ninety gold pieces I'd earned on the minotaur and a lot more besides. Alyce had to part with her beautiful sapphire necklace.

"I consider it an investment," she said. She cocked a thumb at my empty purse and grinned coolly. "You should, too."

I did. A quarter share of Kell's bounty would make the gold I'd paid in bribery seem like the pittance in a beggar's cup.

I was right about Dinn. He joyfully would have given up all hope of freedom for even the slimmest chance of killing me. But Alyce managed him, and it was something to see her go toe-to-toe with that brute, harrying him in hissing whispers like an angry fishwife.

"Use your head, Dinn," she said. And she insisted—often—that he remember why they were here. She demanded—just as often—that he carry through with what he'd promised.

The kender, over his fit of the sulks, came up close to the tall, red-furred minotaur, gestured elaborately. Dinn growled and shook his horns at Peverell, sullenly asking Alyce to translate.

"He's saying just what you know is true, Dinn. We *need* you!"

That made some difference, caused the minotaur to subside. "Arr, well," he growled, glaring at me. "Let's do it then."

"Thank you, my friend." Alyce patted his rough-furred shoulder and rose up on tiptoe to kiss that ugly snout (which made him growl and *harrumph* and shuffle his feet).

I kept one eye on Dinn, for all that everyone seemed happy and friendly together. I'd been the one to shame him by dragging him chained and hobbled into Istar. Minotaurs usually like to erase the memory of shame by killing anyone who knows about it.

* * * * *

An unwelcoming place, the savannah; hot and dry and without landmarks. This is the land of the nomad clans, and there are no borders to cross; nothing to warn you that you're in some clan's territory, for the nomads have no individual territories. Always moving, settling nowhere, the long-braids consider the whole savannah theirs. They have a hard greeting for visitors—a flint-tipped arrow, a lance's stony head.

We went carefully, Alyce and I riding; Dinn loping ahead, a tall, horned outrunner tracking steadily west to the blue-hazed mountains. Sometimes Peverell trotted beside him, unseen but for the parting of the high grass as he went, the wake of a small, mute kender. More often, he stayed by Alyce. Like all kender, he loved to talk, and she had more patience for his silent language—and clearly a greater understanding of it—than the minotaur did.

I was used to riding alone since Toukere and I had parted ways, and I was used to quiet. But soon I found myself liking the sound of Alyce's voice: low because of the danger, thrilling when she was keen on her subject, gentle when she was thinking aloud. Alyce did a lot of thinking out loud, about politics and history and gods.

"I'll tell you something, Hunter-Doune," she said, one blazing noonday when the savannah ran rippling under a hot wind. "I've always heard that gods are about balance, good and neutral and evil all lending their weight in the measure against chaos. I think it's politics that makes heretics, not wrong thinking. Which, if you believe what you hear, is just what this outlaw, Kell, thinks." She glanced at me out of the corner of her eyes. "If you believe what you hear."

She seemed to know a lot about Kell, and I wondered if she'd conceived some romantic fancy for the outlaw. I asked her about this, in a joking way. Peverell, trotting beside us, looked up at me, signing swiftly, laughing silently.

"What'd he say?" I asked.

"Kender nonsense," she said stiffly. "I have no fancies about Kell. A good hunter should know what she's hunting, how the prey thinks, what it will defend, where it goes to hide, where it is vulnerable." She smiled, as though to herself and over private thoughts. "Don't you agree, Hunter-Doune?"

I said I was a bounty hunter, not a boar hunter.

"So you are." She laughed, mocking again. "And a good one who wastes no time thinking about the heretics you hunt. Right?"

"No sense in it. They're nothing more than the promise of gold, payable on delivery." I slipped her a sideways grin. "Thanks to politics."

Again Peverell gestured, his whole bright face a question; this time Alyce translated.

"He wants to know whether heretics are people to you."

I shook my head. "They're profit."

The kender signed again, and Alyce looked at me for a long moment, her eyes all soft and gravely thoughtful, as if she were weighing the balance of me on a scale.

"Empty enough for the wind to howl through, aren't you, Hunter-Doune?"

"Did he say that?"

"No. I did. How'd you get so empty?"

"Tricks of the trade." I shifted uncomfortably to another tack. "Why are you worrying about how I feel? I don't see that *you're* holding a whole lot of mercy for Kell."

She looked away, out across the golden, shifting savannah. "My feelings for Kell are . . . personal," she said. "I'm not a bounty hunter by trade."

"Oh? What'd he do, steal the pennies off your dead father's eyes?"

She winced, and I was sorry I'd said it. I'd come close to some truth, one that hurt.

"Come on, Alyce," I said, and surprised myself to hear how gently I'd spoken. "Don't worry about me and my feelings. They haven't got all that much to do with you anyway, eh?"

The old, taunting light, brittle and bright, came back to her eyes. "Not much," she said, and she laughed.

I thought the laughter was forced.

*   *   *   *   *

That's the way we talked during those long, hot days on the savannah. Sometimes she mocked, as she'd done in the Hart; sometimes she was serious, and I liked that best. Soon I began to wish that the kender would stay with Dinn. I was getting to like Alyce's company, the nearness of her, her voice, even her thoughtful, considering silence.

There were possibilities in her silence. At night, as I slept—Alyce wrapped in rough woolen blankets with a tall fire between us—those possibilities changed into dreams in which the minotaur and the kender had no roles to play.

But the kender was with us more often than not, and so we three were together—Alyce, Peverell, and me—when, at the end of our third day of travel, the sun set in a blaze of red and ahead of us Dinn spotted the nomad woman and her child.

My horse danced skittishly, sidled away from the minotaur's horns. Dinn smiled thinly when he saw that, tossed his head so that a horn came dangerously close to the horse's shoulder . . . and my leg. He pointed to the tall grass where it parted counter to the wind's direction.

"Two," he said to Alyce. "Long-braids."

The nomad woman ran swiftly, though she went hunched over, burdened by the weight of the small boy clinging to her back. The boy's head bounced limply in rhythm to her swift, ground-covering stride. His sun-browned leg was streaked with blood. The woman's course would take her right across our path.

Answering the instinct of fifteen years, I reached for the coil of rope hanging from my saddle. One good cast and I'd have her and the child roped, down, and trussed.

Alyce, seeing my gesture, said, "How much for those two, Hunter-Doune?"

Eighty gold, I told her. Forty for each, the woman not being worth more than the child.

Alyce smiled coldly. "Your share of Kell's bounty is worth ten times that. Are you with me, Hunter-Doune?"

I didn't answer. I was watching the woman run. Although the wind covered our whispering and our mounts were still, something—a silence of birds, maybe—must have spoken to her instincts. She threw a swift look over her shoulder and stumbled, startled to see us. Her eyes were large and dark, like empty holes in a mask of terror. The sight chilled me, squeezed my heart so that it was as if I felt the desperate fear myself. The woman recovered quickly, hitched the boy up higher on her back, and ran faster.

I took my hand away from the rope, saw Alyce watching me—not weighing anything, not taunting. Rather, she smiled the way you do when you first meet someone and you're thinking that you like what you see. Peverell looked from one to the other of us, then gestured something. His hands flew too fast for me to get his meaning, but Alyce did. A dark scowl replaced her smile as she told him to stop talking nonsense.

* * * * *

They say that the red moon, Lunitari, is the daughter of Gilean, the deity who is the keeper of all the knowledge possessed by the gods. Solinari, the silver moon, is Paladine's son, and he watches over all the magic being done in the world. That night, while the others rested, I walked the first watch and saw these two moons—gods' children, if you will—rising. First to rise was Lunitari. When I squinted eastward across the plains, I thought I saw the tall towers of Istar silhouetted against the red disk, dark like a jagged bite taken out of the moon's rim. Second up was Solinari, and he rose a little north of Istar, avoided the teeth of the Kingpriest's city.

Foolish fancy, eh? Well, I had a lot on my mind—too much for sleeping—and I kept coming back to the memory of how I'd felt when Alyce smiled after I'd let the nomads go.

That was just more foolish fancy. Why should I care how I weighed out in her eyes? Aye, she was long-legged and lovely. Her blue eyes, when they weren't mocking, spoke of possibilities, inspired dreams. She was round—and surely soft and warm—in all the right places, but so was many another woman, and I knew that well enough. The only difference between Alyce and them was that she was a good hand with a sword, good to talk to . . . and she was leading me to a quarter share of a fine, large bounty.

Sometimes she looked at me in such a way as to make me want to be what she seemed to hope I was.

Empty? Maybe once. Maybe still, but Alyce, when she looked at me with her eyes soft, a little hopeful, and gravely thoughtful, made me think that she might be able to fill some of those empty places in me.

I shook my head hard, as if I was trying to shake out this nonsense. It *was* nonsense, I told myself. Isn't one woman just as good as another on a cold night?

I was looking at the silver moon when I thought that, so I guess you could say I was praying for something, maybe for an answer, or a way to understand why it mattered to me what Alyce thought.

Of course, Solinari didn't have much to say about it. The children of gods have their own business to tend.

*   *   *   *   *

When the moons were past their heights I left my watch, stepped carefully around the sleeping minotaur, and sat beside Peverell at the campfire. He gave me a sideways look, then signed something to Alyce. When I asked her what he'd said, she didn't answer right away. I had the idea that she wasn't thinking about how to translate, but whether to. Finally she repeated his gestures, slowly, the way you enunciate each word for the hard of hearing. A long reaching up with both hands to cup something, an abrupt dragging down motion.

"Sun setting," I guessed.

"Right."

She raised four fingers, and I suggested that this, coupled with the first gesture, meant four days passing.

"Right again." Her blue eyes danced as she made the fists-and-clasp gesture I knew to mean *friend*. "You know that one. How about this?"

She repeated Peverell's last gesture: slammed her right fist hard onto her level left palm. Then she mimicked his expression: wide-eyed, drop-jawed surprise.

"What do you think that means, Hunter-Doune?"

"I have no idea."

She moved her lips in a secret little smile. "It's the whole point of what Pev said. I'll leave you to consider it."

I spent the night listening to the wind sigh down the starred sky, thinking long and hard about Peverell's gestures. Might be, I thought, that Peverell's fist-in-palm gesture meant an ambush. If so, perhaps he and Alyce were anticipating Kell's surprise to find himself at last taken. And that in only another four days. But nowhere in that interpretation did Peverell's friend-gesture fit.

Last, before I made ready to sleep, I remembered Alyce's secret smile.

Now I remembered this wasn't the first time I'd seen her smile like that. The first time was in the Hart's Leap, right after she'd hunted around trying to find an oath for me to swear. An oath that maybe I wouldn't have given if I'd known it was Dinn I had to help break out of jail.

Cold and creeping came suspicion.

Might be, I thought, that there's another way to interpret Peverell's gestures and Alyce's secret smile. Might be they were having a laugh over how surprised I'd be to find that the oath she took on her father's sword signified nothing but a means to an end—the minotaur's release from jail, the capture of the heretic Kell, and a third share of the bounty instead of a quarter.

Four days. Friendship. And a violent, smashing gesture. Surprise.

Alyce—her considering looks, her soft eyes, her surprised pleasure when I let the nomads go? What were those things? Bait, maybe. Four are better than three on the savannah—until the three got where they needed to go.

Time to get out. Time to cut my losses and get out.

I stayed—for the sake of the gold, I told myself. What I didn't admit—didn't even know then—was that I'd foolishly come too far down the road of fancy to turn back.

Alyce kept to herself after that night. Quiet and brooding, she spoke to Dinn only when she had to, and spoke to me hardly at all. She had something on her mind, and if she talked to anyone about it, that one was Peverell—who seemed to know about, and maybe even sympathize with, whatever troubled her.

They conversed in his silent, graceful language of gesture, and so I had no idea why she'd grown so suddenly distant.

* * * * *

We left the savannah three days after we saw the nomad woman and her child. We made camp that night in a blind canyon, a long slot of stone and tall, rising walls. No need to post watch there. The only way into the canyon was in clear sight of our camp.

We'd no more than built a fire when Alyce looked around to find the kender missing. "Dinn," she said. "Where'd he go?"

The minotaur made the kender's fist-hitting-palm gesture.

"Damn! I *told* him—" She glanced at me, then took another tack. "Dinn, are you sure?"

Dinn shrugged. "I'm never really sure what he's trying to say, but that is my guess."

Ah, she wasn't happy with that answer. Nor was she very happy when I asked her what the gesture meant. Blue eyes glinting, she said, "It means that that kender's going to find himself in some big trouble next time I see him."

She said no more.

As we ate, the red moon cleared the high canyon walls, spilled light over the stone, made the shadows a web of purple. Alyce, who'd displayed a wharfman's appetite at the Hart, picked only absently at her food. When she tired of that, she bunched a rough woolen blanket into a pillow and stretched out before the fire.

She lay silent, staring up at the narrow sky, the gleaming stars. The fire's flickering glow made her pale cheeks flush rosy, her dark hair shine, but I only watched that from the corner of my eye. Dinn, sitting in the night shadows and honing his daggers, had the most of my attention. He worked with sure, even strokes and sometimes sparks leaped from the steel and stone. When that happened, the minotaur would look up at me, his dark eyes gleaming, his large yellow teeth bared in something like a smile.

"Doune," Alyce said after a while. "We're near Kell's hideout. Tomorrow, we'll be playing a whole different game."

I looked away from Dinn, not liking the sound of that. "What do you mean?"

She looked at me, her eyes neither soft and thoughtful, nor brittle and jeering. She wasn't smiling. Her expression was unreadable.

"Doune," she said. "Can I trust you?"

I answered evenly, though I didn't know where the question was leading. (And, no, it didn't remind me of my own doubt. Doubt had haunted me for the past three days.)

"I swore I'd deal honestly with you, Alyce."

She nodded. "On your old friend's memory."

I said nothing, remembering Peverell's fist-hitting-palm gesture, repeated again tonight. Ambush for Kell, or betrayal for me? I didn't know, and I waited to see where Alyce's questions would lead. Dinn put aside his daggers, watched and waited, too. But he wasn't watching Alyce. He was watching me.

Alyce said, "Doune, you also said that bounty hunting is just business. Can we trust you to stand by us, no matter what we find tomorrow?"

I laughed without humor. "Unless this Kell of yours has an army with him. Then you can trust me to do what anyone with sense would do—cut my losses and run.

Live to hunt another day, eh? This is a strange time to be talking about that."

She shrugged. "Not really. Tell me, Hunter-Doune, what would you do if—"

A loud whistle—a sudden pattern of sharp notes, shrill enough to make the hair stir on the back of my neck—broke the night silence.

"Goblins," Dinn rumbled, reaching for his daggers.

I scanned the dark heights, saw nothing but shadows and the baleful eye of the red moon gleaming. I listened hard for Peverell's whistle, but heard only the ghostly echo of night wind trapped in the canyon. Then, darkness become solid, goblins lined the heights, black against the moonlit sky. I counted a dozen. Although distance might fool the eye about details, I knew that the least of them was taller than I and more muscular than even the minotaur.

You might think that none of this mattered much, that we could slip through the shadows and the dark, head for the mouth of the canyon and take our chances running and hiding until we lost them in the dark and the mountains. We couldn't.

A huge goblin stepped forward to the edge of the drop. It held something high, like a dark cleric offering sacrifice. Alyce cursed softly. The goblin held the kender above its head, had voiceless Peverell for a hostage and a shield.

Peverell writhed in the goblin's grip as if he wanted nothing more than to overbalance his captor and send him plunging to a bone-shattered death. So furiously did he struggle that I knew he'd not give a thought to his own bones until he was in midair himself. Yet he was lightly built and had not one tenth of the goblin's strength. His struggling was worth nothing but the goblin's annoyance.

Alyce gestured to Dinn, pointed to the canyon entrance. Wordless understanding passed between them in just one look, as though a whole plan had been unfolded and discussed. The minotaur didn't like it, whatever it was, but Alyce reached up, stroked his red-furred shoulder.

"Don't worry, my friend. I'll be fine. Now, go. Go."

He obeyed, as he always did, but in the fire's light I saw his eyes gleaming, all reflected animal glare and as red as Lunitari hanging high in the sky above the canyon's black walls. A dire warning, that look, and directed at me.

"Don't worry," I said, sarcasm not even thinly veiled. "I'll be fine, too, Dinn."

He exercised admirable restraint, did no more than feint a lunge at me as he passed by—and I still have two eyes today because I kept as still as stone when one of his twisted horns came close to my face. Alyce smiled in a cold, absent way.

"You shouldn't bait him like that, Doune. There might come a time when I'm not near to restrain him."

"Might come a time when I'd welcome that."

She said nothing, likely recognizing bravado when she heard it. I looked over my shoulder at the mouth of the canyon, yawning blackness with silvery stars hanging above. I turned back to Alyce, saw her studying me.

"Is this where a bounty hunter decides to cut his losses and run, Hunter-Doune?"

I snorted. "Could I?"

"Go and try," Alyce said flatly. With her sword's gleaming tip she pointed to the goblins. They'd found a narrow path, a winding way down the black canyon walls. They went slowly, being obliged to keep behind the one who was still shielding himself with Peverell. But they came on steadily, and I saw that my first count was wrong. There were more than a dozen of them; at least twice that. "There's no profit in this for you now, Hunter-Doune."

None at all.

In that moment the silver moon, Paladine's son lagging behind Lunitari as he always does, rose above the stony heights. By Solinari's light I saw Alyce's face in profile, as white as marble. All her attention was on the kender caught in the goblin's clutches.

The big goblin flung the kender to the ground, laughed when he saw him hit the rough stone and tumble the rest of the way to the canyon floor. Peverell lay where he fell, a pitiful jumble of arms and legs. When I looked at Alyce, I saw one thin line of silver on her cheek, moonlit tears.

"Are you with me, Hunter-Doune? Or will you leave me?"

She was not weighing me now, or taunting. She really didn't know how I would answer. By the light of wise Paladine's son, I saw in her eyes the knowledge that with me or without, she'd probably not get out of this canyon alive. I saw her wanting to believe that I would not abandon her here.

I'd be a fool to stay, but that would be nothing new. I'd been a fool for the last three days, should have gotten out when I knew I wasn't sure whether I trusted her. What had made me stay?

It was a jeweled moment, one of those spaces in the soul when you understand that something has happened to change you. Those moments have their sudden, unlooked-for absurdities to send you laughing, if only silently. Once I'd asked the silver moon why I cared what Alyce thought of me. A bit late in answering, was Solinari, but he answered me now, softly, like a whisper in my heart.

What a damned all inconvenient time to finally figure out that I've fallen in love . . .

Maybe Alyce heard the laughter in me. For one moment, swiftly fled, she smiled as though she agreed.

I hefted my sword, took comfort in its trusty balance. "I swore to deal honestly with you, Alyce. By my reckoning, that means sticking by you now."

We stood braced, back-to-back, when the goblins entered the canyon.

* * * * *

Night fighting is a hard thing, all shadows and moon-gleaming steel, all cold sweat and heart leaping in your chest. When the odds are good, it's hard to tell friend from foe, but that wasn't anything for us to worry about. The odds weren't good. There was only Alyce and me, with never the slim breadth of a steel blade between us.

She used her blade like a sword dancer, whirling the steel so that the whistle of it filled the canyon. Any goblin who got too close lost at least a limb. One lost his head. That was all very fine and flashy, but I like the dependable parry and thrust. I spitted the first two of the fanged goblins that came at me, was ready to take on a third when I heard Dinn roaring somewhere near the canyon's mouth. I couldn't turn to see what cause he had for bellowing, but I heard Alyce suck in her breath, a soft hissing counterpoint to her sword's whistle.

The goblin who'd come to take the place of the one I killed feinted from the side, dove in under my guard. He caught me around the neck and did what his fellows couldn't do—separated Alyce and me as he threw me hard to the stony ground. I heard Alyce cursing above me, saw the star-filled sky, felt the goblin's claws raking my face.

The goblin knew how to use his knees. In two thrusts he knocked the wind from me with a knee to the belly—and nearly all the sense with a knee to the groin. I twisted onto my side, hunched over the hurt. The goblin sank his fangs into the muscle between neck and shoulder, gnawed as though he'd like to have chewed his way to my heart.

A dagger whistled past my head, its cold steel stinging my cheek, drawing blood. And the goblin fell off me, the blade through its neck. I didn't stop to marvel over my luck.

I scrambled for my sword and saw Alyce ringed by

three goblins—big as boulders, gray-skinned, clawed, long fangs dripping. Her sword flashed, singing as it cut the air. I ran to her. Limping and listing, still hunched over my pain, I didn't know what I could do for her. Still, I ran. Her fine silk blouse was splattered with blood, and the silver moon's light showed me that it wasn't black goblin blood. It was as red as rose petals, and it was hers.

Alyce cried me welcome. I severed a goblin's head with one chopping blow of my sword, kicked the corpse aside, and Alyce and I were again back-to-back. The goblins came at us howling, nightmares come to life. We were outnumbered, fighting only to kill as many as we could before we fell.

Close by, I heard a piercing whistle—sharp and high and urgent. Peverell? No. It couldn't be. Someone shouted "Kell!" as though it were a war cry, a call to arms.

I looked up, thinking, *Where?* Then, *As if we didn't have enough trouble.*

That moment's distraction cost me. I went down under the weight of two goblins, and Alyce, kicking and hacking at my attackers, yelled, "To me! To me!" as though she were giving an army a rallying point.

The night exploded, as if the moons and every one of the countless stars had burst to rain red and shower silver down on me. In the storm of light, flaring and running, shadows leaped to thrice their height. Alyce's face shone as white as snow, her sword like ice gleaming. A rush and babble of shouting and screaming filled the wildly rocking night, just as though an army *had* come.

Too late for me, though, sword-cut and bleeding . . .

Peverell—bruised and scraped and grinning—threw himself down on his knees beside me, gestured wildly, but I couldn't figure it out. The light, the running, raining red and silver, began to fade, then vanished altogether, taking feeling and sound with it.

*   *   *   *   *

I awoke in another place, a sturdy cottage so light and bright and clean that if I did not have wounds and weakness to gainsay the thought, I'd have believed the canyon no more than a place in a nightmare. The first thing I saw was Peverell, and he was chattering to an elderly woman in his silent way, his hands swooping and flying. After a while, the old woman, her face wrinkled like a winter apple, shooed him away as though he were a pesky hen gotten into the house. I wondered, in a vague kind of way, what they'd been talking about, but I fell asleep again.

I slept often and long. One evening I awoke to find Dinn standing beside me.

"There is no longer debt between us, human," he said. "You kept her safe when I could not. They're right. You'll do, Hunter-Doune, if you live." He said that last grudgingly, with a sullen shake of his horns.

Dinn wasn't the only one who was unsure whether I'd survive my wounds. I wasn't all that certain about it myself, but Alyce wasn't having any of that. She was always near, and one morning I awoke to see her standing in the open doorway, looking out. Her left arm was bandaged above the elbow. She wore a soft blue gown of some light, wide-woven fabric, the hem of it just brushing sun-browned ankles.

I don't know why I remembered it then—with her looking like a breeze-blown flower come to settle on the doorstep, but in memory I heard someone shout, *Kell!* and heard her yell, *To me! To me!*

"Are you Kell?" I asked her.

She turned from the doorway, her blue eyes darkly thoughtful. She was weighing a risk. Finally she said, "Yes. You see, Hunter-Doune, Dinn does know where that terrible heretic Kell hides out."

"But why—?"

She shook her head, laid a finger on my lips, then she

pressed her own lips to my forehead. To check for fever, she said.

* * * * *

Later that day I awoke and Alyce was not in the cottage, but I wasn't alone. I had a visitor. He sat in a chair pulled close to the side of the bed, a tankard of ale in his hand. His eyes, dark and a little flecked with blue, were soft-focused, as though his thoughts were far away.

On second look, I saw that what I'd thought was sunlight glinting in his black beard was the silvering of time's passing. He'd aged, and that shouldn't have been surprising. It had been about seven years since I'd last seen him. When he saw me awake, he turned in the chair, and I saw that he'd lost something since the last time I'd seen him: a leg. In its place, strapped to the stump where a knee should have been, was a carved wooden peg.

Although it hurt to move, I raised my left hand, palm up, and hit it with my right fist. Now I knew the meaning of Peverell's puzzling gesture: A hammer hitting an anvil.

Four days. Surprise. Friend.

Toukere Hammerfell.

"Touk," I said, though hoarsely for trying to sound calm. "Where am I?"

"Ah, well, that's a story." He raised the tankard, drank, and held it out to me.

"No," I said. "I don't drink ale."

Smiling a little, as if he were looking down a long road to an old memory, he said, "Guess you had your fill the night I left Istar, eh? Well, then, listen good, Hunter-Doune. There's a lot to tell about me and the Vale."

He told me there were two mages living in the Vale. They had made the sky over the canyon rain red and silver light. He grinned when he said that, held that those mages did a fine job of scaring the feeble wits out of the goblins with their little light game. He told me there were five clerics, and some declared their allegiance to the gods of good by their white garb. Others wore the red of neutrality. According to Toukere, it was one of the red-robed clerics who had healed the worst of my hurts.

"And there's enough people—young men and old, grannies and mothers and children—to fill up a small town," he said. "Some of 'em you saw in the canyon, which is no great distance from here. Good fighters when they have to be, but mostly they're farmers."

"But this is no town, Touk, is it?"

He allowed as how it wasn't, not exactly. The Vale was a deep, high-sided valley tucked between two rising mountain peaks. The people who lived there hunted the highlands, raised cows and chickens and pigs, had a fine forge at the broad fording place of the river. Kell's father had founded the place.

"Alyce—Kell—told me her father was a mercenary."

Touk shrugged. "He was, once, for a while, but he was a pretty good thinker, and he got to thinking that this habit the Kingpriest has of slaughtering in the name of goodness is a strange one. Once that idea got hold of him, it didn't let go. He opposed the Kingpriest's persecutions with everything he had—heart and soul. He did more than talk about it. He settled this place.

"You call his daughter Alyce," Toukere said, "but that's only a traveling name. Here we name her Kell, for that's what her father called her. Kell o' the Vale."

He told me that all the folk who lived in the Vale were free believers in whatever god or gods they chose. Many of them had come by way of dark paths, hunted for bounty and driven by desperation into the goblin lands. He said that every one of them—men and dwarves and elves, one kender and a minotaur—owed their lives to Kell, the heretic who, like her father, did not believe that torment and execution were fit ways to honor the gods of good.

"We get on well, Hunter-Doune. By which I mean we don't kill each other over the big matters, and we feel free to squabble over the small things."

"We?"

He finished off the ale and thumped the mug against his wooden leg. He winced a little when he did that, and I saw that the wood was newly carved. The amputation wasn't old enough to be used to.

"We're awfully close to goblin lands, here," he said. "That's good and bad. Good because it keeps the Kingpriest's spies and casual visitors away. Bad because we have to keep patrols on our borders against the black-hearted goblins. I am—" He ran his palm along the wood again. "I was the one who led those patrols. No more."

"What happened, Touk?"

He shrugged. "Just what it looks like. Lost my leg to a goblin's axe, lay too long for the cleric to heal me. But I'm not here to talk about me, Doune. I'm here to talk about you."

Now, go reckon this—because I can't. There he sat, my old partner whose advice I'd remembered and lived by even all the years after I'd thought him dead, the old friend whose memory I'd sworn by—and I was suddenly angry. Angry and wondering why he'd not found a moment to spare to let me know that he was not dead.

"You want to talk about me?" I said bitterly. "Why, I'm just fine, Touk. Sword-cut, my ribs broken, gnawed by goblins, and the rest of me feeling like I've been run over by a wagon. But otherwise, fine. How've you been?"

"Now hear me, Hunter-Doune," he said. "Hear me."

"Hear *you*? No, Touk Hammerfell. You listen to me—"

"Hear me!" His dark, blue-flecked eyes flared, as they'd so often done when—as he liked to say—I had the stubborn fit on me.

"It's me who told Kell to bring you here," he said, "and that was a risk. I knew you seven years ago, Hunter-Doune, but I didn't know what you'd become since then.

Still I talked Kell into taking the risk. Ah, blackmailed her, I guess you'd say, told her she owed me for my leg."

"Why, Touk?"

He sucked in his cheeks, as he did when he was thinking, then spoke in a rush, as he did when he was trying to get past sentiment.

"I've never forgotten you, Hunter-Doune, and I hoped . . . I hoped you'd still be the man I remembered. I'd have gone for you myself, but you see I couldn't. We need someone trusty, and someone keen-witted. Someone who—" He shook his head, then went off on another tack. "They're mostly all farmers here, not fighters. The minotaur wanted the job. He wants nothing more than to be killing goblins every chance he gets. But you know how minotaurs are. Hotheaded and not good at leading men. I'll tell you, he didn't much like being the bait in this game."

"Bait? For what? For me?"

"Well, I've been dead these seven years, haven't I? Caught by some bounty hunter in Xak Tsaroth." He grinned, an old familiar twist of his lips. "I don't reckon you'd have believed it if anyone came to say that your old friend Touk Hammerfell wanted to have a chat."

I gave him that.

"So we used Dinn for bait. A nice big minotaur— worth what, ninety gold these days?—wandering your usual stomping grounds and ready for the taking."

I sighed, and he gave me a sharp look.

"I'm not doing a very good job explaining, am I?"

"No," I said. "You're not."

There came a soft sound, a bare foot whispering against the floor rushes. Alyce stood in the doorway, as bright as a sapphire in a golden fall of sunlight. She came to stand beside Touk.

"Let me try," she said. "Doune, we need a new captain for our border patrol"—she rested a hand on Touk's shoulder—"and you come highly recommended."

"Why did Kell himself—herself—come after me?"

She laughed, her blue eyes sparkling. "I told you when we first met that you were a legend where I come from. Touk insisted that you were the man we need, but I like to make very certain about the people who are going to live here. There wasn't all that much danger for me in Istar. They're too busy spinning up legends about Terrible Kell to know who I really am. So, who better to decide whether you were trustworthy?"

"And if you'd decided that I wasn't?"

"Easy enough to lose our way in the canyons." She smiled, her cheeks dimpling. "They're very twisty and winding. You'd have had no trouble believing that Dinn had lost his way."

I looked at the ceiling, trying to get all this into shape.

No murdered party of innocent pilgrims? I asked. None, she told me. No looted shrines and slaughtered clerics? Not a one, she said. No silver pennies stolen from dead men's eyes?

She shuddered. "I hate that story worst of all. No. I have my ideas about what's right, and I see that they get heard out there in the world. That's all."

I nodded. "No bounty then, I suppose?"

"None. Just a job, Hunter-Doune, guarding good people and keeping them safe. A home with an old friend." She glanced away, her eyes hidden beneath the veil of her dark lashes. "And some new ones. Are you with us, Hunter-Doune?"

Touk looked from her to me, raised an eyebrow. "Well, well," he muttered. "So that's the way of it, eh? I thought the kender was just making it up."

"Oh, hush, Touk," she said, her cheeks flushing, but she didn't say it very insistently.

Touk laughed and slapped his knee—his good one. "So what about it, Hunter-Doune? Are you with us?"

Once Alyce had promised me a bounty so great that no place I could stash the treasure would be empty. I'd been thinking about gold; she'd been talking about a home, a place of trust, and an old friend. Now, watching

her smooth white cheek coloring rosy, I understood that
she was offering something more.

I told Touk that I'd sworn a good oath to deal honestly
with Alyce, said that I reckoned that the oath held for
Kell, too.

*   *   *   *   *

Later, when the sky was filled with stars and Solinari's
light shone in though the window, Alyce—the terrible
outlaw, Kell o' the Vale—brushed her lips against my
forehead in such a way that I knew she wasn't thinking
about fever.

"Once I thought it would be impossible to fill up those
empty places of yours," she whispered. "I thought Touk
was wrong, that you weren't the man for us. But when I
saw you watching the nomad woman running, when I
saw you feeling for her, really *feeling* so that you wanted
to turn away but couldn't—"

She smiled, as she had then, as though she were seeing
me for the first time and liking what she saw.

"Welcome home, Hunter-Doune."

She kissed me again, and I felt her lips move in a smile
like a promise.

Off Day

Dan Parkinson

In a place of shadows, small shadows moved.

Sunlight filtered among tumbled stone debris, where great blocks of granite lay in mountains of rubble, braced one against another where they fell. The light shone down through cracks and crevices to illuminate the smooth, damp floor of a meandering tunnel far beneath the ground. Here centuries of rainwater had scoured gullies beneath the rubble, gullies that led downward to larger, cavernous sumps below the massive foundations of a great temple.

In the dim light, shadows wound their way upward—small, furtive shadows moving in single file, moving silently . . . or nearly so.

Thump. The line of shadows slowed, became shorter as trailing shadows converged on those in front. The foremost shadow spun around and said, "Sh!"

"Somebody fall down," a voice whispered.

"Sh!" the lead shadow repeated, emphatically.

Then they were moving again. The source of the eroded gully was a V-shaped opening between squared stones, a seep where stones had settled, pulling apart from one another.

The lead shadow paused, said, "Sh!" again, and disappeared into the cleft. The others followed, into darkness

217

beyond.

Darkness, then dim light from somewhere ahead. With the light, the sounds of voices and the smells of cooking food. The light came through a narrow crack; the lead shadow stopped again. Others piled up behind, and again there were abrupt, soft sounds.

Thud. A hushed voice, "Oof!"

Another voice, "Ow! Careful!"

"Sh!"

"Somebody bump into somebody."

"Sh!"

Thump.

"Somebody fall down again."

"Shhh!"

Silence again, and the little shadows crept one by one through the crack and into a large, lamp-lit, vaulted room where ovens radiated, meat sizzled over coals, pots steamed on blazing grates, and people worked— people far larger than the shadowy little figures that darted across an open space and under a laden cutting table.

One of the tall people in the kitchen glanced around. "What was that?"

"What?" another asked.

"Did you see something just then?"

"No. What was it?"

"Nothing, I guess. Take a look at those loaves, will you?"

A large person turned away and bent to peer into an oven. "A few more minutes. I . . . now where did *that* go?"

"What?"

"Half a duck." The voice sounded mystified, then irritated. "Come on, now. These roast ducks are for the guards' hall. Who took it?"

"I didn't, so don't glare at me. It doesn't matter. Get that tray ready. You know how the guards are when they're hungry."

"All right, but I hope nobody notices that there are only eleven and a half ducks here."

Large people came and went, and the little shadows worked their way from cover to cover, across the kitchen to a half-open pantry door in a shadowed corner. Behind them, another voice shouted, "How many loaves did you put into this oven? I think some are missing."

Through the pantry the little shadows moved, fanning out, investigating everything. Here and there, small items disappeared from shelves and benches. Past the pantry was a wide hall, dimly lit, where linen robes hung from pegs on the walls and pairs of sandals lay beneath them. Curtained cubicles lined the hall. From behind some came the sounds of rhythmic breathing and an occasional snore.

"Oh!" a voice whispered. "Pretty."

"Sh!"

Tools and implements lay on heavy-timber benches in a stone-walled workshop. As the shadows passed, a few of these items disappeared. At the far wall of the workshop, tanned and treated hides stood rolled and bound. Other hides hung on the wall, and others were stacked in piles beside large, covered vats.

A shadow paused near a big elk hide, freshly cured. "Pretty," a whisper said. "Make nice sleeping mat."

"Gorge'll take that for hisself," another whisper noted.

"After th' fight, he will," the first said, determinedly.

Candles lighted a wide eating hall, where large men sat at long tables, wolfing down food and ale as servants carried in laden trays, took them out empty.

"Burnish and polish, scour and shine," a deep voice growled. "I'm about worn out from rubbing armor."

"Captain's orders," another grunted. "Spit and polish all the way. Big things afoot."

"Whole council's here now," a third said. "The ninth delegation just came in. Kingpriest's birthday, the clerics say."

Between ranks and rows of large legs and big feet, small shadows scurried single file beneath a row of tables. Here and there, near the edge of the tables, bits of food disappeared.

Thump.

"Sh!"

"Somebody fall down again," a faint whisper explained.

Above the table a guardsman turned to the one next to him. "What?"

"What, what?"

"Who fell down?"

"Who did *what*?"

"Never mind. I . . . ow! Keep your feet to yourself, joker!"

Beyond the feasting hall, past a crack behind a tapestry, a wide, dim room held ranked cots. Here and there were sleeping men. Suits of armor hung on wooden stands.

Shadows moved about.

"Not much here," a voice whispered. "Nice stuff, but all way too big."

"Sh!"

"Here somethin'. Hey, nice an' shiny." Metal clinked against metal.

"Sh!"

After a time, the shadows were gone, back the way they had come. Except for the ordinary sounds of the temple, now there was only silence.

* * * * *

Through ancient seeps caused by ancient rainfall, shadows moved—small, hurrying shadows laden with bulging net sacks, armloads of various things, and objects of all descriptions. The seeps widened into caverns and ahead were glows of light and the muffled sounds of voices.

Thump . . . clatter. Crash.

The line slowed. "What now?" the lead shadow demanded.

"Somebody fall down."

The shadows moved on, then stopped abruptly as a mighty roar came from somewhere—a roar like the rushing of water. A shout mingled with the sound, then stopped abruptly, only to return as a frantic echo of someone splashing and coughing.

The shadows had disappeared into hiding places. Now, as the sound subsided, they crept forth again, cautiously.

"What that?" one or more whispered.

"Who knows?" the answer came. "Gone now, though. Come on."

Again the shadows moved, hurrying toward the light. Again splashing . . .

"Stop!" the lead one ordered. "What this stuff on floor?"

"Dunno. Wasn't here before."

"Not water. What is it?"

"Smells funny. Tastes good, though. What is it?"

Slurping sounds.

"Who knows? Stop wastin' time! Let's go!"

* * * * *

The Off Day was never planned. Like most historic events in This Place during the long and lusterless reign of His Boisterousness Gorge III, Highbulp By Choice and Lord of This Place and Maybe Some of Those, the Off Day just happened.

It began innocently enough, with a question posed by the Highbulp's wife and consort, Lady Drule. The lady, accompanied by a gaggle of other female gully dwarves, had just returned from an expedition into the Halls of the Talls, in search of something—some said it was roast rice and stew bones, which could sometimes be scrounged from the kitchens when the Talls were distracted; some said it was feathers; some said nice, juicy mice; and most simply didn't remember what it was.

Some things—as far as the Aghar were concerned—were worth remembering, and some were not. Reasons for actions already taken rarely qualified as worth remembering. It was the excursion itself that mattered.

Lady Drule and others had gone as far into the halls as they dared—through middens and pantries, rooms and shops, through a dining place where Talls were having a meal and talking about someone's birthday, and into interesting places where there were cots, personal effects cabinets, and various things just lying about.

The Aghar ladies, instinctively adept at scurrying through half-open doors and under tables, at hiding in shadows and creeping unobserved among the ranked feet of larger species, had quite a successful expedition, by gully dwarf standards. Most of them returned before nightfall—whether all of them returned was not known, because none of them knew for sure how many had gone in the first place—and the treasures they brought back to This Place were a source of great excitement for at least several minutes.

There were two clay pots with morsels of food in them; an assortment of gnawed bones; an ornamented sandal far too large for the foot of any Aghar; two white linen robes, each of which would make marvelous clothing for eight or ten Aghar; a keg nearly half full of Tall ale; half a roast duck; a mirror; a footman's pike three times as long as the height of Gorge III himself; two loaves of bread; a heavy maul; a potato; fourteen feet of twine; a chisel; a Tall warrior codpiece, which would make an excellent tureen for stew; and a complete dressed elk hide, with skull-pan and antlers attached.

This final treasure so delighted Gorge III that he claimed it as his own . . . after the scuffle.

Tossing aside his rat-tooth crown, Gorge pulled the elk hide over his shoulders, squirmed about beneath it for a bit, then emerged with the skull-pan on his head, huge antlers jutting above him. The remainder of the hide trailed far behind as he moved.

Never in his life had he felt so regal. He strutted around in a circle, demanding, "See! All look! Highbulp impres . . . pres . . . lookin' good!"

He was so insistent on showing off that a crowd gathered around him, elbowing aside Lady Drule and the others who had actually acquired the treasure. Murmurs of "See Highbulp," "Mighty Gorge," and "Who th' clown in th' elk suit?" arose among them.

"All kneel!" Gorge demanded regally. "Make obei . . . obe . . . make bow to Great Highbulp."

A few of his subjects dropped to their knees obediently, though most had lost interest and wandered away by then. Some of those behind him, kneeling on the trailing length of the elk hide, discovered that it was a very comfortable mat. Two or three promptly lay down upon it and went to sleep.

"Pretty good," Gorge nodded, satisfied at the attention he was receiving in his regal new garb. Then, "Uh-oh!" The weight of the great antlers above him tipped forward, off balance. The nod became a bow, the bow a cant, and with a tremendous clatter of antlers and oaths, the Highbulp fell on his face, buried completely beneath the great hide.

The opportunity was too much for some of his loyal subjects. Noticing those already asleep on its rearward expanse, others now crawled aboard and curled up for their naps.

With the hide thoroughly weighted down by sleeping gully dwarves, it was all that Gorge could do to crawl out from under it.

His wrath abated somewhat when a sturdy young Aghar came running from somewhere, shouting at the top of his lungs, and skidded to a halt before him. The youth was soaking wet and stained from head to toe—a deep, purplish red.

"Highbulp!" the newcomer gasped, panting for breath. "News from royal mine!"

"You from mine?" Gorge squinted at him. "What is mine?"

"Yes, Highbulp." The red-stained one grinned. "I Skitt. Work in royal mine."

"Fine." Gorge thought a minute. "What is work?" Shrugging, he turned away, trying to recall what had so irritated him just a moment before. Peering around, he walked into a splay of elk antlers and found himself thoroughly tangled.

Lady Drule hurried forward, shaking her head. "Highbulp clumsy oaf," she muttered, and began extricating her lord and husband from his dilemma.

"Highbulp listen!" the red-dripping miner insisted. "News from mine!"

Gorge was in no mood to listen, but Drule turned to the newcomer. "What news?" she asked.

"What?"

"News! News from mine! What news?"

"Oh." Skitt collected his thoughts, then stood as tall as a person less than four feet in stature can stand. "Hit pay dirt," he said. "Mother load. Real gusher."

"Pay dirt?" Gorge was interested now. "What pay dirt? Mud? Clay? Pyr . . . pyr . . . pretty rocks? What?"

"Wine," Skitt said.

Gorge blinked. "Wine?"

"Wine," Skitt repeated, proudly. "Highbulp got royal wine mine, real douser."

Drule finished the untangling of His Testiness from the elk antler trap, then strode to where Skitt stood and moved around him, sniffing. "Wine," she said. "From mine?"

"Whole mine full of wine," he gabbled. "Musta hit a main vein."

Drule stood in thought for a moment, then turned to the Highbulp. "What we do with wine?"

"Drink it," Gorge said decisively. "All get intox . . .

intox . . . inneb . . . get roarin' drunk."

"Dumb idea, Highbulp," a wheezy voice said. A tiny, stooped figure, leaning on a mop handle, came out of the shadows. It was old Hunch, Grand Notioner of This Place and Chief Advisor to the Highbulp in Matters Requiring Serious Thought.

"Drinkin' main-vein mine-wine not dumb, Hunch," the Highbulp roared. "Good idea! Got it myself!"

"Sure," Hunch wheezed. "Drink it all, then what? We all wind up with sore heads an' nothin' to show for it. 'Stead of drink it, trade it. Get rich."

"Trade to who?"

"Talls. Plenty of Talls pay good for wine. I say make trade. Get rich better than get drunk."

Drule found herself thoroughly taken with the idea of becoming rich. Visions of finery danced in her head— strings of beads, unending supplies of stew meat, matching shoes . . . a comb. "Hunch right, Gorge," she said. "Let's get rich."

Outreasoned and outmaneuvered, the great Highbulp turned away, grumbling, and began reclaiming his elk hide by kicking sleeping Aghar in all directions.

"Calls for celebration," Drule decided.

Hunch had wandered away, and the only one remaining to discuss such matters with her was the wine-stained mine worker. Skitt stood where he had been, not really paying much attention, because he had caught sight of the lovely Lotta, a pretty young Aghar female quite capable of making any young Aghar male forget the subject at hand.

Still, he heard the queen's statement and glanced her way. "What does?" he asked.

"What does what?"

"Call for celebration. What does?"

"Ah . . ." Lady Drule squinted, trying to remember. *Something* certainly called for celebration. But she had lost track of what it was. Like any true Aghar, Drule had a remarkable memory for things seen, and sometimes for things heard, but only a brief and limited memory for ideas and concepts. The reasoning of her kind was simple: Anything seen was worth remembering, but not much else was, usually. Ideas seldom needed to be remembered. If one lost an idea, one could usually come up with another. She had an idea now. Turning, she shouted, "Gorge!"

A short distance away, the Highbulp kicked another sleeping subject off his elk hide, then paused and looked around. "Yes, dear?"

It was then that Lady Drule asked the question that led ultimately to that most historic of episodes in the legends of the Aghar of This Place: the Off Day. The question came from a simple recollection of something she had heard in the Halls of the Talls, during her forage expedition with other ladies of the court.

"Gorge," she asked, "when your birthday?"

*   *   *   *   *

It was the acolyte Pitkin who discovered that Vat Nine had been drained of its blessed contents—drained down to the murky dregs, which were beginning to dry and crust over. At first, he simply could not believe it. Making the sign of the triad, he closed the sampler port and backed away, pale and shaking, reciting litanies in a whisper.

"I have been beguiled," he told himself. "It is only an illusion. The vat is not empty. The vat is full."

Murmuring, he knelt on the stone floor of the great cellar and did obeisance to all the gods of good, waiting while his prayers eased the tensions within him, letting the light of goodness and wisdom flood his soul. Still shaken then, but feeling somewhat reassured, he climbed the stone steps to the catwalk and returned to the sample port of Vat Nine. With hands that shook only slightly, he unlocked it again, muttered one further litany, and opened the lid.

The vat was empty. Candlelight flooded its dark interior, illuminating the draft marks at intervals on the inner wall. A dozen feet below, shadowy in the reeking murk, drying dregs lay crusting, inches below the lowest draft mark. Pitkin's pale face went ashen. The vat could not be empty. It was not possible. Yet, there was no wine within.

Easing the sampler lid down again, he locked it and stared around the cavernous vault. From where he stood, on the catwalk, the great vats receded into shadows in the distance. Nine in all, only their upper portions extended above the hewn stone of their nestling cradles. Each of them was many times the size of Pitkin's sleeping cell four levels up in the Temple of the Kingpriest. The huge flattop vats seemed a row of ranked monoliths of seasoned hardwood, their walls as thick as the length of his foot. Each one nestling into a cavity of solid stone, the vats were like everything else in this, the greatest structure of Istar, the center of the world. They were the finest of their kind . . . anywhere.

The wines they held were blessed by the Kingpriest himself. Not personally, of course, but in spirit, in somber ceremonies performed by lesser clerics on behalf of His Radiance. For two and a half centuries the wines had been blessed. Every Kingpriest since the completion of the temple, at every harvest of the vines, had blessed the wines of the nine vats.

Symbolic of the nine realms of the Triple Triad—the three provinces ruled directly by Istar, the three covenant states of Solamnia, and the Border States of Taol, Ismin and Gather—the wines were part of the holy wealth. The best of vintage, produced entirely by human hands and made pure by the blessings of the sun, these were the wines of the nine vats.

The wines that were *supposed* to be in the vats, Pitkin corrected his thought. The wines that vats number one through eight did indeed hold—Pitkin had inspected them himself, as he did every morning—and that Vat

Nine somehow did not.

His mind tumbled and churned in confusion. How could Vat Nine be empty? No vat was ever empty. These were no table wines. Readily available elven wines were used for routine. No, these wines were sacred, used only on rare occasions and only in ceremonial amounts. What was used was replenished by the stewards at regular intervals—always by the finest of human vintage from each of the nine realms.

Made of sealed hardwood, cradled in solid rock, no vat had ever leaked so much as a drop of precious fluid. And there was no way to remove any wine from any vat except by unlocking the sampler port. And only he had the keys. Pitkin wanted to cry.

Slowly, on shaking legs, he made his way to the sealed portal of the cellar vault. A hundred thoughts besieged him—approaches to explaining what he had found, to formulating apologies for such an unthinkable disappearance, to the wording of a plea for clemency—but none had any merit.

There was only one thing for him to do. He must simply report the disappearance of Vat Nine's wine and pray for the best.

* * * * *

"Wizardry," the second warder muttered, staring into the empty vat. "Evil and chaos. Mage-craft. Spells."

"Mischief of some sort," the high warder agreed, "but . . . wizardry? Within the very temple itself? How could that be? There certainly are no mages here . . . save one, of course, but he is sanctioned by the Kingpriest himself. The Dark One would use no such mischievous spells. All the other wizards are gone—driven to far Wayreth. All of Istar has been cleansed of their foul kind."

"Then how can you explain this?" a senior cleric from the maintenance section insisted. "An entire vat of wine—four hundred and, ah, eighty-three barrels' count, by yesterday's inventory—it certainly didn't get up and walk out by itself, and there has been no cartage below the third level for the past week, not even porters."

"Thieves?" a junior cleric suggested, then turned pink and looked away as scathing glances fell upon him. It was well known that the Temple of the Kingpriest was inviolate. In all of Istar, in all of Ansalon, there was no edifice more theftproof.

"Only dregs," the second warder muttered, still staring into the drained vat. He prodded downward with a long testing rod. Its thump as it tapped the bottom of the vat was muted. "Waist-deep, drying dregs. How could this have happened, unless . . ." He lowered his voice. "Unless by magic? Dark and infidel magic."

From below the catwalk a curious voice asked, "Brother Susten, are you aware that you are wearing only one sandal?"

"I can't find the other one," the chief warder snapped. "Please concentrate on the matter at hand, Brother Glisten. This is no time to count sandals."

Far in the distance, beyond the vault doors, a loud, exasperated voice roared, "I'm tired of this game, you bubbleheads! I want to know who took it! Now!"

Heads turned in surprise. Several clerics hurried away toward the sound, then returned, shaking their heads. "It's nothing, Eminence," one of them said to the chief warder. "A captain of temple guards. He, too, has lost some part of his attire, it seems."

Again the irritated voice rose in the distance, "This has gone far enough! What pervert took my codpiece?"

"Gone," the second warder muttered, staring into the emptiness of Vat Nine as though mesmerized. "All that wine, just . . . just gone."

* * * * *

"Sorcery?" The keeper of portals rasped, staring in disbelief at the assembled clerics before him. "Magic? Don't be ridiculous. This is the Temple of the Kingpriest. Mage-craft is not allowed here, as all of you very well know!"

"Our accumulated pardons, Eminence," the chief warder said, shifting his weight from sandaled foot to bare foot and back, "but we have given this matter the most serious of study, and we can arrive at no other explanation."

The keeper of portals glared at them in silence for a long moment, then spread his flowing robes and seated himself behind his study table. He sighed. "All right, we shall review it once again. One: Even if magic were somehow introduced into the temple—and what mage would dare such a thing?—what purpose would be served by draining a vat of blessed wine?"

"Evil," someone said. "The purposes of evil, obviously."

"Two: His Blessed Radiance, the Kingpriest himself, oversaw the evacuation of the Tower of High Sorcery in Istar. Every last mage and artifact was removed, and every magic-user of any degree driven away—not just from Istar but from the nine realms. The tower is empty, and its seals are intact."

"Dire evils have their way," someone said.

"There is the . . . Dark One," someone else whispered, then blushed and lowered his head, wishing he had not spoken.

"Three." The keeper of portals continued grimly, pretending not to have heard. "It is patently impossible for that wine to have disappeared—" He stopped, scowled, and blinked.

"—by any device other than sorcery," the chief warder finished softly, trying to look pious rather than victorious.

* * * * *

"Wizardry?" the master of scrolls whispered, shaking his head. White hair as soft as spidersilk trembled with the motion. Here in the shadows of his deepest sanctuary, where few beside the keeper of portals—and of course the Kingpriest himself—ever saw him, he seemed a very old man. Very different from the dignified and reverent presence who sat at the foot of the throne when the Kingpriest gave audience in the sanctuary of light.

Again the master shook his head, seeming very frail and sad as long as one did not look into his eyes. "After all these years . . . evil still confronts us in Istar."

"There is no other answer, August One," the keeper of portals said, sympathetically. For more seasons than most men had lived, the master of scrolls—next to the Kingpriest himself, the very epitome of all that was good and holy—had born upon his frail shoulders the weight of righteousness in a world far too receptive to wrong. Now he looked as though he might break down and weep . . . until he raised his eyes.

"Evil," the old man whispered. "After all we have done, still it rears its vile head. Do you know, Brother Sopin—but of course you do—that my illustrious predecessor, my own venerated father, died of a broken heart, realizing that even his strenuous efforts as advisor to His Radiance had not stamped out evil forever. He truly believed that such had been done, first with the Proclamation of Manifest Virtue, and subsequently by sanctioning the extermination of evil races everywhere. He believed, for a time, that we had succeeded, just as the third Kingpriest and his advisors believed that *they* had stamped out evil for good the day this temple was blessed in the names of all the gods—of good, of course," he added as an afterthought.

The master of scrolls raised rheumy old eyes—they seemed so at first glance—to gaze at his visitor. "He once even believed the tenet of the first Kingpriest, that by bonding the might of Solamnia with the spiritual guidance of Istar, the forces of evil could be driven from the world."

"It is regrettable, August One," the keeper said sorrowfully.

"Yes. Regrettable. I have said it before, good Sopin. Evil is an abomination. Evil is an affront to the very existence of the gods, and of men. Yet how to eliminate it, finally and forever?" His question was rhetorical. He obviously had the answer.

"Yes, August One?"

"We know now—the Kingpriest himself must know as well—that evil cannot be conquered by unifying states and building temples. Neither by driving away practitioners of chaos, nor even by eliminating evil acts and evil races . . . though that has yet to be thoroughly tested, I understand."

"Such things take time, August Brother. Even the vilest of races resist extermination. As to the practices of evil men, when they believe they will not be found out . . ."

"Time," the master of scrolls rasped, in a voice as dry as sand. "There is so little time, Sopin. This business of the wine missing, this willful and arrogant exercise of a sorcerous spell, right here in the holiest of places in this entire world . . . Don't you understand it, Sopin? Don't you see what it means?"

"Ah . . . well, it might be . . ."

"It is a challenge, Sopin. Worse, it is a taunt. Evil is gaining strength in the world, because we have yet to kill it at its source!" The rheumy eyes blazed at the keeper, and now he saw the fire in them, the eyes of a zealot.

"August Brother! Do you mean—?"

"Yes, Sopin. As has been argued before. It is time to go to the root of evil. The very minds of men."

The keeper went pale. "August Brother, you know that I agree, but is this the time for so drastic a policy? People are—"

"People are children for us to lead in the true path, Brother Sopin, at the pleasure of His Radiance, the Kingpriest." The master of scrolls gathered his robes around him, shivering. He was often cold, of late. "The Grand Council of the Revered Sons, Brother Sopin . . . I believe they are all present now, in Istar? His Radiance has received their respects."

"They are all present, Highest. Each of the nine realms has sent a delegation for tomorrow's festivity, and all the members of the council are present, though I have word today that one of the high clerics is ill. None have been able to heal him. Perhaps tomorrow—at the time of the festivity—he will be better."

"As the gods of good will," the master of scrolls agreed, then looked up again at his assistant. "Ill? Which of them is ill?"

The keeper looked agitated. "Ah . . . it is Brother Sinius, August One. The high cleric of Taol."

The master of scrolls stared at him. "Taol? The ninth realm? The one from whose realm came the disappeared wine?"

"The same."

"By the gods of ultimate good! There lies evil's perfidy, Sopin. It lulls us with subtlety until we expect all of its machinations to be subtle. Then, when we are lulled, it strikes—simple and direct. Through the blessed wine, it strikes directly at us. None can heal him, eh? I must speak of this to His Radiance himself, Sopin. Tomorrow's council of light . . . there is business to discuss."

"It is the Kingpriest's birthday, August. Is such business appropriate?"

"The council is present, Brother Keeper, and so is the evil. Leave me now, Brother. I must prepare a petition. I shall suggest an edict—the same that I have submitted so many times before. But His Radiance must consider it, Brother Sopin. Beyond that, it must have the sanction of the Grand Council of Revered Sons."

"Yes, August One." Sopin felt a chill rise up his back. The Kingpriest require the sanction of council? Only one order of business could explain that. The master of scrolls meant to propose the opening of the Scroll of the

Ancients.

It was the one artifact in the keeping of the priesthood that the first Kingpriest had so feared that it was sealed by a spell. It could be opened, but only by separate, secret incantations recited in unison by all the members of the Grand Council of Revered Sons.

The knowledge contained in the Scroll of the Ancients was a power that the first Kingpriest had found so fearsome that he trusted no man with it—not even himself, or any of his successors. The Scroll of the Ancients, it was said, contained the secret of mind reading. With its power, one could enter and adjudge—possibly even control—the minds of others.

Never in the history of Istar had the scroll been opened. Never had the high council agreed to it, though it had been proposed many times. Among the nine there were always those—notably those of the Solamnic Knighthood—who argued that the altering of free will was an abomination. And usually there were some—generally the elves—who worried that the gods themselves might not condone such a thing. It could, they pointed out, destroy the very balance upon which the universe relied.

Certainly the neutral gods would be outraged, for free will was sacred to them. Even the gods of good and light, some whispered, might consider the exercise of mind control as an arrogance.

The keeper of portals shivered again, realizing that the scrollmaster was looking directly at him now. In those eyes there was no touch of age, no frailty, no question of purpose. The ancient eyes blazed with a zeal as bright as fire and as cold as ice.

"The gods of good rely upon us, Sopin," the old one said. "They entrust us and empower us. We *must* not fail them again. The source of evil lies in the minds of men. It is there that we must stamp it out."

*   *   *   *   *

The great Highbulp Gorge III, leader of all the Aghar of This Place and Maybe Some of Those, was stumped by Lady Drule's question. He hadn't the vaguest idea when his birthday might be—wasn't altogether sure what a birthday was—and had far more important things to occupy his mind . . . if he could remember what they were.

One of them, of course, was the wine mine. Gorge wasn't at all certain, but he suspected that wine was an unusual commodity for mining. Then again, the world was full of mysteries and it was usually best not to dwell on them.

He didn't even know where the mine was, exactly. The combined clans of Bulp always had a mine going somewhere (generally near the town dump), on the off chance of finding something useful, but the mine's location shifted as often as the location of This Place did.

This Place was portable, which served the gully dwarves' purposes. Years of abuse and misuse by other races had built certain instincts into the Aghar, and one was to not stay in any place long enough to be discovered. This week, This Place was here. A week or two ago, This Place had been someplace else, and a week or two hence, This Place might be in some other place entirely. This Place was wherever the Highbulp said This Place was.

Gorge didn't remember exactly why his tribe had left the previous This Place—past decisions based upon past circumstances were seldom worth remembering—but he was proud of his selection of the current This Place. A natural cavern in a limestone formation, its outside entrance was concealed by huge mounds of rubble left by the Talls who built the giant structures soaring above. This Place extended deep beneath the fortress parapets of the great temple of Istar and was joined by ancient, eroded seeps to the pantries of the great structure.

It was a fine place for This Place, and the fact that it had been discovered by accident—several gully dwarves had fallen into it, literally—was not worth remembering. To Gorge III, it was simply one more evidence of his personal genius as Highbulp, on a par with other accomplishments such as . . . Well, whatever they were, he knew there had been any number of them.

Probably the only actual act of genius the leader of the Aghar of This Place had ever managed was to proclaim himself Gorge III instead of simply Gorge. The enumeration had the desirable effect of keeping his subjects thoroughly confused—an accomplishment that all leaders of all nations and all races might envy. Few among the Aghar could count to two, and none could count as high as three. Thus, there was always a certain awe among them when they addressed their lord as Gorge III.

Simply by virtue of his name, they were never quite sure who—or what—he was. That alone eliminated any possibility of competition for his job.

Deciding to be Gorge III had been an inspiration. Now, many years later, the Highbulp sensed another inspiration coming on. He didn't know what it was, but its symptoms were not quite the same as indigestion and it had something to do with the way he felt when he put on his new elk hide with its enormous antlers. Somehow, the improbable attire made him feel like a Highbulp of Destiny.

So, when his beloved consort—what's-her-name— suggested a celebration in honor of his birthday, Gorge readily agreed and promptly forgot the entire matter. He was far more interested in strutting around in his elk hide and feeling important than in planning formalities.

Drule, on the other hand, had no such preoccupation.

"Hunch!" She summoned the grand notioner. "We celebrate Highbulp's birthday!"

"Fine," the ancient said, starting to doze off.

"Hunch!" she demanded. "Pay attention!"

He woke up, looking cranky. "To what?"

"Highbulp's birthday! Celebrate!"

"Why?"

That stumped Lady Drule for a moment, then she countered, "Highbulp say so."

Hunch sighed. "All right. When Highbulp's birthday?"

"Tomorrow," she decided. Other than today and yesterday, it was the only day that came to mind. And the Highbulp certainly had not been born yesterday. "Make plan."

"What plan?"

"Who knows? Ask Highbulp."

The conversation was interrupted by a clatter and a flood of oaths. The great Highbulp, trying to wear elk antlers atop his head, had fallen on his back.

The grand notioner approached and stood over his liege, poking at him with the mop-handle staff. "Highbulp. What you want to do tomorrow?"

"Nothing," Gorge grunted, getting to his feet. "Go 'way."

With his answer, the grand notioner returned to Lady Drule. "Highbulp say for celebrate, all go 'way, do nothing."

It was not exactly what Drule had in mind, but she was busy with other matters by then. Some of the court ladies were bickering over the new stew tureen, and it was obvious to Lady Drule that they should have more than one tureen. An entire table setting might be nice.

Hunch frowned and repeated the Highbulp's order. "For celebrate, all go 'way, do nothing," he said.

Drule glanced around. "No work? Nothing?"

"Nothing."

"Off day, then." She nodded. "Tell everybody, tomorrow is Off Day."

Skitt, the miner, was one of the first to hear the news, and helped to spread word of it. "Tomorrow Off Day," he told everyone he could find. "Highbulp's orders."

"What is Off Day?" someone asked him. "What we supposed to do on Off Day?"

"What we do on Off Day?" someone else asked.

237

Skitt had no answer. He hadn't heard the details. For his own part, though, he intended to go to work.

Among the spoils of the ladies' foray, he had found a reaver's maul and a chisel. Skitt might have been only a gully dwarf, but he *was* a dwarf. The use of tools was strong in his simple soul. He couldn't wait to see what he might do with a reaver's maul and chisel in a wine mine.

Thus it was that on one fateful day, two birthdays were celebrated—one above, in the Temple of the Kingpriest in the city of Istar, seat of clerical power and center by proclamation of all the world, and one below.

* * * * *

The high cleric of Taol had been under the weather, owing to a pardonable excess of elven spirits used to counter the grueling effects of a long and arduous journey to Istar. But when it was announced that the pious festivity of the new day would be preceded by a petitioned meeting of the grand council, his health improved markedly. One did not send regrets when the Kingpriest summoned the grand council.

Thus all nine of the Most Revered Sons—the high clerics of the nine realms—were in attendance in the Hall of Audience when the panels of glowing stone were rolled back to flood the chamber with glorious light, light that seemed to emanate from the throne revealed there, and from the person who sat upon it.

None of them would remember afterward exactly what the Kingpriest looked like. No one ever did. There was always only the lingering impression of immense good, flowing upon waves of light.

In the entire great chamber, there was only one small corner where shadows lurked, a niche among the great floral carvings that rose from the radiant floor. To one who might notice such things—and few did, in the presence of His Radiance—it seemed only a slight anomaly in the magnificent architecture, an inadvertent cleft where the light was blotted out. But to Sopin, who lived daily in the sanctums of the temple, the corner was a source of dread. He glanced that way and thought he saw movement there, among the shadows. He could not be sure, but it seemed that the Dark One was present.

Sopin shivered and turned his eyes away, letting his troubled thoughts evaporate in the brilliance of the light from the throne of the Kingpriest.

There were the prayers and the rituals, the lavishing of appropriate unction toward each of the good gods of the universe, and then it began. "Revered Sons." The voice that came from the source of light was as warm and comforting as the light itself, as resonant as the rays of the sun. "Our beloved brother, the master of scrolls, has petitioned for audience, as is his right. He proposes an edict, one which has been considered before, and one which would require your sanction."

Sopin settled himself into his cubicle, ready for a long and learned debate. He had heard it all before, and now he would hear it again, and he wondered if the outcome would be any different.

Never had he seen the master of scrolls so determined, though, and he wondered if it were possible that evil itself might provoke its own final demise.

Time would tell.

* * * * *

Skitt had about given up on replenishing the source of the wine, which had run dry after an hour's flow. A large part of the cavern of This Place was now waist-deep in wine, but no more had come lately from the pay dirt vein. When he finally managed to widen the vein enough to squeeze through—it struck him as slightly odd that the tunnel had started in stone and ended in wood—he found beyond a sticky, reeking mass of pulp. His maul and chisel had little effect on the mess and, in fact, he very nearly lost them.

He had almost decided that the gusher was no more than a pocket with a dry hole beyond, when splashing sounds behind him caught his attention and he backed from the tunnel to see what was going on. Across a small lake of spilled wine, Lady Drule and a sizable entourage of other Aghar females had launched a makeshift raft and were poling themselves toward the dark seeps that led to the Halls of the Talls. Many of them carried empty sacks and bits of net.

Skitt waved at them from the mine entrance.

Some of them waved back, and Lady Drule called, "Why you here on Off Day, Skatt?"

"Skitt," he corrected.

"Skitt, then," she said. "Why?"

"Dunno," he admitted. "Somebody give me that name, I guess. Where ladies go?"

"Need more stew bowls," she called back. "Lady Grund remember where they are. Place where Tall guards stack metal clothes."

"Have nice day." Skitt waved again.

"Off Day."

"What?"

"Skatt supposed to say, 'Have nice Off Day.' This Off Day, remember?"

"Oh." Skitt waved again. The raft was past him now and approaching the ledge where the seeps began. Having nothing better to do, Skitt went back into his tunnel, took a deep breath, and plunged into the wall of sticky stuff. It had occurred to him that somewhere beyond there might be more wood or rock—something that he could cut with his chisel.

* * * * *

Gorge III was feeling grumpy. He glared around in the dimness of the central cavern, seeing only a few of his subjects here and there, all of them ignoring him. Everybody, it seemed, had decided to take the day off. Nobody was arguing, nobody was scurrying about bumping into one another, and worst of all, nobody was paying him any attention. He was surly and miffed, but he didn't know quite what to do about it.

"This insubor . . . insub . . . in . . . this no fun," he grumbled, and nobody seemed to care.

Even old Hunch was no help. The grand notioner simply had shrugged and said, "This Off Day, Highbulp. Nobody got to do anything on Off Day. Not even put up with Highbulp. Me, too." And with that he had turned his back and wandered off.

For a time, the Highbulp fumed and stamped around. When that gained him no attention, he got his elk hide, pulled it around him with the great antlers jutting upward atop his head, and sat down to sulk.

As usual, when Gorge III set out to sulk, he went to sleep. His eyelids drooped, he yawned, the great antlers teetered and swayed above him, then tipped forward, held upright only by the elk hide on which he was sitting. His mind drifted off into muddy visions of hot stew, cold lizard, stolen ale, and comfortable confusion.

* * * * *

It seemed that Gorge III was alone in the cavern of This Place. It seemed that the cavern had grown darker, and that there was no one anywhere except himself. Or maybe there was someone else, but he couldn't see who it was.

"So *this* is the answer," said a soft voice. Gorge couldn't remember the question.

"Poor Highbulp," the voice whispered. "Gets no respect."

"Right," Gorge tried to say, but it didn't seem worth the effort.

The voice soothed him, weaving its slow way through drifting dreams. "Need to do something special to get respect," it said. "Something grand and glorious. Something great."

"Sure," he thought about saying. "That nothin' new. Highbulp glorious all the time."

"But *special*," the voice purred. "Need to do something special."

"Like what?" the Highbulp considered asking.

"Move," the voice suggested.

"Don't want to," Gorge might have said. "Just got here."

"Oh, but a big move," the voice insisted. "A migration, Highbulp, a great, grand, glorious migration. Lead your people to the Promised Place."

"What Promised Place?"

"Far," the voice whispered. "Very, very far. A long journey, Highbulp. Destiny . . . the Highbulp of Destiny. What is the name?"

"Great . . . Gorge III . . ."

"The great Highbulp who led his people to the Promised Place . . . destiny, Highbulp. *Your destiny*."

"Des'ny," the Highbulp mused and might have whispered. "Great Highbulp. Highbulp of Desi . . . Den . . . Density."

"Destiny."

"Right. Destiny. Where this Promised Place?"

"West, Highbulp." The voice receded, became faint. "Far, far west of here. Very far away."

The voice seemed to continue, but it was no longer speaking to Gorge. It spoke only to itself. "So does the mightiest torrent," it said, "begin with a single drop of rain."

"Drip?" the Highbulp might have wondered.

"Drip," the dream voice agreed.

* * * * *

Once they had crossed the lake of wine, it wasn't far at all to where Lady Grund remembered finding the bit of Tall armor that made such a nice tureen. With Lady

Drule in the lead and Lady Grund guiding, the Aghar ladies made their cautious way through the old seeps to the lowest of the middens, through pantries and stowages, to a hole where a cracked stone had settled into eroding clay. The hole opened into a crawl space behind an ornate cabinet in a huge, vaultlike room where a hundred or more sleeping cots were ranked along the walls. Tables and benches stood in neat rows beyond them, and the open central area was a forest of wooden racks where suits of armor hung.

Dozens of the cots had human men sleeping in them, and the rack nearest each occupied cot glistened with armor.

Drule peered from behind the cabinet, listened carefully to a chorus of snores, then nodded to her followers. With a finger at her lips, she said, "Sh!"

Quietly, methodically and efficiently, the Aghar ladies crept from rack to rack, collecting burnished iron codpieces.

* * * * *

Skitt came near to drowning in pulp before he found solid matter in the wine mine. The pulp shifted and flowed around him as he pushed forward through it, threatening to swamp him. But he kept going and, after a time, bumped into something solid. A wooden wall.

" 'Bout time," he muttered, feeling the surface with his hands. It was like the other wood that had produced the first gusher. With maul and chisel, he went to work.

Beyond was solid stone, and he wondered for a moment if he had gone in a circle and was tunneling out near where he had tunneled in. He was tempted to forget the whole thing and take up rat hunting or something, when a revelation came to him.

"This Off Day," he told himself. "Off Day means don't have to do anything . . . not even quit."

Fortified by this insight, Skitt renewed his efforts,

chiseling away at the stone in reeking darkness. Beyond the stone was more wood. "Give it one more shot," he muttered, "*then* go hunt rats." In his mind, he fantasized that—if he could make a name for himself as a wine miner of note—possibly the lovely Lotta might consent to go rat hunting with him.

At least the wood was easier to chisel than the stone. It was very old, seasoned wood, and he enjoyed the shaping of it as he carved a tunnel, an inch at a time. Gradually the sound of his maul changed, becoming deeper, more reverberant with each blow, and intuition prickled at his whiskers.

"Might have somethin' here," he whispered. "Sounds like maybe pay dirt."

The maul thudded and the chisel cut, and abruptly the wood before him bulged and splintered. Skitt had only time to gulp a breath before a roaring tide engulfed him and carried him, tumbling, back the way he had come— back through the tunnel of wood, of stone, of wood; back through the mushy path of reeking pulp, through wood again, through stone and flung him outward to splash into the frothing, tossing waves of the wine lake in the cavern.

He bobbed to the surface, gasped for air, and stared at the entrance to the mine several yards away. A vast torrent of dark wine was pouring from the hole, roaring and foaming as it met the lake's rising surface.

"Wow!" Skitt gasped. "Whole 'nother gusher!"

Still clinging to his maul and chisel, Skitt bobbed and eddied on the tormented purple surface, trying to stay afloat. His head bumped something solid and he found himself looking up at a raftload of Aghar ladies carrying laden nets and sacks.

"You fall in?" one of them asked him.

"Lake's a lot bigger than before," another commented.

Lady Drule was kneeling at the raft's edge, dipping wine with an iron bowl. She sniffed at it, took a dainty sip, let it roll on her tongue for a moment, then nodded.

"Good," she decreed. "What you say this is?"

"Wine," another told her.

"Wine, huh? Pretty good."

Lady Drule bent to look at the barely floating miner. "Skatt—"

"Skitt," he corrected, blowing spume. "See any dry land?"

She looked around. "Sure. Grab on."

Skitt clung to the raft. The ladies poled for the far shore. A curious crowd of Aghar had gathered on the bank, some to see what the latest expedition had produced and some who had already been there, sampling the wine.

As the ladies waded ashore with their loot, Lady Drule remembered the miner in tow. "Get Skatt," she ordered, pointing.

"Skitt," burbled the clinging Skitt. Half-drowned and becoming more inebriated by the minute, he was having trouble keeping his head above wine. Strong, small hands reached for him, took firm hold on his ears, and lifted him until he could climb onto the raft, then steadied him as he crawled across it to the safety of dry ground.

He sprawled there and looked up into bright, concerned eyes. It was Lotta.

"Skitt all right?" she asked.

"All right." He belched. "Fulla wine, though. Hit 'nother gusher."

Several other young gully dwarves were intently aware of the attention being paid to the wine-logged miner by the fetching Lotta.

"He got somethin' goin'," one of them said.

"Got Lotta goin'," another agreed. "You know anything about mine? Or wine? Or work?"

"What's to know?" A third shrugged. "Just dig, keep diggin'. Somethin' bound to turn up."

With one final gaze at the recumbent Skitt, basking in the glow of Lotta's undivided attention, the other young

Aghar dashed away and went looking for tools. This being Off Day, and having nothing better to do, they had decided to go into the mining business.

* * * * *

The acolyte Pitkin thought that yesterday had been a bad day. Today turned out even worse. His morning duties now included the inspection of only eight vats—the ninth had been sealed the day before by the chief warder—but nagging intuition made him more and more nervous as he worked his way along the catwalk.

It couldn't happen again, could it? Not again?

Somehow he knew, even as he opened the sampler port on Vat Eight, what he would find. Nothing.

Vat Eight was empty.

* * * * *

It was a pale and shaken messenger who ran all the way from the chief warder's quarters in the lower temple to the vast upper halls with their radiant stone, to hand a sealed message to the captain of the guard outside the portals of the great hall of council. The messenger knew what was in the message. The lower levels were buzzing with gossip, and everyone, from the highest maintenance personnel to the lowest cooks and keepers, was worried.

The messenger was almost too worried to notice the odd appearance of the captain of the guard . . . but not quite. As he returned to the lower levels, he wondered why such a magnificently attired soldier would wear one piece of armor so out of keeping with all the other pieces. From polished helm to burnished braces, from fine, oiled chain to fine-worked scabbard, from gleaming gauntlets to glistening plates, every piece of his armor was perfectly matched to every other piece—with one notable exception.

That particular piece looked as though it might have been borrowed.

* * * * *

Within the grand chamber, the sealed message was passed from the clerk of entry to the clerk of the vestry, then carried silently to the clerk of the keep, who handed it across to the aide of the keeper of portals. A moment later the keeper himself rose to his feet, bowed toward the throne and approached it, kneeling at the base of its pedestal. He lowered his eyes and raised the opened message toward the light.

"Share this news," the Voice of Radiance said.

Sadly, the keeper of portals turned toward the Grand Council of Revered Sons. Holding the message at arm's length, he read to them its brief contents.

Vat Eight of the blessed wines—the vintage from the border province of Ismin—was empty, as empty as the vat from Taol, discovered only the previous day.

"Evil strikes at us," the master of scrolls said when Sopin had finished. "So subtle a taunt, yet so direct a challenge. O Most Radiant—O Most Revered Sons—we must respond."

Somewhere beyond, where shadow dimmed the radiance, a quiet voice whispered, "Destiny."

* * * * *

Within hours, at least a dozen would-be wine miners were at work in the royal mine, and more Aghar were on their way. The earliest arrivals found a sizable lake of wine in the cavern below the mine, but only a trickle coming from the mine itself. Armed with various delving tools, they entered single file and traced Skitt's route, going through a long tunnel of rock and a short tunnel of wood, through a sagging tunnel of congealed sludge to another tunnel of wood, which led again to rock, then to wood, then to a seeping mass of wet pulp. Here, dim light filtered through from above and anxious Tall voices sounded muddled, muted by the pulp.

In silence, the Aghar waited until the light and the voices faded. They heard the distant boom of a heavy port being sealed.

When all was silent, the one in the lead said, "Come on. Maybe more pockets of wine. Let's get 'em."

In single file, they trudged through the cavern of sludge, only their heads and candles rising above it, and set to work on the wooden wall beyond. After some tunneling they encountered stone, then wood again.

The caverns of This Place roared with the thunder of released wine, flowing and frothing through two empty vats, spewing outward from the mine shaft into the growing lake beyond, carrying a round dozen gully dwarves tumbling with it. Their shouts and splashes resounded as they hit the roiling, rising surface of the wine lake.

When the commotion finally died down and the drunken gully dwarves had been fished out by their peers, several dozen others picked up tools and headed for the mine. It became a contest to see how much wine could be mined and who could produce the most.

It also was an interesting way to spend Off Day—as good a way as any, since nobody was sure what Off Day was all about, anyway.

* * * * *

By the time the glorious radiances of the grand chamber began to soften, to take on the pastels of evening, a visitor might have thought that the Temple of the Kingpriest at Istar—the most awesome piece of architecture in the entire world—was in a state of siege.

In the upper reaches, white-faced clerics and ashen functionaries rushed here and there, carrying messages, pausing for fervent prayer, gathering in clumps and clusters to whisper among themselves. In the lower levels, daily routine was a shambles. Warders and coding clerks came and went from the wine vaults. A general, emergency inventory had been ordered, an audit of every artifact, every store and every commodity.

And to top everything else off, half a company of temple guards on the noon-to-night shift refused to leave their quarters.

In the evening hours, the final holdouts on the Grand Council of Revered Sons conceded. There was no reasonable explanation for what was happening within the temple, but things were becoming worse by the minute.

There would be no decision reached today regarding the unleashing of the power of the Scroll of the Ancients. Nor would such a matter be decided tomorrow, or even next week. But the zeal of the master of scrolls was having its effect upon the Revered Sons, assisted by the air of chaos in the temple.

It was only a matter of time before the Kingpriest himself conceded that the ultimate power was needed in the battle against evil. Thanks to the master of scrolls, when the power was called for, the council would sanction it.

"Destiny," the whisper in the shadows said again. But in the entire chamber, only the keeper of portals heard it. Intuition told him that it meant something, but reason could not define it.

"Drip." The Dark One in the shadows laughed.

Far beyond the temple, in the skies over Istar, thunder rolled.

*   *   *   *   *

In filtering light of dusk, Gorge III, Highbulp by Choice and Lord of This Place and Maybe a Lot of Others, glared at his subjects crowded around him. It wasn't his presence that had drawn them, as much as that this part of This Place was the only high ground left in This Place, and even here they were ankle-deep in wine.

His elk antlers towering over him and all the rest, the Highbulp muttered every curse he knew . . . which at the moment was two or three. "This abomin . . . abom . . . this no good!" he roared, his voice echoing through the cavern. "Too much wine! Wine all over everything!"

"Should'a traded it off when you had the chance, Highbulp," old Hunch snapped. "Prob'ly too late now."

"This place lousy place for This Place." The Highbulp snorted. "Inoccup . . . unoccu . . . not worth livin' in."

Most everyone else had watched the wine rising through the day, but it had come as a nasty surprise to Gorge III. After sulking for part of the morning, he had slept the rest of the day and it hadn't occurred to anyone to wake him. He had awakened only when he had rolled over and gotten wine up his nose.

Now he came to a decision. "Time to leave," he announced. "All pack up. Let's go."

No one moved. Some simply stared at him, others hadn't heard him at all.

"Matter with you?" he roared. "Highbulp say pack up! So pack up!"

"Don't have to," someone near him sneered. "Don't have to do anything. This Off Day."

"Who says?"

"Highbulp's orders," someone else explained.

"Happy birthday, Highbulp," another said, wiping wine-muddied feet on his lord's trailing elk hide cloak.

"Maybe Highbulp have some stew?" Lady Drule suggested. "Got real nice set of stew dishes . . ."

" 'Nough!" the Highbulp bellowed. "Off Day through! All over! Off Day off! Pack up!"

Status quo restored, everyone scattered obediently to do his bidding. Everywhere in This Place, gully dwarves scurried about, splashing through various depths of wine, stumbling over one another, packing up to leave. When the Highbulp said this place was no longer This Place, it was time to head for another place.

"Where we go this time, Highbulp?" Lady Drule

asked, stacking codpieces. "'Cross town, maybe? Better neighborhood?"

When he didn't respond, she glanced around at him. He was standing very still, gazing off into nothingness, his elk antlers towering above him.

"Highbulp?" Drule said.

"Drip," he whispered, seeming puzzled.

Drule stared. "What?"

"Dest . . . des . . . destiny," he murmured. "Highbulp of Destiny. How 'bout that!"

"Highbulp!" Drule prodded him with a stick.

He turned. "Yes, dear?"

"Where we go from here?"

"West," he said, his eyes aglow. "Great migra . . . mig . . . big move. Long way."

Something in him said that, as of this day, nothing in the world would ever be quite the same again. Destiny was in motion and nothing now could alter it. He didn't know how he knew that, but he did. Without the words or the concepts to voice it, Gorge III had a feeling that the history of the entire world had just begun.

"Destiny," he said, for anyone who wanted to hear.

The Silken Threads

Margaret Weis and Tracy Hickman

Part I

The Tower of High Sorcery at Wayreth is, at the best of times—such as now, with the war's end—difficult to find. Guided by the powerful wizards of the Conclave, the tower roams its enchanted forest, the wildest of the wild creatures within its boundaries. One often sees young mages standing, hovering, on the outskirts of Wayreth Forest, their breath coming fast, their skin pale, their hands nervously clenching. They stand hesitating on the outskirts of their destiny. If they are bold and enter, the forest will permit them. The tower will find them. Their fate will be determined.

That is now. But then, long ago, before the Cataclysm, few found the Tower of High Sorcery at Wayreth. It prowled the forest only in the shadows of night, hiding from the light of day. Wary of interlopers, the tower watched all who ventured within (and there were few) with restive, suspicious eyes, prepared to pounce and destroy.

In the days right before the Cataclysm, the wizards of Ansalon were reviled and persecuted, their lives forfeit to the holy zeal of the Kingpriest of Istar, who feared their power, claimed it was not spiritual in nature.

And he was right to fear them. Long and bitter were the arguments within the Conclave, the governing body of magic-users. The wizards could fight back, but in so doing, they were afraid they would destroy the world. No, they reasoned, it was better to withdraw, hide in the blessed shadows of their magic, and wait.

Wait.

* * * * *

It was Yule, a strange Yule, the hottest Yule anyone in Ansalon could remember. Now we know the heat was the wrath of the gods, beating down upon an unhallowed world. The people thought it was merely an odd phenomenon; some blamed it on the gnomes.

On one particular night, the wind was still, as if the world had ceased to breathe. Sparks jumped from the black fur of the cat to the black robe of its master. The smell of doom was in the air, like the smell of thunder. On that night, a man entered Wayreth Forest and began to walk, with unerring step, toward the Tower of High Sorcery.

No enchantment stopped him. The trees that would attack any other intruder shrank back, bowed low in reverent homage. The birds hushed their teasing songs. The fierce predator slunk furtively away. The man ignored it all, said no word, did not pause. Arriving at the tower, he passed through the rune-covered walls as if they did not exist, alerted no guard, roused no one's interest. He walked unhindered across the courtyard.

Several white-and red-robed wizards walked here, discussing, in low voices, the troubles afflicting the outside world. The man strolled up to them, pushed his way between them. They did not see him.

He entered the tower and began to climb the stairs that led to the large rooms at the very top. Guest rooms and rooms for apprentice mages were located at the bottom. These were empty this night. No guests had been permitted in the tower for a long, long time. No apprentices studied the arcane art. It was far too dangerous. Many apprentices had paid for their devotion with their lives.

The rooms at the top of the tower were inhabited by the most powerful wizards, the members of the Conclave. Seven black-robed mages ruled the evil magic of night, seven white-robed mages ruled the good magic of day, and seven red-robed mages ruled the in-between magic of twilight. The man went straight to one room, located at the very top of the tower, and entered.

The room was elegantly furnished, neat, and ordered, for the wizard was rigid in his habits. Spellbooks, bound in black, were arranged in alphabetical order. Each stood in its correct place on the bookshelves, and each was dusted daily. Scrolls, in their polished cases, glistened in honeycomb compartments. Magical items—rings and wands and such—were stowed away in black-lacquered boxes, every one labeled clearly as to its contents.

The wizard sat at work at a desk of ebony, its finish reflecting the warm yellow glow of an oil lamp suspended from the ceiling above his head. He was at work upon a scroll, his brow furrowed with concentration, his lips silently forming the magical words his pen, dipped in lamb's blood, traced upon the parchment. He did not hear his guest's arrival.

The doors to the wizards' rooms in the tower have no locks upon them. Every wizard is respectful of another's privacy, respectful of personal possessions. Thus the visitor could enter unimpeded, had no need to wait until a bolt was thrown, a lock unlocked—not that there existed any lock that could have stopped him. He stood on the threshold, gazing at the wizard in silence, waiting, respectfully, until the mage completed his work upon the scroll.

At last the wizard sighed, passed a hand that trembled from the reaction to his concentrated effort through his long, iron-gray hair, and lifted his head. His eyes widened; his hand sank nervelessly to the tabletop. He stared, then blinked, thinking the apparition might vanish.

It did not. The man, clad all in black, from the satin-lined cowl to the velvet hem that trailed the stone floor, remained standing in the doorway.

The wizard rose, slowly, to his feet.

"Approach, Akar," said the man in the doorway.

The wizard did so, limbs weak, heart fluttering, though Akar had never before known fear of anything on Krynn. He was in his forties, tall and well built. The iron-gray hair, long and luxuriant, framed a face tight-lipped, resolute, unforgiving, unyielding. He went down on his knees awkwardly; never in his life had Akar bowed to any man.

"Master," he said humbly, spreading wide his hands to indicate he was open to receive any command, obey any summons. He kept his head lowered, did not look up. He tried to, but his heart failed him. "I am honored."

The man standing before him made a gentle motion with his hand and the door shut behind him. Another motion, a whispered word, and the door disappeared. A solid wall stood in its place. The wizard saw this obliquely, out of the corner of his eye, and a chill shook him. The two were locked in this room together, with no way out, except death.

"Akar," said the man. "Look at me."

Akar raised his head, slowly, reluctantly. His stomach clenched, his lungs felt paralyzed, and sweat was cold on his body. He gritted his teeth against the cry that welled up in his throat.

A white face, disembodied within the shadows of the black cowl, hung over Akar. The face was round, with heavy lidded eyes and full lips, and it was cold, as cold as stone that hangs suspended in the vast void of space, far from the warmth of any sun.

"Speak my name, Akar," commanded the man. "Speak it as you speak it when you summon my power to enhance yours."

"Nuitari!" gasped Akar. "Nuitari! God of the black moon!"

The pallid face glowed with a ghastly, unholy light. A pale, translucent hand reached out of the darkness.

"Give me your left palm."

Akar raised his left hand, wondering, as he did so, that he had the power to move it.

Nuitari clasped hold of Akar, the god's pale, delicate fingers closing over the human's tanned, strong hand.

Akar could no longer swallow his screams. Pain wrenched strangled cries from him. The chill that flowed through his body was like the burning of ice on wet flesh. Yet his hand did not move, he did not wrench it from that dread touch, much as he longed to do so. He remained on his knees, gazing up at the god, though his limbs twisted with the agony.

The heavy-lidded eyes flashed; the full lips smiled. Nuitari let loose his grasp suddenly. Akar clutched his chilling, burning hand, saw five livid marks—the fingers of the god—upon the skin.

"My mark will be the sign and symbol of our discussion," said Nuitari. "That you may know, should you by chance ever doubt, that I have spoken to you."

"If I would ever know doubt, it would only be to doubt my own worthiness of such an honor," said Akar, staring at the imprints on his flesh. He looked again at Nuitari. "How may I serve my lord?"

"Rise, be seated. We have much to discuss and we should be comfortable."

Akar rose to his feet, stiffly, awkwardly, and returned to his desk, trying to keep from wringing his wounded hand. He knew what was expected of him, despite his suffering, and conjured up a chair for his guest, a chair that was made of night, held together by stars. This done, he stood humbly until his guest had seated himself, then Akar sank behind the desk, glad to be able to sit before he fell. He kept his hand hidden in the folds of his robes, bit his lips now and then as sharp flames of ice flickered over his skin.

"The gods are angry, Akar," said Nuitari, the heavy-lidded eyes watching the flickering light of the oil lamp hanging above him. "The scales of balance have tipped, threatening the world and all who live upon it. Krynn's destruction has been foreseen. In order to prevent that end, the gods have determined to take drastic measures to restore the balance. Within a fortnight, Akar, the gods will cast down from the heavens a mountain of fire. It will strike Ansalon and split it asunder. The mountain will fall upon the Temple of the Kingpriest and drive it far, far beneath the ground. Rivers of blood will wash over the temple, and the waters of the sea will drown it forever. This doom the gods intend, unless mankind repents, which, between you and me, Akar"—Nuitari smiled—"I do not see him doing."

Akar no longer felt the pain in his hand. "I thank you for the warning, Master, and I will carry it to the other members of the Conclave. We will take such steps as are necessary to protect ourselves—"

Nuitari raised his pallid hand, made a gesture as if to brush away the inconsequential. "Such is not your concern, Akar. My brother, Solinari, and my sister, Lunitari, both walk the halls of magic, bearing the same message. You have no need to fear. Nor," he added softly, "do you have any need to become involved. I have another, more important task for you."

"Yes, Master!" Akar sat forward eagerly.

"Tomorrow night, the gods will come to Ansalon to remove those clerics who have remained true to their faith, those who have not been swayed by the corrupt tenets of the Kingpriest. At this time, the Lost Citadel will reappear, the true clerics will enter, and a bridge will form, leading from this world into worlds beyond. All true clerics may cross that bridge and will be sent to other realms far from this. Do you understand, Akar?"

"I do, Master," said Akar, somewhat hesitantly, "but

what has this to do with me? I have little use for clerics, especially those who serve the god Paladine and his ilk. And there are none left alive who serve Her Dark Majesty. The Kingpriest saw to that with his edicts. The dark clerics were among the first to face his inquisitors, the first to feel the hot fires of the so-called 'purging' flames."

"None left alive. Did you never wonder about that, Akar?"

Akar shrugged. "As I said, Master, I have little use for clerics. Takhisis, Queen of Darkness, was long since banished from the world. I could only assume that she was unable to come to the aid of those who called out her name to save them from fiery death."

"My mother remembers those who serve her, Akar," said Nuitari. "Likewise, Akar, she remembers those who fail her."

Akar flinched as the pain in his hand flared through his blood. He gnawed his lip and cast down his eyes.

"I beg forgiveness, Master. How may I serve our queen?"

"On the night when the bridge forms, good and true clerics will cross from this plane to the next. It will be possible, at that particular moment, for the souls of the dark clerics who wait in the Abyss to cross as well."

"Those who have perished serving the Dark Queen in this world will be able to return to it?"

"As all good and true clerics leave it. And thus, after the fall of the fiery mountain, there will be no clerics left in Krynn except those belonging to Her Dark Majesty."

Akar raised his eyebrows. "Truly an interesting plan, Master, and one that surely will aid Takhisis in her return to this world. But what has this to do with me? Forgive my speaking plainly, but it is the son I serve, not the mother. My loyalties lie to magic alone, as do yours."

Nuitari appeared flattered by this answer. His smile widened, and he inclined his head. "I am doing a favor for my mother. And the wizard who serves the mother will find rich reward from the son."

"Ah!" Akar breathed softly, settled back in his chair. "What reward, Master?"

"Power. You will become the most powerful wizard on Krynn, now and in the future. Even the great Fistandantilus—"

"My teacher," Akar muttered, paling at the name.

"The great Fistandantilus will be forced to bow to your might."

"Fistandantilus?" Akar stared. "I will be his master? How is that possible?"

"With the gods, all things are possible."

Akar continued to look dubious. "I know the tremendous power of this mighty wizard. It is a power that might well rival that of a god."

Nuitari frowned, and the black robes stirred. "So he fancies himself. This Fistandantilus has displeased my mother. Even now he is in the Temple of the Kingpriest seeking to usurp the Dark Queen. He aspires to heights far above him. He must be stopped."

"What must I do, Master?"

"If the blood of a good and true person is spilled in anger upon the bridge, the door to the Abyss will open and the dark clerics may return."

"How am I to find the Lost Citadel, Master? None know its location. It exists only in the planes of magic. None have seen it since the beginning of time!"

Nuitari pointed. "The lines upon your hand."

Akar's hand pulsed and throbbed; skin writhed, and bones shifted. The pain was, for an instant, almost unendurable. He gasped, pressed his lips over a cry. Lifting his hand, he stared at it in silence. At length, drawing a shuddering breath, he was able to speak. "I see. A map. Very well. Have you further instructions, my lord?"

"Steel must draw the blood."

Akar shook his head. "That makes matters more difficult. The only steel weapon we mages are permitted to carry is a dagger."

"You may find another to perform the deed. It doesn't

have to be yourself."

"I understand. But what about guards, my lord? Won't the gods be guarding the bridge?"

"One of the gods of neutrality will stand guard. Zivilyn will not interfere, as long as you or whoever you find to serve chooses to do this deed of his own free will."

Akar smiled grimly. "I see no difficulty. I will undertake this task, Master. Thank you for the opportunity."

Nuitari rose to his feet. "I have long watched and been impressed by you, Akar. I believe I have chosen wisely. The blessing of the god of the black moon on you, my servant."

Akar bowed his head in reverence. When he lifted it again, he was alone. The chair was gone, the wall was gone, and the door was back. He held the pen in his hand; the newly completed scroll lay on the table before him. All was exactly as it had been before. He might have thought he'd dreamed it, but for the pain.

He lifted his hand to the light, saw upon it the marks of the god's fingers. The marks formed roads that led up to the hills of his knuckles and over and around to the crisscrossed valley of his palm. He studied his hand, attempting to decipher the map.

Outside his door, he heard shuffling footfalls pass, robes brush against the stone floor. Someone coughed, softly.

A visitor, now, of all times.

"Go away!" Akar called. "I'm not to be disturbed!"

He brought out a sheet of parchment, began to copy the lines on his hand onto the scroll.

The person standing outside his door coughed again, a smothered sound, as if he were trying to stifle it.

Irritated, Akar raised his head. "To the Abyss with you and that coughing! Be off, whoever you are!"

A moment's silence, then the footfalls, the whisper of the robes, continued past the door and down the echoing hall.

Akar paid it no further attention.

Part II

The high cleric frowned, and the lines of his frown extended down his mouth, creasing the numerous chins that rolled over his breast, above the mound—enveloped in rich cloth of gold—that was his belly.

"And this is your final word on the subject, Sir Knight?"

The knight to whom these words were spoken looked troubled, lowered his head to stare unseeing at the still-full chalice he held in his hand. He was a young man. He "rattled in his armor" as the saying among the knights went, referring to the fact that the youthful body didn't quite fill out the breadth and width of the breastplate that had been his father's. The young man had been accepted into the knighthood early, to take over the responsibilities of that father, who had left this world and its many burdens to his son.

The burdens were heavy ones, to judge by the careworn expression that prematurely aged the young face. But he was not bowed down or crushed beneath them. He raised his eyes, faced the high cleric steadfastly.

"I am sorry, Revered Son, but that is my final word. My father donated generously to the building of the temple in Istar, more generously than he ought, perhaps, but he could not have foreseen the bad times to come."

A young woman, who had been standing behind the knight's chair, suddenly stepped forward, faced the priest.

"Nor could my father have foreseen that the time would come when the Kingpriest would go back on his sworn word to those who placed him in power!"

The woman's features were so like those of the young knight that many people meeting the two for first time thought they met twin brothers. Both were of equal height and nearly similar in build and weight, for the twins were each other's companion in everything they did, including swordsmanship.

The one marked difference between the two was the woman's sheaf of long, wheat-colored hair that, when she let it down from its tight braid around her head, fell in shining cascades almost to her knees. Her brother's hair, the same color, was kept short, falling to his shoulders.

The sister's beautiful hair and the beginnings of the long moustache of a Solamnic Knight growing upon the brother's upper lip marked the difference in their sexes, but in all else they were alike—moved alike, spoke alike, thought alike.

"Peace, Nikol," said her brother, reaching out to take hold of his sister's hand.

But she would not be placated. " 'Give to the temple,' you say. 'Increase the glory of Paladine!' It isn't Paladine's glory you've increased, but your own!"

"Take care how you talk, Daughter," said the high cleric, glaring at her. "You will bring down the wrath of the gods."

"Daughter!" Nikol's skin flushed in anger; her hands clenched. She took another step toward the priest. "Don't you dare call me daughter! The two people who had the right to speak that dear word to me are dead, my father in the service of your lying Kingpriest, my mother of hardship and overwork."

The high cleric looked rather alarmed at the sight of the impassioned young woman advancing on him. He glanced uneasily behind him at his two bodyguards, wearing the military insignia of Istar, who stood stalwartly near the door. Reassured and, perhaps reminding himself that he was, after all, a guest in the castle of a Knight of Solamnia, the high cleric turned back to the brother.

"I do not blame you for this unseemly outburst, Sir Knight. If your sister has not learned to speak respectfully to men of the cloth, it is not your fault, but, rather, the fault of the one who has her religious training in his care."

The high cleric's narrow-eyed gaze shifted to another man in the hall, a man clad in the humble clerical garb of a family healer. He was young, near the same age as the brother and sister, yet the gravity of his expression made him seem older. His robes were not fine, as were those of the visiting clerics of Istar. He wore no jewels on his fingers. His only emblem was a holy symbol, shining with a soft blue light, that hung from a leather thong around his neck. He looked troubled by the high cleric's accusation, but made no comment and bowed his head in silent acknowledgment of the rebuke.

Nikol flushed, glanced at the young healer. "Do not blame Brother Michael for my sharp tongue, Revered Son of Paladine," she said, her voice low. "Forgive my outspokenness, but it is hard to see those left in our care suffer and know that there is little we can do to help them."

"There is something you can do, Sir Knight," said the high cleric, talking to the brother, ignoring the sister. "Turn your lands and estates over to the church. Release your men-at-arms from their service. The time of warring is past. Peace is at hand. All evil has been—or soon will be—eradicated from Ansalon.

"Face reality, Sir Knight. Once the knighthood was necessary. Once we relied upon you and those like you to keep the peace, protect the innocent. But that age is ended. A new age is dawning. The knighthood is outdated, its virtues admirable but strict, rigid, old-fashioned." The high cleric smiled, and his chins waggled. "People prefer more modern ways.

"Give your lands to the church. We will take over control, send priests well qualified"—the high cleric cast a scathing glance at Brother Michael—"to collect the rents and maintain order. You will, of course, be permitted to live in your ancestral manor as caretaker—"

"Caretaker!" The knight rose to his feet. His face was pale, and his hand trembled on the hilt of the sword he wore at his side. "Caretaker of my father's house! Caretaker of a noble estate that has been handed down in honor from father to son for generations! Get out! Get out or, by Paladine, I will—" He drew the sword halfway from its scabbard.

The high cleric's fat face mottled over with red and white splotches; his eyes bulged. He heaved himself up out of his chair. His guards drew their weapons, and steel rang in the hall.

"Revered Son, allow me to escort you to your carriage." Brother Michael strode forward, taking care to place his body between that of the outraged knight and the offended priest.

Nicholas, with an effort, restrained himself, slid his sword back into its scabbard. His twin sister stood at his side, her hands clasped over his arm. Brother Michael, talking smoothly, politely, was hastily ushering the priest from the hall. At the door, the high cleric of Istar paused, looked back, his gaze hard and stern.

"You dare threaten a man of the cloth in the name of Paladine? Beware, Sir Knight, lest the wrath of the gods descend upon you!"

"This way, Your Reverence," said Brother Michael, clamping his hand over the high cleric's fleshy arm.

The healer steered his superior out of the hall, into a corridor that was devoid of furnishing. Only the Yule branches, drooping in the heat, and a few relics of a bygone era—an ancient suit of armor, faded tapestries, a torn and blood-stained standard—decorated it. The high cleric sniffed, glanced around in disdain.

"You see, Brother Michael, how run-down this fine manor has become. The walls crumbling about their ears. It is a shame, a waste. It will not be tolerated. I trust, Brother, that you will counsel these two prideful young persons, make them see the error of their ways."

Brother Michael folded his hands in the sleeves of his shabby robes, did not answer. His gaze went to the numerous sparkling rings worn on the high cleric's fat fingers. The healer's lips tightened, keeping back words that would have done no good, maybe much harm.

The high cleric leaned near him. "It would be a pity if the inquisitor was forced to pay a visit to this knight and his sister. Don't you agree, Brother Michael?"

The healer lifted his eyes. "But they are devout followers—"

The high cleric snorted. "The church wants these lands, Brother. If the knight truly was a worshiper of Paladine, he would not hesitate to grant all he owns to the Kingpriest. Therefore, since this knight and his foul-tongued witch of a sister thwart the wishes of the church, they must be in league with the powers of darkness. Bring them back to the paths of righteousness, Brother Michael. Bring them back, or I will begin to wonder about *you*."

The high cleric waddled out the door, accompanied by his heavily armed bodyguards. He rolled to his carriage, waving his hand in lethargic blessing to several peasants, who humbly doffed their caps and bowed their heads. When the priest disappeared inside the carriage, the peasants stared after his rich equipage with grim and angry faces in which could be seen the cruel pinch of hunger and want.

Brother Michael stood a long time in the doorway, watching the cloud of dust raised by the carriage wheels. His hand clasped the holy symbol around his neck.

"Grant me understanding, Mishakal," he prayed to the gentle goddess. "You are the only light in this terrible darkness."

Brother and sister, within the hall, heard the carriage wheels rattle over the flagstone of the courtyard and each breathed a sigh. The knight drew his sword, stared at it ruefully.

"What have I done? Drawn steel against a holy father!"

"He deserved it," said Nikol stoutly. "I wish I'd had mine. I'd have relieved him of a few chins!"

Both turned at the sound of footsteps entering the

hall. The family healer paused in the doorway.

"Come in, Brother Michael. As always, you are one of us," said Nikol, mistaking his hesitation for a reluctance to intrude on their private conversation.

Michael was, in reality, wondering how he would tell them, wondering whether or not to impart the terrible threat. They were so young, already struggling with the burdens of a manor and its poverty-stricken people. There was little Nicholas could do for his tenants. He had trouble enough supporting the men-at-arms, who kept marauding goblins from plundering what meager stores the people had remaining.

Michael looked at the young knight, the healer's eyes dimmed with tears. Nicholas should have been riding to tourneys in his shining armor, wearing the favors of his lady. He should have been winning renown in gallant contest, but the only contest this knight fought was an inglorious battle against hunger and deprivation. The only horse he rode was a plow horse. The healer closed his eyes and bowed his head.

He heard a rustle of skirts, felt gentle fingers on his hand.

"Brother Michael, are you in trouble with the Revered Son? It's all my fault. My tongue's sharper than my sword. I'll send a note of apology if you think it will help."

Michael opened his eyes, stared at her dumbly. As always, she took his breath away. His love for her and his longing, his admiration, pity, and compassion, surged inside him, tangled up his voice. Gently, he removed her hand from his, took a step away from her. She was the daughter of a knight; he, a cleric of the lowest standing, with no money to pay the temple to rise higher.

"Brother Michael, what is it? What's wrong? What did that man say to you?" Nicholas strode across the room.

Michael could not bear to look at either of them. He lowered his gaze to the floor. "He threatens to send for the inquisitor, my lord."

"If we don't give up the lands to the church?"

"Yes, my lord. I'm deeply sorry that one of my own kind—"

"Your kind!" Nikol cried. "That man is not like you, Michael, not in the slightest! You work tirelessly among the people. You share our poverty. You take nothing, not even what rightfully belongs to you. Oh, I've seen you, Brother! I've seen you slip the salary we pay you for your services back into my purse when you think I'm not looking."

She laughed at the foolish expression on his face, though there was a catch in her laughter, as if she might weep.

"M-my lady," Michael stammered, face burning, "you make too much of it. I need nothing. You feed me, house me. I—" He could not go on.

"Come, Nikol," said her brother briskly. "You'll unman us all if you keep this up. And we have urgent matters to discuss. Will the high cleric make good his threat? Will he send this inquisitor?"

"I fear so," said Michael reluctantly, though he was thankful to Nicholas for changing the subject. "It has been done to others in the past."

"Surely only to evil men," protested Nikol, "clerics of the Dark Queen, wizards, and those of their ilk. What have we to fear if they do send an inquisitor to us? We have always worshiped Paladine faithfully."

"There used to be nothing for the faithful to fear, my lady," said Michael. "In the beginning, the Kingpriest truly meant to try to rid the world of darkness. He did not realize, however, that to banish darkness he would have to banish us all, for there is a touch of darkness in each of us. We are none of us perfect, not even the Kingpriest. Only by recognizing that darkness and constantly striving against it do we keep from being overwhelmed by it."

Michael had his own darkness, or so he considered it. His love for this young woman was not pure, not holy, as he wanted it to be. It was tinged with burning desire. He wanted to take her in his arms, press his lips to hers. He wanted to undo her crown of hair and feel it cascade down around them both.

"I understand," said Nikol softly. "I long for a beautiful new dress. Isn't that terrible of me, when people are starving? Yet, I'm so tired of wearing this one poor gown." Her hands smoothed the well-worn, oft-mended fabric. She sighed, turned to her brother. "Maybe we are wrong, Nicholas. Maybe it is proud and sinful of us to want to keep these lands. Maybe we should give them to the church. After all, if it is the will of Paladine—"

"No," said Nicholas firmly. "I cannot believe it is Paladine's will. It is the will of the Kingpriest and his Revered Sons."

"How can you be sure?"

"Because, my lady," answered Michael steadily, "the Kingpriest claims to know the minds of the gods. How can any mortal claim such a thing?"

"You serve Mishakal."

"I follow the laws of the goddess. I obey her commands. I would never presume to speak for her, my lady."

"But is it wrong to want to rid the world of evil?"

Michael hesitated before answering. This was a question he himself had long argued internally, and it was not easy to utter his innermost thoughts and feelings.

"How do you define evil, my lady? Too often, we define it as that which is different from ourselves, or that which we do not understand. You said before that we should rid the world of wizards, but it was a wizard, one Magius, who fought at the side of the great Huma and who was the knight's dearest friend.

"In the land of my birth, near Xak Tsaroth, there live a band of nomads called the Plainsmen. They are barbarians, according to the Kingpriest. Yet a more generous, loving people never lived. They worship all the gods, even the dark ones, who are supposedly banished from this world. When one of their people falls ill, for example, the Plainsmen pray to Mishakal for healing, but they pray also to Morgion, evil god of disease, to withdraw his foul hand."

"What is their reasoning?" Nicholas's brow furrowed. "Morgion, along with the Dark Queen, was driven from the world long ago."

"Was he?" asked Michael gently. "Have plagues and illness left the world? No. What do we say, then? We say that it is the unworthy who suffer. Was your mother unworthy?"

Brother and sister were silent, absorbing this thought. Then Nicholas frowned and stirred. "What is your counsel, then, Brother Michael? Do we defy the Kingpriest? Think well before you answer." The knight smiled wanly. "As the one in charge of our spiritual guidance, you will be in as much danger from the inquisitor as my sister and I."

Michael did not respond immediately. He rose to his feet, paced thoughtfully about the hall, hands clasped behind his back, as if again wondering what to say, how to say it.

Brother and sister drew near each other, held hands. At last, Michael turned to face them.

"Do nothing. Not yet. I . . . I cannot explain, but I have had strange dreams of late. Last night, Mishakal came to me as I slept. I saw her clearly. Her face was grieved, her eyes sad. She started to say something to me, to tell me something. She reached out her hand to me, but, at the last moment, she faded away. I will pray for her return tonight, pray that she will speak to me. And then, hopefully, I will be able to guide you."

Nicholas looked relieved; the burden lifted, for a time, from his shoulders. Nikol smiled tremulously at Michael. Reaching out her hand, she took hold of his, pressed it warmly.

"Thank you, Brother. We have faith in you."

Michael's hand tightened on hers. He couldn't help

himself. She was so lovely, so caring. Nikol, looking into his eyes, flushed, removed her hand from his grasp.

"Nicholas," she said, "it is time for our sword work. I, for one, could use the exercise."

Her brother went to the weapons rack, lifted a sword. "Yes, and I feel the need to sweat the touch of that fat priest out of my pores."

He tossed the weapon to her. She caught it expertly. "I'll change my clothes first. It wouldn't do to put any more rents in this poor dress of mine." Teasing, she glanced demurely at Michael. "You need not come with us, Brother. I know how fighting, even in practice, disturbs you."

She didn't love him. Liked and respected him, but she didn't love him. How could he expect her to? What was he? A healer, not a warrior. How often he had seen her eyes shine when she listened to tales of courage and valor on the battlefield. Her dreams were of a bold knight, not a humble cleric.

The twins ran off, laughing and jesting, leaving him behind, empty, lonely, and afraid. Sighing, he went to the family chapel to say his prayers.

Part III

"You know what it is you must do?"

"I know," growled the goblin chief. He was some part human, and thus smarter and more dangerous than most of his kind. "Give me the money."

"Half now. Half when you deliver the knight. Alive!"

"You didn't say anything about that!" The goblin glowered, his face hideous in the bright light of the red moon, Lunitari. "You just said bring you the knight. You didn't say you wanted him alive."

"And what would I do with him dead?" Akar demanded testily.

"I don't know what wizards do. And I don't care." The goblin sneered. "Alive will cost you extra."

"Very well." Akar gave in with an ill grace. Reaching into a black velvet pouch, he carefully counted out a few gold pieces.

The goblin stared at them with deep suspicion.

"They're real," snapped Akar. "What do you expect them to do? Disappear?"

"It wouldn't surprise me. If they do, so do I. Remember that, wizard." The goblin chief thrust the coins into a hairy pouch at his belt. "Tomorrow night. Here."

"Tomorrow night. Here," repeated Akar.

The two parted, both skulking back into the dark shadows that bred and sheltered them.

*   *   *   *   *

It was the hour before dawn. Brother Michael's sleep had been restive. He woke often, thinking he heard a voice calling him. He sat upright, holding his breath, staring into the darkness of his small, windowless room.

"What? Who's there?"

No answer.

"Am I needed? Is someone ill?"

No response.

He lay back down again, telling himself he'd imagined it, and drifted into sleep, only to be roused again by the same call.

"Michael . . . Michael . . ."

He sat up, weary, sleep-dazed. "What now—" he began, then stopped and stared.

The image of a beautiful woman, surrounded by a radiant blue light, glimmered at the foot of his bed. He had seen her image before, but never this clearly, never this close. He knew, now, that she would speak to him, that she had come to comfort and guide him. His prayers had been answered.

Michael had no care for his nakedness, for the goddess sees all men naked, when they come into the world, sees the nakedness of their souls, their hearts. He slid from his bed and fell to his knees upon the cold stone floor.

"Mishakal. I am your servant. Command me. What is your bidding?"

The goddess's voice was lovely, like the song of myriad birds, like his mother's whisper, like silver bells on a bright new morning. "Truly you are my servant, Michael. One of my faithful servants. I need you. Come with me."

"Yes, of course, Holy One." Michael rose swiftly, began dressing himself, hardly knowing what he was doing. The blue light surrounding him was blinding, filled his heart with uplifting joy. "Is someone sick? Someone in the village, perhaps?"

"Put aside the cares of this world, Brother Michael. They are no longer yours." The goddess held out a hand of surpassing beauty and wondrous softness. "Come."

Michael heard horns blowing the call to battle. He heard shouts and voices, the rattle of armor and of sword. He heard feet pounding on the battlements. He paused, looked behind him, looked toward the door that led to the family chapel.

"Yes, Lady, but there is fighting! They will need me—"

"Not for long," said the goddess. "Paladine has them in

his keeping. He will gather their souls to him, remove them from a world that soon will erupt in fire. Lay down your burden, Michael, and walk with me."

"And I will see them again? Nicholas, Nikol?"

"On the other side. You will wait for them. It will not be long."

"Then I will come." He was glad to leave, glad to give up the pain of living, the pain of his desires. Soon, he would be able to love her purely. He reached out his hand to take the hand of the goddess. . . .

A scream shattered the dawning. Fists pounded on his door.

"Michael! Brother Michael! You must come! It's Nicholas! He's hurt! He needs you!"

"Nikol's voice!" Michael trembled; his hand shook.

"There is nothing you can do, Brother," the goddess told him sadly. "True, the valiant knight is wounded, but, even as his sister stands here, pleading for your aid, the knight is being carried away by his attackers. You will arrive too late to save him."

"But if Nicholas has taken ill, who will lead the men? The manor will fall—"

"Brother Michael! Please!" Nikol's voice was raw with shouting.

The goddess gazed at him with cool eyes. "What will happen, will happen. You can do nothing to prevent it. Have faith in us, believe that all is for the best, though you do not understand. You said yourself, 'What mortal can know the mind of a god?' If you refuse, if you lack faith, if you stay and interfere, you run the risk of dooming yourself, the woman, and the world to a terrible fate!"

"Michael! I need you!" Nikol cried. Fists pounded on the wood.

"Then so be it, Lady," he said heavily, "for I cannot leave them." His hand dropped to his side. He could no longer look on the radiance of the goddess. It hurt his eyes. "I love her. I love them both. I can't believe that their deaths would be for the best! Forgive me, Misha-kal."

He started toward the door. His hand was on the handle. His heart ached. He longed to go with the goddess. Yet, outside, he heard Nikol crying. He placed his hand upon the door. The light around him seemed to soften. He glanced back.

"Tomorrow night, the Night of Doom, the bridge at the Lost Citadel will open to all true clerics. Only those who have faith may pass."

The blue light glimmered and died. Michael yanked open the door.

Nikol clutched at him. "Where have you been? What have you been doing? Didn't you hear me call?"

"I was . . . at my prayers," Michael said lamely.

Her eyes flashed. Daughter of a knight, she could not understand the soft cleric who fell to his knees and prayed to his goddess to save him, when other men were grabbing shield and sword. Catching hold of his hand, she began running down the hallway. He stumbled to keep up with her. She was clad in her nightclothes. Her long gown whipped around her ankles, nearly tripping her. Blood stained the white cloth. Michael had no need to ask whose it was.

"They carried him inside," Nikol was talking feverishly, as they ran. "We stripped off the armor. His wound is deep, but not mortal. We have to hurry. He's lost so much blood. I left old Giles with him. . . ."

No, we don't need to hurry! Michael cried silently. Too late. We will be too late! But he found himself running all the faster, as if he could outrun destiny.

They reached a room on the ground level, near the entrance. They had not carried the wounded man far.

"Giles!" Nikol cried, pushing on the door. "I've brought the healer. I—Nicholas? Where are you? Giles! Oh, god, no! Paladine, no!"

Her heartbroken cry went through Michael like iron. Nikol caught up the body of the elderly servant, lifted him gently from the floor.

"Giles! What happened? Where's Nicholas?"

Michael knelt beside the old man. A goblin arrow stuck out of his chest, the shaft buried deep.

"Mishakal, heal . . ." Michael's voice cracked. The holy medallion of Mishakal he wore around his neck, the symbol of his faith that gleamed blue with the radiance of the goddess, was dark, its light gone. He stammered; his words halted.

The old man gasped. "They . . . took him!"

"Who took him? Giles, answer me!" Nikol cried.

"Goblins . . ."

The old man stared at her, but his eyes no longer saw her. His head lolled in her arms. She laid him on the floor, her face expressionless, shocked past hurt and sorrow.

Michael stood, looked around the room. Broken glass littered the floor; the window swung crazily on its hinges. It had been smashed open with a heavy object, probably a club or mace. Blood smeared the windowsill.

"They carried him out this way," he said.

"But why?" Nikol stared at the empty bed, the bloodstained, rumpled sheets. Her face was whiter than the linen. "Why would they take him? Goblins butcher and kill. They never take prisoners. . . . Oh, Nicholas!"

A shudder swept over her. She buried her face in the still-warm bedclothes, twisted the cloth in her fingers. Michael ached to comfort her. He drew near, reaching out to her. His hand touched her shoulder.

"My lady—"

Nikol rounded on him with a savage cry. "You! This is your fault! If you had been here, instead of hiding behind the skirts of your goddess, my brother would be well! He would be alive! He could have fought them—"

A bowman, bloodied and disheveled, appeared in the doorway.

"Where's my lord?" he demanded harshly. "The enemy is assaulting in force. What are his orders?"

Michael straightened, was about to give the man the terrible news that his lord was gone.

Sharp nails dug into his skin. Nikol pushed past him.

"My lord will be with you presently," she told him, her voice cold and level. "We are binding his wound."

"Pray Paladine he comes swiftly," said the bowman, and dashed off.

"Katherine!" Nikol cried. "Katherine—There you are."

The woman who had been nursemaid and nanny to the girl, lady-in-waiting to the young woman, hastened into the room at her mistress's call.

"Fetch me the men's clothing I use when I practice with Nicholas! Be quick about it! Hurry!"

Katherine stared at her, confused and upset. "Oh, my lady, there is no time! We must flee—"

"Go!" Nikol shouted at her. "Do as I command!"

Katherine cast a frightened look at Michael, who shook his head, bewildered. The woman fled, her wooden clogs clattering over the stone floor.

Nikol glanced about the room, found what she sought. Catching hold of her brother's leather belt, she drew a sharp knife from its sheath and held it out to Michael. He stared at it, then at her.

"My vows forbid me to carry sharp weapons, my lady—"

"You weakling! I'm not asking you to fight with it!"

Nikol thrust the knife into his limp hand. Lifting the heavy braid of long, golden hair, she twitched it around, held it out to him.

"Cut it. Cut it to match the length of my brother's hair."

Michael understood suddenly what she intended. He stared at her, aghast. "Nikol, you can't be serious! You're not thinking—"

"No, it's you who's not thinking!" She turned, faced him. "This is my only chance to save Nicholas. Don't you understand? They've taken him away. Now they're launching an assault to cover their escape. We must drive them back, then I can lead a party to go rescue my brother."

"But you're a woman. The men won't follow you."

"They won't know they're following me," Nikol said calmly, turning around again. "They'll think they're following my brother. We look enough alike that I can fool them, beneath the armor. And don't worry, Brother," she added bitterly. "You can stay here in safety and pray for me. Now, cut."

Her sarcasm was sharper than the blade. He realized now how wide was the gulf that separated them. He had sometimes dared to hope that she was fond of him. He had sometimes fancied that she had responded warmly to his touch.

If I were noble or if she were common, might we not love?

But now he knew the truth, he saw it in her eyes. She despised him, despised his weakness.

Michael grasped the knife awkwardly. Lifting the heavy braid of hair in his hand, he felt its silk beneath his fingers.

How many times have I dreamed of this moment, he thought to himself bitterly. The grace, the privilege of touching her beautiful hair.

He heard frantic shouting outside. A spent arrow whistled in through the window. Gritting his teeth, Michael hacked away at the shining, twisted strands.

*   *   *   *   *

"My lord!" A grizzled sergeant caught hold of the knight's arm. Blood streamed from a cut on the sergeant's head. He limped from either a new wound or an old. "My lord! It's hopeless. There are far too many of the fiends! Sound the retreat!"

"No!" The knight shook him off furiously. "They're falling back. Rally the men for another charge!"

"My lord, they're regrouping, making ready for the

killing blow, that's all," said the sergeant gently.

Michael realized then that the sergeant knew the truth. He knew he wasn't following his lord, but his lady.

The cleric edged closer, to listen to the conversation. The battle had been brief and brutal. He had done what he could to ease the pain of the dying, but that hadn't been much. The situation had been too dire, too confused, for anyone to notice that their cleric had tucked his medallion of faith inside his robes, that no prayers passed his lips. Merciful death came to most swiftly. Michael's one panic-stricken thought was that Nikol would fall, wounded. And then what could he do for her?

"What are your orders, my lord?" the sergeant asked, respectfully.

Nikol did not immediately answer. Exhaustion had taken its toll. The ragged blond hair that fell to the metal-armored shoulders was wet with sweat. Any other knight would have removed the heavy helm, wiped his face. This knight kept her helm on.

Michael joined them, stared out over the battlements into the woods beyond. Day had dawned. The vast numbers of the enemy could be counted easily; they made no secret of their strength. The knight glanced around at the pitiful number of men who remained.

"Release the men from duty," said Nikol, in a low, toneless voice. "If they leave now, they can make good their escape. The goblins will be too busy looting and burning to chase them."

"Very good, my lord," said the sergeant, bowing.

"Give them my thanks. They fought well."

"Yes, my lord." The old sergeant's voice was choked. "My lord will be coming with us?"

Nikol made no response. Michael stepped forward, prepared to argue, prepared to tell everyone the truth, if necessary. Anything to save her. He caught the flash of blue eyes from behind the helm. Nikol's gaze held his a moment, warned him to keep silent.

"No, not immediately," she replied. "And don't wait for me. I will try to save what little of value remains."

"My lord—"

"Go, Jeoffrey. Take my thanks and my blessing."

The knight held out a gauntleted hand. The old man caught hold of it, pressed it to his lips.

"Never did a noble knight fight with such courage as you have fought this day, my lord! May Paladine walk always at your side."

The sergeant bowed his head. Tears streamed down the weathered cheeks. Then he was gone, running through the smoke, shouting orders.

Michael stepped forward, out of the shadows. "You should go with them, my lady."

Nikol did not even glance at him. She stood staring out into the woods, crawling with evil creatures. "Your prayers did little good, Brother."

Michael's face burned with shame. Did she know the truth? Suspect? He turned away in unhappy silence.

"Don't go, Michael," she said softly, remorsefully. "Forgive me . . . and ask the gods to forgive me. It's just . . . so hopeless!"

She leaned against him, thankful for his support. He couldn't very well take an armored knight in his arms. He made do by squeezing her hand tightly. "We must get away, my lady."

"Yes," Nikol murmured. She talked as if she were in a daze. "There is a cave, not far from the castle. Nicholas and I used to play there, when we were little. It is well hidden. We will be safe."

"Is there anything you want to take with you?" Michael asked, feeling helpless. He looked at the castle walls. Even now, they appeared stalwart, impregnable. It was difficult to imagine that they could no longer offer the shelter they promised. "What about the servants?" he asked.

"I sent them away long ago," said Nikol. They were

alone now. The men had fled. She removed her helm. Her face was ashen, grimy with dirt and blood and sweat. "Most of them have family in these parts. They'll warn them, hopefully in time to get away safely. As for the jewels, we sold them years ago. I have with me what matters to me most."

Her gaze went fondly, sadly to the sword in her hand—her brother's sword, which once had been her father's and his father's before him.

"But we'll need food, water skins . . ."

A hideous yell went up from the goblins in the woods. A black wave started to roll across the torn and trampled grasslands in front of the castle. The gate was shut. It would take them some time to storm the walls, even though they were no longer defended.

Nikol's lips tightened. She replaced the helm over her head, gripped the sword. "Stay behind me and keep clear of my sword arm. I may need to fight our way out."

"Yes, my lady."

They hastened to stairs, leading downward. Nikol paused, turned to him, grasped his hand.

"We'll find Nicholas, and you will heal him," she said.

"Yes, my lady," Michael replied. What could he say?

She nodded abruptly and disappeared into the darkness of the spiral staircase. Michael followed after her, his heart aching, heavy.

"It's hopeless!" he wanted to shout. "Hopeless! Even if we did find him, I can't heal him! Don't you see? Don't you understand?"

Grasping the blue holy symbol of Mishakal, he drew it forth from beneath his robes. Once it would have lit the darkness. Once it would have glowed brightly, radiantly. Now he could barely see it for the thick shadows surrounding him.

He let the medallion fall heavily to his chest. "You will see, soon enough. Now you despise me. Then you will hate me."

He stumbled after her through the darkness.

Part IV

Night crept over the land. Nikol stood at the entrance to the cave and watched the lurid red glow of flames lighting the dark sky, at first brilliantly, then gradually growing dim. The smoke of the burning stung the eyes, bit into the nostrils. Occasionally, raucous shouts and wild laughter could be heard, carried on the wind.

"You should rest, my lady," said Michael gently.

"You sleep, Brother," she told him. "I'll keep watch."

Her spirit was strong, but it could not lend its strength to muscle and bone and sinew. Even as she spoke, her knees buckled beneath her. Michael caught her in his arms, eased her to the cavern floor. He pried her fingers from the sword she still held, fingers gummed black with goblin blood. He washed her hands, bathed her face with cool water.

"Wake me before the dawn," she murmured. "We will follow them . . . find Nicholas." She slept.

Michael sat back, closed his eyes. Tears of weariness and despair filled his eyes; a lump grew in his throat, choked him. He loved her so, and he must fail her. Even if they found Nicholas and saved him—and how could they do that, against a goblin army?—Michael could not heal him.

Tomorrow night, the Night of Doom, the bridge at the Lost Citadel will open to all true clerics. Only those who have faith may pass. Mishakal's voice came to him. The goddess had given him a chance to redeem himself.

Tomorrow night. The cleric had until tomorrow night to find the bridge, the Lost Citadel, a place remembered only in legend, from the beginnings of the world. He would cross the bridge. The light of the goddess once more would shine on him, envelop him, end the pain of this hopeless love, this useless existence. Once he was there, he would rediscover his lost faith.

"Good-bye, Nikol. Tomorrow, when you wake, I will be gone," he told her. Reaching out his hand, he touched the rough-cut hair. "Don't be angry with me. You don't need me. I would be a liability to you, a weak man who cannot even call upon the power of the goddess to aid you. You will travel faster alone."

He propped himself up against the cavern wall, fully intending to stay awake, watch for the gray light of dawn, when he would sneak away. But easeful slumber stole over him. His head drooped; his body slumped to the ground. He did not see it, but in the darkness, the holy medallion he wore began to glow a soft blue, and no harm came to them during the night, though many evil creatures skulked about their hiding place.

With the dawn, however, the medallion's soft light faded.

* * * * *

The black-robed wizard squatted on a cleared patch of ground in the middle of the forest. It was midmorning. The sun shone through a haze of smoke that drifted among the treetops. Akar sneezed, glanced up at the smoke irritably, then turned his attention back to the divining rocks he had tossed on the ground. Leaning over them, he studied them carefully.

"This is it, the Night of Doom. The true clerics will depart Ansalon. I have one night to find the Lost Citadel. Where are those blasted goblins anyway?" Akar looked once again, grimly, at the smoke. "Enjoying themselves, I fancy. We'll see how long they do if they fail me—"

The rustling of tree branches interrupted him. Akar gathered up the stones in one swift movement of his hand, thrust them into a black leather pouch. The words of a deadly spell on his lips, he crept back swiftly into the protection of the trees and waited.

A group of four goblins burst into the cleared space. They moved loudly, with the confidence of those engorged on victory. They bore between them a litter on which lay the body of a human male. The wizard, seeing the litter, cursed.

The goblin chief shoved past his men, looked around the forest. "Wizard? Show yourself! Make haste! I want my money!"

Akar stalked out of the woods. Ignoring the chief, he strode over to the litter, which the goblins had dropped on the ground. The young man on the litter groaned in pain. He was conscious, though he seemed to have little idea what was happening to him. He looked up at the wizard with dazed puzzlement.

Akar regarded him coldly.

"What's this?" he demanded. "What have you brought me?"

"A Knight of Solamnia. They stripped him of his armor." The goblin sounded bitter. He could have used that armor.

"Bah! He's too young to be a knight. Even if I believed you, the man is wounded, near dying! What use is he to me in this state?"

"Lucky you are to have him in any state!" hissed the goblin. "Did you expect us to take a Knight of Solamnia without a fight?"

Akar bent over the young man. Roughly, he lifted the blood-soaked bandages wrapped tightly around the abdomen, peered at the wound. The man cried out in agony, clenched his fists. A ring flashed in the light. Akar grasped it, stared at it, grunted in satisfaction.

"Well, well. You are a knight."

"What do you want of me?" the wounded man managed to gasp.

Akar ignored him. He felt for the lifebeat in the neck, noted the fever burning the blood. The wizard sat back on his haunches.

"He won't last another hour."

"I suggest you do what you must do with him quickly, then," advised the chief.

"Impossible. I need him alive all night."

"Oh? I suppose now you'll want us to go out and capture you a cleric?" The goblin chief sneered.

"It would do no good. No cleric you would find this night on Krynn could heal him."

The goblin chief gestured. "Then you take care of him. You're a wizard, after all. I suppose your magic's good for something. Pay us what you owe us and let us be gone. We plan to make something out of this deal. The castle was picked clean before we got there. Not a woman to be had."

The knight cried out, struggled to rise. His hand went for his sword, but it was no longer at his side.

"Save your strength." Akar shoved the knight back down. The wizard stood up. He was in a better mood, almost smiling. "Here's your pay." He tossed a few gold coins at the goblin chief.

The chief found this sudden change in the wizard suspicious, apparently, for he eyed the money dubiously. "You pick it up," he ordered one of his cohorts, who did as he was told.

The goblins slunk back to their looting, their chief keeping a careful eye on his man who held the wizard's money.

Akar turned to the knight, who lay still and silent, fighting against the pain, refusing to show weakness.

"What do you want of me?" he repeated hoarsely.

"This night, I must spill the blood of a good and true person on the bridge of the Lost Citadel. You have the misfortune to be, Sir Knight, a good and true person. At least that's what your people say of you. Something of a rarity these days, I must admit. Don't trouble yourself over the how and why, but, with your murder, the clerics of Her Dark Majesty will at last be able to return to this world."

The knight smiled. "I am dying. I will not live long enough to be of use to you, thanks be to Paladine."

"Ah, now. Don't give up hope. My magic is good for something. I cannot heal you, Sir Knight. Nor do I necessarily want you healed. You would, I fancy, prove a most troublesome captive. Yet you will remain alive until I can transport you to the Lost Citadel.

"A wish spell will accomplish what I want. Yes, a wish will do nicely. The spell will cost me a year of my life." The wizard shrugged. "But what is that? When I have the power of the great Fistandantilus, I will gain that year back, with interest!"

Akar lifted his hands, gazed up at the sky, to the black moon, Nuitari, the moon that only those with the vision of darkness can see.

"My wish is thus: Let the knight remain alive until he meets death at the point of this dagger." Akar removed the dagger from its sheath at his belt, held it up to the sky. The metal darkened, as if a shadow fell across it, then it flashed with a terrible, unholy light.

"My wish is granted!" Akar said in satisfaction.

"No! Paladine, forfend! Take my life! Kill me now!"

The young knight struggled to his feet. Ripping the bandages from his wound, starting the blood flowing freely, he lurched across the clearing, heading toward the forest.

Akar made no move, watched calmly.

Nicholas fell to his knees. His lifeblood flowed from him. He stared at it, watched it soak into the ground. The pain was intense, excruciating. He doubled over, cried out to die.

Death did not come. Nicholas lay in his own blood, writhing in agony.

Akar whistled. A horse as black as goblin's blood—which was, indeed, the steed's name—cantered into the clearing, drawing behind it a small wooden cart. The wizard grasped hold of the knight by the shoulders, dragged him across the bloody grass to the cart, and heaved him up into it. Removing a length of rope from the cart, Akar bound the suffering knight's hands and feet securely.

"Not that I think you're in any shape to do me harm,"

said Akar. "But you're a tough breed, you knights. I'm sorry I can do nothing to ease the pain. But, look at it this way. After a few hours of agony, you'll be more than ready to die. Try not to groan too loudly. Foul creatures roam the countryside these days. And now, to find the Lost Citadel."

Akar mounted the cart, lifted the reins in his hands. Once again he gazed up at the sky. As he watched, a shadow crossed the sun, like the moon eclipsing it, but it was a shadow only he could see. He stared at it, squinting against the sunlight, until he found what he sought.

The shadow extended downward from the sun, formed a shaft of darkness that pierced the daylight. Whatever that shadow touched instantly burst into flame. Fire roared through the forest. Smoke, foul and poisonous, hung in the air. Akar sniffed its perfume. Behind him, he heard the knight choke and retch.

When the smoke dissipated, blown aside by a death-cold wind, Akar saw that a trail had been burned among charred trees, a trail of blackness, a trail of night in day.

"Nuitari be blessed," said Akar.

Slapping the reins on the horse's back, he drove the cart onto the shadow-shrouded path.

Part V

The goblins' trail was easy for Michael and Nikol to follow . . . too easy. The army had cut a swath of destruction through the forest surrounding the burned and gutted castle. Their numbers were strong; they had no need to hide or conceal the path that led back to their lair in the mountains. They feared no retribution. Neighboring knights, in neighboring manors, had their own lands and people to consider.

Michael stared in dismay at the broken trees, the trampled brush, the bodies of dead goblins, who, wounded, had been left behind by their loutish comrades. Nikol roamed the path, her gaze fixed on the ground, searching for any clue of her brother.

"My lady, if they did take him, what chance do you have of rescuing him? There must be . . . hundreds of them!" Michael waved his hand at the destruction.

"Then at least I will have the comfort of dying with him," Nikol returned. Straightening, she brushed her hair back out of her eyes. "You knew what we faced. I warned you this morning."

Michael didn't want to be reminded of the morning. The two had awakened, clasped in each others arms. Confused and embarrassed, each of them kept the other well at a distance. He meant to tell her, then, that he was leaving her, but somehow he couldn't find the words.

The silence between them grew uncomfortable. Undoubtedly she was thinking of this morning as well.

"Nikol," he began, longing to say what was in his heart.

She turned away from him hurriedly, began looking with self-conscious intensity back at the ground.

"Have you ever known goblins to take hostages, Brother?" she asked him abruptly, putting, he thought, a heavy emphasis on his title.

Michael sighed, shook his head tiredly. "No, I haven't. It takes a subtle mind to plot exchanging hostages for ransom. Goblins think only of looting and killing."

"Precisely. And yet they took Nicholas, stole him deliberately. They took him alone. They didn't want anyone else. They killed poor old Giles. Why? Unless they were under orders to capture Nicholas . . ."

Her face was flushed with her new idea. She forgot the strained formality. "That's it, Michael! The attack on the castle was a diversion to cover their real intent: capturing Nicholas. Which means that someone wants him and that someone must want him alive!"

"Yes, my lady." Michael agreed.

No need to tell her that her twin, if he was still alive, might well have good reason to wish himself dead. A few hours fruitless searching and Nikol would be forced to admit defeat. Then, perhaps, he could persuade her to take refuge in some neighboring manor, while he himself prepared to leave. . . .

"Michael!"

Her excited voice rang like silver in the still air. He hastened through the brush toward her.

"Look! Look at this!" Nikol pointed to a splotch in the trampled grass. Blood. Red blood. Human blood.

Before Michael could say a word, Nikol had dashed off, following a trail that broke from the main one. He hurried after her, not knowing whether to give thanks or curse the gods that had put this sign in her way.

They came upon the clearing. Both stopped. Although the sun shone brightly, the evil that lingered in the place covered it with a dark cloud. Nikol put her hand to the hilt of her sword, but nerveless fingers slipped from it. Unconsciously, she reached out to Michael. His hand closed over hers, and they drew close together, shivering in the chill, sunlit darkness.

"Oh, Michael," Nikol whispered brokenly, "where is he? What have they done to him? I—"

She gave a cry. The large puddle of red blood glistened in the light. Near it lay the bandage she had wrapped with her own hands around her brother's wound. Nikol covered her face with her hands, slumped against Michael's chest. He put his arms around her, held her shivering body close.

"My lady, we must go away from here." Michael's love for her, his pity, was agony. "Let me take you to Sir Thomas's manor. You will be safe—"

"No!" Hastily, Nikol wiped her eyes, pushed herself away from his comforting embrace. "I was weak for a moment. This dreadful place . . . " She looked around, shuddered. "But Nicholas isn't here. His body isn't here," she continued, her tone grim, resolute. "They've taken him off somewhere. He's still alive. I know he's alive!"

She began searching the clearing. It did not take her long to find the tracks left by the wheels of the cart, or the spoor of blood that led to it. She followed the signs; Michael followed her. Both found the opening burned into the forest, the opening of darkness. They stopped, stared at it, blood chilling in their veins.

"I think this is what it must be like to gaze into the Abyss," said Michael in awe.

Nikol's face was ashen, her eyes wide and terrified. She stood close to him, and he could feel her body tremble beneath the armor. "I can't go in there. . . ."

Wind moaned in the tops of the blackened trees, a cry of pain, as if the trees were screaming. And then Michael realized, with a thrill of horror, that the cry came from a human throat. He hoped against hope that Nikol had not heard.

"Come, my lady, let us go away from this evil place—"

"Nicholas!" Nikol called out in anguish. "I hear you! We're coming!" She took a step forward, into the noisome shadows.

Michael caught hold of her. "Nikol, you can't!"

She struck at him, hard, shoved him back. "I'm going. And so are you, you coward!" Her hand closed over his wrist with a grip of iron. "You will heal him—"

"I can't!" Michael cried savagely. "Look! Look!" He yanked the holy symbol from its hiding place beneath his robes, held it up for Nikol to see. "It's dark, as dark as that path before us. Do you know what that means? The goddess has turned away from me. She won't answer my prayers. Even if we did find Nicholas, I could do nothing for him."

Nikol stared at him, not comprehending. "But . . . how? How could the goddess abandon you?"

Because I abandoned the goddess! I did it for you, for you and Nicholas! Michael wanted to shout at her, vent his frustration, his fear and anger—anger at her, anger at the gods. . . .

He shivered suddenly. He shouldn't be angry. That was wrong. The faithful were never angry, never questioned. Again, he'd been found lacking.

"I can't explain," Michael said tiredly. "The matter is between myself and my god. But, now, you must come away from this place. As you see, there's nothing we can do. . . ."

Nikol let go of him, as she might have tossed away a piece of rubbish.

"Thank you for accompanying me this far." Her voice was cold, bitter with disappointment. "You needn't go on with me. This place holds far more danger for you than for me, for now it appears that you are defenseless against its evil. Farewell, Brother—I mean, Michael."

She turned and walked, with firm step, into the fearsome, fire-ravaged forest. The shadows surrounded her instantly. He lost sight of her, could not even see a glint of her armor.

Michael stood shivering on the outskirts of the blackened woods. Mishakal's words, forgotten until now, came back to him suddenly, as if spoken for this very time, this very place. *If you lack faith, if you stay and interfere, you run the risk of dooming yourself, the woman, and the world to a terrible fate!*

He had stayed. He had interfered. He had helped bring this evil upon her, upon himself, perhaps upon the world!

"I should have faith," he counseled himself. "If I did, I'd let her go. Paladine is with her. Love armors her. She will only lose her life. I might lose my soul! I should turn away, seek the Lost Citadel, beg the goddess to forgive me. I have only until tonight to find it, to retrieve my faith. . . ."

He did turn away. He turned his back on the dark and fearsome woods into which she had vanished. He took a step away from her and then another. And then, he stopped.

He could not leave her. He could not leave her to die alone, in pain and in terror. Although it would cost him his soul, he would go with her, be with her until the end.

Until doom fell upon them . . . and the world.

Part VI

Michael was blind. Darkness, thick and suffocating, fell over his sight the moment he entered the fearsome woods. His loss of vision was utter and instantaneous. He could see nothing—not vague shadowy outlines, not movement. He could see neither the shine of Nikol's armor nor the sheen of her golden hair. So strange and terrifying was his sudden blindness that he involuntarily put his hand to his eyes. It seemed to him that they must have been plucked out.

"Michael?" Nikol was frightened. "Michael . . . is that you? Michael, I can't see!"

"I'm here," he said.

He tried to sound reassuring, but he choked on the words. Yes, he was here. A lot of good it would do her, do either of them. He reached out with groping hands toward the sound of her voice, the silvery jingle of the buckles on her armor. "I . . . can't see either, my lady."

He paused, blinked. Suddenly, he could see. He could see the way out, the way back. He could see the hot sunlight shining in the clearing, see the ruts left by the wagon wheels leading into these woods. He gasped aloud in thankfulness. He had feared, for a moment, that his sight had been stolen from him forever.

"What is it, Michael?" Nikol heard him, caught hold of his hand.

"Turn around, my lady," he said, guiding her.

She did so, slowly, feet shuffling in the charred undergrowth and ashes. Her eyes widened, she clasped his hand tightly.

"I was so afraid!" She breathed, shifted to look at him. Her smile slowly faded. "I can't see you!" She moved her head around. "I can't see anything ahead of me. . . ."

"We can see the way out—"

"But I don't want to go out!" she cried angrily. "I—"

The sound of the scream came again, but it sounded farther away, came from deeper within the wood. They could hear a horse's hooves and the rattle of a cart being driven at a slow pace over uneven ground. Letting go of Michael's hand, Nikol ran forward.

"Nikol! Come back—"

He heard her running footsteps, then heard her stumble, fall, heard the sound of angry, frustrated sobbing. He made his way toward her, fumbling through the terrifying darkness that seemed to become darker the farther into it he ventured. He almost fell over her, knelt beside her.

"Are you hurt?"

"Leave me alone!" Nikol started to get to her feet. "I'm going after him."

He lost patience. "Nikol, be reasonable. It's hopeless! Even if you could see, could you keep up with a cart on foot? You can't find the trail! You can't see what obstacles or dangers lie in your path. You could step off a cliff, fall into a chasm—"

"I will not abandon him. I will go after him if I have to crawl!"

He felt her, so near him, turn. He knew she was looking back the way they'd come. He turned as well. Never had sunlight looked so bright or so beautiful. The clearing, which had seemed a place of terror before, was now a haven of peace and safety.

Thus do we take our blessings for granted, until they are gone, he thought in bitter sadness, putting his hand to the symbol of Mishakal that lay, a heavy burden, on his chest.

"What is causing this?" Nikol demanded in frustration. "What evil has created this darkness?"

"Nuitari," answered a soft and whispering voice, "god of the unseen. You walk in the light of the dark moon."

"Who is it?" Nikol was on her feet. Michael heard the ring of steel. She had drawn her sword. "Who is there?"

"Your weapon is useless, Sir Knight." The voice was heavily ironic. "I've been sitting here, watching you two bumble about for the last ten minutes. I could have slain you both twice over before now."

Michael stood, grasped Nikol's sword arm. He could feel her trembling in frustration and fear. She shoved him away, swung the sword in front of her wildly, more to relieve her own sense of helplessness than in hope in hitting anything. He heard the blade whistle harmlessly through the air.

The unseen watcher began to laugh, a laugh that caught suddenly in his throat, changed to a racking cough. After long moments, the coughing spasm ceased. Michael heard a ragged, indrawn breath.

"My lady," Michael counseled, reaching for her, finding her arm, holding it firmly. "If this person has watched us, as he claims, then he must be able to see."

"That is true," said Nikol, lowering her sword. "Can you see?"

"I can," answered the voice calmly. "To those of us who walk in Nuitari's night, this wood is lit as brightly as the day. For you, it will grow ever darker with each step you take. But, perhaps you have wandered in here by accident. I suggest you leave, while you can still find the way out."

"If you have been watching us, as you say, you know that we did not enter this wood by accident," said Nikol coolly. She had turned in the direction of the voice, her sword still in her hand, her guard raised. "Someone has been taken into this wood, someone dear to us. We have reason to believe he is being held captive by goblins."

"A young man?" asked the voice. "Comely, well made, with a grievous wound in his side? He is wrapped in bloody bandages. . . ."

"Yes," said Nikol softly, her hand closing over Michael's, holding him tightly for support. "Yes! That is my brother. You've seen him?"

"I have. And I offer you this counsel. Turn back. There is nothing you can do for him. He is a dead man. You will die yourselves. Nothing you can do will save him. Isn't that true, Revered Son of Mishakal?" The voice seemed to sneer.

"I am not a Revered Son," answered Michael quietly, "only a humble brother."

"Not even that, seemingly," said the voice.

Michael felt eyes staring at him, strange eyes that he swore he could almost see, eyes like hourglasses. Self-consciously, the healer put his hand over the medallion on his chest, thrust it hastily beneath his robes.

"Let him alone," Nikol retorted angrily. "He has no reason to be here, not as I do. He comes with me not out of love, but out of loyalty."

"Is that so?"

Michael could see the hourglass eyes laughing at him.

"So you come in here for your brother, Sir Knight?" the voice continued, soft, hissing. "Give him up. You can do nothing for him except die with him."

Nikol spoke steadily. "Then I will do so. I could not live without him. We are twins, you see—"

"Twins?" The voice was altered, low and dark, darker than the woods. "Twins," it repeated.

"Yes," said Nikol, hesitant, uncertain at the sudden change she sensed in the speaker. Did it bode good? Or ill? "We are twins. And if you know anything of twins, you know that we are close, closer than most siblings."

"I know . . . something of twins," said the voice.

The words were spoken so softly that the two might not have heard them, but both were straining every sense to make up for the loss of their eyesight.

"Then you know that I will not abandon him," said Nikol. "I will go after him, to save him if I can, die with him if I cannot."

"You cannot save him," said the voice, after a moment's pause. "Your brother has been captured by a powerful wizard of the Black Robes, a man named Akar. He needed a virtuous person. Is your brother, by chance, a knight as well?"

"My brother is a knight," answered Nikol. "I am not. I am a woman, as you well know, for I can feel your eyes on me, though I cannot see them."

"One twin born to a body fragile and frail, one twin strong and powerful. Did you never resent him?"

"Of course not!" Nikol answered too fast, too angrily. "I love him! What are you talking about?"

"Nothing important." The voice seemed to start to sigh, but the sigh was broken by a cough that seemed likely to rend the man apart.

Involuntarily, forgetting that he was powerless, Michael reached with a hand toward the stranger. He heard a hissing laugh.

"There is nothing you could do for me, healer! Even if you retained the favor of your goddess. It is the wrath of heaven that batters this poor body of mine, the anger of the gods that will soon cleanse this world in fire!"

The voice changed, abruptly, becoming cool and business-minded. "Do you speak truly, Lady? Will you follow your brother, though the way be dark and terrifying, the end hopeless?"

"I will."

"How can we go anywhere?" Michael demanded. "We cannot see the way."

"I can," said the voice, "and I will be your eyes."

Michael heard a rustle of cloth, as of long robes brushing across the ground. He heard odd sounds, objects hanging from a belt, perhaps, clicking and rubbing together. He heard a soft thud that accompanied whispering footfalls—a staff, helping the speaker walk. Michael sniffed, his nose wrinkled. He smelled the sweetness of rose petals, and a more horrible sweetness—that of decay. He sensed an arm moving toward them.

"Wait a moment," Michael said, halting Nikol, who had sheathed her sword and was reaching out to the stranger. "If you can see in the light of Nuitari, then you, too, must be a mage of evil, a wizard of the Black Robes. Why should we trust you?"

"You shouldn't, of course," said the voice.

"Then why are helping us? What is your reason? Is

this a trap?"

"It could be. What choice do you have?"

"None," said Nikol, her voice suddenly gentle. "Yet I believe you. I trust you."

"And why should you do that, Lady?" The voice was bitter, mocking.

"Because of what you said about twins. One weak, the other strong . . ."

The stranger was silent a long moment. Michael might have thought the man had left them, but for the rasping breathing of sickness-racked lungs.

"My reason for helping you is one you would not understand. Let us say simply that Akar has been promised that which is rightfully mine. I intend to see he does not acquire it. Will you come or not? You must hurry! The Night of Doom approaches. You have very little time."

"I will go," said Nikol. "I will follow where you lead, though it cost me my life!"

"And you, Brother?" said the wizard softly. "Will you walk with me? The woman has pledged her life. For you, as you surmise, the cost will be greater. Will you pledge your soul?"

"No, Michael, don't!" Nikol said, interrupting the cleric's answer. "Go back. This is not your battle. It is mine. I would not have you sacrifice yourself for us."

"What's the matter, my lady?" snapped Michael, suddenly, irrationally angry. "Don't you think I love Nicholas as well as you? Or perhaps you think I don't have a right to love him or anyone else in your family? Well, my lady, I do love! And I choose to go with you."

He heard her sharp intake of breath, the jingle of armor, her body stiffening.

"The decision is yours, of course, Brother," she said in a low voice. She reached out to hold the mage's arm.

The wizard made a raspy sound that might have been a laugh. "Truly, you *are* blind!"

Michael reached out, and his hand closed over the wizard's arm—as thin, frail, and fragile as the bones of a bird. Fever burned in the skin; the sensation of touching the mage was an unpleasant one.

"What is your name, sir?" Michael asked coldly.

The wizard did not immediately answer. Michael was startled to feel the arm he held flinch, as if the question was a painful one.

"I am . . . Raistlin."

The name meant nothing to Michael. He assumed, from the wizard's hesitation, that he'd given them a false one.

The mage led them forward into a darkness that grew impossibly darker, as he had warned. They walked as fast as they dared, not entirely trusting him, yet holding tightly to his guiding arm, listening to the rustle of his robes, the soft tapping sound of his staff.

In their nostrils was the smell of roses and of death.

Part VII

No harm befell them. They began to trust Raistlin and, as their trust increased, they started to move with incredible speed. Michael's feet barely skimmed the ground. A chill wind blasted in his face, stung his blind eyes. Branches scratched his cheek, tore his hair. Thorns and brambles caught at his robes. He pictured vividly what it would be like to smash headlong, at this speed, into tree or rock, or hurtle into some boulder-strewn chasm. He grasped harder the mage's frail-boned body.

Michael had no idea how long they traveled through the darkness. It might have been the span of a heartbeat, or it might have been eons. He wondered how much longer he could keep going, for though it didn't seem that he exerted himself, his body was growing more and more fatigued. He was forced to lean heavily on the mage's shoulder, wondered that such a frail body could support his own. His limbs were stones; he could barely move them. His feet stumbled. He tripped, lost his grip on Raistlin, and fell.

Sobbing for breath, Michael started to try to regain his footing. He lifted his head and stared.

Before him stood a building, a structure of beauty and simplicity and elegance. Columns of black, white, and red marble supported a domed roof whose shining exterior was a mirror for the night sky. Reflected in it, the constellations wheeled about its center. The two dragons, Paladine and the Queen of Darkness, each kept careful watch upon the other; in the middle, Gilean, the book of life, turned; around them wheeled the rest of the gods—good, neutral, evil.

A bridge of shining starlight burst, gleaming, from beneath the dome. The bridge spanned up and over the temple, extended to the night sky. An open door appeared in the starlit blackness. Beyond it, strange suns burned fiery red and yellow against deep blackness. Strange planets circled around them.

The beauty of the vision made Michael weep, and only when he felt the tears cold on his cheek did it occur to him that he could see again, that his sight was restored.

When he realized he could see, he noticed a dark shape mar the radiance of the temple.

A mage in black robes, tall and powerfully built, was untying the hands and feet of another man, lying in a horse-drawn cart. They stood in deep shadow. The black-robed mage could barely be seen, a shape of darkness against night, but the light of the temple fell on the face of the man in the cart. The young face was pale, drawn with pain and suffering. Sweat glistened on the pallid skin.

Michael could see Raistlin now as well, and the healer was considerably astonished to note how young the wizard appeared. Young and weak and ill. The thin face was blanched; feverish spots burned in the cheeks. His breathing was shallow and raspy. He leaned on a wooden staff, the top of which was adorned by a dragon's claw clutching a faceted crystal. Soft, pale light shone from the crystal, glittered in the mage's cold brown eyes.

Odd, thought Michael. I could have sworn they were the shape of hourglasses.

"Nicholas!" cried Nikol.

She would have run to him, but Raistlin grasped her tightly by the wrist and held her fast.

Nikol had been her brother's partner and equal in all his sports and training. She was as tall as Raistlin and was far stronger physically. Michael expected her to break the wizard's weak hold easily, and the cleric steeled himself to try to stop her impetuous rush to what undoubtedly would be her death.

Already, the other wizard, the one called Akar, had paused in his work and was peering about in alarm.

"What was that? Who is there?" he called in a deep, harsh bellow.

The thin, frail hand of Raistlin remained closed over the woman's wrist. Nikol gasped in pain. She seemed to shrink in his grasp.

"Make no sound!" he breathed. "If he knows we are here, all is lost!"

Raistlin dragged the young woman back into the shadows of the blackened, burned trees. Michael accompanied them reluctantly, unable to wrench his rapt gaze from the radiant splendor of the shining temple and the wonderful bridge that soon would take him away from pain and suffering, despair and fear.

"You're hurting me," Nikol whispered, trying ineffectually to pull away. "Let me go!"

"You would be hurt far worse than this if I did," said Raistlin grimly. "Akar is powerful and will not hesitate to destroy you if you interfere in his plans."

Nikol cast a stricken glance at her brother. Akar, apparently deciding he'd been hearing things, had returned to his work. He took rough hold of the young man, pulled him from the cart, and dumped the knight on the ground. Nicholas cried out in agony.

"Soon your torment will be ended, Sir Knight," said Akar, rubbing his hands on his robes to cleanse them of blood.

Akar removed an object from his belt, held it up to the light. Steel glinted, bright and sharp. He inspected the dagger and thrust it back into his belt with a grunt of satisfaction. He bent down, started to lift the knight by the ankles, intending to once again haul him over the ground.

Nicholas struck out; his feet knocked the wizard backward. Caught off guard, astonished that his feeble victim should have fight left in him, Akar stumbled, off balance. He tripped on the hem of his robe and fell heavily.

Nicholas began, pitifully, to try to crawl away, to lose himself in the hideous darkness from which he had come.

"I'm going to him. You can't stop me." Nikol, her right hand still held fast in Raistlin's grasp, reached for her sword with the left.

Sparks jumped from the hilt. She snatched her hand back, wringing it in pain. Again she tried; again the sparks. She glared at the mage.

"You foul wizards are in league! I should have known! I never should have trusted—"

"Silence!" ordered Raistlin.

His gaze was intent on Akar. His entire being seemed concentrated on his counterpart. He had even ceased, for the moment, to cough. A faint tinge of color burned in the thin cheeks. He didn't seem to notice the woman struggling in his grasp, though his hold on her never loosened.

Nikol twisted around to face Michael.

"Why are you standing there? Go to Nicholas! Save him! This wicked man has no hold on you! He cannot fight us both!"

Michael started forward, reluctant to turn away from the shining bridge, yet his heart ached for the gallant young knight and for the sister who suffered with him. The voice of Raistlin stopped him, held the cleric as completely as the mage's hand held Nikol.

"Far more is at stake here than the life of one brave knight. The fate of the world hangs in the balance on Gilean's scales." Raistlin glanced at Michael. "What do you see, healer?"

"I see . . . a sight more beautiful than anything I've ever seen in my life. A temple stands before me, its columns of black and white and red marble. Its dome is the heavens, its roof the constellations. A bridge of starlight extends from this world to worlds beyond. People walk across that bridge—men, women, human, elven. They look back at this world with regret, their faces sad. But Paladine is with them, and he reassures them, and they turn to the door with hope."

"What have you done?" Nikol demanded of Raistlin. "You've bewitched him!"

Michael himself took a step forward, as if he would

follow. An outraged cry jolted him back to this world. Akar had regained his feet. He glared at the knight in anger.

"Truly, as I said, a tough breed. Come, Sir Knight, I am losing patience. Time grows too short for more games."

Akar kicked Nicholas in the face. The knight fell back without a sound and lay still and unmoving. Akar grasped Nicholas, this time by the shoulders, and began hauling the limp body across the ground.

"He's taking him to the temple! What does he plan to do?" Michael asked Raistlin, who watched all with an expression grim and stern.

"He plans to murder him!" Nikol cried, trying again to free herself.

"My lady, please—" Michael began gently.

"Leave me be!" Nikol's eyes flared. "You're ensorcelled. The wizard's cast some sort of spell on you! Bridge of starlight! Radiant temple! It's a broken ruins, probably an altar of evil, consecrated to the Dark Queen!"

Michael stared at her. "Can't you see? . . ."

"No, she cannot," said Raistlin. "She sees a ruined citadel, nothing more. You alone, cleric, see the truth. You alone can stop Her Dark Majesty in her efforts to return to this world."

Michael didn't believe the wizard. How could Nikol not see what was so obvious and beautiful to him? And yet Nikol was staring at him angrily, fearfully, as if he were indeed a person acting under a spell.

"What must I do?" he asked in a low voice.

"The lady is right. Akar intends to murder the knight, but the mage must commit the crime within the precinct of the ruins or, as you see it, on the bridge of starlight. If the blood of the good and virtuous is spilled on the sacred bridge, the dark clerics, long held prisoner in the Abyss, will be free to return to Krynn."

"Will you help me?" Michael demanded.

"Don't trust him!" Nikol cried, twisting in the mage's grasp. "His robes are cut from the same black cloth!"

"I brought you here," said Raistlin softly. "And without my help, you will not succeed. Your brother will die, and all of Krynn will fall into the hand of the Dark Queen."

"What must we do?" Michael asked.

"When Akar drops the dagger, pick it up swiftly and do not allow him to retake it. He has foolishly bound the knight's life in the weapon."

"I will seize it," said Nikol.

"No!"

Perhaps it was a trick of the light shining from the temple, but the wizard's brown eyes, staring at Michael, gleamed suddenly golden, as if that were their true color, the other, only a disguise.

"The cleric alone must take the dagger, else the spell cannot be broken."

"What do I do then?" Michael's gaze shifted back to the black-robed wizard, laboriously dragging the body of the dying knight across the grass.

"I do not know," said Raistlin. "I cannot hear the voice of the gods. You can. You must listen to what they say.

"And you, my lady"—the wizard released Nikol's hand—"must listen to your heart."

Nikol sprang away from Raistlin, drawing her sword in the same motion. She held it, blade toward the wizard, as she began backing up. "I don't need either of you. I don't need your gods or your magic. I will save my brother."

She ran off, sword flashing in the temple light, a light that, to her, was darkness.

Michael took a step after her, fear for her and for himself and for them all constricting his heart. Then he paused, turned to look at the wizard.

Raistlin stood leaning on his staff, regarding the cleric intently.

"I don't trust you," said Michael.

"Is it me you do not trust?" asked the wizard, his thin lips twisted in a smile. "Or yourself?"

Michael turned without responding, ran after Nikol. There came to him the words, "Remember, when the dagger falls, pick it up."

Part VIII

Sweating and straining, stumbling over the hem of his black robes, Akar dragged the unconscious knight across rough and uneven ground. The mage, though strong, was more accustomed to spending his time studying his spells. Akar was forced to pause a moment in his exertions, rest aching muscles. He glanced over his shoulder to judge the distance to his destination.

He could see, by Nuitari's dark light, a ruined citadel, its stone walls crumbling into dust. A bridge extended outward from the broken floor, a bridge that glimmered with a ghostly, wraithlike glow. On the far side of the bridge, shadowy figures reached out eager hands to him. Hollow voices shouted for him to free them, release the legions of darkness.

"A few moments more, Knight, and you will be free of this life and I will be free of you, for which we both will be grateful," Akar grunted, bending once again to his task.

Nicholas had regained consciousness, pushed back the shadows that would have brought him blessed relief from the agony he suffered. But worse than the pain of his wounds was the bitter knowledge that he would be, however innocently, responsible for the resurgence of evil in the world. He kept his gaze focused on the face of his enemy.

"Why do you stare at me so?" Akar demanded, somewhat disconcerted by that burning-eyed gaze that never left him. "If you are afraid you will not recognize me when our souls meet on the other side, save yourself the trouble. I will be more than happy to introduce myself."

It took all the knight's will to release each indrawn breath in a sigh and not a scream. Nicholas managed a smile, through lips caked with blood, parched and cracked from thirst. "I watch you as I would watch any opponent," he whispered hoarsely. "I wait for you to slip, to lower your guard, to make a mistake."

Akar laughed. "And then what will you do, Sir Knight? Drool on me? Or do you have the strength to do that much?"

"Paladine is with me," said Nicholas calmly. "He will give me the strength I need."

"He had better hurry, then," said Akar, grinning.

Perhaps it was the urging of the dark voices, but Akar found himself suddenly anxious to have this task done. He allowed himself no more rest, but manhandled the knight up the broken stairs of the citadel, listened to the cries of agony wrenched from the man with a certain satisfaction.

"I do not think Paladine hears your cries"—Akar sneered—"for here we are at the bridge. And here, Sir Knight, your life ends."

Dreadful moonlight shone upon the knight's face and bandaged, bloodied body. The unholy radiance washed out all color, turned red blood black, reduced waxen flesh to bone, glistened in the eyes like unshed tears. The light blinded Nicholas with its vast and terrible darkness. He cried out, clutched at nothing with groping hands.

"Know despair!" breathed Akar, drawing the dagger from his belt. "Know defeat. Know that your god has forsaken you and the world—!"

"Halt, foul servant of evil! Stay your hand or I swear, by Paladine, I will cut it from your arm!"

Akar stopped, peered out into the darkness. He was not arrested in his movement by the living voice, though it was stern and commanding, as he was halted by frantic, whispered warnings coming from the shadow voices on the other side of the bridge. What threat did they see?

The wizard's gaze flickered over the figure of a knight in armor, sword in hand, who ran forward to challenge battle. Strong enchantment surrounded the Lost Citadel. Akar doubted if the knight could break through it. As he expected, the armored figure came up against a barrier that was like an explosion of stars, was thrown suddenly and heavily backward.

"Nikol!" cried the knight, straining to reach her, but he only managed to fall forward on his bloodied breast.

The woman hurled herself once again into the barrier, cried out in pain and frustration when she could not get through, and she began to hack at it with her sword. A cleric in nondescript blue robes appeared to be trying to remonstrate with her. Akar paid them scant attention. He saw, by Nuitari's dark light, something far more disquieting.

A mage clad in black robes stood leaning heavily on a staff that had at its top a crystal clasped in the claw of a dragon. Akar recognized the staff, the Staff of Magius, a powerful magical artifact that was, the last he had heard, in safekeeping in the Tower of Wayreth. Akar recognized the staff, but not the mage who held it, and that disturbed him, for he knew all who wore the black robes.

"So you would try to usurp me, would you, Akar?" said the mage. Raistlin strode closer.

Who was this stranger wizard? His voice sounded familiar, yet Akar could swear he had never before seen him. The words of a killing spell were on Akar's lips. He shifted the dagger to his left hand; the fingers of his right slid into his pouch, gathering components. The voices from the darkness shouted cries and warnings, urged him to destroy the silent onlooker, but Akar dared not kill the stranger without first ascertaining who he was, what his purpose. To do so would be against all the laws of the Conclave. In a world in which magic is mistrusted and reviled, all magi are loyal to one another for the sake of the magic.

"You have the advantage of me, Brother Black Robe," shouted Akar, trying in vain to see more clearly beneath the shadows of the hood that covered the mage's face. "I do not recognize you, as you seem to recognize me. I would be glad to renew old acquaintance but, as you see, I am somewhat busy at the moment. Allow me to dispatch this knight and complete the spell and then I will be happy to discuss whatever grievance you think you have against me."

"You don't recognize me, Akar?" came the soft, whispering voice. "Are you sure?"

"How can I if you do not remove your hood and let me see your face?" demanded Akar impatiently. "Be swift. My time is short."

"My face is not known to you. But this, I believe, is."

The strange mage lifted an object in his hand and held it forth to be illuminated by Nuitari's dark light. Akar saw it, recognized it, felt the chill hand of fear close around his heart.

In a thin and wasted hand—a hand that seemed, to Akar, to gleam with a golden light, as if the skin had a strange gold cast to it—the mage held a silver pendant, a bloodstone.

Akar knew that pendant. Often he'd seen it hanging around the neck of his teacher, one of the greatest, most powerful wizards who had ever lived—and one of the most evil. Akar had heard the whispered rumors about that bloodstone, how the ancient wizard used it to suck life out of an apprentice, infuse his own powerful life into a new, younger body. Akar had never believed the rumors, never believed them until now.

"Fistandantilus!" he cried in recognition, and fumbled for the spell components with fingers gone numb while his brain fumbled for words that eluded his grasp.

A jagged bolt of lightning streaked through the night, struck Akar's left hand. The jolt knocked the dagger from the wizard's grasp, flung him backward, momentarily dazed.

Nicholas made a feeble effort to try to escape. Crawling on his hands and knees, he dragged his suffering, tortured body out of the ghastly light. He reached the edge of the stairs, tried to crawl down, slipped in a pool of his own blood, and plummeted down the steps. His death-shadowed eyes sought and found his sister. He stretched his hand out to her.

She dropped her sword, tried to clasp him, but the magical barrier kept them apart.

From behind them, out of the darkness, came the urgent command, "Pick up the dagger!"

Part IX

Michael heard Raistlin's command, remembered the mage's instructions.

When the dagger falls, pick it up!

"But how can I?" Michael cried. "How can I cross the barrier?"

The cleric had been attempting to keep Nikol from injuring herself, flinging herself again and again into the magical wall that kept her from her brother. Her hands were burned and blistered, yet, even now, she ignored the pain, trying her best to reach Nicholas, though every time she did so, a cascade of sparks burst around her.

Michael looked past her, looked past the tortured Nicholas, and saw the dagger that lay gleaming on the citadel steps, near the bridge. The black-robed wizard who had wielded it, who sought to bring into the world the dark clerics that shouted and gibbered from the other side, was recovering from his shock, was starting to look around and take stock of his situation. He was much closer to the dagger than Michael.

"You can enter, fool cleric!" Raistlin cried. The words were his last, however, tearing the breath from his body. The spell he had cast had weakened him. A violent fit of coughing brought him to his knees, near where Nikol stood.

Akar saw his enemy falter. His eyes glinted. He lurched to his feet.

Michael grasped his holy medallion, the medallion that was dark and lifeless, and plunged forward, gritting his teeth against what he knew must be a surge of magic that would most likely kill him.

To his amazement, nothing happened. The barrier parted. He ran up the stairs and plunged forward to snatch the dagger from beneath Akar's clutching fingertips. The mage's chill touch brushed the cleric's skin. Michael shrank from the horrible feel and the sight of the burning enmity in the black eyes, but he had the dagger.

Clasping the weapon in his hand, hardly knowing what he was doing, only wanting to escape the wizard, Michael stumbled back down the stairs.

At the bottom lay Nicholas. Michael looked down at the pain-twisted face, lost his fear in his compassion for the young man's suffering, his admiration for his courage. He knelt, lifted Nicholas's hand in his, held it fast. The dying knight managed a pain-filled, weary smile.

"Paladine, help me!" Nicholas said, gasping for breath.

A blue light bathed Michael, bathed the knight, washed the dreadful lines of pain from the gaunt face, as if he had been immersed in a lake of placid water. Time ceased its flow. Every person was arrested in motion, from Nikol, striving desperately to reach her brother, to the evil wizard, trying still to achieve his heinous goal. Michael, his heart filled with thankfulness, raised his eyes to the radiant blue goddess who stood at the entrance to the shining bridge.

"Mishakal," Michael prayed, "grant me the power to heal this man, Paladine's faithful servant."

The blue light dimmed. The goddess's face was sorrowful.

"I have no power here. The knight's life is bound by the magician's cursed wish to the dagger you hold. Only the dagger and the one who wields it, for good or evil, will bring this young man ease."

Michael stared at the dagger in his hand with horror and the sudden, sickening realization of what he was being asked to do.

"You can't mean this, Lady! What dread task is this you give me? I am a healer, not a killer!"

"I give you no task. I tell you how the knight's pain may be forever ended. The choice is up to you. You can see the bridge, can you not?"

"Yes," said Michael, looking with longing at the radiant, shining span and the peaceful, serene features of those ethereal figures who walked it. "I see it clearly."

"Then you may cross it. Throw aside the dagger. The concerns of this world are no longer yours."

Michael looked down at Nicholas, who lay still, eyes closed, in peaceful sleep . . . as long as the light of the goddess shone on him. When it was withdrawn, the terrible spell that bound him to his cruel suffering would be empowered once more. Nikol had ceased her bitter struggle and was on her knees, as near her brother as was possible for the magical barrier that barred her way.

"You can heal him, Michael," she was saying.

Near her, the strange, black-robed mage, Raistlin, who had fought one of his own kind, watched Michael with glittering eyes that reflected back the goddess's light, seemed to see and know all that was passing.

Who was this Raistlin? What was his purpose? Michael didn't know, didn't understand. He didn't fathom any of this, knew himself suddenly to be nothing more than a frayed thread in a tangled skein.

Anger stirred in him again. What was his life or any of their lives worth to the gods, who live forever? How could he be expected to know what was right and what was wrong if he stumbled through life as blind as he'd been in that enchanted forest?

"While I am in the world, its concerns are mine," cried Michael. "When I took your vows, Lady, I accepted responsibility for the world and its people. Those will be mine, as long as I live. How can you ask me to break them?"

"But by killing this man, Michael, you do break my vows."

"So be it," said the cleric harshly. He gripped the dagger with hands that trembled. "Must . . . must I stab him?"

"No," said the goddess gently. "Draw blood only. That will break the spell."

"And my vows?" Michael looked up at her again, calmly, not pleading, but in deep sadness. "Will I lose your favor?"

The goddess did not reply.

Michael bowed his head. The blue light faded. Time began its ticking, like the beating of a heart. He heard, behind him, Akar's trampling footfalls, the rasping of his breath. He saw, before him, Nikol regarding him hopefully, expectantly. He felt the knight's hand, still clasped in his own, stiffen in agony, saw the young man's face twist.

"Strike now!" ordered Raistlin, so weak with coughing that he could not stand. "Or else all is lost!"

"Strike? What do you mean?" Nikol sprang to her feet. She saw the dagger in Michael's hand, suddenly understood his intent. "What are you doing? False cleric! You have betrayed me!" She turned to Raistlin. "Help me! You understand what I feel! Don't let him kill my brother!"

She wasn't watching. Michael must strike now, while she wasn't watching. Barely able to see for the tears in his eyes, Michael rested the dagger's tip on the knight's sweat-covered brow and pressed the point into the flesh. A thin trickle of blood oozed from the scratch.

Akar cursed bitterly.

Nicholas opened his eyes, turned his head. The light of the bridge shone on his face.

"Paladine is merciful," he said. "He gave me strength."

At the sound of his voice, Nikol turned swiftly. "Nicholas!"

His eyes had closed. His breath left him in a sigh. The lines of pain and suffering were smoothed away, as if by some immortal, soothing hand.

She saw Michael lay the dagger reverently on the knight's bare breast.

"Nicholas!"

Nikol's voice, ragged with grief, pierced Michael more deeply than the dagger had pierced her brother's flesh. The barrier was lifted. She fell upon the lifeless body. The hair that she had shorn for his sake mingled with the hair that was so like it that it was impossible to tell them apart.

Suddenly, she raised her head, stared at Michael and Akar.

"The cleric killed your brother!" Akar cried. "It was my spell that kept him alive. The cleric broke it!"

Michael could say nothing, couldn't explain, if she didn't understand.

She stared at him, eyes empty of all feeling.

Rough hands grabbed hold of Michael from behind, jerked him to his feet. A black-robed arm wrapped around his neck.

"Here, cleric!" Akar said. "Come up here to the temple. Away from that evil wizard, Fistandantilus. You don't know him. He's dangerous!"

Michael started to cry out a warning. Akar's hand covered the cleric's mouth.

"Yes, I've captured you. The good and virtuous!" Akar laughed beneath his breath. "I saw the goddess speak to you! You are in her favor. Your blood will do as well as the knight's!"

Michael tensed, prepared for a struggle.

"I wouldn't try it," breathed the wizard, "unless you want to see the young woman die in flames! There, that's better. Come quietly. And you, Fistandantilus!" Akar sneered, all the while dragging Michael backward, up the stairs. "You are too weak to stop me!"

Raistlin was on his knees, clutching the staff to keep from falling. Blood flecked his lips. He could not speak, yet he smiled and pointed.

Michael, clasped close against the mage, heard Akar draw in a sucking breath.

The dagger. The dagger lay shining on the knight's lifeless breast.

Steel must draw the blood.

Akar halted, ground his teeth in frustration. Michael saw the bridge beneath his feet. And now that he was this near to the other side, he could hear cold voices calling for his death, see shadowed shapes writhing in eagerness to be free.

Michael had, at first, thought it was his fevered imagination, but now he was sure of it—the light of the bridge was growing gradually dimmer, the clamoring shouts of the dead growing louder, more frantic. The Night of Doom was ending.

"Girl!" Akar's voice was suddenly soft, sweet and thick and warm. "Girl, bring me the dagger."

Nikol shifted her gaze to him, blinked. Slowly, she lowered her eyes to the dagger that rested on her brother's body.

"The false cleric killed him, this knight that was dear to you. Bring me the dagger, girl, and you will have your revenge."

Nikol reached out with her hand, lifted the dagger in fingers that trembled. She stared at it, looked from it to the wizard, from the wizard to Michael. Her eyes were dark. Slowly, she rose to her feet and began to climb the stairs of the Lost Citadel, coming toward them, the dagger in her hand.

Was she ensorcelled? The wizard had spoken no words of magic, had cast no spell that Michael had heard.

"Come, girl, swiftly!" Akar hissed.

Nikol did as he bade. She walked forward steadily, her eyes as empty as her brother's. Something within her had died with him.

Akar's grip around Michael's throat tightened. "I know what you're thinking! But if you break free, cleric, it will be her blood I spill on the bridge. Make your choice. You or her. It matters little to me."

Nikol was level with them, the dagger held loosely in her limp, outstretched hand. Her left hand. Her sword hand, her right, was free.

The light of the bridge was fading fast. A pale glow in the far distant sky presaged morning, a gray morning, a dawning of unhappiness and fear for those left in a world where man had forsaken the gods.

Akar had seconds only. He made a grab.

Nikol's grasp tightened on the dagger. She stabbed. The blade tore through the wizard's palm, tore through bone and tendon and muscle, thrust out, blood-blackened, on the other side of the hand.

Akar howled in pain and rage. Michael broke free of the mage's weakening grasp, flung himself to the ground. The only help he could offer Nikol was to keep clear of her sword arm.

Nikol's blade, which had been her brother's and his father's before him and his father's before that, swept past Michael in a shining silver arc. The wizard screamed. The blade drove deep into his vitals.

Michael rolled over, was on his feet. Akar stood spitted on Nikol's sword, his hands grasping at it, his face distorted with fury and pain.

Nikol jerked the sword free. Blood burst from Akar's mouth. He pitched forward on his face and lay dead on the steps of the Lost Citadel.

Her face pale and set, as rigid as the stones, gray in the morning light, Nikol nudged Akar's body with the toe of her boot.

"I'm sorry if I frightened you," she said to Michael. "I had to play along with him. I feared he'd cast a spell on me before I could slay him."

"Then you do understand!" was all Michael could think to say.

"No," Nikol answered bitterly. "I don't understand any of it. All I know is that this Akar was the one responsible for my brother's death and, by the Oath and the Measure, that death is avenged. As for you"—her lifeless gaze turned to Michael—"you did what you could."

Nikol turned and walked back down the temple steps.

Sickened by the terrible death he had just witnessed, shaken by his ordeal, the cleric tried to follow, but his legs gave way. Sweat chilled on his body. He leaned weakly against a crumbling pillar, his wistful gaze going back to the shining bridge, that line of peace-filled, serene figures leaving this world of pain and sorrow and suffering.

The bridge was gone. The door amid the stars was closed.

Part X

The morning was deathly quiet.

Quiet.

Michael raised his head. The dread voices of the dark clerics were silenced. Their threat to take over the world, now that all the true clerics of the gods were gone, was ended.

All true clerics gone. Michael sighed. His hand went to the symbol of Mishakal that hung dark and cold about his neck. He had questioned when he should have believed. He had been angry, defiant, when he should have been humble, submissive. He had taken life when he should have acted to save it.

Michael drew a deep breath to dispel the mists that blurred his vision. One more task was left for him to perform, the only task for which he was seemingly worthy now—composing the body of the dead for its final rest. Then he could leave, leave Nikol alone with her bitter grief, remove himself and the knowledge of his failure from her sight. It was poor comfort, but all he could offer. He pushed himself away from the pillar, slowly descended the stairs.

Nikol knelt beside her brother's body, his lifeless hand clasped fast in her own. She did not glance up at Michael, did not acknowledge his presence. Her armor was splattered with the blood of the dead mage. Her skin was ashen. The resemblance between the twins was uncanny. It seemed to Michael that he looked on two corpses, not one. Perhaps he did. Daughter of a knight, Nikol would not long outlive her brother.

A shadow fell across the two, and a gasping cough broke the stillness. Michael had forgotten the black-robed mage who had led them here, was startled to find the man standing quite near him. The smell of rose petals and decay that clung to the soft black robes was unnerving, as was the fevered heat that emanated from the frail body.

"You got what you wanted?" Michael asked abruptly, bitterly.

"I did." Raistlin was calm.

Michael rounded on him. "Who are you, anyway? You gave us one name. Akar gave you another. Who are you? What was your purpose here?"

The mage did not immediately answer. He leaned on his staff, stared at Michael with the brown eyes that glittered gold in the chill light of a sad dawn.

"If I had met you a year ago and asked you the same questions, cleric, you would have answered glibly enough, I suppose. A month ago, a day ago—you knew who you were—or thought you did. And would you have been correct? Would your answer be the same today as it was yesterday? No." Raistlin shook his head. "No, I think not."

"Stop talking in riddles!" Michael said, fear making him angry, frustrated. "You know who you are, why you came. And we served your needs, whatever they were, since you were too weak at the end to stop Akar yourself. I think you owe us an explanation!"

"I owe you nothing!" Raistlin snapped, a flush of color mounting in the pale cheeks. "It was I who served your needs, far more than you served mine. I could have dealt with Akar on my own. You were a convenience, that is all."

The mage lifted his right arm. The black sleeve fell away from the thin wrist. A flash of metal gleamed cold in the sunlight. A dagger, held on by a cunning leather thong, slid into Raistlin's hand when the mage flicked his wrist. The movement was so fast that Michael could scarcely follow it.

"If she had tried to murder you," the mage said, turning the dagger, making it flash in the light, "she would not have succeeded."

"You could have slain Akar."

"Bah! What good would that have done? He was never anything more than a tool for the Dark Queen. He was not needed, only the blood of the good and virtuous, spilled in anger."

"You would have killed Nikol!" Michael stated in disbelief.

"Before she killed you."

"But, then, the curse would have been fulfilled anyway. Her blood would have fallen on the bridge."

"Ah," said Raistlin, with a cunning smile, "but it would no longer have been the blood of a good and virtuous person. It would have been the blood of a murderer."

Michael stared at him, shocked. The calculating coldness of the mage appalled him.

"Go away," he said thickly.

"I intend to. I am needed in Istar," said Raistlin, briskly. "Events will move fast there in these last thirteen days before the Cataclysm, and my presence is essential."

"The Cataclysm? What is that?"

"In thirteen days' time, the gods in their wrath at the folly of men will hurl a fiery mountain down upon Ansalon. The land will be sundered, seas will rise, and mountains topple. Countless numbers will die. Countless more, who will live in the dark and terrible days to follow, will come to wish they had died."

Michael didn't want to believe, but there was no doubting the calm voice or the strange eyes, which seemed to have witnessed these terrifying events, though they had not yet come to pass. He recalled the words of Mishakal. *He will gather their souls to him, remove them from a world that soon will erupt in fire.*

Michael looked back down at the two motionless figures, who seemed to personify the wizard's prediction: one who was dead, one who could not bear the pain of living.

"Is there no hope?" Michael asked.

"You are the only one who can answer that, my friend," the mage responded dryly.

At first it seemed to Michael that there was no hope.

Despair would cover the world in a black tide that must drown all in its poisonous waters.

But as he looked at the brother, the cleric saw the peace and serenity on the pallid features, the knowledge of a battle well fought, a victory won. The goddess had not forsaken Michael. The Dark Queen had been defeated in her ceaseless efforts to reenter the world.

Michael, Nikol, Nicholas—three silken threads, stitched together for a time. Raistlin, Akar—two more threads, crossing theirs from opposite directions. None of them could see beyond their own insignificant knots and tangles. But in the eyes of the gods, the individual threads formed—not a tangled skein—but a beautiful tapestry. If the gods chose to rend that fabric, it would no longer be as beautiful. But it might, when it was mended, be far stronger.

Gently, Michael removed her brother's lifeless hand from Nikol's grasp, laid the still hand across the still breast. A soft blue radiance surrounded them. Nicholas opened his eyes. He rose. He was once more clad in knightly armor, the symbol of the crown glittering on his breastplate. All marks of his suffering and pain were gone.

Nikol reached out to him, joy lighting her face. But Nicholas backed a step away from her.

"Nicholas?" Nikol faltered. "Why won't you come with me?"

"Let him go, my lady," Michael told her. "Paladine waits for him."

Nicholas smiled at her reassuringly, then he turned away and began walking toward the stairs, toward the Lost Citadel.

"Nicholas!" Nikol cried in anguish. "Where are you going?"

The knight did not reply, but kept walking.

Nikol ran after him. "Let me come with you!"

The knight paused on the steps of the ruined temple, looked back at his sister sadly, pleadingly, as if begging her to understand.

The blue light grew stronger. The radiant figure of the goddess materialized, standing beside the knight.

"For now, you two must part. But take with you the knowledge that someday you once more will be together." Mishakal's gaze went to Michael. The goddess held out her hand to him. "You may come, Brother, if you choose."

The holy light that surrounded them shone from the medallion around Michael's neck. He clasped his hand around it thankfully. He recalled with aching heart the beauty and the wonders of the worlds beyond. The light of his medallion strengthened, shone on Nikol's face. He saw her standing alone in the darkness, bereft and forlorn, not understanding. There would be many, many more like her in the dread days to come.

"I will stay," said Michael.

Mishakal nodded wordlessly. The bridge flashed back into being, the door to the stars opened. The knight set foot upon the shining span, turned for one last look at his sister, one reassuring smile. Then he was gone. The bridge vanished. The blue light faded.

Next to Michael, the mage began to cough.

"Finally!" Raistlin muttered.

He wrapped his black robes closely about his thin body and clasped the magical staff. He spoke a word of magic.

The crystal's light flared, nearly blinding Michael. The cleric held his hand before his eyes to block out the painful glare.

"Wait!" he called. "You claim to know the future! What will happen to us! Tell us what you see!"

The mage's image was starting to fade. For a moment it wavered, and, as it did so, it altered, startlingly. The black robes changed to red, the hair whitened, the skin glistened gold, the eyes had pupils the shape of hourglasses.

"What do I see?" Raistlin repeated softly. "In a world

of the faithless, you are the only one who is faithful. And, because of that, you will be reviled, ridiculed, persecuted." The golden eyes shifted to Nikol. "But I see one who loves you, who will risk all to defend you."

"You see this happening to us?" Nikol faltered.

Raistlin's mouth twisted in a bitter smile. "To myself."

He was gone. Nikol and Michael stood in the chill dawn of a gray morning.

They stood alone, together.

MEETINGS SEXTET

Volume Four

An excerpt from

The Oath and the Measure

Michael Williams

On sale May 1992

Chapter 1

LORD ALFRED MARKENIN GREW RESTLESS AS HE
stood before his place at table. He shivered and rubbed his
hands back to life and let his eyes wander through the
Council Hall. Tonight it was a cold sea of banners.

The standards of the great Solamnic houses hung ghostly
and strange in the wavering torchlight. The old fabric, once
brilliant and thick, now gossamer with age, lifted slightly
and floated as the winter wind trickled through the drafty
hall. The sign of MarKenin was there, of course, and the
far-fetched signs of Kar-thon and of MarThasal, interwo-
ven designs of suns, kingfishers, and stars. Among them
hung proudly the intertwined roses of Uth Wistan and the
phoenix of House Peres. The lesser houses—Inverno and
Crownguard and Ledyard and Jeoffrey—were also represented, and their colors passed dimly across one another as
the banners settled. The first solemnities were observed,
and three hundred Knights of Solamnia seated themselves
to wait out the death of the year. So many were present that
even the servants from the grounds and gardens had been
brought in to wait upon them.

For wasn't that the beginning and end of the Yuletide?
Lord Alfred asked himself, as simple Jack, a transplanted
gardener, awkwardly lit the candles on the table. The death
of another year?

The powerful knight, High Justice of the Solamnic Order, shifted uncomfortably in the high-backed mahogany chair at the head of the longest table. He dreaded the unexplainable, and the unexplainable was no doubt approaching as the candlelight swelled and lengthened. He looked about, into the faces of his cohorts and lieutenants. They were numerous and varied as gemstones, and in their eyes he saw their reflections on this ceremonial night.

Lord Gunthar Uth Wistan sat at his left, stocky and scarcely thirty, though his hair was already steely gray. After Lord Boniface Crownguard, whose honor was legendary, Gunthar was the most skillful swordsman at the banquet. Such men were always impatient with ceremonies like these, finding them somehow too settled and pretty. Lord Alfred sympathized and continued to watch his friend. Gunthar plainly wanted it over—all of it, from meal to ritual to the grand disruptions. Uneasily he stared out across the vast armada of standards, to where darkness swallowed the silk and linen and damask, to where Lord Boniface, his marginally friendly rival, also sat with an entourage of youthful admirers—squires who mimicked his attitude and envied the great man's swordsmanship.

No doubt a similar impatience rose from those shadows. Though Gunthar claimed that Boniface wore the waiting more gracefully in his ardor for Oath and Measure, there was something else to the big knight's restlessness and silence, thought Alfred. To Gunthar, ceremony was the delay between battles, but to Boniface, it was the battle proper.

To Lord Alfred's right, Lord Stephan Peres, an ancient veteran on his last but extraordinarily durable legs, had seated himself with an audible creak and a quiet groan. Alfred leaned back, drumming his gloved fingers across the dark arms of the chair, then raised his right hand. At his signal the music began. It was a ponderous march, slow and melancholy as befit the dirge for the year, the three hundred forty-first since the Cataclysm.

Beside the High Justice, old Lord Stephan smiled faintly in his forest of a beard. He was a tall man and lean, having parried gracefully that tendency of the older knights to sink into heaviness and dreams. They said it was eccentricity that had kept him healthful—that and the gift of being amused at just about anything that came to pass.

Tonight, though, the old man's amusement was strained. The death of his eighty-fifth year approached, and with it, as always, this ceremony of memory, where the halls were decked with banners. He was weary of it all: the pomp and the trumpetry, the abyss of winter, Frostkalt's winds fully bitter in the Vingaard Mountains.

Lord Stephan raised his glass, and, with lowered eyes, Jack filled it once more with amber Kharolian wine. Through its glistening gold, Stephan watched the squire's table nearest that of Lord Boniface, focusing on a solitary wavering candle in the ceremonial darkness.

A young man sat by the flame, lost in thought. Sturm Brightblade, it was. A southerner from Solace, though his family was northern, ancient in the Order.

The image of Angriff Brightblade, Lord Stephan thought. Of Angriff Brightblade and of Emelin before him, and of Bayard and Helmar and every Brightblade all the way back to Bertel, to the founding of the line in the Age of Might.

Sturm would have been pleased with Stephan's thoughts. For, after all, it was to find his place in that chain that he had returned to beleaguered Solamnia after six years in exile. Smuggled from Castle Brightblade one winter's night in his eleventh year, he remembered his father in images and episodes—as a series of events rather than a living person. From the beginning Angriff Brightblade had concerned himself with Solamnic duties, leaving the lad to the care of his mother and the servants.

Sturm, though, had fabled a father from scattered memories, from his mother's stories, and no doubt from sheer imagining. Angriff grew kinder and more courageous the longer the boy dreamed, and dreams became his refuge in Abanasinia, far away from the Solamnic courts, among indifferent southerners in a nondescript hamlet called Solace. There his mother, the Lady Ilys, reared him with more tutors than friends, schooling him in courtesy and lore.

And ruining him, Lord Stephan thought with a smile, for

anything except Solamnic Knighthood.

Ilys had died of the plague. They said the boy had dismissed his few friends and grieved alone, in silence and with the proper vigils. That fall, Lords Gunthar and Boniface, who had been Angriff Brightblade's closest friends, arranged to have Sturm brought back to Thelgaard Keep, where he could be trained further in the ways of the Order.

Sturm had not taken to the North at first. He was smart, that was certain, and the years of genteel poverty had toughened him in ways that the northern boys secretly envied: he was smart in the woods, and rode horseback like a seasoned knight. But his southern ways and old Solamnic charm seemed like a relic of the last generation to the urbane younger men, squires and knights from prominent Solamnic families. They called him Grandpa Sturm, and laughed at his accent, his storehouse of remembered poetry, his attempts to grow a moustache.

They once laughed at his father, too, Stephan mused. Some laughed right up until the night of the siege.

It was hard going at Sturm's table, this or any night.

"Where is *your* banner, Brightblade?" Derek Crownguard hissed mockingly over the boards. He was nephew to the great swordsman, and exceedingly proud of his family ties, though he had not yet proved whether he shared more than blood and a name with his legendary uncle.

Derek sneered, and his burly companions, all hangers-on to the Crownguards of Foghaven, stifled their laughter. Two of them looked nervously to the High Table, where the assembled lords sat lost in memory and ritual, from the oldest loremaster and counselor to the younger war leaders, such as Gunthar and Boniface. Assured that their masters' gazes rested elsewhere, the squires turned back like hyenas, grinning and eager to feast.

"Be still, Derek!" Sturm Brightblade muttered, his brown eyes averted. It was a weak retort, the lad knew, and yet it was all he could summon against the other squires' vicious teasing. Derek was the worst—all puffed and proud at being Lord Boniface's chosen squire—but all were difficult, all scornful and superior. His friends Caramon and Raistlin had warned Sturm in long conversations over firelight and ale that talk at the High Clerist's Tower was quick and sharp and often political. This was indeed the case in the Solamnic North, and when Sturm's fellows turned upon him with their edged words and jests about his missing father, he felt rural and awkward and disinherited.

And in fact, was he not all those things?

Sturm flushed angrily, clenching his whitened fists under the table. Derek snorted in triumph and turned to the center of the hall, where the ceremonies continued, as they had for a thousand years in this very room. The harpist—a silver-haired elf in a plain blue tunic—had stepped out from the swirl of banners, and there in the red tilt of light cast by the encircling torches, had begun to play the time-honored "Song of Huma," that old contraption of myth and high-blown heroics. "Out of the village," it began,

> out of the thatched and clutching shires,
> Out of the grave and furrow, furrow and grave,
> Where his sword first tried
> The last cruel dances of childhood,
>   and awoke to the shires
> Forever retreating, his greatness a marshfire,
> The banked flight of the Kingfisher always above him . . .

Quietly the knights began to mouth the words, and slowly the song rose in the torchlit room—the tale of Huma's love and sacrifice and enshrinement. Sturm's anger subsided as he, like the rest of the young men who sat around him, entered the world of the story.

Sturm knew the tradition. If the song were sung perfectly and in unison on a night of special auspice—a night such as Yuletide or Midsummer—Lord Huma himself would return and be seated among the singers. That was why the foremost place at the foremost table was always left empty. Slowly the lad joined in, breathing the words as the room filled with the sound of a soft wind, of one clear elven voice raised in song and three hundred others whispering. Only the youngest held out hope that extraordinary things would happen. Only the oldest knew they would.

So they continued, chanting monotonously, until the outburst of the flute startled them all.

From the rafters the harsh tune tumbled, frenzied and playful, and with the music a rain of light, green and golden, dispersed the shadows in the great hall and dazzled the astonished knights. At once the whispering faded into silence, along with the song of the bard as the new, discordant music rose and quickened, and the chamber swelled with its notes. It was like the trilling of birds, or the droning of bees, or the whine of wind through the high evergreen branches—all of the knights remembered it differently later, and whatever their description they knew the song eluded it, for it was shifting and large and ever-changing.

Dumbstruck, Sturm braced himself heavily against the table. The wood shuddered beneath his stiffened hands, and the goblets chimed absurdly as they dropped to the stone floor and shattered. The sweet wood smoke in the air turned suddenly to a sharp and watery perfume—the odor of spilled wine, then of fresh grapes and strawberries, then the sudden and pungent freshness of leaves. The torches around the table extinguished, and suddenly the Great Council Hall was awash in moonlight, silver and red.

"Great Solin and Luin!" Sturm exclaimed, exchanging shocked glances with Derek Crownguard.

Then Lord Wilderness appeared in the rafters above them, bristling with music and green sparks.

* * * * *

Sturm had never seen the likes of him. The man's armor glistened with the waxy, depthless green of holly. Embossed roses, red and green, intertwined on his breastplate, and leaves and scarlet berries cascaded from his gauntlets and greaves, trailing behind him like a rumor of spring in the lifeless midwinter hall. About his face, more leaves flared and clustered like green flame, like a glory of grassy light, at the center of which his wide black eyes darted and glittered and laughed. He was a huge green bird or dryads' consort, and again he raised the flute to his lips and again the music burst forth limitless, out of the dusk and cedars and pines. He leapt to the floor with astonishing lightness.

Slowly, their faces stern and forbidding, Lord Alfred, Lord Gunthar, and Lord Stephan rose to their feet, their hands riding lightly on the hilts of their swords. Sir Adamant Jeoffrey and Lord Boniface of Foghaven stepped from behind their tables, moving toward the center of the room, then suddenly stopped, their expressions uncharacteristically cautious. Servants scattered to the far corners of the hall as more crystal broke and silver jangled on the stone floor. The strange, leafy monstrosity ignored the commotion, crouching comically in the center of the hall as the elven minstrel scrambled away in a flurry of oaths and twanging strings, his coat tangled with holly thorns.

"Who are you?" Lord Alfred asked, his voice thunderous. "How dare you disturb this most solemn of nights?"

The green man pivoted full circle, his flute vanishing somewhere in the jungle of leaf and armor that covered him. Faintly, Sturm heard its music echoing up the stairwell, as echo doubled back upon echo until the melody finally traveled beyond his hearing.

"I am Vertumnus," said the intruder, in a low voice. "I am the seasons turning and home of the past years."

"And the belfry for a thousand bats," Derek muttered, but a glance from Lord Gunthar silenced the young man.

"And what," Lord Alfred asked, "does . . . m'lord Vertumnus want of us this Yuletide?" The High Justice was tense, ceremonious, his fingers playing across the gold pommel of his sword.

"I wish to make a point," Vertumnus announced, seating himself on the floor, "near and dear to my heart."

He removed his helmet, and green fire danced at his temples.

Sturm frowned nervously. He knew that dark enchanters were wizards of merriment, urging you to be less somber, less gloomy. Finally less good. Then, when they had you lost in their laughters and songs, they would . . .

"You Solamnics gather like owls in these halls in the dead

of the year," Vertumnus said, "hooting of dark times and times past and how far the world has tumbled from ages of dream and might. Look around you—the Clerist's Tower is a hall of mirrors. You can see yourselves from all vantages and angles, preening and garnishing and admiring your own importance."

"By your leave, Lord Alfred," Lord Gunthar interrupted, his sword half drawn from its sheath. "By your leave I shall show this . . . this *pasturage* the door, and perhaps the shortest way down the mountain, if the high wind in this room continues blowing insults!"

Vertumnus smiled menacingly, his windburned face crinkling like the bark of an enormous vallenwood. The banners drifted in a warm, unseasonable breeze. "Never let it be said," he announced calmly, the faint rustle of his voice surprisingly audible in the farthest corners of the enormous chamber, "that when there is sword or mace or lance available, Lord Gunthar will settle for words or wit or policy."

"Mild words will not avail you, Vertumnus," Gunthar menaced, oblivious to the insult.

The green man only laughed. Rising with a creak of armor and a rustling of leaves, Vertumnus waggled his flute at the foremost table, at the empty chair. It was a clownish gesture, but unsettling, even obscene. The older knights gasped, and several of the younger ones drew swords. Calm, unhurried, Vertumnus turned gracefully about, brandishing the flute like a saber. It whistled hauntingly as he waved it through the air, and Sturm, watching him in fascination, noticed at once how strange it seemed when larksong rose from beyond the Tower walls as though the bird, out of time and out of season, was answering.

"To my point: There is a seat where no one sits," Vertumnus observed. "Nor guest nor beggar nor orphan nor the foreigner—none whom you have sworn by the Oath to guard and to champion. And the chair is empty this night and all others, a seat for the parrot and popinjay."

Lord Alfred MarKenin glowered at the green man, who continued serenely.

"For the Oath you swore in this nest of oaths," Vertumnus

claimed, his wild eyes riveted to the empty chair, "is the call and response of owls—dark and grim and wise in the depths of the night. You have no joy in following it. Even your festivals say so."

"Who are you, outlander, to tell us our joys and our festivals?" Lord Alfred boomed. "A thing of leaf and patch and tatters, to speak of Huma's waiting chair?"

Gunthar and Stephan turned suddenly toward the shadows, then back again, their faces unreadable in the shifting light. Suddenly Lord Alfred stepped from behind the table, and, pointing at the green man, addressed him in a voice usually reserved for horses and underlings and untrained or untrainable squires.

"Who are you to question our customs, the thousand-year waiting of our dreams? You *walking, tooting salad!*"

"Old man!" Vertumnus retorted and lurched, stopping mere inches from the High Justice. "You empty, gilded breastplate! You vacant helmet and flapping banner! You mask of laws and absence of justice! You tally sheet! You plodding ass with a snout for letters, foraging honor in a barren plain! If a prophetic breeze passed by you, you would mistake it for the flatulence of your brothers!"

Sturm shook his head. The strange name-calling was too fanciful, almost silly, as though it was a duel of bards or, even worse, a quarrel of birds in the rafters. Lord Alfred MarKenin was the High Justice of the Solamnic Order, to be addressed with respect and deference and duty, but the green man rained words upon him, and, stunned and spellbound, the High Justice staggered and fell silent.

All about Sturm, his comrades fidgeted and coughed, their eyes on the windows and rafters. For a band of lads who delighted in banter and wrangling, they, too, were strangely quiet. Occasionally a nervous laugh burst out of the shadows, but no squire dared to look at another, and certainly none dared to speak.

Now Lord Stephan stepped forth, his eyes bright with a sudden amusement. Sturm frowned apprehensively, for the old man was half wilderness himself, teasing the young knights from the strictest observance of the Oath and laughing at the outreaches of the Measure, where grammar and manners were set for even the youngest Solamnics.

It was a head wound sixty years back, suffered in some obscure Nerakan pass, that had rendered him oblique and irreverent. He seemed to be enjoying this shrill exchange, and Sturm realized, with rising embarrassment, that the old man was clearing his throat.

"What, Lord Vertumnus, would you have us do?" the old man asked, his voice still loud and firm after eighty-five years. "What would you have of us, if we are hypocrites and masks of justice? I see no widows, no orphans with you. What have *you* done for the poor and the outcast?"

"I have made you ask that question," Vertumnus replied with a sly smile. "You are an old fox, Stephan, full of more wisdom than a bloodhound could find in the rest of this room. But the fox doubles back on his trail, turning on his own stink until he goes nowhere."

"Poetry instead of policy, Lord Wilderness?" Stephan asked, his white beard rising like spindrift as he settled himself with a grunt and creaking of knees directly in front of the green man, who neither flinched nor back away.

"What I do for orphans is not your concern," Vertumnus answered calmly, "for it does not change the ruinous shires of Solamnia, the vanishing villages and the fires and the famines and the new, unspeakable dragons. No orphan here would question *me*. No, he would second my outcry."

He paused, his dark eyes searching the room.

"That is, if there were aught of orphans here."

You are wrong, Lord Wilderness, Sturm thought, shifting his feet, preparing to step forward. . . .

But no. "Orphans," he had said.

"Besides," Vertumnus continued, "*I* have sworn no oaths to protect them."

A torch fluttered and gasped in a sconce by Sturm Brightblade and Vertumnus raised the flute again to his lips.

His melody hovered, sad and haunted, and within it Sturm thought he heard something of autumn and dying and an impossibly vanished time. It was a thin, melancholy music, and the dead leaves whirled about the hall like ghosts fleeing an enchanter, yellow and black and red.

He is an enchanter, Sturm thought. He speaks in double-talk and riddles. Do not listen to him. Do not listen.

Vertumnus took another step forward. He stood face-to-face with the ancient Solamnic lord, and their eyes met without anger, and words passed between them, so hushed that even Lord Alfred, who stood not two strides away from them, swore later that he could not hear what was said. Then the green man rocked back on his heels and laughed, and Lord Peres unexplainably sprouted foliage.

Shoots and tendrils and branches flourished in the old man's armor, so that leaves intertwined with his beard and vines entangled his fingers. Vertumnus stepped back toward the center of the hall and again played his flute—this time a merry summer's air—and the elegant old man who had served long years as the steward for the missing High Clerist blossomed sweetly with a hundred blue flowers, and a navy of yellow butterflies descended from the winter rafters and settled happily on Lord Stephan Peres.

" 'Tis enough!" Lord Gunthar exclaimed and stepped forward, his fists raised and doubled, but the legs of his table were sprouting, too, and corded roots snaked and tangled about his ankles, slowing his progress toward the center of the room. Stephan gestured, but his meaning was lost among the flowers. Vertumnus whirled from the charging Solamnic lord gracefully, as Gunthar crashed into a table where the Jeoffrey brothers were seated, sending glassware and crockery and Jeoffreys scattering in all directions. Young Jack, who had apparently crawled beneath the table in search of better banquet leavings, scrambled to safety as the table collapsed, then began to take root in the floor, its dark boards branching and budding..

Someone pushed Sturm aside. "For the Oath and the Measure!" Lord Boniface shouted, and surged rashly into the center of the room. His sword was drawn and his shield ready, his cold blue eyes bright as tempered steel with the prospect of battle. Vertumnus spun about, winked at the knight, then turned to face the onrush of one of the Jeoffrey brothers as Boniface fell face-first onto the stone floor, his leggings mysteriously fallen about his ankles.

The Jeoffrey reconsidered, fainted, and wordlessly Vertumnus leapt atop another table, hurdling the grasp of the other Jeoffrey, who suddenly found himself rooted to the floor like a sapling. The young knight cried out, and the room fell to an ominous stillness, a dozen men poised for attack, their single adversary dancing on one foot atop the table, flute raised to play again.

It is an indignity! Sturm thought. An indignity past the telling and enduring. He caught Derek's eye as he stepped forward, scarcely knowing what he was doing, and drew his short sword. Aside from that of the thoroughly embarrassed Boniface, it was the only bare blade in the room. It had never been blooded.

Vertumnus twirled to face the lad, and then ceased his dance. A mournful shadow passed over his face, and he nodded. As though in reluctant agreement, he stepped down, set aside his flute, drew his own enormous sword, and moved to the center of the great hall. The Knights of Solamnia stood rooted and helpless amid the green thicket of broken tables. Peering through the leaves, they watched the swordsmen circle, green man and green lad.

Sturm knew at once and too late that he was overmatched. Vertumnus had the thoughtless grace of an expert swordsman, and the blade took life in his hand. He spoke to the lad as they circled each other, his words as soft and insinuating as the wind, his gaze locked on Sturm's.

"Set it aside, boy," Vertumnus whispered, the dark eyes flickering. "For you know not the forest you're bordering . . . where the blade fails against darkness and thorn. . . ."

"Enough poetry!" Sturm muttered. "For Brightblade and the Order!" He would at least make a good show of it.

But his thrust was tentative and slow. Vertumnus brushed it lightly away.

"For *Brightblade* and the Order?" the wild man hissed, suddenly behind the lad, who wheeled to face him. "For the Order gone bad in the teeth and botched? For a father . . . who had no business with Solamnic honor?"

"No business?" Sturm's hand wavered with his voice.

Vertumnus backed away from him, eyes on the main entrance to the Council Hall, to the stairway and the winter night. He thought he heard Derek snicker. "No business? Wh-what do you . . ."

The green man's dark stare returned, fierce and almost predatory. With a swift turn of his wrist, bright and elusive as summer lightning, Vertumnus's sword flashed by Sturm's uncertain guard and plunged deep into his left shoulder.

Dazed, breathless, Sturm fell to his knees. His shoulder, his chest, his heart blazed with green fire and lancing pain. The air hummed about his ears like a choir of insistent gnats, their song mournful and menacing.

So this is dying . . . I am dying . . . dying, he thought, and suddenly the pain subsided, no longer unbearable, but dull and insistent, and to Sturm's consternation, the wound in his shoulder closed swiftly and cleanly, the fresh blood fading from his white ceremonial tunic. But the pain burrowed and seared, as insistent as the humming in the air.

"Look about you, boy," Vertumnus said. "Where is a place for a man like *your* father among the likes of these?"

Sturm forgot his wound at once. He shouted and surged to his feet, his young voice cracking with emotion. He rushed toward Vertumnus blindly, both hands bracing the short sword. Calmly his opponent stepped aside, and the blade lodged deeply in an oaken limb, recently sprung from the heart of Huma's chair.

The lad tugged at the sword and tugged again, glancing frantically over his throbbing shoulder as Vertumnus stepped menacingly forward. Then, slowly, the green man lowered his own sword. He measured Sturm as the boy labored his blade from the hard wood, and smiled when the young man whirled awkwardly to face him.

Vertumnus's grin was baffling, as unreadable as the edge of the wilderness. It angered Sturm even more than the green man's words. With another cry, he lunged at his adversary, and Vertumnus's knees buckled as the lad's blade drove cleanly into his chest.

The flute clattered to the floor and lay still. Instantly, the chill of winter returned and settled painfully about the knights' feet. The hall lay silent, as if the air were frozen.

"Sturm . . ." Lord Stephan began in astonishment. The young man staggered, wrenched free the sword, and Vertumnus fell forward solidly and quite lifeless. Gunthar rushed toward the green man, and Sturm winced as the strong hand of Lord Alfred clutched his shoulder.

The smear on Sturm's blade was clear and wet, and the resinous smell of evergreen rose from its blood groove. He turned wildly, marking the puzzlement of Alfred, of Gunthar, Lord Stephan's strange, wounded stare and, by the sundered table, the anger of Lord Boniface, who glared incredulously and jealously at the lad, then stooped to wrench up his leggings.

"What have you done, lad?" Alfred bellowed. *"What have you . . ."* The question rang in the hall, again and again, the only sound in the abject, cavernous silence.

Then Vertumnus sprang up and pushed the astonished Lord Gunthar aside. Throughout the hall rushed an enormous intake of breath, as though the room itself had gasped. As the green man touched the wound in his chest, it puckered and closed like a scar in living wood. Serenely, his eyes sought Sturm's.

"It has come to this, young Brightblade. You have made your point and mine," Vertumnus announced, and the stones at his feet grew over with thick moss. "It has come to this, though I would have had it otherwise. But it is my doing, my wound as well as yours.

"The rest is your own foolishness. You have entered my game. Which, alas, you must now play to its end, as your shoulder will tell you daily and nightly."

Outside the window the songbirds choired again. Wide-eyed, Sturm looked from the green man to his unwiped sword, from the sword back to the green man. In great perplexity, with controlled focus, the young man touched his blade. It was dry and clean.

"Meet me on the first day of spring," Vertumnus ordered, again with a strange smile, "in my stronghold amid the Southern Darkwoods. Come there alone, and we shall settle this, sword to sword, knight to knight, man to man. You have defended your father's honor, and now I challenge yours. For now I owe you a stroke, as you owe me a life. For it is written in your cherished Measure that *any man who returns a blow must stay the course of battle*."

Sturm looked about him in confusion. Gunthar and Alfred stood frozen on the dais, and Lord Stephan opened his mouth to speak, but no words came forth.

Hawk-eyed, expectant, Lord Boniface nodded. What the green man had said concerning "return of the blow" was indeed enshrined in the Measure. Sturm was trapped by his impulsive deed in an ancient statute.

"I will lead you to that place when the time comes," Vertumnus announced. "And you might learn something of your father in that place and time. However, you must make your own way. If you fail to meet me at the appointed place, on the appointed night . . . your honor is forfeit.

"Nor is your honor alone in jeopardy," the green man continued with a mysterious smile. "For, indeed, you owe me a life, Sturm Brightblade, and you will pay it whether or not you arrive at the appointed time."

Dramatically, he gestured at the lad's shoulder.

"You can come like a child of the Order and meet my challenge," he pronounced, "or you can cower in the halls of this fortress and await . . . the greening of your wound. For the deeds of my sword bloom forth in the spring, and their blossoms are dreadful and fatal."

The hall filled with more leaves and vines and tendrils, with briar and root and branch enough to take a week to clear. The green man closed his eyes, bowed his head, and vanished amid the rustle, as the torches on the walls burst suddenly into a cold white flame. Astonished, Sturm squinted through the shadowy thicket, but Vertumnus was truly gone, leaving behind mist and wood smoke and the watery, metallic smell of the woods after lightning.

"Of all the trouble you might have uprooted, lad," Lord Alfred proclaimed sorrowfully, "of all you might have done or left undone, this indeed was the worst of things."

DragonLance® Saga

The sweeping saga of honor, courage, and
companions begins with . . .

The Chronicles Trilogy

By *The New York Times* best-selling authors
Margaret Weis & Tracy Hickman

Dragons of Autumn Twilight
Volume One
Dragons have returned to Krynn with a vengeance
An unlikely band of heroes embarks on a perilous
quest for the legendary *Dragonlance!*

ISBN 0-88038-173-6

Dragons of Winter Night
Volume Two
The adventure continues . . . Treachery,
intrigue, and despair threaten to overcome
the Heroes of the Lance in their epic quest!

ISBN 0-88038-174-4

Dragons of Spring Dawning
Volume Three
Hope dawns with the coming of spring, but then
the heroes find themselves in a titanic battle
against Takhisis, Queen of Darkness!

ISBN 0-88038-175-2

tail Each $4.95; CAN $5.95; £4.99 U.K.